Ingram #14 12/17

THE PEAR TREE

D1512188

By K.M. Sandrick

The Pear Tree/K. M. Sandrick

ISBN: 978-1-947605-01-5
Ebook: 978-1-947605-02-2

For My Father

CONTENTS

AUTHOR'S NOTE

The Pear Tree describes actual incidents that occurred in 1942 and 1945 in Nazi-Occupied Czechoslovakia and Germany. The events have been researched and are presented as accurately as possible in time, location, and sequence. They also present some of the individuals who were directly involved. While the expressions of the thoughts and feelings of these individuals are fictional, they have been constructed on the basis of historical sources of information. The names of these individuals are listed on the following pages; a partial list of the sources of information for each chapter is provided in a reference section at the end of the book.

Fictional characters have been placed at the events to depict the reactions of ordinary individuals as they would have experienced and expressed them. Many turns of phrase, terms, and titles as well as locations are given with Czech or German spellings. A glossary at the end of the book provides definitions to help guide readers as they retrace a series of wartime incidents that have been largely forgotten.

K. M. Sandrick

May, 2017

HISTORICAL FIGURES

Alexander Commichau—head of the work force responsible for demolition and cleanup of Lidice.

Edvard Beneš—leader of the Czechoslovak Government in Exile in Britain.

Richard Bienert—member of a delegation formed by Karl Hermann Frank that attempted to secure a separate peace for Nazi leaders of Occupied Czechoslovakia with American Forces in 1945.

Gustav Binder—overseer of the straw-weaving workshop in the Ravensbrück work camp. Binder was tried, convicted, and sentenced to death along with other overseers of the work camp in Hamburg in 1947.

Josef Bublík—member of the Czechoslovak Army in Exile who parachuted behind Wehrmacht lines in 1942. He was killed by Gestapo and SS in the raid at St. Charles Borromeo Church that also killed assassins of Reinhard Heydrich in June 1942.

Karel Čurda—member of the Czechoslovak Army in Exile who presented himself to the Gestapo in June 1942 and led SS and Gestapo to Heydrich's assassins.

Kurt Daluege—head of ReichsProtektorate named by Hitler after the death of Reinhard Heydrich.

Karl Doenitz—Hitler's successor.

Bohuslav Ečer—Colonel Judge Advocate for the post WW II U. N. War Crimes Commission. He represented Czechoslovakia.

Karl Hermann Frank—Secretary of State for Occupied Czechoslovakia after the assassination of Reinhard Heydrich. Frank ordered the Lidice massacre. He was executed by hanging in Pankrác Prison, Prague, on March 23, 1946.

Josef Gabčik—one of two members of the Czechoslovak Army in Exile who succeeded in assassinating Heydrich.

Hans-Ulrich Geschke—commander of the Gestapo in Prague who formed the committee to investigate Heydrich's assassination. He disappeared after the war and turned up as a senior public prosecutor in Frankfort/Main, Germany, in 1959.

Emile Hácha—president of Czechoslovakia during the Occupation. He died in Pankrác Prison one month after his arrest in 1945 for collaboration with the Third Reich.

Reinhard Heydrich—head of Occupied Czechoslovakia. He was severely injured when his limousine was bombed on May 27, 1942 on the outskirts of Prague. He died 8 days later from blood poisoning due to his injuries.

Heinrich Himmler—head of the SS and immediate superior of Reinhard Heydrich. In his eulogy at Heydrich's funeral, he said: "It is our holy duty to atone for his death, to take up his tasks, and to pitilessly destroy, without any sign of weakness, the enemies of our Volk."

Adolf Hitler—Führer of the German Third Reich. He bestowed the German Order on Heydrich at his funeral, saying: "As leader of the party and as leader of the German Reich, I give you, my dear comrade Heydrich, the highest recognition I have to bestow: the uppermost level of the German Order...You are the second person to receive this award."

Ernest Hochwald—interrogator of Karl Hermann Frank. The interrogation took place in Wiesbaden on June 11, 1945.

Horák—a farmer in Lidice with two sons in the Czechoslovak Army in Exile in Britain. The Horák farm was the site where the men of Lidice were executed en masse.

Adolf Hrubý—member of Frank's 1945 delegation to the American Forces.

Albert Kesselring—Wehrmacht Field Marshall in Bavaria in

1945 who received members of Frank's delegation but was not able to direct them to the American Forces.

Vladmir Klecanda—member of Frank's 1945 delegation to the American Forces.

Jan Kubiš—one of two members of the Czechoslovak Army in Exile who succeeded in assassinating Heydrich.

Ana Maruščáková—resident of Lidice who received a love letter from her lover and fellow coworker Václav Říha. The letter was considered to be suspicious by investigators of the Heydrich assassination.

Norman Miles—a first lieutenant in the U.S. Army War Crimes Branch who was involved in the interrogation of Karl Hermann Frank.

Bernard Montgomery—head of the British Army in WW II.

The Moravecs—one of the families who hid members of the Czechoslovak Army in Exile in Prague. Marie committed suicide while under arrest by Gestapo on June 14, 1942. Her husband and son were executed in Mauthausen concentration camp in October, 1942.

Adolf Opálka—member of the Czechoslovak Army in Exile who parachuted behind Wehrmacht lines in 1942. He was killed by Gestapo and SS in the raid at St. Charles Borromeo Church that also killed Heydrich's assassins in June 1942.

Heinz Pannwitz—criminal investigator for the Gestapo in Prague who led the investigation into the Heydrich assassination. He authored a memoir of the Heydrich assassination and investigation in 1959.

Vladimir Petrek—pastor of the church where Heydrich's assassins and other members of the Czechoslovak Army in Exile were found and killed.

Josef Pfitzner—former Czech mayor who was tried and hanged in September 1945 for collaboration with the Nazis. He was the first Czech to be prosecuted, convicted, and sentenced for crimes committed during the Occupation.

Hermann Raschofer—member of Frank's 1945 delegation to the American Forces.

Václav Rihá—author of the love letter to Ana Maruščáková that led Gestapo investigators to the town of Lidice.

Max Rostock—commander of the execution squad in Lidice. After the war, he lived with his family in Heidelberg, Germany. After being discovered by American forces in 1946, he was transported to Czechoslovakia for trial but escaped on the way. In 1948 he was arrested for black-marketeering and sent to Czechoslovakia, where he was sentenced to death for war crimes. He was released by order of amnesty by president Antonín Zápotcký and welcomed in Germany as a victim of "judicial error." He died in West Germany in 1986.

Siegfried Seidl—commander of Terezín Jewish ghetto near Lidice. Inmates of the ghetto were taken to Lidice to dig the communal grave for the men who were executed. He was arrested and prosecuted in Austria in 1946 and executed on February 4, 1947.

Fritz Suhren—commander of the Ravensbrück work camp where many of the women of Lidice were taken after the attack on the town. He was tried and hanged in 1950.

Fr. Sternbeck—73-year-old pastor of St. Martin's Church in Lidice.

Karl von Treuenfeld—commander of the troops that attacked and killed Heydrich's assassins and other members of the Czechoslovak Army in Exile at St. Charles Borromeo Church in Prague in June 1942.

Harald Weismann—SS leader who addressed riflemen before the mass execution of the men of Lidice: "It is the will of the Führer which you are about to execute."

1942

ASSASSINATION

CHAPTER ONE

Reinhard Heydrich caught a glimpse of himself as he passed what was left of the hall mirror in his chateau in Panenské Březany. Stopping to stare at distorted reflections, he inhaled sharply. Despite the evidence of his standing as the leader of Nazi-Occupied Czechoslovakia on his uniform, he was overcome by disgust at the images in the shards of glass: his nose appeared wide and crooked instead of long, narrow and straight; his face seemed broad and square instead of lean, smooth and oval.

Impatient to remove the offending pieces of glass, Heydrich withdrew his sidearm from its holster hanging on the coat rack next to the mirror, grabbed the barrel and struck down with the pistol grip, hammering at the jagged scraps until none was left in the mirror frame and grinding each of them into slivers with the heel of his boot.

Reversing the position of the gun in his hand, he pushed the nose of the barrel into the bullet holes in the wall as he recalled the flash of anger and self-loathing that had overcome him when he returned from the previous night's bout of drinking, saw his reflection and remembered the taunts from his youth: Filthy Jew.

While replacing the gun in its holster, Heydrich glanced at a photo of his family that had been knocked askew. All because of that silly old woman, he thought as his finger traced the outline of the figure in the foreground of the photograph—his grandmother.

"Foolish old hag! Whore to a Jew! How could you? How could you marry again after Opa died? And leave us, your family, *me* to argue every day of my life that I don't have tainted blood. Just so you could have a dalliance with a Jew!" He slapped the edge of the picture frame and sent it crashing to the floor.

Wiping his fingertips on his trousers, Heydrich made his way down the hallway to the bathroom, where he performed his morning ritual: He opened the medicine cabinet, pulled out a bottle of hydrogen peroxide and unscrewed the cap. Lifting it to his mouth, he poured out a small amount of liquid, then leaned his head back and gargled, forcing the harsh liquid against his tonsils and down his throat in the hope that the peroxide would granulate the tissue of his voice box and coarsen his troublesome high-pitched voice.

He spit out the foam, twisted the cap back on the bottle, placed it on the shelf and closed the cabinet door, pausing to scrutinize his image in the mirror and assure himself again that there was no sign of Jewish blood along the edges of his lips, his cheeks and chin, his slicked-back blond hair, his spare and linear eyebrows and the narrow bridge of his nose. Jewish? Hah! No Jewish blood in him. Nor in his father. Nor in his mother.

Back in the hallway, he picked up his sidearm, wrapped and fastened the holster belt around his waist and adjusted the position of the gun. Checking on the preparations for his trip to Czechoslovak ReichsProtektorate Headquarters in Prag, he glanced out the window and saw a guard, a new recruit, loosening the stays that held open the cloth cover of his Mercedes convertible.

"Stupid," he sputtered as he leaned out the window. "You," he called to the recruit. "You!" he said more loudly when the recruit continued to raise the cloth. "Didn't anyone tell you to leave the cover the way it is?"

"But, Herr Gruppenführer..." The recruit turned to speak to Heydrich, who had already slammed down the sash, rattling the windowpane.

"Leave it," a Nazi sergeant admonished the recruit.

"But he doesn't want to drive in an open car all the way to Prag, does he? Isn't he worried about the Resistance?"

"Why would my Czechs shoot at me?" Heydrich interrupted, raising his cap to examine the crown and bill and brush them clean before he placed the hat on his head. "My Czechs are like blades of grass," he said as he approached the driver's side of the car and waited for the recruit to open the rear door. "They move whichever way the wind is blowing."

While twirling his hand as if flicking a fencing foil, he stepped into the car and began the speech he repeated regularly to the men under his command. "The winds of the Third Reich have blown the Czech government away. The Reich has swept up and destroyed the Resistance and sent the Czech Jews to the ghetto at Terezín. And the Gentiles? They love the Third Reich, now that their invalids and old people and widows

ASSASSINATION

get pensions, and their workers get better rations and theater tickets and vouchers for vacations. The Czechoslovaks may be grinning brutes, but they know they can't afford to raise their heads against the Reich or pretend to play good soldiers. The racially good and well-intentioned Czechs should know by now that they will have the opportunity to become Germans. The rest? The mongrels? The Slovaks? What does it matter what they think? They will be gone ... to the East ... away from here." He never tired of delivering this message and worked to fine-tune it. He was particularly pleased with the latest turns of phrase—"winds of the Third Reich," Czechs as "blades of grass."

Satisfied that the recruit had been sufficiently schooled, Heydrich sat back against the seat cushions, crossed an ankle over a knee, tapped the driver on the shoulder and waved a salute to the recruit and his sergeant as the vehicle pulled away from the chateau, traveled down the gravel path and through the iron gates, passing the wild-boar stone carvings with their bared fangs that he had specially designed as guards for the front entrance to the grounds.

Between gaps in the shrubbery, Heydrich could see his pregnant wife lead their three children to the stone kiosks at the edge of the swimming pool where they would change into their bathing suits. In the past Heydrich had enjoyed many women and had paid a high price for the pleasure: He had been forced to resign his naval commission for impregnating and refusing to marry the daughter of a shipyard director. How could he marry a woman who would give herself so easily? he had said at the time. But Lina—Lina at the age of 19 had so captivated him that he could entertain no other women, and he rushed to the altar within a year of meeting her.

Heydrich watched her now, her hair pulled back in a tight bun, holding 3-year-old Silke's hand. He followed the path of his rambunctious sons—8-year-old Heider and 9-year-old Klaus—down the stone steps as the sun glinted off their glossy white hair. He was happy that he and Lina had reconciled after his commitment to the Reich and his workload had, only a few years ago forced a divorce, assured that he and his wife and family would lead the New Germany.

His wife and family hidden behind the trees that lined the drive to the chateau, Heydrich turned his attention to the stack of file folders on the car seat next to him, their top layers sliding away. Ever since his early days in the SS, he had carefully amassed information about aristocrats,

Catholics, Communists, Conservatives, Jews, Socialists and even enemies within the Reich's high command. He created "poison" files on Nazis who might not be loyal enough, had too many debts or had been too flamboyant with their scandalous behavior. As second-in-command in the Schutzstaffel, Heydrich used his dossiers to identify what SS Reichsführer Heinrich Himmler called the "lowest species of humanity" and impose "preventive detention" on thousands of criminals, politicians and enemies of the state, so many, in fact, that his orders quickly filled the prisons beyond capacity, and he had to convert an abandoned munitions factory at Dachau into a concentration camp.

Heydrich opened the first file and began reading, tapping a pen on his knee as he flipped pages. He reached into a pocket and rifled through a series of index cards until he found the kind he was looking for: one with a red tab on the right side and a black tab on the left. Carefully copying the name of an identified political operative from the first page of the file onto the card, he muttered, laughing to himself: "Sedláček? You thought I wouldn't find out you're a Marxist? Hah! See how you like planning the Communist takeover of the world with your friends in Dachau."

Swaying slightly as the limousine slowed to make its turn on to Rude Armady VII Kobylisky and enter the road that curved along the bend in the Vltava River in the near Prag suburb of Holešovice, Heydrich pushed protruding papers back into their folders, opened the flap of his satchel, slipped them inside and rested his fingers on the buckled leather straps. He relaxed in the seat as the sedan followed the wide arc of the road and then slowed to a crawl to make the sharp turn into V Holešovičkách Street. Surprised there were so few people on the street or waiting for the tram, he glanced at his watch: 10:35 a.m. Well, he said to himself, they are all good Czech workers. They are already on the job. *He* was the one who was late.

He had to admit, if grudgingly, that Czechoslovakia had its charms. Prag itself was cosmopolitan and cultured in a number of ways, with many examples of magnificent architecture. The suburb of Holešovice was serviceable—its buildings part lackluster—and maddeningly slow in operation with trams that were aged and inefficient, but its design, with large green areas on both the north and south sides of the town, was refreshing. Its residents were for the most part pleasant and passive, at least now that they knew who was in charge. But there wasn't a Germanizable Czech among them. Except maybe, he thought, for that

ASSASSINATION

one.

Heydrich had let his eyes trace the two-story shops lining Rude Armady and the shoppers adjusting their string bags as they walked along the cobbles and spotted a young man with a high, smooth forehead, slim and pointed nose and softly curling lips standing partially hidden in a doorway, a coat covering his body down to his shins. But what was such a young man doing here? And wearing such a heavy coat? It was nearly the end of May. Heydrich looked away from the man with contempt. Stupid Czech! This man clearly did not meet RuSHA racial criteria! He should not be walking the streets of a small town in Czechoslovakia! He should be working in the steelworks or laboring in the camps in the East! Heydrich decided he would tell the head of RuSHA—the Rasse- und Siedlungshauptamt unit of the SS responsible for Germanization and racial profiling—that its investigators needed to do a better job of applying tests for racial purity. Better yet, he would suggest that the Race and Settlement Main Office add more tests—ones for intelligence.

*

Czech Resistance fighter Josef Gabčík turned his head to the left and made a quick nod to his compatriot, Jan Kubiš, who was standing at the corner of V Holešovičkách Street rummaging through a worn rucksack. Gabčík shrugged the arm of the coat off his shoulder and raised a 99-mm automatic submachine gun. With his left hand under the fore piece of the weapon and the stock against his shoulder, he peered through the sight and aimed the barrel of the weapon directly at the side of Heydrich's face. He smiled as he watched Heydrich's head turn and eyes rest on him, at first squinting in surprise, then gradually hardening with the realization of what they were observing. The years of preparation in the Czech Army in Exile in Great Britain, the months of planning with the Czech Resistance, the weeks of hiding in the hills and forests of Bohemia, the days of indecision and apprehension were finally being translated into action: He was about to become an assassin.

Gabčík gently squeezed the trigger and waited for the recoil. But there was no sound or rebound. He squeezed the trigger again, but felt no response. He looked nervously at Kubiš, his eyes wide, his head shaking, his shoulders rising as if to ask a question. Then he released the fore piece and let the weapon drop to the side of his body, tugging the sleeve of his coat back onto his shoulder and hiding the weapon underneath. He was prepared for death, assuming it would come quickly by his own hand or an enemy's weapon, and for flight and concealment until then. But he was not prepared for failure. Since he had been airdropped into Nehvidzy by British pilots in March, he had thought of nothing but the bullet-shattered face and body of Reinhard Heydrich. Yet here at the perfect spot and the perfect time for the assassination, he could do nothing but turn away from his quarry and run down Rude Armady to the next side street.

*

Heydrich fumbled with the flap of his holster and finally unsnapped the catch, withdrawing the pistol. With his hand on the handle of the sedan's rear door, he paused slightly when he heard the clank of metal striking metal, a thump and then a scraping sound.

"There!" he called out to his driver. "He's over..." An overpowering rush of air took his words away. A sharp, sudden roar deafened his ears. Reverberations distorted his orientation as the back of the car rose a foot off the ground and crashed back to the earth, a passenger-side tire flattened, the windshield cracked.

Heydrich fell out of the car onto his shoulder, straining against the acute bursts of pain in his side and abdomen. He rose to his knees and held his breath as he forced his legs to raise his body. Hugging his torso with his left arm, he placed his hand on top of the sites of pain and pressed down to make it easier to move. Catching sight of a long coattail, he lifted his pistol and fired off several rounds aimed at the middle of the flapping cloth.

A stab of pain. A loss of breath. He grasped his side, stumbling on the cobblestones and falling back onto his knees. Then his body lurched forward, his pistol hand crashing to the curb.

Lying on his side, Heydrich wrenched open his uniform jacket. Running his fingers gingerly along his shirt front, he probed his injuries. In an area dark with blood, he saw small bits of metal protruding from his skin: shrapnel from the grenade and the interior of the car's rear door. The tips of his fingers felt tufts of material—strings of horsehair

ASSASSINATION

stuffing—and tiny curved pieces of metal—sections of the automobile's seat springs.

He rose on an elbow and looked back towards the car. There, in the gutter and on the street and sidewalk were index cards, fluttering in the breeze, dotted with spots of his blood.

CHAPTER TWO

Stones skittered along the path next to the grain storage building at the edge of the Lidice creek bridge and bounced onto the backs of their intended targets.

"You're not throwing at those geese, are you?" Chessie Sabel asked her son as she raised the cast-iron pump handle of the communal well.

She looked sidelong at Ondrej as he picked up a pair of small stones and massaged them in his palm.

"Well?" She pressed down on the pump and watched water splash into the wooden tub.

Ondrej stole a glance at his mother as he hefted a stone in his hand, working it between his thumb and forefinger and extending his arm out to the side, preparing to skim the pebble along the ground.

"Leave those geese alone. You know how Paní Nemeç is about her birds."

"Yeah, until she chops off their heads and cooks them up for Christmas dinner."

"I don't want to hear any more about it," Chessie complained, an edge to her voice. Ondrej had already raised Paní Nemeç's ire. "That hooligan," the old woman had told Chessie on more than one occasion, pointing a crooked finger at Ondrej. "Boys in my day had respect." Paní Nemeç had sniffed, thrusting her hand inside the bib of her apron. "But then again, their parents knew how to keep them in line. Your mother would have known how to discipline your boy. Too bad you didn't learn anything from her."

It was hard enough to raise Ondrej without his father Václav, dead now for two years. As for her mother, Chessie tried as much as possible not to dwell on the things her mother had taught while she was alive. She certainly didn't need that old stada baba Nemeç hectoring her about her mother or her son, especially now when she was so worried about him. Ondrej was at a crossroads, she felt. The Occupation and the war were

ASSASSINATION

forcing him to make decisions about himself he was not prepared for, and she didn't know how to help him.

When the Third Reich annexed the largely German Sudetenland in the autumn of 1938, 7-year-old Ondrej had been too young to understand why people in his town felt so vulnerable. He overheard his father and other men fret about the loss of a third of the country's perimeter to Nazi Germany, with the acquiescence of Czechoslovakia's supposed allies Britain and France, leaving what remained of the united territories of Bohemia, Moravia and Slovakia to fend for themselves. But the Sudetenland was 90 percent German anyway, Ondrej had read in his history book. So, the boy had wondered, wasn't it a good idea to let the Germans have it anyway?

Still, Ondrej did smart with shame in the early months of 1939 when he heard that Nazi troops had crossed the northern Bohemian border, invaded Prag, and within hours had established machinegun outposts overlooking the city from the Hradčany Castle district. The only opposition from Prag citizens? A few snowballs and slashed tires. Pitiful! Gutless, the older boys at school had said.

Rumors about old farmer Horák's sons, Josef and Filip, impressed him. Although Ondrej's father and other men in the town hushed as soon as Horák approached, Ondrej could not ignore fragments of their conversations: "Czech Army and Air Force units." "Britain." "Paratroopers" "Resistance." His Czech countrymen perhaps weren't cowardly after all.

But the actions of Czechoslovaks flew in the face of all he was learning in the classroom. Soon after the Occupation, he and his classmates were learning and speaking only German in the schoolhouse. The focus of their history lessons was on Germany, much of it centered on the betrayal of the bureaucrats in the loss of WW I, the unfairness of the Versailles Treaty, the subjugation of the German people. Current events classes highlighting the latest Wehrmacht victories in France and Africa replaced experiments in science and exercises in mathematics. Daily lessons stressed German superiority, national pride and dominance as the country's armies swept over Eastern Europe. The red and black swastika took the place of the red, white and blue national flag of Czechoslovakia. Schoolyard play shifted from stickball to organized calisthenics and lockstep marching.

Ondrej's father had interceded. Sitting across from the boy at the kitchen table, Václav urged his son to question what he was learning in school. He created and led Ondrej through mathematical calculations, told him about Czech and European history and tempered the Reich versions of the war.

After her husband's death, Chessie tried to continue the lessons, but she could feel her son pulling away from her. He told her he was too tired to take lessons at school and at home, too. He was bored with all the Czech heritage. The country hadn't even existed until after WW I. What great accomplishments or battles or culture could it point to? Why did he need to study math? No one else in class had to bother with it.

Ondrej soon was instructing her: the proper pronunciation of the German umlaut; the overpowering victories in the 1870 Franco-Prussian war, including decisive Prussian defeats of the French on August 4, 5 and 6, the siege of Metz on August 30 and Paris on September 19; and equating her with his teacher Paní Blazek. His mother, like his teacher, wasn't showing enough respect for the swastika or the salute to Adolf Hitler, or appreciating the progress of the Wehrmacht against the Soviets.

Chessie lately wished he was still lecturing her. Though she had felt diminished by his dismissiveness, she would have preferred it to his current obstinacy. These days, Ondrej gave one-word answers to her questions about his schoolwork. He spent much of his time trying to ingratiate himself with the older boys who hung around the town garage and the mechanic Zelenka—an uncompromising supporter of Nazi Germany—despite having to endure harsh taunts when he could not completely hide his youth.

In the past few weeks, her son had become agitated yet secretive. He refused to tell her why Paní Blazek was replaced by a new schoolteacher, Magda Marik, in the classroom. From what Chessie could piece together in conversations with other parents, she learned that someone had reported Paní Blazek to the SS for dereliction of duty as an educator of pupils for the New Germany because she had failed to lead the class in the Nazi salute each morning. Chessie was afraid that person had been Ondrej.

Chessie drew the last burst of water into the nearly overflowing tub, straightened the straps and hoisted it onto her back. She looked around for her son and saw him running up the hill next to St. Martin's Church. He takes after his father, she noted. Lanky for his 11 years, he

ASSASSINATION

would probably grow to be tall and muscular—and good looking, with his thick blondish hair and mischievous gray-blue eyes.

"Watch out for that tree." She indicated a stalk a few meters high jutting up in front of Ondrej.

"Why? It's just another one of those stink trees."

"No, it's a young pear tree."

"It's just like that one, isn't it?" Ondrej pointed to widely spreading tree with dark green leaves crowding out the few remaining bursts of white spring blooms.

"Yes, it is."

"Well, that's a stink tree. So if this thing," he rubbed his foot along the stalk and its fledgling branches, "is the same as that, it will smell bad, too." Ondrej held his nose and danced around the stalk.

"Yes, it does smell awful now, but it will be beautiful when it's fully blooming," Chessie insisted. "It will sway in the wind like a twirling dancer, and it will have nests of mockingbirds..."

"Who likes mockingbirds?"

"Oh, just stop," she said.

"You just like it because that's where daddy first kissed you." Ondrej skipped along next to Chessie. "On May Day, 'when a girl should be kissed under a blooming tree so she will be beautiful all year round,'" he sing-song quoted the Czech traditional saying.

"'It was late evening on the first of May,'" Chessie began a rhyme.

"Oh no. You're not going to recite *that* old thing," Ondrej groaned.

"'The eve of May was the time of love,'" Chessie continued as Ondrej made an exaggerated frown and stuck his fingers in his ears.

"'The turtle-dove's voice called to love.'" Chessie tugged his hands away from his head. "Come on," she prompted, "you know the rest."

"'Where rich,'" she paused. "Come on—'Where rich *and*...'"

She waited for her son to chime in, but he was already running ahead of her. Impatient as usual, she thought, ready to test the limits, whether they were in the schoolroom, on the playground or at home, in a hurry to shed his childish years and become a man. How she wished he had his father's hand to guide him.

ASSASSINATION

"Be careful," Chessie shouted, as he darted across the hard-packed dirt road toward the narrow bridge spanning the spring-rain-swollen creek. He zigzagged in front of a pair of teenage boys who had just stepped off the bus that transported workers to and from the munitions and steel plants in Kladno.

She was nervous around the two boys: Ignáce Tichy, a short, thick—in body and mind—16-year-old, who masked his ignorance with insouciance and combativeness; and Vit Kaspar, tall for his 15 years—5' 11"—and not as heavyset as Ignáce, nor as obviously aggressive, but edgy and volatile.

She watched now as the pair scuffed their blackened boots on the ground and stumbled over their loosened bootlaces and the unrolled cuffs of their dingy dungarees. She glanced quickly at the time on the church bell tower clock—10:45 a.m. They must have worked the midnight shift and spent a few hours in the tavern afterward, she thought, noting their unsteadiness.

"*Be careful.*" She stiffened when she heard Ignáce repeat her words and add the taunt "little man" directed toward her son, but then breathed more easily as she saw Ignáce turn his attention elsewhere.

"How's that Resistance business, old man?" Ignáce asked farmer Horák, who rested on his cane while talking with his friend Urbie Maruščáková at the side of the bridge. "How's that going for Josef and Filip? They parachuting in any time soon? From England? To save our country?"

Horák's two older sons had not been seen in Lidice for almost 3 years, ever since the Nazis started rounding up Czech doctors and lawyers, professors, teachers and university students and editors and journalists. The boys had tried to turn the town against the Nazis and organize an opposition group, but the people of Lidice hadn't gone along. Most of the townspeople didn't support the Nazis—most resented them, in fact, for taking away their jobs and farms and autonomy. But they didn't want the Czechoslovak Resistance in their backyard. That belonged in the big cities—Brno or Olomouc or Prag—not in a tiny village like theirs.

Some, like Ignáce, denigrated the Czech Resistance. It was a penny-ante movement, responsible for scattered work stoppages and

ASSASSINATION

rail disruptions, the mysterious appearance of flags or graffiti bearing the Resistance's trademark—the single capital letter V—but nothing pivotal. Or so Ignáce said. Chessie suspected that Ignáce, and maybe Vit, thought more highly of the Horák boys than they let on. Stuck in a small town, working long hours amid sulfurous molten slag, the boys might very well have wished they, like Josef and Filip, were thousands of kilometers away, learning how to fly airplanes and shoot rifles and break enemy codes.

"What do *you* know?" Ondrej piped up. "You couldn't be a soldier or a Resistance fighter in a million years. You're just grubby old steelworkers."

"And you could?" Ignáce nudged Vit with an elbow and laughed.

"You bet I could."

"Sure, sure, little man."

"I'm not a little man."

"Look pretty little to me," Vit spoke more to Ignáce than to Ondrej.

"Little man, little man, little man," Ignáce began to chant.

Ondrej rushed at Ignáce, his arms wide, his aim to grab Ignáce by the waist and pull him to the dirt. As Ondrej approached, Vit turned his body toward the boy and thrust a foot in his path. Ondrej tumbled forward just as Ignáce swung his arm into Ondrej's nose and cheeks, and Vit elbowed him in the ribs. Ondrej's knees buckled and he fell onto his side, gasping for breath.

"Even littler! ... Oh, Jesus Christ," Vit howled as the knob of Horák's cane crashed into his knee.

"So you think you're big men?" Horák asked, lifting the cane a few inches off the ground.

Vit took hold of the cane and tried to wrestle it away from the old man, but Maruščáková landed a series of punches in quick succession on both teens.

Ignáce and Vit shrunk from the blows and backed away, wiping sweat and blood from their faces and hair.

"Christ. We were just having a little fun. Can't you take a joke?" Ignáce said.

"It's not funny," Ondrej sputtered.

"I don't know. You all look pretty funny to me," Ignáce said, smirking. He turned to Vit. "Let's get out of here. Go to my grandmother's. She'll be out with the old ladies. We'll have the place to ourselves. She's got some good homemade gin, you know? Doesn't think I know where it is, but I do." He slung his arm over Vit's shoulder, sniggering and nodding in Ondrej's direction.

With his legs curled in close to his body, Ondrej watched the teens walk away. He rose on his knees, got to his feet, then quickly hunched over, covering the front of his pants and the spreading yellow stains as he ran across the bridge.

Chessie watched him pass the church, turn the corner and disappear down the street toward home, mortified that she had stood immobilized, her body frozen, her pulse pounding, her mind so overcome with uncertainty and fear she had been unable to help her son. She turned her face toward Horák and Maruščáková. "I…"

Horák nodded in acknowledgment of her distress, leaned once again onto his cane and spoke to his friend. "Felt good to take on those two, eh, Maruščáková?"

"Still a ball-buster," Maruščáková replied, tipping his hat in apology for the profanity to Chessie.

Chessie busied herself positioning the wooden tub on her back, then followed the men across the bridge and into town, parting ways with them in front of the butcher shop. In the middle of the street in front of the garage, she saw some boys bent over, with their elbows on their thighs, pointing and laughing at a departing figure. Her heart ached when she heard their jeering voices: "Piss Pants. Piss Pants."

ASSASSINATION

CHAPTER THREE

Secretary of State and Chief of Police for the ReichsProtektorate of Bohemia and Moravia, Karl Hermann Frank hurried across the square toward Petshův Palác, the imposing, roughly finished grey stone and brick building that had been transformed from the Petschek and Company Banking House into the headquarters for the Nazi secret police in Prag. He stiff-armed the front door and rushed up the main staircase three steps at a time.

He strode into the office of Senior Criminal Investigator SS-Hauptsturmführer Heinz Pannwitz, head of the Special Gestapo Committee charged with finding and making an example of Reinhard Heydrich's assassins.

Although Frank had been among the first Bohemians to push for German annexation of the Sudetenland by organizing the Sudeten-German Homeland Front as far back as 1933, he had not moved up in the ranks of the ReichsProtektorate leadership as he wished. Hitler had passed him over for promotion twice. First, when Hitler decided to replace the tactful and diplomatic ReichsProtektor Konstatin von Neurath with someone who could take a more strong-armed approach, he opted for Reinhard Heydrich. Frank could almost understand that. When Heydrich died, Frank was certain that he would take Heydrich's post. But Hitler had not replaced Heydrich with the radical German jingoist Karl Hermann Frank. No, Hitler had appointed Kurt Daluege. "Daluege, the engineer," Frank mocked him in private. Daluege, the man Heydrich called Dummi-Dummi, Frank had told his wife. Daluege! Hitler let *that man* take Heydrich's place and left *him* as the Czechoslovak Protektorate's state secretary, the *second in command*.

Smarting at the insult, Frank felt that he had to prove himself—yet again—and he struggled to tamp down his feelings of desperation. He and Emil Hácha, puppet president of Occupied Czechoslovakia, had advised Hitler to stay mass executions after Heydrich's death, arguing that such tactics would play into the hands of enemy propagandists. But

ASSASSINATION

Hitler was becoming uneasy, yearning for the Reich to act boldly, decisively, unforgettably. Frank needed to show Hitler he was the man for the job. He was the man who would find Heydrich's assassins, drag them down the streets of Prag and hang them in the courtyard of Hradčany Castle. He was the man who would make the Czechs suffer for their audacity.

"First, we got nothing," Frank heard Senior Criminal Investigator SS-Hauptsturmführer Heinz Pannwitz complain from the head of a mahogany conference table where he sat flanked by the other members of the Special Gestapo Committee. "And now this." Pannwitz eyed the piles of more than 600 reports that had been delivered in the past 48 hours.

Frank and Pannwitz were initially shocked when the Special Gestapo Committee received only a handful of reports from citizens of the Czechoslovak Protektorate in the first few days after the assassination. They thought the Reich had sent a clear message about the consequences of continued silence when 100 Czechs were shot immediately and another 1,800 were executed within days of Heydrich's death. Entire families were still being lined up and killed, including grandparents, teenage sons and daughters and children, and their names were broadcast on the radio, printed in the local newspapers, blazoned on posters in cities and small towns and nailed to trees and farm fences. The Gestapo warned that if the assassins were not found soon, every tenth Czech would be shot.

Still, it wasn't until the committee promised huge rewards—up to 2 million Reichsmarks—that information started flowing, and even then, the amount of information that might actually lead to the assassins' identities was small. The committee knew that the assassins were moving from place to place, hidden and protected by Czech families. The reports they hurried out to investigate took them to "hiding places" in abandoned buildings so full of cobwebs it was clear they had not been used in years.

Frank watched Pannwitz rub his cheeks and chin, then pull his hand away from his face in disgust at the touch of his budding bristles. No matter how often or how closely he shaved, Pannwitz always had dark

ASSASSINATION

shadows of whiskers, stains almost, that set him apart from the Gestapo leadership. To Frank's mind, this perpetual beard served as an outward reminder of Pannwitz' tenuous grasp on the proper New German credentials. The man had been a metalworker incapable of holding down a factory job, a student barely able to complete his high school studies, the product of an illegitimate birth by a poor German girl. Probably his only claim to investigator status in the Nazi police, and later the Gestapo, was his dubious paternal link (who could prove it one way or another?) to Prussian nobility and a decorated German general. That link would do him little good if he couldn't speed up the search for the assassins. Pannwitz had better have something solid this time, Frank thought.

Pannwitz looked across the table at the fresh-faced Soldat who held a letter bearing the logo of the Palaba battery factory in Slaný, along with a handwritten note.

"The letter," he told Frank, "is from the factory owner, uh, a Jaroslav Pála. As you can see from the signature on the company letterhead, Pála found a note that had been sent from one of his employees to another. The letter was intended for a woman—Ana Maruščáková."

"What does it say?" Frank demanded.

"The letter from Pála or ..."

"Just tell me."

"A factory hand named Václav Říha sent this note to his girlfriend ... to Ana ... the one I ..."

"Go on."

"Well, the note said, 'I had to do it. We shall not meet for a long time.'"

Pannwitz took the letter from the Soldat and read: "'Dear Annie. Excuse me for writing you so late, but maybe you'll understand because you know that I have had many worries. What I wanted to do, I have done. On the fatal day, I slept somewhere in Čabárna. I'm fine. I'll see you this week, and then we will never see each other again.'"

"Where is this..." Frank indicated the name on the page, "This Ana? Where is she from?"

The Soldat reached over to point out the address.

"Yes, yes, I see," Frank said. "Lidice... So?"

Pannwitz rubbed the side of his nose. "Lidice. It is a small town not far from Prag. You probably have not heard of it before, but... " He tapped a black leather binder that lay open on the table in front of him and let his finger trace down a list of names. "There." He stabbed at several lines of type.

Pannwitz turned the binder as Frank leaned forward to see it more clearly. "It's a list of the men who left the Protektorate to join the Czechoslovak Army in exile in Britain." He sat back and smiled. "Look down to the H's. Do you see it? The name Horák? Lt. Horák, a Czech pilot?"

Pannwitz waited until Frank was hunched over the binder.

"You see? Where he is from?"

Frank nodded, sat back and rubbed his temples.

"Lidice."

Chapter Four

"Zzzzz. Zzzzz. Zzzz." Fourteen-year-old Milan Tichy turned his head to determine the source of the sound.

He stopped and listened. "Zzzzz. Zzzzz. Zzzzz." There it was again, this time followed by childish giggles.

Milan placed his hedge clippers against his shoulder and followed the noises to the edge of the Lidice schoolhouse. He walked alongside the 3-story, stucco building, noticing through an open window that the schoolteacher, Magda Marik, was at the blackboard writing out verb conjugations for the next day's language class. He sidestepped a bicycle, its handlebars balanced against the wall, its back tire almost flat. He'd better tell the teacher before she tried to ride it home.

Behind the building, in a corner of the playground, he saw his friend Fat Ceslav crouching down with his arms close to his body, his hands next to his face, his fingers fluttering.

"It was a fly," Ceslav said to a group of small children watching him with rapt faces. "A fly," Ceslav moved his arms up and flexed them at the elbows, then let his fingers hang down limp from his wrists. "Caught in a web." He twisted his shoulders as if they were held fast. "And a hu—u—u—ge spider," he cringed, "was coming."

The Tale of the Three Doves, Milan thought, or at least Ceslav's version of it. Milan put the clippers on the ground and leaned against the building to watch Ceslav as he fell down on all fours, spread his arms and legs wide and scowled. Ceslav curled one hand like a claw and made a sudden move toward the children, who shrieked and scrambled to get out of reach.

"But our hero," Ceslav paused, looking up at the faces of the children, "His name was Ceslav."

"That's *your* name," the children shouted.

"Well, isn't that the strangest thing?" he said, scratching his head.

Ceslav stood and smoothed his shirt over his bulging frame. "Our hero," he patted himself on the top of his shoulder, "He came right up to that big old thick cobweb, and you know what he did?"

"What?" the children called out.

"He stuck in his hand, right in between the fly and the spider, and pulled the web totally apart." Ceslav reached into an imaginary cobweb, took hold of its elusive strands of silk, ripped them up and rolled them into a ball.

"The spider? He was really mad." Ceslav went back down on all fours, turned his hands into fists and pounded them on the ground.

"But our hero," Ceslav said, jumping up again. "He just gave that spider the back of his hand. 'Take that, Mean Old Spider.' " Ceslav brushed his fingertips together. As if he heard something, he turned his head suddenly to look behind him. Wiping a hand across his forehead, he whispered to the children, "Whew, I was afraid that spider was still there."

"A hero can't be afraid," one of the children asserted.

"Sometimes it's smart for a hero to be a little afraid," Ceslav advised.

"Now the fly," he returned to his story, "You remember that fly … that was caught in the web? Well, our hero set her free." Ceslav put his hands in his armpits and flapped his elbows up and down. "She was so happy, she told hero Ceslav, 'If you ever need any help, you just call me, and I will be there.' "

"How can a fly help with anything?" one of the children piped up.

"You will be surprised."

"He's leaving out the first part of the story," said Paní Tichy, who, like Milan, has been drawn from Michalská Street by the sounds of the children. "He's left out the whole part about the birds," she complained to her walking companion, Paní Smida.

"Oh, it's all right, Luka. He's telling a good story. Don't you think so?" Paní Smida asked her daughter Emília.

"Oh yes, Mama," Emília said.

"You remember it?" Paní Smida asked her daughter. "The story you learned when you were just a girl?"

Emília sucked on a curl and shook her head.

ASSASSINATION

"She probably remembers the story the way it's supposed to be told, not like this," Paní Tichy said as she turned her back on the scene and started walking home. "You'd better be coming along soon," she called out to Milan. "I don't want to have to wait all day for you." She cast a critical eye on the young boy, examining his curly brown hair, his dark and thoughtful eyes and his gangling adolescent frame. She frowned. "Nothing like his brother or his father," she muttered to herself.

"Yes, Grandma," he said, shifting his eyes from her to Paní Smida, who was speaking slowly and carefully to Emília. "It's the Tale of the Three Doves," she said. "You learned it at school."

Emília was almost the same age as Milan's older brother, Ignáce, but she still hadn't finished her studies. No one ever told Milan what was wrong with her. She just wasn't like everyone else her age. She came to school regularly and sat in the front of the room, next to the schoolteacher, marking up a blank notebook with thick black lines and curlicues and humming while the rest of the class read history or social studies. When the teacher brought out one of the old primers, Emília would concentrate on the pictures and the words, sucking on her lower lip. She would copy the letters on lined paper, working hard to keep the markings straight and evenly spaced. She would sit with the younger children at story time and rock back and forth while the teacher read aloud.

"I want to hear the story, Mama," she said to her mother.

"Not now, dear. We have to go home."

She pointed at Milan. "Story time?" she asked expectantly. "Are we going to have story time? I like story time."

"I do, too," he said.

"Come, Emília," her mother said.

"But," she said, trying to pull away from her mother's grasp.

"Not now," her mother said, tugging on her arm.

Emília's eyes probed Milan's.

"It's all right, Emília," he said. "We will have other stories."

Emília shifted her gaze from Milan to Ceslav. She put a thumbnail between her teeth and kept looking back as her mother pulled her away from the playground.

"And what do you think our hero did now?" Milan heard Ceslav ask the children.

"He helped the wolf get his tail out from under the log," the children cried.

"That's right. And do you know what the wolf said?"

"'If you need help, call me,'" the children sang.

"Oh, you are so smart. You're ahead of me."

"Now," Ceslav lowered his voice to a sinister whisper, "Our hero had to go into a deep, dark forest..."

Milan's mind shifted to an earlier time, when birch branches filtered and blunted the sunlight, when a small metal trap lay open on the ground.

He stepped away from the children but could still hear Ceslav's words: "A forest where there were bad things ... like ... the Devil's Grandmother."

"Don't be such a cry baby," Ignáce hissed. "You'll like this." He waved the bloody body in front of 10-year-old Milan's face. "You like wild hare, don't you?"

Milan shook his head violently to protect his face from the cascade of blood pouring out of the slash in the animal's gut. He squeezed his eyes shut but still felt the liquid fall onto his eyelids and run alongside his nostrils and the edges of his mouth. He struggled to free his arms and roll his body out of the way, but he was trapped by Vit, who sat on top of his abdomen and legs, holding his arms down with his knees and pressing his shoulders to the ground.

"You like this bunny, don't you?" Vit laughed, his eyes dancing with malice.

For weeks, Milan had been carefully approaching the skittish hare. He had left bits of food in the same spot at the edge of the forest at the same time every day and watched from the mulberry bushes as the animal nibbled on the morsels. Every few days, he had taken a position closer to the feeding spot and had sat completely still while the hare fed. When he was only a few meters away, he had begun taking pieces of food and holding them out to the animal. At first, the hare had knocked Milan's hand to make the food drop to the ground. But as Milan had continued to keep his hand steady, the animal had grown comfortable with him and soon began to leave its hiding place in the underbrush as soon as

ASSASSINATION

it saw Milan sit down.

Today Milan sat in his usual spot, but he did not see the hare. He waited for several minutes, peering between the leaves for a rustle of motion, a wiggling whisker. He placed the food on the ground and rose on his knees. He slowly pushed back branches and leaves, then stood up and cautiously moved into the underbrush, clicking his tongue as a call to the animal.

Milan saw it then, the trap, with the hare inside. The trap was resting in a clearing between pine trees. He ran to the trap and spoke softly. "What's happened to you? This shouldn't be here. I'll get you out." He fumbled with the latch that kept the trap closed, worried that his movements would scare the animal even further.

Milan heard a belittling voice: "I'll get you out." And another: "Oh, poor bunny. What's happened to you?"

He turned suddenly to see Ignáce and his friend Vit step from behind a pine tree.

"Help me," Milan said to his brother. "I can't get the trap open."

"Help me," Ignáce whined. "Help the poor little bunny."

"We'll help the poor little bunny," Vit echoed.

Vit grabbed Milan's shirt collar and pulled him away from the trap. "Watch us help the bunny," he sneered.

Ignáce flipped the trap over so the hare fell backward. He unlatched the trap door and pulled on the animal's ears to detach it from the wire frame. He held the animal high in the air and thrust it toward Milan.

Milan pushed against Vit, but was not strong enough to get past him. "Leave my bunny alone," he cried.

"Oh, so it's your bunny," Ignáce taunted. "I should take care of your bunny? Here's how I take care of it." He shook the animal up and down.

"Stop it," Milan cried. "Stop it," he wailed, tears springing from his eyes.

Ignáce reached into the bushes and withdrew a large knife.

Milan began pounding on Vit's chest, trying to get past him to reach his brother.

Ignáce poked the hare in the side with the tip of the knife. "He would make a good dinner, wouldn't he?" he said.

"NO," Milan cried. "He's my friend."

ASSASSINATION

Ignáce curled a lip. "Your friend," he jeered, as he thrust the knife into the animal until its legs stopped moving and it hung limp.

Milan reached in vain toward the bleeding body, sobs choking his chest.

"Let's do this," Vit said to Ignáce, relishing the words.

Ignáce nodded. "Do it," he agreed.

Vit knocked Milan to the ground and pinned his body, arms and legs. Ignáce slit the hare's belly fully open and held it over Milan's face, shaking it to propel the blood more quickly. He pushed his hand into the animal's belly and withdrew its innards, pressing them down onto Milan's cheek and then sweeping the organs across Milan's nose and mouth. "A treat for your lunch," he said.

"I don't think so." Fat Ceslav stepped into the clearing. "No, I don't think so," he said.

"And what are you going to do about it, Fatso?" Ignáce taunted the newcomer.

"This," Ceslav said as he pitched a rock into Ignáce's face.

Ignáce staggered from the blow. He dropped the animal to the ground as his nose began pouring blood and he tried to stanch the flow.

Ceslav took advantage of the distraction to grasp Ignáce's wrist, wrench the knife away and pull his arm behind him. He kicked Ignáce's knee, then elbowed him forward and forced him onto the ground. Stepping on one of Ignáce's hands, Ceslav ground his heel into his wrist, not caring that Ignáce's yelps were swallowed by the earth.

Ceslav then hefted the knife in his hand and looked at Vit, who had released Milan and was turning toward him with clenched fists. Ceslav held the knife close to his body, thumbing the handle. "You really want to try that?" he asked Vit.

Vit bounced on the balls of his feet, his eyes looking for an opening to attack.

Milan rolled over on his stomach, then onto his knees. As Vit stepped back to set himself to deliver a punch, Milan thrust his head and shoulders into Vit's legs.

Vit fell onto his fists, gasping as painful reverberations ran up his arms to his shoulders. He twisted on his side, cringing as Ceslav pushed a foot onto his knee. He froze as the knife blade ticked his cheek.

"Never again," Ceslav warned, as he pressed the blade more deeply into

Vit's skin. "Understand?"

Vit whistled, more in fear than in pain.

"Understand?"

"Yes. Yes," he breathed. He curled into a ball as soon as Ceslav rose.

Milan picked up the hare's body and replaced the entrails. He cradled it in his palms and walked with Ceslav's arm around his shoulders to find a burial site.

"'You came at the right time,' the Devil's Grandmother told our hero." Milan turned his attention back to Ceslav and his words. "'I need someone to herd my horses,' she told him. And she promised to give him plenty of food if he did a good job. 'But if you don't herd the horses well,'" Ceslav warned, wagging a finger at the children, "'You will lose your head.'" His fingers made a slashing motion across his neck.

Milan once again wondered whether he should have told his mother about the incident with the hare. If she knew what Ignáce was really like ... if she knew .... then maybe her eyes wouldn't dance when she saw him at the end of his workday or her fingers wouldn't curl his hair when he sat next to her on the sofa reading the newspaper or...

Milan retrieved the hedge clippers and began walking toward his grandmother's house. If his mother knew, then maybe she wouldn't love Ignáce so much and she would love him more.

Chapter Five

Prinz-Albrecht-Strasse was quiet, solemn even, in anticipation of the funeral later in the day. Reichsfürher Heinrich Himmler saw no traffic on the street or pedestrians on the sidewalks as he looked out the window of his office at Gestapo Headquarters in Berlin.

Himmler pulled a handkerchief from his pocket and shook it out. He unhooked the round, wire-rimmed spectacles from his ears, fogged the lenses and wiped them absently. Who would have thought Heydrich could be felled by an assassin? Heydrich of all people: his second in command in the SS; the lieutenant who had sat directly to his right when he convened the round table of Teutonic Knights in his castle outside Paderborn; the confederate who had shared his goal of creating a network of spies that would infiltrate every aspect of life in the New Germany.

Heydrich was exactly who he wanted in the SS. Himmler formed a picture of Heydrich in his mind: tall, slim, athletic and a skilled fencer, equestrian, swimmer and pentathlon champion. And Nordic—blond hair, blue eyes, oval face, clear white skin. More Nordic than the Nazis at Wannsee who decided the fate of every Jew in Europe. Himmler smiled as he lined up the leaders of the SS at the 1934 Wannsee Conference in his memory: Milch, Wolff, Bonin, Krügel, von Schütz. All of them shorter, fatter—straining their uniforms at the buttons—and plainer than Heydrich. Far less trim. Himmler reflexively squeezed a bicep that refused to tone up to his liking despite his determined weight-lifting routine. And far more healthy. He kneaded his stomach with his knuckles in response to a sudden surge of cramping.

Himmler realized he would miss Heydrich, but certainly not because he liked the man. Himmler knew that Heydrich did not embrace the philosophy he tried so hard to instill in members of the SS—his wish that SS officers would believe they were not just a political arm of the Third Reich, but a brotherhood of Nordic men, a new breed of Teutonic Knights who were inspired by medieval legends. He had felt Heydrich's impatience when he held rituals and torch-lit parades and

ASSASSINATION

presented ceremonial swords and daggers inscribed with pagan runes. On more than one occasion, Himmler had noted a glint of scorn at the edge of Heydrich's eye, a smirk on Heydrich's lip. It was as if Heydrich had been undressing Himmler in his imagination—and laughing at the inadequacy outlined in Himmler's undershorts.

No, Himmler would not miss Heydrich's vanity and contemptuousness. He would miss Heydrich's drive and determination to make the SS an elite and disciplined corps of loyalists and his tireless efforts to identify and eliminate enemies of the Reich. No one had worked harder than Heydrich to collect and collate even the smallest bits of information that might reveal subterfuge, betrayal, weakness or insincerity. No one had been more committed to distinguishing the Aryan from the Mongol or the Slav. No one had been more ingenious at devising solutions that would breed and disperse a new Germanic population throughout Eastern Europe.

Heydrich had been proud of his work to rid Germany of the elements that were eating away at the country's spirit and eliminate once and for all those who were racially imperfect or asocial. As head of the Occupation government, he gladly accepted his mission to make Bohemia and Moravia a "bulwark of Germandom" and a "sentry facing East." He recognized the urgency: Some in the SS had been too quick to label all non-native Germans as inferior, suitable only for being displaced from their properties and turned into slave laborers. But as the Wehrmacht moved inexorably eastward, it was becoming clear that there were not enough native Germans to resettle the confiscated lands. The Third Reich needed more Aryan Germans—whether they came from breeding programs between SS officers and suitable Czech women or through the assimilation of the 40 to 60 percent of ethnic Czechs considered racially qualified for Germanization. He relished the complexity of the task: the need to create a racial and national census; to find ways of classifying entire populations by nationality and race; and to use scientific as well as common-sense methods for screening individual physical characteristics and examining bloodlines. He welcomed Himmler's challenge: to ensure that all of Eastern Europe was populated solely by men with Aryan blood. He was content to be called "The Blond Beast."

Himmler consequently had bristled when he heard Hitler's private comments about Heydrich's death. "Idiotic," Hitler called Heydrich's recklessness in exposing himself to unnecessary danger. "Such heroic gestures as driving in an open, unarmored vehicle or walking about the streets unguarded are just damned stupidity, which serves the Fatherland not one whit," Hitler said to Himmler.

Heydrich had not contributed to his death! Himmler huffed. The man was sacrificed, hunted down by the treacherous English and the cowardly Czechs. Himmler fumed. He had to make that clear. He had to make sure there would be retribution for this heinous act.

Himmler snapped the handkerchief against the windowpane, then turned back to his desk. He pawed through a sheaf of typewritten sheets until he found the place in the eulogy where he would recount the assassination. He held the paper out in front of him, his fingers tightening as he read.

He walked to the other side of the desk and sat down, then opened a drawer, took out a blank sheet and spread it out smooth. He uncapped his fountain pen and wrote: "On May 27th, an English bomb hit him from behind. A paid person from the ranks of..." Himmler paused and lifted up the pen point. He thought for a moment, then pressed the point down heavily and continued, "...from the ranks of the most worthless subhumans brought him low." That's the way to do it, he thought. The blame must lie at the feet of the Czechs and the British who support the Czech Resistance and the government in exile.

Himmler placed the top of the pen against his lower lip and chewed on it absently as he gathered his thoughts. "Fear and excessive caution were foreign to him," he wrote, underlining the words to add emphasis. "With courage and energy he defended himself and shot twice at his attackers, though he had been gravely wounded." He wrote more rapidly now, sure of his message. "For days," he added to the page, "we hoped that his hereditary strength and disciplined, healthy body would overcome his horrible injury. On the seventh day, June 4, 1942, destiny, Almighty God the ancient, ended the life of Heydrich, a deep believer, but the greatest opponent of the use of religion for political purposes."

Himmler read over the paragraph, his pen hovering over each word. Satisfied he had defended Heydrich's actions but would not incur Hitler's disdain, he capped the fountain pen and placed it alongside the blotter, parallel to the leather portfolio that would house the completed eulogy.

He picked up the rest of the papers and scanned the text, rising from the desk and walking with them in his hand as he reread sections aloud to test his pronunciation and oratorical skills. "How incomprehensible

ASSASSINATION

to us is the thought that this shining, great human, scarcely 38 years old, is no longer with us and unable to battle alongside his friends."

Himmler cleared his throat. "For all Germans, he will bear witness as a martyr that Bohemia and Moravia are and always will be German lands, as they have been since time immemorial. It is our holy duty to atone for his death, to take up his tasks, and to pitilessly destroy, without any sign of weakness, the enemies of our Volk."

Himmler scanned his last, personal paragraph of farewell to Heydrich. "Your unwavering loyalty..." he began.

CHAPTER SIX

The breeze rippled across the rows of budding barley in the field next to the Tůma farmhouse. It tickled the blooms in the flower-beds that edged the farm buildings and drove pungent drafts of hyacinth toward Katrenka Becke.

Katrenka sat in the rocking chair she had dragged from the living room of her mother's home to the grassy area underneath the front windows. She propped up her heels on a wooden milk crate and sifted through the string bag of home remedies her friend Chessie had left for her. There were ginger and chamomile leaves to make tea, sprigs of lavender and peppermint to sniff and the needle, fastened to a swatch at the bottom of the bag, to let her know if the end of her pregnancy, now at 34 weeks, would produce a boy or a girl.

She opened the jar of freshly made lemonade and took a sip, then withdrew a cracker from the bag and took a small bite. Then she sat back, waiting for the nausea to pass. Throughout her pregnancy, she had been able to eat only sparingly. Even this close to term, she was still vomiting several times a day, and at times, she was too nauseated to drink water. Her legs and ankles were so swollen she had difficulty walking and her skin was raw, red, and flaky, tender to the faintest touch. In the last weeks, she was often weak-kneed and wobbly, disoriented and seeing double.

She looked forward to the birth, even though she was bringing a new life into the world alone. But the death of her husband just six months ago was overwhelming. She watched the sun shining off the new leaves of the linden trees and the trail of the wind among the flower stalks. In her mind, she knew this was beautiful. In her heart, she felt nothing.

Katrenka rested the string bag of remedies on the ground, reached into the pocket of her smock and removed a small carved wooden bird. She rubbed the wings of the bird, then closed her fingers around the figure and pressed her hand to the side of her pregnant belly. A picture of her husband formed in her mind: his sandy blond hair, thick and

ASSASSINATION

tousled; his fingers, long and thin, marked by calluses and small cuts from whittling and wood carving; his eyes, pale blue, magnified by round reading glasses, with lashes so light you could hardly see them; his body, sinewy legs, strong chest, flat stomach; his smell, yeasty, a little like bleu cheese. How she loved the smell of bleu cheese. She thought about her own dark-blond curly hair and blue-green eyes, and pale, pinkish skin.

"You will be beautiful, my love," she said to her pregnant belly, "if I do say so myself."

She pressed the carving to her heart and let herself remember the last time she had been with her husband, wrinkling her nose again at the smell of the jaeger schnitzel and sauerkraut soup she had prepared for their dinner. She tasted the grains of sugar from the strudel he had so carefully removed from the bakery wrapping and felt the sting of the slivovitz passing along the sides of her throat. She recalled the long, slow sex, the entangled fingers, overlapping legs, tender kisses. And the letter he had left for her—on his pillow the next morning. "I didn't want to make you cry, so I didn't wake you," it had said. "Here is *Slét*." The letter introduced the carved bird. "To keep with you. Every time you touch him, you will touch a piece of my heart. *Sléthnout se*," Johann had signed the paper. "We will one day come together, come together by flying."

The door to the farmhouse opened and Silvie Tůma, Katrenka's sister-in-law, stepped through.

"Mooning over your dead husband?" Silvie said, as she placed a cigarette in her mouth, lit it, then shook out the match flame and tossed it into the flowerbed. Silvie was an imposing bear of a woman, her hair black, curly, and dense, her body squat, more heavyset than muscular, and her disposition snappish and demeaning, particularly toward her sister-in-law. She bent forward, held the cigarette inches away from Katrenka and sent a stream of smoke into her face. "A lot of good that's going to do."

Having to return to Lidice still smarted for Silvie Tůma—even though it had been 3 years since her husband had lost his tobacco business and they had returned to run his family's farm. Silvie had been happy in Prag. She *belonged* in Prag, with all the diversions it had to offer, not in this backwater town. Didn't she *deserve* to be there? Wasn't she just as good as the Sudeten Germans—the ones who were taking over the city, the Sudeten "Germans" who had lived their entire lives in

Czechoslovakia and were more Czech than German?

Silvie scorned Sudeten Germans. Their wives were Czech. Their children were Czech. They talked and walked like Czechs. None of that German officiousness or that stand-on-the-street-corner-until-the-traffic-light-changed-even-if-there-wasn't-a-car-for-kilometers kind of respect for authority. No, the Sudetens were Czech. The Sudeten Beckes, Katrenka's full-of-himself husband and his mother, were Czech.

And don't think Sudetens considered themselves anything but Czech—before the Nazis invaded, that is—when all you heard from them were complaints about the Germans. And now? Silvie scoffed. Those same Sudetens couldn't be *more* German. They couldn't be happier to be part of the new Reich. Well, why not? They could get more and better rations, the best jobs in the factories and quicker promotions in the new Oberlandrat government.

The only way for Czechs to keep at least *something* of their own, Silvie felt, was to grease the German pan and find a way to link up with the Germans without losing their shirts. And for Silvie, that's where Katrenka should have come in. She with her fancy-dancy, book-store-owning Sudeten husband. But the stupid bitch couldn't seem to develop any German connections, or get any black market Reichsmarks, or help her own brother keep his business and make it possible for Silvie to stay in Prag, kicking up her heels to oompah bands and downing mugs of Hofbräu in the beer halls of Nové Město.

So Silvie had to move back to Lidice and that meant blending in with the townspeople—going to bingo games, for god's sake, with the good ladies of the Sokol society! At least it had been working. The people of Lidice had warmed up to her, tamping down their suspicions and treating her almost like a life-long resident, not a turncoat who had moved to Prag and become a Nazi sympathizer.

But then *Katrenka* had shown up and Silvie's dumb-ox, bleed-ing-heart of a husband had taken her in. The Good Samaritan! And did he get anything for it? No! Katrenka didn't help out around the farm. She followed the same routine—other than visits to the midwife and church for mass and confession, she spent most of her time weeding her mother's garden, picking apples in the nearby orchard and reading (over and over) a pair of books she had taken from her husband's bookstore.

All that hard work, sucking up to every goddamn woman in the town, was now for naught. Take the wife of a Sudeten German into your

ASSASSINATION

house and you might as well plaster an SS on your sleeve! That's what a lot of these ignorant townspeople thought. To many of the self-righteous women of Lidice, Katrenka was nothing more than a Nazi whore, and Silvie and her husband Kornel were whoremongers of the Third Reich. She was tired of it. Tired of the shoppers who crossed to the other side of the street rather than approach her and her family face to face. Tired of the churchgoers who refused to sit in the same pew with them. Tired of the people who cringed at any mention of Katrenka's name. Tired of being a pariah like her sister-in-law.

Well, she might have to put up with the bitch, but at least she could keep the woman in her place.

"Doing anything today?" Silvie asked Katrenka, puffing to stoke the cigarette. "Like cleaning up after yourself?"

CHAPTER SEVEN

"Your unwavering loyalty." Himmler's words reverberated off the walls of Mosaic Hall in the New Reichs Chancellery in Berlin as he spoke into the microphone atop the podium that stood to the left of Heydrich's casket and directly below a bronze eagle and swastika.

"And wonderful friendship," he continued, letting his voice rise, "which united us in this life and which death cannot obliterate."

Himmler finished his remarks, placed the papers inside the portfolio and slipped it under his arm, then moved to the front of the casket. He extended a Nazi salute, turned, stepped down the red marble stairs past cascades of flowers and approached the first row of dignitaries at the state funeral for Reinhard Heydrich. He took his place next to Josef Goebbels, head of the Gestapo, and Czech President Emile Hácha.

*

Adolf Hitler waited for Himmler to settle in his seat before he rose and made his way to the podium. Standing straight and silent, his head bowed, he made sure he had the full attention of every person in the hall. "I have only a few words to dedicate to this dead man." His voice was clipped, abrupt; his fingers grasped the podium tightly. "He was one of the best National Socialists, one of the strongest defenders of German Reich thought, one of the biggest opponents of all the enemies of the Reich, who fell as a martyr for the preservation and safeguarding of the Reich."

Hitler opened a polished wooden box and withdrew a heavy, iron cross medal. "As leader of the party and as leader of the German Reich, I give you, My Dear Comrade Heydrich, the highest recognition I have to bestow: the uppermost level of the German Order. You are only the second person to receive this award."

Hitler placed the medal on top of the casket and waved a Nazi salute. He stepped down from the podium and turned toward Heydrich's two young sons. He patted the first on the top of his head, squeezed the

ASSASSINATION

face of the second and waited while the SS honor guard surrounded the casket and led the procession down the center aisle. A hand on his chest, moved by the opening sounds of the processional music—Siegfried's Funeral March from the fourth and final opera in Richard Wagner's *The Ring Cycle*—the Führer let his chest inflate with pride as he listened to the trumpets, trombones and tubas capture the theme of Siegfried, the hero who represented all that was superior about a master race. How satisfying to honor Heydrich—an Aryan hero—with the same music. Hitler let the sounds embrace him as they rose from the woodwinds, spread to the strings and with a clash of cymbals, finally burst into the brasses, moving from a mournful dirge to commemoration. Then he fell in line behind the casket with Hácha, Himmler and Goebbels, and let his anger seep through his words.

"Nothing can prevent me from deporting millions of Czechs," he sputtered to Hácha.

"But the war effort," Hácha implored. "Mass deportations or killings will endanger our armaments industry. We rely so much on the Czechs..."

"I don't want to hear it. You know what I did after that German was killed by the Resistance in France," Hitler said. "Ten French inmates executed. Ten French deaths for one death—of a minor official in the Third Reich. This..." he pointed to Heydrich's casket. "*This* requires an example. A massive demonstration of our power and how we will use it."

"But what about...."

Hitler raised his arm quickly to cease all comment. "The assassins must be found." He glared at Hácha. "Czechs must pay ... now!"

Himmler placed a hand in front of his face to hide his smile, then scanned the assembled SS for the man charged with the task: Karl Hermann Frank.

*

"What are you waiting for?" Himmler asked Frank.

Frank traced for Himmler the flimsy links between the assassination and Lidice. "Not much there," he concluded.

"Well, you're not going to find anything more if you keep standing around here."

REPRISAL

Chapter Eight

Chessie sat back on her haunches and rubbed dirt from her hands onto her skirt while surveying her garden. The spring colors had waned. Petals had fallen from tulips, revealing ovaries and engorged stigmas at their tips as filaments and leaves dried up and died back. Yellow fronds of forsythia had been replaced by swaths of green. Tufts of grass camouflaged isolated stalks of purple crocus.

She covered the rows of summer vegetable seeds she had sown with a little compost and a sprinkling of water, pulled some early new green beans from their stalks and pinched a few sprigs of parsley, placing them in a wicker basket and taking them into her kitchen. At the washstand, she rinsed the greens and set them on a towel to dry and began pulling leaves and roots from a kohlrabi she had brought up from the root cellar.

A rumble of engines—automobile engines—caught her attention as they grew steadily louder. Whiffs of exhaust fumes irritated her nose. A pair of brakes scraped on their pads, a clutch popped, an engine gulped as it switched off, car doors squeaked on their hinges.

The vegetable still in her hand, Chessie moved to the front windows of her house and peered through the lace curtain. She stepped back quickly, trying to hide herself in the shadows when she saw that boxy black sedans, one after another, were rolling into the streets of her town, disgorging soldiers into the streets, soldiers with jagged double S's on their collars.

*

A rap on her front door. "Everyone must come out of their houses and go to the town square," a harsh male voice called out.

Katrenka rolled onto her hip and leaned a shoulder into the sofa cushions. She pushed down on the soft fabric to raise herself up, swooning with waves of dizziness and nausea.

"What's taking so long in there?" the voice demanded. Heavy blows rattled the door in its frame.

"I'm coming," Katrenka said weakly as she carefully lifted one knee and eased her foot onto the floor, then raised the other knee.

"Kick it in," the voice ordered. "There. Hit it there."

Thumping. Whacking. Smacking sounds. Wood splintering. The door flew open. Coal-scuttle-helmeted men in green woolen uniforms stood on the threshold.

*

"For Christ sake, Milan, hurry it up," Ceslav admonished his friend. He stood with his body angled so he could look around the edge of the schoolhouse. "The SS are all over the place. They've been to your house—and mine. They're pushing people, knocking down doors, dragging the old ladies out of the church. Jesus."

"Why the hell are they doing that?"

"Like I know?" Ceslav inched his head forward and peered toward the front of the schoolhouse.

"But what can it be?"

"What does it matter? The SS are *here*, for Christ sake. They tell us to jump, we jump." Ceslav tensed. "There they go," he said as he pulled his head back. "They're going into the school, Milan. Jesus. The kids." He turned toward Milan. "Come on. We have to..." Ceslav didn't wait for a reply. He looked around the corner of the building again, and seeing that the coast was clear, moved along the side of the schoolhouse.

Milan dropped the hoe he had been using to till the garden behind the playground and hurried after his friend, who was just about to round the corner of the schoolhouse and enter the town square. "Ceslav," he called out. "Come back this way."

"Why?" Ceslav mouthed.

"Just do it."

Ceslav looked back and forth between Milan and the SS charging through the schoolhouse doors.

REPRISAL

Milan dropped his head and quickly nodded twice.

Ceslav flattened his back against the stucco and backed up, keeping his eyes toward the square.

At the edge of the building, Milan grabbed Ceslav's sleeve and pulled him onto the playground.

"There." He pointed to a space in the shrubbery. "We can get all the way to the back of the dry goods store from here—through the bushes."

"But the SS."

"What do you think you can do about them?"

Ceslav shook his head and shrugged.

"Come on. We can watch what's going on, and they won't see us. Maybe then we can figure out something to do."

Ceslav eyed the space between the branches. "You sure I can fit?"

"No."

*

The townspeople of Lidice assembled in front of the buildings surrounding the town square. Prodded by rifle butts, they formed an irregular series of lines. Motivated by uncertainty and fear, they spoke in quick, hushed bursts and squirmed restlessly. The men, women and children of the town stood—exchanging querulous glances with neighbors, pressing anxious hands together—and waited.

*

The driver of a Mercedes limousine stepped out, opened the rear door of the vehicle and stood behind it, snapping his heels together. From the backseat, a Gestapo captain swung his black-booted legs onto the ground, pulled on a pair of leather gloves, slipped one hand into the sling handle of a riding crop and grasped a black visor cap with the other. The officer emerged from the vehicle, placed his cap on his head and ran his right hand over his uniform jacket. He straightened his back and dipped his head in acknowledgment to the driver, tugged on the fingers of his gloves and strode on the hard-packed dirt, his eyes unblinking, facing forward.

In the middle of the square, the officer turned and slowly scanned the rows of townspeople, stopping only to peer into the faces of the young women. He removed his cap and took out a handkerchief to wipe the inside headband. Returning the handkerchief to his pocket, he twisted the cap in his hands, then said softly, "We are looking for Ana Maruščáková."

Questions murmured through the crowd:

"Ana? Why Ana?"

"She's hardly more than a teenager. What could they want with her?"

Little sighs of relief eased the tension, as if to say, "Thank heaven. They're not looking for me."

The officer placed the cap back on his head and asked, more loudly, "Which of you is Ana?"

The townspeople were silent.

The officer began pacing in front of the crowd, slapping his hand on his thigh. "Are you Ana?" he asked, pointing at a girl in the back row. "Or *you*?" he shouted, thrusting a finger into the face of a girl in the front.

A slight movement swayed the crowd. What was that? the officer wondered. The soft rustling of fabric by a nervous hand? A change in position to protect or hide someone? He scoured the bowed heads. There. He noted a slight twitch, a wary glance out of the corner of an old man's eye, a barely noticeable head movement.

"You there." The officer pointed.

Heads rose.

"You." He pointed to the mechanic Zelenka.

"You have something to say?"

An undercurrent of grumbling led to a shove and a murmured, "Keep your mouth shut, Zelenka."

"Come out here," the officer demanded.

Under his overhanging brow, Zelenka's eyes darted back and forth as he took a tentative step. Townspeople standing in front of him squeezed together more closely to block his way. Fists held onto his shirt and tried to pull him backward.

A pair of soldiers elbowed bodies out of the way, grabbed Zelenka's arms and dragged him forward.

The officer raised Zelenka's head with the tip of the riding crop and searched his face. "Who?" he demanded.

Voices rose:

"Don't do it, Zelenka."

"Stop, old man."

"Think what you are doing."

Ignoring the susurrations, Zelenka tilted his head to one side. "There," he said. "She's that one." He turned and pointed a palsied finger.

The voices burst like cherry bombs:

"Bastard."

"I spit on you."

"Turncoat."

An agonizing "No!" as Ana was pulled from the crowd.

The Gestapo officer extended his arm and spread out his fingers. "Enough!" he said sharply.

He turned back to Zelenka. "Now, who is Horák?"

The voices whispered:

"Isn't he the one who has sons with the exile government?" a man muttered.

"Hush," a woman hissed.

Zelenka scanned the faces in the crowd.

"There." He pointed to the hunched and grizzled farmer standing with both hands on the knob of his cane at the end of a line of Lidice men.

The officer shoved Zelenka aside.

"Where do you live?" the officer shouted at Horák.

"At the end of the town," Horák replied.

"And you?" he asked Ana.

"Just there. The ... the third house," she stammered.

"Take him," the officer ordered a group of soldiers, "take Horák to his house."

"Ana." He tapped the crop on the side of a boot as he moved next to her. "Let's you and I go and have a talk in your house." Putting an arm around her shoulders, he looked along the side of her face, following her gaze as it fell upon a middle-aged couple. "Your mama and papa?" he asked, noting the woman's fluttering hands and the man's attempt to bull his way past his neighbors into the line of soldiers.

"No mama and papa," the officer said to them. Then he turned back to Ana. "It is just going to be you and me." Holding her tightly against his side, he began speaking brusquely: "We have the letter."

"What letter?"

"The letter from Říha ... your boyfriend from the factory in Slaný."

"I don't have..."

"Now don't lie to me. I know you have a boyfriend. I know what he wrote to you. I know what he did. You may as well tell me your side. We already have Říha in custody." Ana shrank away from the officer. "He will tell us ... eventually ... if you won't."

Ana shook her head and turned her frightened eyes to her mother and father, breathlessly uttering denials: "I don't know anything. I didn't do anything. He's not my boyfriend. He's just someone I know." She tripped over the front step of her house. "What," she asked as she and the officer followed two Gestapo soldiers through the doorway, "What has happened ... to Říha?"

*

Until the officer shut the door to Ana's house, Chessie had been afraid to scan the crowd for her son. She had been pushed by the SS into the front row of the crowd along with the other women from her street. As stealthily as she could, she moved from one row to the next, further and further back toward the buildings. She now stood in the last row of townspeople, her knees flexed, head bowed, arms close, sweat trickling down the sides of her body and accumulating under her breasts.

As soon as she heard the click of the lock to Ana's front door, she began to move closer to the schoolhouse, steal glances at the children as she passed between the rows of frightened, angry neighbors. At last she saw Ondrej. He was on the top step of the schoolhouse, next to his teacher Magda Marik. His eyes were focused on an SS soldier who was standing a few meters in front of him. He was balancing himself against his schoolteacher, on tiptoes, his face shining with admiration.

*

Katrenka stood alone, separated from the townspeople by a rough circle of physical space, as well as a cloud of suspicion. Cells of distrust metastasized through the crowd:

"I warned you something like this would happen, that Katrenka would get us in trouble with the Nazis. She looked down on us even before she went off with that German. Now she thinks she *is* German—better than everyone else."

"Who else in town is so close to the Germans? She was in Prag for more than a year. Plenty of time to make contact with the Gestapo. Then she's back here for what? Six months? The Gestapo hasn't been anywhere near Lidice until now, only a few months after *she* came back."

"Didn't her family have trouble with Horák?"

"Yeah, yeah, yeah. He worked the Tůma farm after her mother got so sick. There was a fight over the way he was keeping the books—or something. Katrenka probably had it in for him."

Silvie moved within Katrenka's earshot. "Why the hell didn't you open the door for them?" she asked. "You know what a mess you've created in that house?"

*

From his hiding place in the underbrush close to the Maruščáková house, Milan could hear crashing sounds within: drawers pulled open and dropped to the floor; furniture tipped over; glass shattering. "My mother's crystal from Prag," he heard Ana cry.

Then the officer's voice, soft, almost soothing: "If you would just tell me what you know, I will leave you and your mother's crystal alone."

"I can't tell you anything. I don't know anything," Ana moaned.

Heavy boots pounded down the steps to the root cellar. A crate crashed against a wall. Vegetables thumped and bumped as they fell and rolled across the floor. A wooden stave groaned against a metal hoop as a barrel was rocked from side to side.

Rustling in the weeds behind Milan, a muffled curse arose. "Keep it down," Milan muttered.

"You know how hard it is for me to crawl through this stuff?"

"Ssh," Milan warned, as an SS guard appeared in the doorway.

"I'm sure you were just trying to help Říha," the officer said as he held Ana's elbow and pulled her out of the house.

"No ... No ... We never ... .He wouldn't ... " Ana flinched against the pressure on her arm. She turned to the crowd of her neighbors and friends and saw some accusing faces. Surprised, she shook her head. "I didn't do anything. Říha didn't do anything." Her eyes scanned the townspeople seeking confirmation. "You know me. You know I wouldn't do ... "

"Mama?" she called out when she saw her mother's face.

Ana's mother pushed the people standing in front of her, but her husband held her back. "We can't help her. We can't help her here. Not now. We can't do anything. Not now," he said quietly, gazing at Ana and the Nazi officer. "It will come out," he insisted, holding his wife's arm. "It's Říha's fault. They will see that. They will see that." His voice trailed off. His eyes filled with tears. He raised his hand as if to wave to Ana until his wife grasped and held it between her breasts. He raised her fingers to his lips, all the while watching mournfully as the officer led Ana down the street to his car, opened the car door and put her in the backseat.

Until then, Ana's father hadn't even noticed that soldiers were also guiding Horák to the car. What did Horák have to do with this? he wondered. Did he know Říha? No, it was his sons. The sons who left the country to join the Czechoslovak Army in exile in Great Britain. He was the one, not Ana. The one who brought the Gestapo here. He and his sons caused this.

"Horák, you bastard," he called out to the old man. "What have you done? What have your good-for-nothing sons done? Get my Ana out of this. You know she didn't do anything. Horák? You hear me?"

Horák did not respond. The old man walked slowly, dragging the

REPRISAL

leg that had been twisted by the treads of a tractor when he was a boy.

"Horák," Ana's father pleaded. "Help her."

Horák shook his head as if to push the words out of his ears and kept walking.

"You were my friend," Ana's father continued to call out. "We worked our fields together. We drank together at The Three Crows. We stood across the aisle from one another with our families in St. Martin's Church." Ana's father had admired the way Horák had accepted his deformity without complaint, how he had overcome his grief after his wife died, how he protected his sons.

"You were the one who told Ana how to watch for witches on Christmas Eve. You told me to spread extra honey on Ana's holy bread at Christmas dinner so she would be sweeter for suitors in the coming year. You were ... you were ... my friend," he finished bitterly. He watched without sympathy as Horák lost his footing and fell, as Horák refused a Gestapo's hand, as Horák came to his knees, put his weight on his cane, and hauled himself up. Ana's father watched as the Nazi officer pointed to the backseat of the car and Horák shook his head. "My bad leg. I can't get in on this side of the car." Then he watched Horák slowly and painfully shuffle to the other side of the car, bend his head, and with a glance back at the crowd, lean into the doorway. He watched as the soldier waited for Horák to sit down, then slammed the door, climbed in the front seat and took his place behind the wheel.

Ana's father pushed his way to the front of the crowd as the car turned around, wheels spinning in the dirt. He strained to see Ana in the backseat and reached out his arms toward her. He saw her fingertips pressing against the window.

The car slowed. The front window rolled down. "Preventive custody," the officer called out the window to Ana's father. "Preventive custody ... for their own good."

The window rolled up. The car accelerated. The dust settled.

CHAPTER NINE

On his way to the office of SS-Standartenführer Hans Ullrich Geschke, Secretary of State and Chief of Police for the Reichs Protektorate of Bohemia and Moravia, Karl Hermann Frank moved briskly past office staff, ignoring proffered salutes. He paused only long enough to finger the nameplate on the wall next to Geschke's office before rapping smartly on the wood, twisting the knob and flinging the door open. He took three quick steps into the room and stationed himself directly in front of Geschke's desk.

"Well?" he demanded.

Geschke raised his eyes to meet Frank's. Angered by the abrupt interruption, he reached lazily over to a box of chocolates that lay open at the edge of his desk and lifted the corner of the container toward Frank.

Frank shook his head, pulled off his leather gloves and held them in one hand.

"Suit yourself," Geschke said as he examined the candy nestled in paper cups. He took the measure of one of the small mounds and nudged it with his finger but decided against it. Instead, he chose a neighboring morsel, releasing it from its paper and turning it slowly back and forth in front of his face before lifting it to his mouth. He took a bite and let his tongue curl along the edge of the chocolate coating and probe into the center, enjoying not only its taste but the discomfort he sensed in Frank. Karl Hermann Frank might be the Secretary of State of Occupied Czechoslovakia, second in command to Heydrich's replacement, but to Geschke and others in the Third Reich, he was a pretender to the Aryan brotherhood. The man wasn't born in Germany; he was Bohemian. A failure in law school and a menial laborer moving from job to job until he "discovered" the right-wing, pro-Nazi groups after WW I. Sure, he was one of the loudest voices pushing for German annexation of the Sudetenland and the Fascist state and helping to organize the Sudeten German Hoelan Front in 1933, but wasn't that just so much tough talk to cover some racial inferiority? Geschke wouldn't be at all surprised.

"Caramel," Geschke smiled. "I chose well." He rubbed his fingertips

REPRISAL

together and turned to his assistant, who was standing at attention next to his desk. "We'll finish this later." The Soldat struggled to keep a grip on the papers and files he had been reviewing with Geschke, trapping loose pages against his body as he tugged on the doorknob and then drew the door closed.

Geschke folded his hands on top of his desk and looked at Frank. "How can I help you?"

"The investigation," Frank said. He turned and began to pace in front of Geschke's desk, nervously twisting his wrist under his watchband. "Give me something." He stopped in front of the man, put his hands on the desktop and leaned forward. "I need something."

Geshke once again perused the array of candy as Frank straightened and resumed pacing.

"What about that fellow, Říha?" Frank asked. "What did he have to say about the Resistance and the assassination plot?"

"Him?" Geschke laughed, licking chocolate from his fingertips. "He's no Resistance fighter. He pissed himself before we asked the first question."

"But the letter. The one he sent to the girl." Frank peered at Geschke.

"It was nothing but a kiss-off to end his affair with her. His wife found out he was fooling around and turned him out of their bed. But he still wanted to impress the girl, so he pretended to be in the Resistance, pretended that he had to give her up for 'The Cause and Our Beloved Country.' That bullshit."

"Horák?"

"He's a tough old bird, I'll say that for him. Barely flinched when Schütze started on him. And he held up—didn't give us anything. Nothing in his home, either. We didn't find any letters from his sons or a wireless radio. No suspicious writings, no scribbled V's on papers shoved behind the crockery. Nothing ... anywhere."

"So. Nothing," Frank repeated. "So the assassins are out there and we have," he said, mimicking Geschke's voice, "nothing ... anywhere."

Frank twisted his gloves with his fingers, tightening the fabric until his tendons bulged. Then he suddenly raised them in the air and slammed them down on top of the box of chocolates. Surprised by the smack of leather on empty candy papers and the flurry of spilled choco-lates, Frank lowered his head and paused, breathing heavily.

"The Schupo?" he asked quietly.

"They're on alert," Geschke replied.

"How soon? How soon can they ... ?" Frank lifted his head and looked at Geschke.

"Tonight," Geschke said.

Frank examined the jumble of candy pieces, absently nudging one, then another, back into their crumpled paper cups. "And Rostock?"

"Before daybreak tomorrow."

"So," Frank pulled himself upright. "Tonight." He turned toward the door but didn't move, waiting for a final acknowledgment.

"Tonight then," Geschke said as he reached for the telephone.

Frank placed his cap on his head and adjusted it. "It begins..."

*

In the squad room doorway of the Kladno Sicherheitsdienst Security Police Station, SS-Obersturmführer Max Rostock watched ap-provingly as his men prepared their Karabiner 98k rifles. He appreciated their diligence. Schneider was carefully removing the floor plate and cleaning his weapon's receiver. Klein was slowly pulling an aluminum chain through the barrel, all the while talking Keitel through the process of oiling the bolt mechanism and testing the turn-down-bolt handle. Müller was checking the internal magazines and loading cartridges into a stripper clip.

Rostock was proud of his men. Klein was a natural leader, able to show newcomers the ropes without disparaging their inexperience or uncertainty. Schneider and Müller were raw but enthusiastic and eager, almost too eager sometimes, moving with a nervous, kinetic energy that Rostock could feel spreading like a contagion from one man to the next. Except for Bach. Rostock appraised Bach as he hefted the stock of his rifle and stared through the hooded sight. Emil Bach was steadfast, serious and soft-spoken, a seasoned former Sudeten German policeman who went about his duties without comment or complaint,

REPRISAL

placid, meticulous down to the smallest detail, rote almost. He never had a worry when it came to Bach and yet ...

Rostock thought about the other Security Police unit leaders in the Protektorate who were having problems with their men. His men, he was happy to say, weren't breaking down or refusing to perform their duties. His men weren't succumbing to alcoholism or desertion or suicide. But then again, his men weren't in Poland or the East, where the Sturmmann had to march Jews over hundreds of kilometers of frozen ground or in blistering heat. Nor did they have to deal with the stink of bodies in the death train boxcars—sometimes as many as 2,000 bodies on a single train—or perform strip searches in the undressing barracks of the death camps.

Like other members of the Sicherheitsdienst Security Police, Rostock's unit had to round up Jews, but more often than not, they didn't have to pull them out of their homes. The Jews were already assembled at designated collection points waiting for "registration," clutching meager belongings. And where did they have to dispatch them? To Terezín, for goodness sake. That's not such a bad place, Rostock thought. A gazebo in the center of its park where the inmates could hear string quartets. A bakery, a bank. Poets writing poetry, composers writing music, artists painting pictures. Better than where he lived, he grumbled to himself. And besides, the Jews ran the place. None of it is on us.

Rostock was a little nervous about the next operation, though. He had been surprised to get the call from Geschke telling him where his men would be going. He had never been to Lidice, but he knew no Jews lived there. And he was worried that this seemed like a much larger operation than usual. When the Kladno Security Police were called in for field operations, he typically needed only a few men. But Geschke wanted all his men involved, and had sent scores of extra ammunition, as well as two companies of reinforcements from Prag—the Ordnungspolizei. A rough crew, Rostock thought, observing a hardness in the eyes of the reserve-unit soldiers that his own men did not have. And then the units had to be ready so quickly. They had to arrive in Lidice by seven in the morning. My men will be up to the task, he said to himself with more conviction than he actually felt, as he turned away from Bach, rubbing the bags under his eyes and trying to wipe away his misgivings.

*

Kommandatur of the Terezín Jewish ghetto Siegfried Seidl dropped the telephone receiver back in its cradle and shoved the phone across his desk. He was irritated. He didn't like receiving commands from Geschke and the Reich Security Main Office, especially in the middle of the night, especially when he was in the midst of bluffing his sergeant out of a sizable poker pot with a lowly pair of nines.

Wasn't *he* the one who was in full charge of the ghetto? Hadn't *he* been Kommandatur since Himmler and Adolf Eichmann had ordered him to relocate the 7,000 Czechs living in Terezín, and transform the former garrison city of Theresienstadt into a "model" community for Czech Jews? And hadn't he *done* that? Hadn't he made the best use of the Aufbaukommando construction crews? Didn't Eichmann and those other dolts in Berlin know how much *progress* he had made?

In a little over a year, the AK, under Seidl's command, had expanded kitchens that were originally designed to feed 3,500 soldiers into centralized cooking operations capable of accommodating 40,000 to 50,000 Jewish inmates. The Kommandos had converted soldiers' barracks, concrete storehouses and public buildings into separate communal housing units for men, women, children and infants. The AK had constructed a ghetto bakery, waterworks and a power plant, added a 1,000-bed surgical and general ward to the 18th-century garrison hospital and built sick bays in every housing complex.

Seidl himself had established the Jewish Council of Elders to oversee the ghetto's internal affairs. The Council and the Jewish directors of administrative departments were responsible for the day-to-day operations of the ghetto—child care, finance, food and water, gardening, health care, housing, recreational activities, engineering and construction, water works, gas works, the sewage system.

All the elements were in place to support the myth that Terezín was a spa, a retirement and nursing home for the elderly and infirm—a "Paradise Ghetto" —and a prime example of just how well Nazis were treating Jews. Landscaping was nearly finished in the ghetto's central Hohenelhe Park, its gazebo repaired and refurbished, the crisp white paint hardly even dry. The apple, apricot, cherry and pear orchards were blooming; the gardens were ready to yield bushel baskets of tomatoes and cabbages, beans and broccoli, potatoes, squash and peppers. Small cottage factories offered Jews meaningful work such as splitting mica

REPRISAL

for electric parts, sewing uniforms, woodworking, architectural planning and drawing. And just this week, the Bank of the Jewish Autonomy had started printing savings books so inmates could deposit the wages they earned from their work, and it was issuing paper camp money so inmates could pay for showers, concerts and coffee at the café.

Outsiders didn't have to know that Seidl gave the Jewish Council of Elders its marching orders every day and severely punished any infractions, or that housing units were crowded with as many as 100 to 300 people to a room and furnished only with excelsior-filled mattresses on wooden slats in two- and three-tier bunks. They didn't have to know that the ghetto's fruit and vegetables only appeared on SS guard tables, or that the main meal of the day for Jews consisted of soup, a potato and a dumpling. People living outside Terezín didn't have to know that the ghetto was bound on three sides by high walls and moats, that the bank money was fake, or that it was not a permanent community but a way station for Jews who would eventually be transported to the East, to Auschwitz.

That's why Seidl was so annoyed by the "outside" assignment he had just received. He didn't want his Jews to get a taste of life beyond the walled city. Jews in Terezín needed to get used to living with ghetto routines and rules. He also didn't appreciate getting an assignment from Karl Hermann Frank. The man had never come to Terezín, didn't have a clue what was going on. The whole "Paradise Ghetto" idea was Himmler's. What would Himmler think if outsiders saw the Terezín Jews? If outsiders saw that Terezín Jews were no different from any other Jews—wearing gray stripes with yellow stars, emaciated, dirty and rank? What would they say then about the "Paradise Ghetto?" Did Himmler know what this Frank character was ordering? Did he understand how this assignment could jeopardize the work here?

Seidl sat back. Well, he thought, maybe no one would see his Jews. He reached in the drawer of his desk for a local map and found the destination: Lidice. Nothing but farms and forests around there. He circled the area with his finger. The roads to and from the town didn't have much traffic and the trees were pretty close to the roadway. He traced the route with his pen. Not much chance the Jews would be seen on the way to or from the town.

Except maybe from the trains. Seidl pictured in his mind the road to Terezín from the train station. Trains stopped only in Bauschowitz, which was at least 2 kilometers from the ghetto. And besides, he realized, the truck loaded with Jews would be hidden on the winding roads behind the hills that topped the old garrison fortifications. The truck wouldn't be visible until it approached the gate to the ghetto, well removed from view by anyone on the passenger trains. He smiled. Good, good, good.

Seidl read the notes he had made during the telephone conversation. He numbered the items he would need: (1) a truck from the motor pool, fueled up and ready to go early in the morning; (2) enough picks and shovels for 30 men; (3) quicklime; (4) a work crew. He circled the second item. What kind of burial duty needed 30 men? That's one helluva big hole they're going to dig in some little town that didn't have any Jews.

Chapter Ten

Chessie woke with a throbbing in her chest, the same kind of gasp or hiccup she experienced as a child when she lay on her stomach on the ridge above her mother's family farm. She would press her fingers into her ears, close her eyes and let her body feel the tremor that spread underground from the tractor her grandfather piloted as he hauled hay bales across the fields. She liked to trace the pulse of the movement and sense the machine's path without opening her eyes or unplugging her ears.

Her grandfather had been dead for many years, and she no longer had time to spend on foolish thoughts and feelings. So why was she reliving those moments?

Chessie lay quietly, gradually recognizing what her body was telling her. Heavy machinery, that's what she was sensing—the movement of heavy machinery. Coming steadily closer. She could feel the small gaps in vibration as gears shifted, the quivers of acceleration and deceleration as engines pulled weight over bumpy surfaces. Trucks, she realized, and many of them, groaning as their axles turned, shuddering as their motors slowed, pock-pocking as their wheels rumbled over the dirt road leading into Lidice, flapping as their canvas panels slapped against their metal frames.

Chessie almost never heard trucks on the main road from Kladno. She couldn't remember the last time she had. Even after the Nazis invaded the Soviet Union and started sending massive numbers of troops across Germany and Czechoslovakia to the East on their way to attack the Soviets, a single truck coming toward Lidice in the middle of the day was rare. This many—how many—at night? Stopping here!

"Mama?" Ondrej stood in the doorway to her bedroom. "Why are the Schupo here? They're jumping down from the backs of all those trucks outside."

There was a time when we weren't afraid of the Schupo, Chessie thought, when they were just the ordinary policemen you'd see in the big city, directing traffic, chastising litterers, chasing down pickpockets. But that was before the Nazis turned the Schutzpolizei into the Nazi Protective Police and replaced policemen with beer hall brutes and young toughs. That was before routine police matters became excuses for finding enemies of the Third Reich. A Schupo questioning a young mother because she seemed to be carrying too many grocery bags for a single household now led to a Gestapo pounding on her door in the middle of the night to find out if her family was hiding Jews. A Schupo hearing too many noises at odd hours coming from the back of a store led to a Gestapo search of the premises to learn whether the store owner was listening to forbidden radio broadcasts. Once the Schupo became Nazi Protectors, it wasn't long before people started hunching their shoulders and picking up their pace, and shuttering their windows and doors as soon as they caught sight of the peak of a grayish-green Schupo cap, the tip of a shiny black boot, or the edge of an eagle insignia on a green woolen sleeve.

And the Schupo were now in her town, rushing toward her home.

She pulled Ondrej behind her, walking quickly and quietly through the kitchen to the back of the house. Her hand on the doorknob, she looked up to see a broad, whiskered face peering at her through the window in the door.

"Who is here?" the man asked.

"Me ... and my son," she answered, backing away.

"Open the door," he demanded, jiggling the knob.

She shook her head.

The man's eyes appraised the room, beginning with the washstand, a cast-iron frying pan upended in the basin. He took in the rectangular pine dining table littered with Ondrej's geography homework, the four high-back chairs, the pot-bellied stove, the open cupboard crowded with tins and jars. His gaze rested on Ondrej, then rose to Chessie's face. He scratched the side of his chin with the butt of his pistol, then slammed the weapon into the window and thrust his shoulder into the door, cracking it open.

*

REPRISAL

Milan followed his mother Marketa out of their home and into a town in chaos. The Schupo were dragging men out of their houses, marshaling them into lines, and frog-marching them to the end of town. They were pulling women away from their husbands and sons, ignoring the cries of children reaching for their fathers and grandfathers or asking their mothers for the simplest things:

"My shoes. Can't I even get my shoes?"

"My rosary. It's on my nightstand."

"My dolly."

*

A commotion in front of the church revealed a small, thin figure running down the main street away from the city, past the granary. The Schupo were chasing, firing warning shots in the air. It was Emília, approaching a welt in the road in front of the bridge, followed by three policemen leveling their rifles at her back.

Cracks of gunfire.

Emília's head jerked backward as her body convulsed. She staggered and tripped, arms thrust forward, fingers grasping at the air, knees collapsing, chest falling, her head hitting the ground. Her body sprawled on the cobblestones—her arms shuddered, her fingers twitched—then there was calm.

"Keep going. There's nothing to see here." A Schupo captain stepped in front of the bridge and stood with his legs widespread. He pulled his rifle from the sling on his back and held it in front of him, bouncing the butt lightly in one hand. "Nothing here."

More shots, this time at the edge of the woods. A boy—Ignáce—staggered into a tree, hugging the trunk while his body slid slowly down the bark.

*

Milan did not understand what was happening. His brother was on the ground at the edge of the woods. Why wasn't he moving?

"Ignáce?" he called out. Then his mother screamed and pulled away from him. He saw her running toward Ignáce. Her legs gave way and her body crumpled, one hand covering her mouth, the other kneading her skirt.

"Mama!" Milan cried, putting his arms tightly around her and burying his face in her chest as he sobbed. But she did not respond.

"Mama?" he asked, pulling his head back so he could look into her eyes. "Mama, it's me. It's me!" But now she sat silent and still, her eyes open but unseeing, her palms open and flaccid at her sides, alongside her swollen, pregnant belly. He laid his head in her lap and stroked her legs. "Mama," he moaned.

*

Chessie led her son into the steadily growing throng of women and children being shoved toward the schoolhouse by the Schupo and their weapons. A rifle butt in the middle of her back thrust her roughly forward, sending her into the bowed back of her neighbor Paní Soucek and the outstretched but trembling hands of Paní Benda. Inside the schoolhouse, Chessie stutter-stepped Ondrej through the crowd, resisting his attempts to squirm away from her. "Stop it," she said.

"But my friends are over there." He pointed to Jarmil and Jindrích Janda.

"No, you stay with me."

"Ma," he moaned.

"We don't know what is happening," she said, shaking his shoulders. "This is not a game."

*

"My bird, my bird," Katrenka cried out in anguish. "Where is it?" She turned out her pockets, searched the floor and the classroom desks next to her. "Please," she implored the women around her. "Please help me find it."

"This?" asked Milan's grandmother, Paní Tichy, lifting the bird in her hand. "This silly little thing?"

REPRISAL

"Yes, yes, please." Katrenka reached out for it. "Johann carved it for me."

"Some Nazi thing, then," Paní Tichy said as she flung the bird across the room.

"No," Katrenka cried. She turned and pushed her way through the women, following the bird's trajectory.

"See if you can find it." Her sister-in-law Silvie laughed as she caught the bird and threw it to the other side of the classroom.

Katrenka watched the falling bird land in the outstretched hand of Jana Maly, Silvie's cousin and friend.

Jana turned the bird over and over, inspecting it. "Doesn't look special to me." She reached her hand out toward Katrenka, then let the bird fall to the floor and kicked it into the corner where it slid under a chest of drawers.

Katrenka waddled awkwardly toward the chest, her heavy pregnancy and breathlessness impeding her progress.

"Wait, Katrenka." Václava Janda took hold of her elbow. "Let my boys do it." Václava directed her sons Jarmil and Jindrích toward the chest and led Katrenka to an easel covered with maps. "Here, lean against this," she said.

Thirteen-year-old Jarmil dragged the chest away from the wall, while his younger brother sifted through puffs of dust until he found the carving. "Here, Ma." He carried the bird to his mother. Václava nodded toward Katrenka. "It's hers," she said.

The boy rolled the bird in his hand. "It's nice," he said, placing it in Katrenka's hand.

*

"Bitch."

"Whore."

"Nazi cunt."

The words rained down on Chessie like razor cuts in the back of her mind, even though they weren't aimed at her. She was brushing past

Hana and Berta Najman, two of Katrenka's most vocal critics. The twins had known Katrenka all their lives—they had gone to school with her, taken their First Communion along with her, played dolls and dress-up with her. But all that was forgotten when Katrenka married a German and moved away. To their way of thinking, she had turned her back on her birthplace and her friends; she had taken the side of the Occupiers. The only reason for her to come back to Lidice last January, they continually muttered to themselves, was to spy on them and their town. Wasn't the visit from the SS proof enough of that? The Nazis would never have come to Lidice if it hadn't been for her.

"Don't give them any mind." Chessie's friend Klaudie Cizek told her, nodding toward Hana and Berta. "There will always be people who see the worst, who try to find someone to blame. They're just afraid."

"And you're not?"

"This is bound to end soon."

"How can you be so sure? It seems to me they'll stop at nothing. They've already killed two people. God knows what they've done to Ana and Horák or what they'll do to..." Chessie swallowed references to Klaudie's husband Ctibor and her older sons Radomir and Bohan who had been rounded up with the other men in the town. "...next," she said finally.

"But that's it. Don't you see?" Klaudie answered. "They've already done what they're going to do. The killings were clearly mistakes— Schupo shooting at people running. The men in the Schupo police nowadays are not that smart. They don't know what they're doing. You should hear my Ctibor talk about them ... the kinds of things he has seen. And Ana and Horák being involved in some plot against the Third Reich? How ridiculous. Horák's sons may be in Britain, but that old man couldn't do anything for them or the government in exile. As for us, you think the Gestapo is going to do something to a whole town? We're not in the Resistance. We're not Jews."

*

Milan sat next to his mother, her back propped up against the wall of the classroom behind the teacher's desk. Marketa stared straight ahead, her eyes wide and glassy, unresponsive to the touch of his hand.

REPRISAL

She didn't see him. She didn't know him, he thought with bitterness.

He hurried over to Paní Vasko and begged her to come to his mother's side.

"I will talk to her, son," she said.

"It's Milan," Paní Vasko explained to Marketa. "He's worried about you."

Marketa remained limp and unfocused.

"I know it's hard for you to see Ignáce ..."

Marketa tensed and uttered a low keening sound. She began rocking, clenching and unclenching her fists. She looked at Paní Vasko.

"But Milan. He is here. He needs you," Paní Vasko said.

Marketa searched her eyes, then turned her face away, withdrawing her sight and her awareness.

*

Sudden sharp sounds: banging, thumping, scraping; metal clanging, wood creaking and snapping, glass and pottery shattering; men laughing.

A Schupo guard stood in the doorway, surveying the room, feeling along the wall for the light switch. "No," the women begged, "please don't shut off the lights."

"My girl is afraid of the dark."

"*Please...*"

The Schupo flipped the first switch.

A small girl began shrieking in fear, soon joined by other children. Calls of: "I'm here." "It's all right." "Ssh. Ssh," came back from their mothers.

"Here, Ondrej," Chessie reached for her son in the waning light. "Come closer." She pulled him onto her lap. She hugged and rocked his restless body, kissing the top of his head, as the Schupo flipped the next switch.

*

Milan nestled his head on his mother's shoulder, wrapping his fingers around her elbow and tugging on her arm. His movements intensified.

The bank of lights on the left side of the room snapped off.

"Mama," he pleaded, pushing against her breast. "Mama," he said more harshly, shaking her shoulder.

The second bank of lights switched off.

Milan raised his mother's hands so he could rest his head on her thighs, next to her belly. He placed her palms and fingers on his head and pulled them down slowly to stroke his cheeks and face.

The door to the schoolhouse slammed shut, erasing the remaining light from the room.

Milan felt the darkness fall upon him like a blanket. He welcomed it. In the dark, he could block out the view of his mother. In the dark, he could pretend that she knew he was there.

CHAPTER ELEVEN

Thundering noises. Reverberating voices. Banging shutters. Doors bursting open. Sunlight shattering the darkness.

Men shouting: "Time to move." "Get up." "Hurry."

Ondrej, shaken awake, cowered, holding Chessie's arms. Chessie, jerking out of a dream, cradled her son, then twisted the cramped muscles in her neck and back. Scanning the room, she stared uncomprehendingly at bodies rousing from sleep. Her eyes fell on the children's desks scattered throughout the room, book shelves bulging with texts and workbooks, the blackboard with a grammar lesson smudged but still visible, a globe of the world on a stand. The classroom, she realized, was crowded with Lidice women and children. There was Magda Marik, her son's teacher, lying next to Paní Kolar and Paní Benda—their eyes blinking open, first alert and alive, and then quickly clouding over. Her friend Klaudie was embracing her mother, Johanna Kolar, in fear and solidarity. Klaudie's son Tomás was holding hands with a pair of small, whimpering children. Young Ivona Mares was soothing a baby crying out in hunger. All the while, the Schupo were rushing through the open doorway, gesticulating and kicking the shins of women still huddled on the floor, urging them to get moving.

*

Milan held his mother's arm and directed her toward the schoolhouse door. He took a step, then stopped as women in front of him tugged reluctant children by the hand, lifted toddlers into their arms and hushed cranky babies.

Milan was anxious to get through the crowd. He had not seen Ceslav in the schoolhouse. He was worried about him. On the threshold of the schoolhouse door, he stood on his tiptoes and craned his neck to see over the heads of the women in front of him. His mother before him, he pushed into the crowd, searching for women he knew or school friends.

Paní Vasko walked wearily behind Paní Mares and Paní Benda. "Ceslav," he asked the women. "Have you seen Ceslav?"

They shook their heads.

The crowd turned the corner onto Dykova Street. At the far end, Milan saw Schupo propped up against the sides of their trucks, smoking, laughing, punching one another on the arm. From the household doorways, the Schupo were balling up clothing and throwing it into the street. They were breaking windows and flinging canisters of coffee, sugar, flour and tea into the street. Crockery was smashed, releasing puffs of powder in the air, rainbows of crystals, streaks of coarse grain, flutters of small green leaves. Loaves of bread, handfuls of vegetables and fruit, baskets of pies and pastries were skimming over the ground, plummeting into bushes and flower beds. Eggs were flying, colliding with one another, shattering, creating pools of white and yellow.

In front of him, the Schupo were herding the women and children of his town, keeping them in more or less orderly ranks.

In line to Milan's left, Paní Smida slumped against Magda Marik's shoulder, muttering between soft sobs: "She didn't understand. My Emília. I tried to make her understand."

"You couldn't stop her, Paní Smida. She ran when she was afraid," Magda said.

"But for them..." Paní Smida raised her head and looked into Magda's face. "For them... to..."

Magda tightened her hold on the woman's waist.

"*Promint*," Milan excused himself for the interruption and waited until the teacher turned toward him.

"Do you know where Ceslav is?"

"No, I'm sorry, Milan. I haven't seen him."

"Grandma," Milan caught up to Paní Tichy, in line to his right. "Have you seen Ceslav?"

"Oh, it's you," she said disdainfully. "What's wrong with your mother?"

"After Ignáce ... she collapsed."

"Knew she was weak."

REPRISAL

Milan stiffened. He grabbed his grandmother's arm as she turned away.

"What is it, boy?"

"Ceslav. Have you seen ... ?"

"Oh, they took him. He's with the men at Horák's farm. They locked them all up in the stable and the barn last night."

"But he's a kid. Like me."

She shrugged and turned away.

*

"Take enough for three days," Chessie heard a Schupo say as she left the schoolhouse. "Get what you need from there." He motioned toward the heaps of clothing littering the street.

"NO!" she heard a Schupo shout at Paní Kolar, who was walking toward her front door. "You can't go inside."

"Why not? Why can't I get my things?"

The Schupo grabbed Paní Kolar's arm and pushed her toward the mounds of blouses and shirts, brassieres and undershorts, coats and jackets all jumbled together. "Take things from there—anything you need—and hurry up. We need to get moving."

"What about food?" Paní Kolar asked. "We're hungry. The children are hungry."

The Schupo pointed at the conglomeration of cast-off food accumulating under the windows of the shops and houses. "Take some of that," he said.

"But it's in the dirt. You expect us to eat that?"

"Take it or not. If you want to eat, find something. If it's dirty, wipe it clean. Or don't eat."

*

Chessie scrounged the ground for food. A small packet of nuts, she jammed into the breast pocket of the man's shirt she had thrown over the top of her nightgown. Handfuls of blueberries and a can of beans, she thrust into the side pockets of the overalls dangling off her body. A jar of pickled beets, some slices of ham and a wedge of bread, she shoved into the crown of a hat.

"Mama." Ondrej ran up to her. "Come on. Jindrích and Jarmil are already on the truck."

"What truck?"

"They're taking us for a ride to the city," he said excitedly, pulling on her arm. "Come on. I don't want to miss the truck."

"A few more minutes," she said. "I just want to get past Pan Marushak's house. I'll be right there. Just a few minutes."

*

"Where's Ondrej?" Chessie asked Paní Vasko.

"He's with Jindrích and his brother. On that truck." She pointed to a lorry with its canvas panels already tied down, its exhaust pipes coughing out fumes.

"Wait," Chessie shouted as she began to run. She stumbled over the cuffs of the oversized overalls as they unrolled, staggering to keep her balance, even as the bottoms of the overalls bunched up underfoot. She tripped, falling to her knees and pitching forward. Thrusting out her hands to break her momentum, the jar of beets flew out of her hat and skittered out in front of her.

"Wait!" She waved at the departing truck. "My son is on that truck!"

Chapter Twelve

Chessie scrambled up and rushed after the truck. A hand reached out and clutched her arm but she wrenched it away, shouting, "Leave me alone. I need to find my son." A pair of arms encircled her waist. "Chessie. Chessie. Ondrej is there ... there ... with Katrenka.... He is not on the truck," Paní Benda explained.

Chessie whirled around, searched Paní Benda's face, and then followed the line of the woman's outstretched arm until she could focus. There, at the side of the road leading to Lidice creek was Katrenka, and standing at her side was Ondrej, hunching his shoulders and looking worriedly at Chessie.

"I didn't do anything wrong," he whimpered.

"Of course not," Chessie cried. "Of course not."

She looked questioningly at Katrenka. "I saw them filling up the truck," Katrenka said. "Ondrej was next. He was standing with the Janda brothers. But I didn't see you. So I pulled him out of line and kept him with me."

Chessie collapsed onto Katrenka and Ondrej. "Thank you. I don't know ..."

"I know," Katrenka said. "I know." She patted Chessie's back.

Someone tugged Chessie's arm. "The beets ... you lost your beets," Ivona Mares said, holding the jar to Chessie.

Chessie wiped her eyes and bent down to the girl. "Well, I don't know what I would have done if I'd lost these."

"Could I have some later on? I love beets," the little girl said.

"Of course," Chessie laughed. "You come see me when you want to, and we will all share the beets." The girl smiled, waved and ran back to her mother.

"Fine. Fine," a Schupo said. "Have a feast with the damn beets when you get to Kladno. Now it's time to get on the truck." He pushed

Chessie and her son toward the back of a near-empty truck, a step ladder propped against the tailgate.

*

"Can you climb up?" Schupo Sgt. Albert Kleinschmidt asked Katrenka, eying her belly.

She shook her head.

"All right," he said, pushing her against the tailgate. "Weber," he called to a corporal positioning the human cargo in the back of the truck. "Take care of this one."

Schupo Cpl. Wolfgang Weber took hold of Katrenka's forearms, put his hands under her armpits and raised her high enough to sit on the edge of the truck bed.

"You hardly weigh a thing," he said, surprised. He guided her shoulders. "Pull up your legs ... yes ... that's right. Now to the side ... right here."

With a hand on her elbow, Weber helped Katrenka rise and led her to the side of the truck where women were sitting on a wooden bench that ran along the full length of the bed.

"You sit here," he told Katrenka. "Make room for her," he told the women.

"Why should I make room for her? She's nothing but a Nazi whore," Paní Tichy said.

Weber turned sharply, glared at Paní Tichy and waved her away. "Get up. Get to the back of the truck," he said.

"Look how she's getting special treatment," Paní Tichy whined as she pulled herself up.

"She's on the truck, isn't she? Like the rest of us," Magda Marik retorted.

"Bah. She's a Nazi, mark my words," Paní Tichy replied.

Weber eased Katrenka down on the bench, asking softly: "You are German?"

Katrenka shook her head. "No, I was born here. In Lidice. My husband is German."

"What happened to him?" Weber held her shoulder as she leaned back against the side panel. "Why are you here and not with him?"

"He went to Moscow ... Barbarossa."

"My brother also."

"You know about Barbarossa?" Katrenka asked, raising her eyes to meet his.

Weber hesitated. Could he speak about the Eastern Front? About his brother? To a Czech? Maybe. Maybe to this woman, a woman with such pain in her eyes.

"My brother was one of the first ... to go ... to die ... on the way to Moscow. There were so many ..." He shook his head.

Katrenka reached out, took his hand and squeezed it.

"More than 100,000 in the first month," he continued hesitantly, waiting for a sign of understanding. She squeezed his hand again. "Three thousand in one *day*," he said. "It was the cold, you know, and then there were the Siberians, dressed in white." He bowed his head. "We lost ... so many," he paused. "We couldn't see them in the snow."

"Maybe you know something about my Johann. Maybe you can tell me ... something." She paused and looked from Weber's face to the Schupo in front of the truck, then to the women at the back, puzzled. "Something ..." Katrenka frowned. She turned back to face him. "What was I saying?"

Noticing her bewilderment, Weber touched her shoulder lightly, indicating that she should slide to the end of the bench, close to the tailgate.

"You can stick your head outside ... when the truck is moving and the canvas is down," he explained. "I will leave this side of the canvas untied." He pointed to the back covering of the truck. "You understand?"

Katrenka gazed at the canvas he was holding and the dangling ropes.

"Johann? You know him?" She looked into Weber's eyes.

"You understand? About this?" Weber placed her hand on the canvas.

Katrenka moved her eyes from Weber to the canvas and back

again. "Yes," she nodded. "But Johann?" she implored. "Tell me," she took hold of his arm. "Please."

"Finish it up, Weber," Kleinschmidt called to him, as he dislodged the step ladder. "This one's full."

"No, madam. I do not know your Johann." Weber lifted Katrenka's fingers off his arm.

"No." She reached out for him again. "You must know. Please, please tell me."

Weber backed slowly away from Katrenka, away from her desperate fingers.

"Don't leave me." Her voice cracked. "Don't..."

Weber reached the tailgate, turned and jumped down to the ground. He yanked on the canvas flaps, pulled the ropes tight and secured them to their moorings along the back of the truck. On the side where Katrenka was sitting, he let the ropes hang. Raising the patch of canvas, he saw Katrenka glancing quickly from side to side, confusion in her eyes, rubbing her fingertips against her temples. He raised a hand and touched his helmet, stepped back and slapped the side of the truck.

"What was that all about?" Kleinschmidt asked Weber.

"Her husband. He was German. He died—in Barbarossa."

"Really?" Kleinschmidt stared at the back of the truck.

*

Chessie adjusted her eyes to the shadows and gradually made out the shapes of the women huddled next to her, holding onto each other as the truck swayed and bumped into motion. She sat with her knees butting up against the edge of the bench and Katrenka's legs. She twisted to free her arms from her shirt sleeves and folded the bottoms of the baggy overalls, then searched its pockets for bits of food. From one of them, she withdrew morsels of bread and small slices of ham.

"Ondrej," she motioned. "Open your hand."

Ondrej corkscrewed his arms out of the oversized shirt he had taken from the clothes pile. "I thought this was going to be fun, but it's hot and stinky," he said, coughing as exhaust and gasoline fumes swirled in the air.

"It hurts to sit," he said. Giving up his attempt to find a comfortable spot between the metal supports, he crawled to the back of the truck.

"Quit pushing me," Silvie complained as he passed her.

"Give me some space," Jana groused.

Ondrej lifted the canvas flap and watched his town recede: Tiny azalea bursts were half hidden behind overturned milk bottles, white liquid beads staining the dark green leaves in Paní Kolar's garden. Water from the faucet on the side of Houbová's butcher shop dripped onto torn and crumbled sheets of butcher paper on the ground. Shutters on the dry goods shop windows hung open, twisted and broken.

As the truck turned on to the road to Kladno and drove up the incline out of the Lidice valley, the archway at the entrance of Horák's farm appeared, then the farm buildings and the grounds.

"Looks like they're going to have fun," Ondrej said.

"Who are you talking about?" Katrenka asked.

"The people over there. The ones at the farm."

Katrenka leaned over to see out of the back of the truck.

"See there," Ondrej directed. "They're going to be sleeping outside."

"What are you talking about?"

"There, on the ground and the side of the farmhouse. All the mattresses."

The Schupo were pulling mattresses from nearby homes, dragging them on the ground and propping them on the outside walls of Horák's farmhouse.

"They will be able to sleep outside. On the mattresses. See?"

*

Ondrej called out, "Mama! You should see this." He pushed out the canvas flap.

"There's a truck? That's turning on to the road toward town? Can you see? There are all these people wearing gray and white stripes."

REPRISAL

*

The truck in Ondrej's line of sight shifted gears and lurched ahead, turning onto to the main road from the entrance to Bauschowitz and the Terezín ghetto. Its canvas panels were rolled a quarter of the way back, revealing a row of passengers and the tools they were holding.

"A goddamn traffic jam," said the driver, SS Sgt. Arno Engel, as he hit the steering wheel with the heel of his hand. "First, we get all these troop carriers coming *from* Kladno. Now we've got *this.*" He flicked his fingers at the canvas-covered truck going toward Kladno from the direction of Lidice.

"Did you see that last batch? The ones on the troop carriers from Kladno, I mean?" Engel asked his corporal as he moved his foot to the clutch.

Cpl. Casmir Lorenz remembered the men they had seen on the back of the carriers in their green uniforms with brown collars and cuffs. "Yeah. You know," he said, turning to Engel, "those Ordnungspolizei look as bad as I heard they were."

Engel eased the back wheels of the vehicle over a rut and checked his progress in the rearview mirror, noticing a gap in the canvas at the back of a vehicle and the profile of a small boy, his blond hair ruffled by the wind.

Chapter Thirteen

"It's the work crew from Terezín," SS Sgt. Engel announced to two Schupo sentries standing at the mouth of the road leading to Lidice, a troop carrier parked to one side, half on and half off the embankment.

"You need to see Rostock," one of the men said. "He's at a farm. Number 13. Drive down that road, the one to the side there." The sentry indicated the way with an outstretched arm. "Take a left and then stay on the road until you pass the houses and the cemetery. You'll start seeing the entrances to the farms. Number 13 is easy enough to find."

Engel waved a Nazi salute with his right hand and rolled up the window with his left. He turned on to a wide, smooth, dirt-packed road, gullies and gorse on either side.

*

Rostock led his men under the arch of the brick and stone entry gate and into the courtyard at Number 13, the Horák farm. Several meters from the main house, he started dividing the men into two lines. He stationed the first group so the men stood directly in front of a row of mattresses that had been propped against or laid on the ground in front of the farmhouse wall. He arranged the second group a few steps behind and to the right of the first.

*

Through low-hanging branches of linden trees, Cpl. Lorenz could see the narrow side streets of Lidice. Just beyond hillocks of wildflowers and a privet hedge were rows of two-story stucco houses under peaked, dark red or brown-tiled roofs, neatly groomed gardens beside each one, a single-story shed behind.

"Can you see that?" Lorenz asked. Engel slowed the vehicle so he could look past the corporal's head. Dull green vans were parked haphazardly in the middle of the streets, at the intersections, near the hedgerows. Schupo were removing large metal cans and slatted wooden crates from the rear of their vehicles.

"Smell it?" Lorez asked, turning toward Engel.

The sergeant nodded. "Kerosene."

"Look over there," the corporal added. At the far end of the street, a pair of Schupo shook out the last drops of liquid from one of their cans, struck a match and tossed it. Engel and Lorenz felt the whoosh of ignition before they saw the dance of flames at the base of the buildings.

Engel let the truck roll forward, and on street after street, he and his corporal saw similar tableaux. Schupo were combing through belongings that had been pulled from the houses and salvaging valuables for themselves; toting gas cans, setting charges and flinging incendiary devices; posing for photographs in front of flaming and scarred facades.

*

Each of the men in the first of Rostock's two groups released his rifle from its shoulder harness and let the weapon lean against his leg. The men relaxed, bouncing up and down to release the tension. Each of the men in the second group dropped down to his knees and removed a series of cartons from his canvas pack. The men pried open the lids from boxes of ammunition and began freeing rounds from their packaging.

*

Trees soon thickened and encroached as the road in front of Engel's truck dipped slightly and curved, but then fell away to expose a flat grassy area to the right, with the confines of the town cemetery in the foreground, an imposing four-story, Baroque graystone church in the distance. Beyond were rolling hills in shades of green—olive patches separated from light green oblongs by thin pale scratches of earth.

Engel tamped down on the brakes and tightened his hold on the

REPRISAL

steering wheel as a rolling current of air shook the cab of the truck. The earth sighed as it rose and fell beneath the truck's wheels. He barely recovered his composure before the air was filled with an insistent shriek as stones and bricks grated then ripped away from one another and the clapper of the church bell bounced back and forth against its sound bow. Out of his side window, Engel could see the dark green bell tower of the church tremble, slowly tip to one side, tear away from the reddish-brown roof, and slide along the side walls of the building until it disappeared behind a stand of bushy pear trees. Mesmerized, Engel and Lorenz watched stained-glass windows splinter, walls explode, sections of roof cave in.

"What's happening?" Engel whispered to his corporal. "Don't the people in this town work for us in the steelworks?"

*

Rostock paraded slowly up and down the rows of men, stopping occasionally to adjust a helmet or smooth a lapel. Satisfied that his men were presentable, he stepped aside and made room for his superior officer, SS Hauptsturmfürher Harald Wiesmann. Wiesmann ran a critical eye over Rostock, the farmhouse, the rows of Sturmmann. He nodded curtly to Rostock, then positioned himself in front of the men. "It is the will of the Führer," Wiesmann made sure they understood, "which you are about to execute."

*

Engel guided the truck past the city proper and entered the Lidice farming area, passing Number 11 with its fields of sprouting beans and Number 12 with its rows of squash. At Number 13, he stopped in front of a stone archway, a linden tree to one side, its branches slanting across one of the columns.

"You stay here," Engel told the corporal as he opened the driver's side door and stepped onto the running board. "Not that they're ...," he indicated the passengers huddled on the bed of the truck, "going anywhere, but still ..."

He walked into the courtyard in front of the farm buildings and past the stable, pausing when he heard voices inside the walls. Men's voices. A lot of men's voices. He turned the corner of the building and entered the yard, where an Obersturmführer and a Hauptsturmfürher were eyeing the policemen, straightening out the rows, swatting at sagging buttocks or slouching shoulders. "Herr Obersturmführer Rostock?" Engel approached the officer warily.

"What?" Rostock barked.

"Engel. From Terezín." He saluted the Obersturmführer.

"Well, it's about time," Rostock appraised Engel, tightening the collar of his uniform.

"We had—"

"I don't want to hear it," Rostock silenced Engel. "I need you to get those men started."

Rostock led Engel to a garden area on the other side of the farmhouse. "There," he indicated a spot between walnut trees and pines, next to mulberry bushes and sprouting spring vegetables. "I need a plot 20 by 30 meters, 10 meters deep."

"That will take all day."

"It will take all day before we can start filling it."

Chapter Fourteen

German Police Corporal Wolfgang Weber stood on the cobblestones at the side entrance to the Kladno high school watching the women from Lidice. Two truckloads had already been emptied. He was getting snappish as he watched the women climb down from the back of this truck, due more to the conversation with his fellow Schupo Anton Gruber than because of the operation.

"They think they're going to get something they can Germanize from this crowd?" Gruber nodded in the direction of the women. "Look at them. Look at that one." He pointed to Silvie who was pulling the hem of her skirt down over her piano legs and thick-veined ankles. "That doesn't even look Slavic, let alone Czech, or anything remotely German."

"All this 'processing' they're calling it," Gruber continued. "All this nonsense about interviewing and measuring noses and heads and doling out different colored badges. A waste of time, if you ask me, with people like that anyway." He waved to encompass all the women and children lining up on the street and filing into the school gymnasium under Schupo guard. "These people should all get black badges and be done with them—send them off to the death camps." Gruber fiddled with the buttons of his jacket. "They were responsible for Heydrich, after all." He looked at Weber. "What else do you do with assassins?"

"How do we even know that?" Weber asked. "Heydrich was just buried, and the assassins got away. We don't know that these people had anything to do with it."

"Watch yourself, Weber." Gruber narrowed his eyes and glanced sidelong at him. "We just follow orders around here. We don't think about such things. The Gestapo does all the thinking."

Weber watched Ondrej jump off the end of the truck and walk behind a Schupo, mimicking the man's movements.

"I don't know," he said under his breath. "Some look Germanizable to me."

He turned his attention back to the truck. Schupo Sgt. Albert

Kleinschmidt was calling him.

*

"This is the one? The one with the German husband?" Kleinschmidt asked Weber.

Weber nodded.

"Help me with her," Kleinschmidt told him. "She seems confused."

Weber clamored on the truck and crouched down to speak to Katrenka. "Can you get up? Get down the steps of the ladder?"

Katrenka concentrated her gaze, straining to focus, to understand what was happening. Her eyes fell on Weber's hand, followed the line of his sleeve up past the forearm to the upper arm and the insignia. Her eyes widened as she raised her head and saw blond stubble on a chiseled chin, a thin moustache, and close-set, light-blue eyes behind round glasses. "Johann." She relaxed. "You've come back to me."

Katrenka leaned on Weber's legs and let him pull her upright. She clutched his arm with one hand and patted his face with the other. "You have been gone so long." She rested her head on his chest. "I was so worried."

His arm around her waist, Weber led Katrenka forward with a gentle push on the small of her back, but she moved haltingly, scraping one foot on the floor of the truck and dragging the other behind, stopping every few meters to take a breath and adjust her grip on his arm.

Weber guided her to the edge of the tailgate above the stepladder. "Here," Kleinschmidt called from below. "Can you step down here?" he asked Katrenka, pointing to the top rung.

Katrenka shrank back and tightened her grip when she felt Weber's body withdraw. "Aren't you coming with me?" She turned toward him. "You can't leave me again." She wrapped her arms around his body.

A Schupo corporal scrambled up the ladder and stepped to her side, trying to peel her hands and arms away from Weber.

"No," she shrieked, slapping his away.

The guard pulled on her more forcefully.

"Don't let him take me..." Katrenka raised her head and peered

REPRISAL

into Weber's eyes. She squinted in confusion as she touched his chin and mouth and the rim of his glasses. "You're not Johann!"

She stumbled and fell against the other man. "Who are you? What do you want?" She twisted her head back and forth. "What is happening? What are you trying to do to me?"

"Pick her up," Kleinschmidt directed Weber. "Get her moving. Get her out of there."

Weber placed one arm around Katrenka's waist and the other behind her knees. In one quick motion, he had her in his arms. He turned around and stepped backward, inching his heels toward the ladder, struggling to keep his balance as Katrenka pounded her fists into his face and chest and kicked her legs.

"That's right," Kleinschmidt encouraged. "The step is right below you."

Weber tested the space with his foot.

"A little more—you're almost there." Kleinschmidt placed a hand on Weber's ankle. "There. You've got it."

Weber teetered under Katrenka's weight as he took the first, then the second step. He steadied himself with the help of Kleinschmidt's hands on his back as he took the last steps to the ground. He let go of Katrenka and stepped away from her.

She stood uneasily, holding her arms away from her sides until she gained her balance. Once steady and settled on her feet, she rushed forward and struck out at Weber—first slapping him across the face with open hands, dislodging his glasses—then with closed fists, pummeling his chest.

Kleinschmidt moved next to Weber so Katrenka could see him. He gently put his hands on top of hers and pushed against her punches until they quieted. He let go of her fists so he could rest his fingers on her shoulders. Then he cradled her face. "You are all right now?"

Katrenka shuddered and pulled away from him, shifting her eyes from him to Weber.

"You are in Kladno," Kleinschmidt said softly. "You are here for processing."

"Why? Why do I need processing?"

"We are going to find the best place for you and your baby."

"Why isn't Johann here? I saw him..."

"No. You saw my soldier Weber. He looks like your Johann, ja?"

Letting her eyes travel over Weber, she nodded. "He is like my husband."

"Your husband is not here," Kleinschmidt said.

"Why not? There are so many soldiers here." She noted the Schupo on the truck, along the street, in groups, standing alone.

"He is ...," Kleinschmidt struggled to find words, "... in another regiment."

"Will he be coming here?" she asked with pleading eyes.

"We will see what we can do." Kleinschmidt turned her body and looked into her eyes. "Now, you must come with us—with him." He motioned to Weber. "He will take you inside ... over there." He indicated the door to the gymnasium. "We will let you rest for awhile."

Kleinschmidt bent forward and kissed the tops of her hands. Taking a step back, he stood at attention and knocked his heels together. He led Katrenka as if she were a dance partner, letting the tips of his fingers guide her to Weber's arm.

"You go with him now, ja? And don't beat up on him too much."

With her hand on his arm, Weber took a step forward and waited. Katrenka shifted her weight from side to side and began to lift her foot, but stumbled, losing her balance. "You will let me carry you?" he asked, opening his arms.

She gazed down, willing her legs to make a forthright stride, but they could only quiver in response. "Yes, I think that would be better."

Weber moved to her side and raised his arms. Katrenka let her back fall into his body and his arms support her shoulders and knees.

"I'm sorry," she said to Weber. "I thought you were my Johann."

*

"Did you hear that?" said one of the women standing behind Chessie on the walkway next to the gymnasium. "They are going to 'process' Katrenka and her baby. What did I tell you? She's one of them. They're going to take special care of her."

"Do you see how that soldier was treating her?" another woman said. "So *careful*. He *bowed* to her. He *kissed her hands!*"

"She's playing that sick role pretty well, don't you think? 'Oh, no, I can't walk. You have to carry me.' " The woman mimicked Katrenka's voice.

Chessie felt hostility, isolated in pockets, rising like bubbles on the bottom of a pan of slowly boiling water, percolating among the women.

One of them turned to her. "That's right. You've been spending a lot of time with her. At her house. Just you and her. So, are you in on it, too? Are you one of *them*? Another collaborator?"

Enmity erupted as a group of women surged toward Chessie, shrinking the distance between them. Chessie pushed toward the dwindling space and ducked her head as if to fend off a blow. She took a step and felt a burst of anger wash over her, enveloping even her child. She hunched over her son and wrapped her arms around him, fashioning a sort of cocoon, holding him tightly.

*

Milan felt pressure on the side of his body—a Schupo nudging him and his mother forward. "Over there. Follow them." the Schupo directed him to the wall on the far side of a gymnasium where boys, girls, toddlers, babies and young women were gathered. Opposite him were more of the same; to his left, in an alcove, was a group of old women. To his right was Katrenka Becke, seated on the floor, her back propped up against a mat, her legs splayed out in front of her.

He eased his mother to the hardwood floor, then sat down beside her and scanned the room: heavy mats hung from hooks halfway up the white plaster walls; wire netting covered the overhead and sidewall light fixtures, an open door at the end of the wall behind him revealed rows of lockers and shower stalls beyond; a pair of doors in the wall to his right were closed. Above the alcove was a loft fronted by a polished wooden railing. Overhead was a dark wood-paneled ceiling.

He followed the actions of the Schupo as they herded the remaining women and children through the dark-wood, double-doored entry and directed them to fill empty spots in the crowd of nearly 300. Then they stood, waiting for orders. Also watching carefully, he noticed, was Silvie Tůma, who stood on the other side of the room directly across from him. Silvie's eyes were fixed on Weber, who was bundling a pair of towels he had retrieved from the locker room and positioning them under Katrenka's legs. Her gaze intensified, Milan noticed, when she saw that Kleinschmidt was focused on the same thing.

Chapter Fifteen

"Where did you get those?" Milan asked Václava Janda.

"Those ... ?"

He pointed to the clothing she was folding and stacking and the bits of food she was lining up in front of her on the gymnasium floor.

"In the street—from the piles in the street. You didn't ... ?" Václava took a look at Milan and his mother, noting that they were wearing flimsy nightclothes and soft-soled slippers.

"Here," she took some clothing she had fashioned into a pillow and handed it to Milan. "Slide it behind her. Your mother can rest easier that way." She grabbed a rozky and some bread and urged it on him. "For her," she said, noticing his reluctance. Nodding toward Marketa, she said: "And the baby."

"Mama?" Milan put the food to his mother's mouth, but her lips did not move.

*

"Here," Klaudie called out to Chessie, patting the space on the floor next to her and her mother.

"You're still not worried?" Chessie asked. "Now that we're in this ... place?"

Klaudie shook her head. "Men like my Ctibor are probably talking to the Schupo right now. You know how well it's been working out for Ctibor and my boys in the factories—here in Kladno. They have been doing all right. Don't tell anyone about this," she lowered her voice, "or those bitches Berta and Hana will hate me as well as Katrenka. But Ctibor gets extra rations from the Nazis. He knows how to get around them."

Irritated that Chessie wasn't more impressed, Klaudie continued, "Now don't you get all high and mighty with me. My Ctibor deserves those extra rations. He's a good worker. When the Nazis first came in, they purged hundreds of Czechs from the factories so they could bring in more Germans. But not my Ctibor. They kept him because he knows a thing or two about those machines. He knows how to keep them working. He knows how to get on the right side of the Nazis."

She paused. "So just you wait and see. My Ctibor has probably already made the Nazis realize this is all a mistake and is arranging to get us home."

She stopped at the sounds of bumps and scrapes outside the main entry to the gymnasium. "What did I tell you? I bet you Ctibor has gotten this all straightened out," she said to Chessie, smoothing her mother's skirt over her shins. "We'll be out of here anytime now."

*

"Look, I know how these things go," Ctibor Cizek told a Schupo guard standing at the door of the stable on Horák's farm. "I've been working with the shift captain at the Kladno steelworks for years. So have two of my sons. I'm sure there's been a misunderstanding. If you would let me talk to your superior, I can clear this all up."

When the guard did not respond, Cizek's voice rose. "Hey, corporal, I *know* people, people in high places at the factory. You don't know how much trouble you're in..."

Father Sternbeck, the St. Martin's parish priest, began the Lord's Prayer.

"We don't need that, Father," Cizek chastised the old man. "I can take care of this." To the guard, Cizek whispered, "If it's just a matter of money, I have a few hundred Reichsmarks ... in my house. So do my sons. Other people in this town have a little money, maybe not much, but we've been working in the factories since the first days of the Occupation. Nowhere to spend it." He smiled, but a laugh died in his throat when a Schupo sergeant and four guards approached.

Cizek slipped back into the stable, flattened himself against the hay bales, and watched from the shadows as the sergeant ordered ten Lidice men to emerge from the building and guards muscled them into a single-file row.

REPRISAL

*

Surprised by the sound of sharp blows and a commanding, clipped voice, the women shrank back from the gymnasium doors, huddling in groups, unsure where they should stand, what they should do. They watched in silence as two Schupo guards pushed the doors open wide, then stood at attention in front of them. The women watched the parade of Schupo that followed: men in single file carrying portable chairs; men in pairs carrying large folding tables.

Schupo Cpl. Anton Gruber told the men to drop the tables at the far end of the gymnasium, pull out the metal supports, and upend the table-tops, open the chairs and set them up behind the tables—two chairs in front and two chairs behind each of three tables. The corporal tested the sturdiness of the tables and adjusted their position so they lined up and were equally distant from one another. After surveying the arrangement of the furniture, he tapped his helmet as a sign of satisfaction and walked briskly back to the doorway.

He didn't even break his stride when he heard a woman's voice call out, "Bitte?"

"Please." The woman persisted, stepping quickly up to him.

"Ja?" he asked.

"The guards told us we would be able to get food in Kladno."

"I know nothing about that," he said, walking away from her.

"But we have so little ... here," she said. "Aren't you going to get us more?"

He kept walking, ignoring her plea.

"Aren't you going to help us get food? We have children here."

"Nein."

"What are we going to do?"

"I don't know." He walked through the doors in front of the Schupo guards.

*

"What did he say?" women asked Václava after the doors slammed shut.

"They aren't going to get us any food," she answered.

"But they said they would, ... in Lidice. They said we would get food when we got to Kladno."

"Yes, well, they aren't going to do it," Václava replied.

"I don't have much left," Dorota lamented.

"My boys are hungry," Berta complained.

"The baby. What will I do about her? She's crying so much. She's so hungry," Klara Hruska said.

"We're going to have to share," Václava said, as she grabbed a man's shirt from a pile of clothing, tied the sleeves and shirttail together to make a pouch, and walked over to a group of old women sitting on the floor who were eager to contribute, adding pieces of bread, small sausages, a jar of applesauce.

"I'm not going to put anything in there," Paní Tichy snapped when the pouch was in front of her. "I'm old. I need my own food."

"But this is for the children. The little ones. Surely you can spare something for them or your daughter-in-law. What about her? She's pregnant, isn't she?"

"She's fine on her own."

"She's clearly not. Look at her." Václava pointed to Marketa, who was sitting unaware, her eyes open but unfocused.

"So?" Paní Tichy took a quick look at Marketa and shrugged. "Never was worth anything to my son. Or to me. Always whining and complaining. 'Urbie is so mean to me,' " Paní Tichy said in a mocking tone. ' "He beats me.' Like my son would do anything like that. And even if he did, I'm sure Marketa deserved it." Paní Tichy held her body stiff and wrapped her arms across her chest.

"How can you say that?" Václava challenged.

"Oh, you don't know." Paní Tichy turned to face Václava. "You don't know what that—that woman—is like. You think you know her? Hah. You don't know anything."

Václava stepped back and began to turn away, then stopped.

"But your grandson? Milan? Don't you want to...?"

"Him? You ask about *him*? He's nothing like his brother. Nothing,"

REPRISAL

Paní Tichy insisted. "I tell you, the Nazis shot the wrong boy out there in the woods. The wrong boy died."

*

Kladno Security Police Officer Emil Bach's hands shook as his fingers pushed under the flap of a sealed box of ammunition. He tugged sharply at the edge of cardboard to free it from the glue and lost his grip on the box, sending the top row of bullets into the air. He dropped forward on his knees and swept the spilt rounds into a pile, then picked up one of the bullets and placed it next to the clip but dropped it before he could snap it into place. He picked up another bullet but immediately lost control of it. He rested the backs of his thighs on his calves and rubbed his palms on his uniform tunic. He crossed his arms, placed his hands in his armpits and began rocking back and forth.

The Ordnungspolizei rifleman standing to Bach's left thrust his weapon to the side and waited for Bach to replace it with a reloaded weapon. He tapped his fingers nervously on the rifle butt, finally turning his head to look at Bach. The rifleman raised the butt of his weapon and slapped the side of Bach's helmet, but Bach did not move. The rifleman called out to Rostock, "Get somebody else here—somebody who can do the job."

Rostock hurried to the rifleman's side, grabbed the man's weapon, and quickly loaded the clip. He shoved Bach out of the way and motioned for Müller to take his place. Rostock grabbed Bach by the collar of his uniform and dragged him away from the line of fire. He stepped in front of him so Rostock's superior, Harald Weismann, could not see him and whispered harshly, "Pull yourself together, Emil. For your sake—and mine."

Bach pressed his palms on the ground and raised his body to his knees. He flinched when he heard Rostock ordering more Ordungspolizei to join the firing squad. "Our work of art," said Rostock, "is not moving fast enough."

Bach looked at the lines of bodies. There were six lines already: the first reddening the mattresses with their blood and brains, the next five despoiling the ground with shattered bones and expelled feces. And more Lidice men were coming to the killing field: young and old men, boys barely in their teens. Czech, they were, like his wife, her father, her brothers, their sons. What can they be thinking? What would he himself think, if these were his neighbors and friends, sons and fathers? What would he think if he knew he was about to die—like this—shot by people who not so long ago were like him?

Bach backed away from the farmhouse and entered the garden. He heard the dry rattle of spades and pickaxes loosening dirt from stones and turned to see, through the trees, Jews in gray-and-white-striped uniforms. Some were dragging away uprooted bushes and underbrush, others were flinging soil out of the ground, their heads barely visible above the deepening hole. An SS sergeant and a corporal were talking with each another, their backs to the burial plot.

He heard the snap of a twig behind him. It was Rostock, standing in a clump of bromegrass, holding a pair of boards forming a cross. Rostock flung the boards toward the SS sergeant. "For him," Rostock said, jerking his head in Bach's direction.

Bach saw Rostock raise his automatic weapon and bowed his head in understanding as the hammer clicked, the barrel flamed and the bullet pierced his chest and tore open his heart.

*

Klaudie sat with her mother Johanna between her legs, pulling wispy strands of her mother's hair off her face and into a braid down her back. "I wish I had something to tie this off. It will unravel before too long."

"Here, dear," Paní Tomasek said, holding out a thin strip of cloth.

"What are you doing?" she asked, noting a pile of cloth strips in front of her mother.

"Making dolls ... for the little girls," Paní Tomasek said.

"Dolls? Really?"

"Yes," Paní Tomasek said. "This is how our mothers made toys for us in the old days, when times were hard."

Klaudie watched, fascinated, as arthritic fingers lined up eight large cloth strips and tied a smaller strip around them in the middle, "to act as the headscarf," Paní Tomasek explained. She folded all the strips

REPRISAL

of cloth in half so the headscarf was at one end and then tied another strip of cloth about an inch above the scarf to fashion the doll's neck. She took four of the long strips of cloth and braided them together to create one arm, and another four strips to create the other arm. A strip about four inches long wound around the remaining unbraided strips of cloth marked the doll's waist and braided strips below the 'waist' formed the doll's legs.

"Too bad we don't have anything to draw the face," Paní Tomasek said, holding out the doll at arm's length.

"Well, Andrea, its owner will just have to use her imagination," Klaudie's mother said as she picked up some cloth and started on a doll of her own.

*

Klaudie picked up the finished dolls and looked around the room at the children. Seven-year-old twins Nika and Lizveth were following the leader Ondrej as he crawled in between chairs and tables. Nine-year-old Ona sat on the floor watching Jarmil explain patiently to his brothers Radek and Nicholai why they could not use their hands to touch a soccer ball. Four-year-old Elina stood on her mother's lap, her head buried in her mother's hair. Six-year-old Adriana hugged her mother's leg, her eyes wide with worry and confusion.

Klaudie held out one of the dolls to Adriana, but she shrank back and hid her face in her mother's skirt, so Klaudie placed the doll on the floor in front of her and stepped away.

Klaudie gave the other doll to Elina's mother, who brushed her daughter's hair with her hand. "Elina." The little girl turned a tear-stained face toward her mother. "Here," her mother said, waving the doll back and forth. The little girl plopped down on her mother's lap and grabbed the doll with both hands, putting its braided arms in her mouth.

Looking back at Adriana, Klaudie saw that the little girl had moved so she could see the doll with one eye. Adriana extended a foot and nudged the doll closer, then released her mother's skirt, bent down and cupped the doll with her hand. She brought the doll close to her face and ran a finger along its head, arms and legs. With the doll on her chest, she again wrapped both arms around her mother's leg.

K. M. Sandrick

REPRISAL

*

"Alexandra," Paní Vacek nudged Paní Smida. "See what they're doing."

Paní Smida scratched a path through her hair with her fingertips. "Oh, yes. The dolls. I used to make them ... for Emília. She loved them. Even when she was no longer a child. Of course, she was always a child ... in her mind."

"Let's do it. Let's make dolls, too," Paní Vacek said.

"Yes," said Paní Smida, who was already pulling off an over-blouse and tearing at the seams. She started humming *Když jsem koval koníčky.*

"When did you ever put horse shoes on a pony?" Paní Vacek laughed. "When did you ever have a pony?"

"Stop it, Lucia. It's a nice song," Paní Smida said.

"Yes, it is," said Paní Mares, as she joined Paní Smida and Paní Vacek in the refrain.

*

When she heard the women singing, Katrenka opened her eyes. She adjusted the towels the Schupo had placed at the small of her back, then rubbed her thighs and slapped her calves on the wooden floor to increase her circulation. Her eyes panned the room, seeking out her friend Chessie. She so much wanted to talk with her, to chat about silly things from their past—their trips to the beauty shop or the school dances, or the times Chessie and her Václav had snuck off to neck in the trees. She was so worried—about what the Schupo were doing, about what was happening to her body and what might be threatening her baby.

There, finally. Katrenka spotted Chessie. She was kneeling next to Ondrej and the younger Janda boy and his mother. They were pulling food from the makeshift pouches and arranging them in piles: breads, pastries, cheeses, meats, jars, tins.

REPRISAL

*

Chessie searched the folds of the shirt she had used to collect and carry food, then shook out the cloth. She sat back and glanced around the gymnasium, past the corner of the room where Katrenka was smiling and waving. Chessie did not let her eyes rest on Katrenka. She noticed how other women huddled together, stealing glances at Katrenka and speaking in hushed tones, warning one another about the "German spy in their midst." In that moment, she turned away from her friend. She could kid herself into thinking it was because she wanted to protect her son. In truth, it was because she was afraid for herself.

*

"And the giant asked the shepherd, 'What are you looking for?' " Ceslav said to the men being led from Horák's stable.

" 'Your big, fat head,' the shepherd said. 'I'm going to knock it right off.' "

Ceslav took his place in line and continued his story. "The giant took a hammer and threw it at the shepherd's head, but he caught it. And..." He paused when he saw Vit stumble, his shoulders heaving, his nose dripping onto the front of his shirt.

"...he swung that hammer and hit the giant in the head..." Ceslav took hold of Vit's hand and pulled it to his chest. "...and the giant swayed and swayed, and then he fell right over. The shepherd searched the giant's pockets and found a silver key. Know what he did with it, Vit?"

Vit slumped against Ceslav, burying his head in the younger boy's shoulder.

Ceslav put his cheek on top of Vit's head and continued his story. "The shepherd opened the castle door and went from room to room. Know what he found?" The boys turned the corner of the stable and walked toward the back of the farm house.

GERMANIZATION

CHAPTER SIXTEEN

Morning light streamed down from the windows high in the exterior gymnasium wall. It slanted across the center of the hardwood floor where Schupo Cpl. Anton Gruber stood guard. He shifted his weight and relaxed his stance. At last, he thought, he was finally invisible.

He always did disappear from the awareness of the people under his surveillance. How long it took depended on whom he was guarding. Children were the quickest to stop taking note of him. They either ignored him entirely and immediately got involved with their play or they pestered him with questions about his uniform and his weapon, got bored with the lack of response and then moved off with their playmates. Men were next: blustery and demanding until they felt they had saved face in front of their friends. Women were last, always a bit cautious and quick with a wary eye, but anxious to do whatever they could to make their surroundings more normal: sharing food, grooming one another, singing, praying. From his vantage point near the doorway, he took stock of how the women and children in this room were adapting.

A tiny young woman, ash-blond curls swept carelessly behind her ears—the schoolteacher, he suspected—was drawing an imaginary finishing line with her foot. "We're going to have a contest," he heard her tell a group of little ones, "to see who can be the fastest animals, who can get up to this line quickest. All right?" Small heads nodded.

"We'll start by being frogs. Get down on your hands and put your backside down, like this, and jump forward." She demonstrated. "Now you try it."

"That's it. You've got it," she said after a few minutes of falls and false starts.

"Now for our contest ... On the count of three: One. Two. Three. Go!"

The children jumped and slipped and fell and laughed at one another:

"You don't look like a frog."

"You're running, not hopping."

"I'm the best frog."

"No, you're not. I am."

Frogs indeed, Gruber agreed.

In one corner of the room, Gruber spied a pair of boys testing one another in multiplication. "Fourteen times 167?" asked a boy wearing a pair of dark-rimmed eyeglasses. The other, dark-haired with intense brooding eyes, traced 167 in the air with 14 below it and drew a line. "Four sevens are 28. Carry the two. Four sixes are 24, plus two is 26. Carry the two. Four times one is four plus two ..."

Gruber wondered why the boys were learning arithmetic. All these kinds of people needed was a fourth-grade education that taught them how to write their names, count to 500 and do whatever the Reich told them to do.

A girl, barely in her teens, was huddling with two other girls, glancing sideways at the dark-haired mathematician, tossing her head back and shaking out her silky hair, unhappy that he paid her no heed.

"Hello, Adéle," a short, fat, nervous girl said as she approached the group.

The one called Adéle cast her eyes down at the interloper and sighed, nodded a perfunctory greeting, then drew her friends together and walked away.

The plump one trailed behind until the group stopped, put their heads together and started whispering, their lips moving rapidly, pursing and stretching across their teeth, hissing barely audible catty comments. The girl flattened her shirt collar, opening and closing the top button, wound her hair behind her ears and stared at the group, trying to understand why they had turned their backs on her. Her eyes filled with tears when she saw Adéle jerk a thumb in her direction and laugh.

Gruber raised his eyebrows and tilted his head to the side. Who knew the mongrels could be so discriminating?

GERMANIZATION

A rough-looking boy sat back in one of the chairs, his ankles crossed and balanced on the edge of a table. Stroking his chin, he laughed. "Jindrích," he called out. "That's no way to pin him down. Here," he said, dropping the chair to the floor. "Here's how you do it," he told Jindrích and the other would-be wrestler. He grabbed the waistband of the smaller grappler's trousers and pulled him away. With his foot, he rolled the younger wrestler onto his stomach, kneed him in the back and pinned his shoulders to the floor. "Can't get out of it, can you?" he said, grasping and twisting a clump of the boy's hair and sending a quick jab to his ribs. "That's how you take somebody down," he told Jindrích.

He would have to inform Kleinschmidt about this, Gruber told himself. The Kommandants of the concentration camps in the East were always on the lookout for guards who could keep the inmates in line. That boy had possibilities.

At the sound of voices just outside, Gruber leaned his head close to the crack between the gymnasium doors, then jumped back as bolts released, doors flung open and two Schupo pushed through the doorway, leading the way for Sgt. Albert Kleinschmidt and a group of four men dressed in white coats and carrying satchels. RuSHA investigators, Gruber realized as the men hurried into the room, approached the folding tables, adjusted the chairs behind them and took their seats. The men dropped their satchels on the tabletops, opened the flaps and withdrew stacks of printed paper, pens, folders, ink pads and rubber stamps. Meanwhile, Kleinschmidt stood in the center of the room and announced: "We begin processing today. We go as far as we can, and then come back tomorrow. You go there—to the tables—when they call you. Ja? When they call you."

"Ja?" he asked again when he heard no response.

"Yes, yes," women answered.

Gruber helped Kleinschmidt corral the women and children into two lines, then stepped to the side and watched the process unfold. A RuSHA interviewer spoke with each woman and her children, took notes, scanned color charts, checked off boxes, filled out forms, stamped documents. When the interviewer was finished, he handed out a small triangular badge, either red, black or blue.

"At least they aren't yellow stars," said one of the women near Gruber. "Those are for the Jews, and you know what happens to the Jews."

Gruber turned toward another woman, sitting in front of one of the tables, the bespectacled mathematician and the one called Adéle flanking her.

*

"You don't understand," Klaudie's voice rose in anger. "You have to talk to my Ctibor. He knows people. I shouldn't have to go through all *this*." She grabbed a handful of printed forms and shook them in the air. "My Adéle and Tomás aren't just *any* children. They are Ctibor's. Ctibor's," she stressed. "You." Klaudie pointed at the interviewer sitting on the opposite side of the table. "*You* need to go talk to someone who is in charge. Someone who *knows* what has been going on, someone who knows who we are and the kind of treatment we deserve. Not this.... this...," she picked up a tin and dumped out the triangles, "...*processing*. We are not like other people," she sneered.

*

Gruber made a game of the RuSHA interview process, guessing which color badge each interviewee would get. It was obvious with the old women. They weren't strong enough to be sent to a labor camp and certainly not material for the Lebensborn breeding program. Black badges for them, for sure. The same for the short, dark, ugly children who couldn't possibly have any Aryan blood. To his mind, none of the children or young women from Lidice was suitable for Germanization. Well, there was the one woman carrying a German soldier's child. But the others getting blue badges? They didn't deserve them, as far as he was concerned. He didn't understand why those people were being singled out.

Gruber eyed the next ones in line—a mousy woman holding on to

GERMANIZATION

a feisty blond boy. No question about the color of the badges they would get.

*

"You are Czech?" the interviewer asked Chessie.

"Yes," she replied, suddenly becoming uncomfortable under the man's gaze.

"Your husband? Czech also?"

"Yes. Well, he was. He's dead now."

The interviewer pulled three printed forms from the stack. "And your surname?

"Sabel."

"Your given name?"

"Chessie." The man wrote Chessie's full name on the top of one of the forms.

"And your boy?"

"This is Ondrej." The interviewer wrote his name on the top of another form.

"Where is your family from?"

"České Švýcarsko."

Another interviewer raised his head and looked at Chessie. "The Bohemian Switzerland," he said. "I know it well. I ...," he patted his chest, "... and my family are from Rosenthal. Just a few kilometers away. When I was young, my brother and my father and I would go to one of the 'rock cities' and hike over the bluffs and into the mini-canyons. It was a great place for rock climbing. So many rocks in so many different shapes." The man paused. "Did you go there? To climb?"

"Yes, a few times." Chessie smiled, remembering how she had scrambled over the rocks, struggling to keep up with her father.

"Where exactly did your father come from?"

"My father's family lived in Děčín."

"And your mother?"

"From Gablonz."

"I know the area well. There is that big apple tree in the village green."

Chessie nodded.

"There are a lot of Germans there."

"Yes, my mother's neighbors were German," Chessie said.

"What did your father do?"

"He made jewelry ... before the war." Chessie saw her father in her mind's eye, huddled over the workbench in the back of his father-in-law's jewelry store, slipping stones into gold settings, polishing silver, raising the pieces to the light, admiring their glitter.

"And after?"

"He wasn't ... he didn't ... He lost an arm in the war. He couldn't work ... with the jewelry ... anymore." Chessie recalled how different her father seemed after he returned from WW I: how quiet he was; how he sat and looked at her and her mother with clouded eyes; how he watched the new, young jewelers while he clasped and unclasped the cuff of the empty sleeve that hung limp, covering what was left of his shattered arm; how distant and unwilling he was to engage with her or her mother.

"Your husband?"

Chessie shook away the memory of her father.

"What? What about him? My husband."

"Where was ... he from?"

"He was born and raised in Lidice. He worked his father's farm ... we both did ... after his father died."

"Brothers and sisters?"

"Václav has an older brother and a sister. They both live in Prag."

"And you?"

"No. I am an only child."

"And the boy? He is your only child?"

Chessie nodded.

Ondrej pulled out one of the forms. "You look like this," he said to the interviewer, holding up the form and pointing to one of the sketches

GERMANIZATION

of different types of noses. "This one." He stabbed a finger at a picture of a long thin nose with the word *gerade* written under it.

"Well, so do you," the interviewer replied.

"No. Mine is more like this." Ondrej placed his finger on the drawing of a pointed nose.

"Leave that alone," Chessie admonished Ondrej as she pulled him away from the sheet of paper.

The interviewer smiled at Ondrej. On the form that bore his name, the man began drawing circles around pictures of an oval face: a head with a high crown and forehead; light-colored, almond-shaped eyes; and a straight nose, jaw and chin. The interviewer opened a pair of calipers and measured the width of Ondrej's nose, the space between the edge of his nose and the beginning of his ears, his forehead, the space between his eyes, the line of his jaw from his ear to his chin. He wrote down each set of numbers in designated boxes on the paper, asked him to stand, and then measured his height, his girth, the length of his fingers, the circumference of his head.

"What do you like to study in school?"

Ondrej frowned and scratched the side of his face. "History, I guess," he said reluctantly. "I like the stuff about the wars. I'm going to be a soldier, you know."

"I guess you need to know about the wars, then ... if you're going to be a soldier," the interviewer said.

"Like this." Ondrej jumped up from the chair and started marching in place, his back straight, his chin tucked in toward his chest.

"That's enough," Chessie said, uncomfortable with Ondrej's demonstration. She extended a hand and rested it on his arm.

"You never let me do anything," Ondrej whined. "Just because you don't like the Germans and what happened in the war, what happened to Otec. You want me to be all serious and smart—and B—O—R—ING. I don't know why I can't be a soldier."

"Not now, Ondrej. We will talk about it later."

"Later. Later. Later," Ondrej snapped, plopping down next to Chessie, hanging his head, banging the tips of his shoes against the legs of the chair, shrugging off her touch.

GERMANIZATION

The interviewers gathered and signed Ondrej's forms and measurements and placed them in a file, then selected two different colored badges. "You put this on your shirt—over here," the man told Ondrej, handing him a blue triangle. "You wear this ... all the time. You understand? It is important."

"It's like a medal," Ondrej said proudly, positioning the badge on his left shoulder. "It's like I'm in the army."

"This is for you." The interviewer handed Chessie a red badge.

"What does this mean?" she asked. "Why is mine red and his is blue? We are a family. We should have the same..."

"It is just our procedure," the interviewer said, closing the portfolio and waving to the next woman and her children. "Come," he called out to them.

"But ..." Chessie said worriedly.

"That is all," the interviewer told Chessie. "Move along now." A Schupo guard nervously changed the position of his rifle and took a step toward the table. "She is going," the interviewer called over his shoulder to the Schupo. "You go now," he said to Chessie.

"Don't worry," Ondrej said to the Schupo with a wink. "She doesn't know what it's like with us—with us soldiers."

*

Gruber shifted position, his eyes tracing the movements of a fellow guard who was speaking to a dark-haired pregnant woman. The Schupo nudged her shoulder, then lifted her chin in his hand, crouching in front of her so he could look at her face. The man gazed into her eyes and raised his voice. "You understand?" he asked, shaking her shoulder when she didn't respond. He tried again. "You hear me?"

Frustrated, the Schupo waved to Gruber. He pointed to Marketa. "I don't know which one ..." he held up a red badge and a black one, "... to give to her. She's young enough to go to—"

"Ssh," Gruber said, holding up a hand and shaking his head. "No, no." He put a finger to his lips. "Not in front of the others."

"But she doesn't understand," the Schupo went on. "I don't know if

GERMANIZATION

she's deficient." He tapped a finger against his temple. "Or ..."

"Just give her a black one," Gruber said. "What do we care?"

"She's pregnant." The Schupo pointed to her swollen belly.

"So?"

"But that means..."

"Yes, I know what it means."

*

"What are you doing here?" Gruber asked Milan. "Why aren't you in line with the others?"

Milan twisted away from the Schupo's grasp.

"Oh, no, you don't. You're not getting away from me."

Gruber pulled Milan to the middle of the gymnasium.

"Where is your mother?" he asked.

Milan stood in silence, his eyes focused on the floor.

The Schupo shook Milan's body, grabbed his chin and raised his head. "Where is she?" The guard pulled Milan's face to the right. "Is she over there?"

Milan did not respond.

The guard squeezed Milan's chin hard. "You tell me," he insisted.

Milan closed his eyes and shook his head.

Gruber released the boy's chin and clasped his arm. He raised it and held it in the air. "Who does this one belong to?" he asked.

The women turned slowly toward Milan. A few swept the gymnasium with their eyes, searching for Marketa. Silvie raised her arm and pointed. "That one. That's his mother," she said.

The Schupo saw Marketa sitting motionless at the end of the gym, the black badge pinned to her blouse. He ran his eyes up and down over Milan's thin frame. He squeezed his shoulders and tested the strength of his bicep. He reached in a pocket and thumbed through a jumble of red and black badges. He pulled out a red triangle and put it in Milan's hand.

"All right," he said. "You have your badge. Move along." Gruber pushed Milan away.

"It's not black." Milan looked at the badge, turning it over in his hand.

"Move along boy," the Schupo urged.

"But ..." Milan protested, holding out the red badge.

Chapter Seventeen

Ondrej took a circuitous route toward Anton Gruber, who stood with his back to the boy at the door of the gymnasium. Ondrej meandered to the left, then to the right, all the while keeping his head turned to the side, his eyes gauging whether the corporal would welcome conversation or not. Standing parallel with the Schupo, he asked tentatively, "How long have you been a soldier? Do you like being one?" He dragged a foot back and forth in front of him while waiting for a response. "I want to be a soldier," he declared. "I can be one. Just watch." Ondrej pulled his legs together, straightened his back and tucked in his chin. "See," he said. "I can stand like you. I can march, too." He thrust out one leg, then another and raised his right arm in salute. He took three steps, then turned smartly and marched back to his position next to Gruber, who stood unmoving, his face expressionless.

Exasperated, Ondrej stepped behind the Schupo, pulled the edges of his mouth down with his fingers and stuck out his tongue.

He gasped as a firm hand grabbed his shoulder. He scrunched up his shoulders, dropped his head and rose on the balls of his feet, preparing to bolt.

*

"That's all right," said Schupo Cpl. Weber. He turned Ondrej around to face him, then bent down to whisper in his ear. "I did the same thing when I was a boy."

Weber stood and led the boy away from Gruber. "So you want to be a soldier? Let's see." The corporal put his on Ondrej's upper arm and pumped the bicep. "Very strong." He lifted Ondrej's face in his hand and looked in his eyes. "Smart, I can see, too. Yes, you would make a good soldier. Maybe you could be one of the new recruits. Would you like that?"

Ondrej jumped up. "Oh, yes, yes, yes," he said.

"All right. Let's go over here." He led Ondrej to a corner of the room and crouched down. "Let's talk," he said as he patted the wood next to him. "What do you know about soldiers?" the corporal asked.

"I know a lot. I read all about the Great War. And I saw the soldiers—just last week—in our town ... the Gestapo," Ondrej said excitedly. "The Gestapo came to our town."

"What happened?"

"They came in these big black cars. And they all jumped out and ran to the ends of the town. And they lined up—like this." Ondrej jumped up and stood at attention, pretending he held a rifle.

"Then an officer came out of one of the cars. He was very tall." Ondrej raised his hand over his head "And he had these tall shiny boots. Up to here." Ondrej indicated his shins, a few inches below the kneecap. "And he walked so straight and strong." Ondrej mimicked a strut, thrusting out one shoulder, then the other. "He must have been really important. He had these medals." Ondrej pointed to the left side of his chest. "And a big cross up here." He pointed to his throat. "And on his cap—I saw it when he took it off. There was a skull—right in the middle."

"What about these soldiers here ... my men. Wouldn't you like to be one of them?" the corporal asked.

"They're not *real* soldiers," Ondrej said. "They have those drab green uniforms. Not like the one I saw in our town with his tall black boots and the skull on his cap."

"But that is a Gestapo officer, a captain. Other Gestapo are not so ... so flashy."

"Well, I'm going to be a Gestapo," Ondrej said firmly. "I'm going to be the best. The most important one. A Gestapo captain."

"It's not just wearing uniforms and riding in big black cars, being in the Gestapo," the corporal warned. "And it's not like being in the army or in the police. The Gestapo—they don't fight in the war."

"They don't? But they're soldiers."

"They are special kinds of ... of ... soldiers, I guess you would say. But they don't go to the front lines of the battles."

"What do they do, then?"

"They ... they are here ... in the Occupied countries." He glanced at

GERMANIZATION

his fellow Schupo to see if anyone was listening, then lowered his voice anyway. "They are like a special police—they look for enemies—behind the lines."

"They're like investigators," Ondrej concluded. "I can do that. I'm good at finding out things."

"They are not always ... so nice."

"Stop bothering the man," Chessie said to Ondrej as she approached them. "Your teacher wants to see all the children—over there," She pointed to the opposite side of the room. "Maybe you can get some schoolwork done."

"What do I care about school? I'm going to be a soldier. He...," Ondrej nudged the corporal's thigh, "...he said I would be a good soldier."

"But good soldiers are smart. They go to school. They finish school," the corporal said.

"Did you go to school?" Ondrej asked.

He nodded. "I finished university. In Hamburg. Before I moved here to be near my wife's family in Unhošt. And you should finish up your school, too. You should go." The corporal leaned his head toward the gathering group of children. "You should learn all you can—to be a good soldier."

"You heard what the man said. Now go." Chessie gave Ondrej's rump a couple of soft slaps and watched as he reluctantly made his way toward Magda and the other children.

"Thank you," Chessie told the corporal. "Thank you for helping me to convince him to go to school. He doesn't like it, you know. School."

The corporal smiled. "Neither did I."

"Weber," Sgt. Kleinschmidt called out. "Come."

"I need you," the sergeant told Weber as he led Katrenka toward the corporal. "You take care of this one. Watch her. Make sure she is all right. Ja?"

*

Milan folded the red badge over and over in his hand as he walked over to his neighbor Joshko. "What kind of badge do you have?" Joshko pulled a red triangle out of his pocket.

"What about Radek? What kind does he have?" Milan asked as he looked around the gymnasium.

"There he is." Milan followed Joshko's glance and saw a red badge on Radek's shoulder.

"Why does it matter to you?" Joshko asked.

"I need to get a black one."

"Why?"

"Because my mother has a black one. I need to be sure I will be with her. I need to have a badge like hers."

*

Milan scanned the gymnasium and saw that most of the older boys, boys his age, had red badges. A few of the girls, toddlers and babies had blue badges. The rest of the children, including Klaudie's son Tomás, had black ones.

Milan took Tomás to a corner of the room. "Can I have that?" Milan asked, pointing to Tomás' black badge. "I'll give you this one."

Tomás shook his head and turned to walk away.

Milan grabbed his shoulder. "Tomás, Tomás, listen to me. It's important that I have a black badge."

"No," Tomás insisted.

"But my mother." Milan pointed to Marketa. "She has a black badge. If I don't get one, we won't be together."

"My mother—my mother made a big deal about the badges. She talked to that Schupo man ... Kleinschmidt. He told her I should have a black badge. She will kill me if I change anything."

"Yeah, I remember. I remember all that—when your mother made such a fuss," Milan said. "All right." He patted Tomás on the back.

"Sobeslava—over there," Tomás offered. "Maybe she will switch with you."

GERMANIZATION

Milan approached the girl who had been rejected by Adéle and her friends where she sat folding clothing. He sat down next to her, put his arm around her shoulder and asked softly, "Your badge," he pointed at the black triangle, "... would you trade it with mine?"

Sobeslava looked down at the triangle in Milan's hand. "No," she said. "It would be different." She looked up at him. "Different from those." She nodded toward her friends. "We all have the same ones."

"Yes. Yes. I see," Milan said, withdrawing his arm from around her shoulder.

He stood and looked at the other children in the room, searching for someone who might switch with him.

*

"No, I won't do it." Ondrej turned and began to walk away from a small group of children.

"Why not?" they asked.

"Don't want to." Ondrej sulked. "Don't have to."

"But Jindřích is your friend."

"Not anymore," Ondrej insisted.

"What's going on?" Chessie asked.

"Ondrej," one of the children answered. "He won't play with him," the boy said, pointing to Jindřích who stood a few steps away, his thin arms jutting out from an oversized plaid shirt, his eyes glancing from Ondrej to the floor, one foot rubbing the side of the other.

"What happened?" Chessie asked Ondrej.

"He's not like us." Ondrej jerked his head in Jindřích's direction. "He's not like me."

"What do you mean?"

"Look." Ondrej pointed to Jindřích's chest.

"What are you talking about?" Chessie squatted in front of Ondrej and held his shoulders. "You tell me what is going on right now."

"His badge." Ondrej sputtered. "He's one of the black ones. Not

GERMANIZATION

one of us." He indicated a group of three children who wore blue badges.

"Ondrej, he's been your friend since you were five years old."

"Well, I didn't know any better then. I didn't know he wasn't as good as us."

"You stop that kind of talk right now, young man," Chessie said.

"Hey, it's not my fault. They..." Ondrej pointed to the interviewers at the tables. "They're the ones."

Chapter Eighteen

Schupo Sgt. Albert Kleinschmidt was examining the results of the RuSHA interrogation. Six children had been categorized as Germanizable. There were a few babies and, he counted on his fingers, ten women who were destined for Lebensborn.

"Gruber," he called out.

Kleinschmidt scribbled his name on a pair of order sheets. "One standard size bus should be enough for the ones going to Lebensborn. And we'll need an ambulance. Don't forget the ambulance for the pregnant one," he added. "She will be going to the infirmary with that sister-in-law of hers."

"Why the other one, the sister-in-law? Why is she going? She's hardly Lebensborn."

"But she will be useful as midwife. That infirmary is small. Not very many nurses, and they are busy with other things."

"There aren't that many guards there, either. Who's going...?"

"Weber."

"Right. Weber. He's been getting pretty cozy with that one."

"What?"

"Nothing. Nothing."

*

Since he had been assigned to watch out for Katrenka, Schupo Cpl. Weber had been at her side while she paced from one end of the gymnasium to the other.

"Don't you want to sit?" he asked, pointing to the spot in the corner of the room near the entry to the locker room, where he had left her the previous morning. The towels he had given her were bunched together there in a small heap.

"It is easier if I walk." She leaned against him.

Weber glanced around the gymnasium, growing uncomfortable as he noticed women's eyes flashing back and forth between him and Katrenka, lips compressing, bodies turning toward one another, mouths spitting out words, minds passing judgment.

He tilted his head toward the women and said, "Maybe it would be better for you if we didn't talk to one another."

Katrenka took a look around the gymnasium. "They couldn't think any worse of me than they already do." She paused when she saw Chessie talking with the interviewers, then stared straight ahead when Chessie dropped her eyes to the floor, ignoring their brief connection.

Weber noted how slowly Katrenka moved—how she shuffled along the floor—how she braced the outside of her calf against his leg and lightly brushed her hand along his trousers to keep herself oriented, balanced. He waited while she stopped every few steps and watched how her shoulders rose and fell with her breath. He saw how her hips rotated in a wide and awkward manner as she swung each leg out to the side before moving forward. It reminded him of his wife's cousin, Martina.

Martina's legs also had been terribly swollen, and she had been similarly breathless and confused in the last days of her pregnancy. No one knew what was wrong or what to do when her time came: her arms and legs started jerking; her head tossed from side to side; her eyes rolled back in her head. Weber had tried to hold her down but the shaking wouldn't stop. She was such a little thing, but she was so strong then, her back arching in spite of his hold on her. Then, all of a sudden she went limp. Drool and froth appeared at the corners of her mouth, urine and feces between her legs. She hadn't responded when Weber and his wife and Martina's husband shook and pinched her, or even when they placed the newborn on her chest. He wondered if the same thing would happen to the woman walking by his side.

Tracing Weber's profile with her eyes, Katrenka commented, "You are so like my husband." She raised her fingers to his cheek and chin. "It was so easy for me to think Johann was back with me ... you know, when you came to me on the truck." Katrenka withdrew her hand, distracted by a puffy area just behind her knuckles. She pressed down with a finger and watched curiously as the area remained white and indented even after she released it.

"Your husband was not from around here, ja?"

She shook her head.

"So how did you meet?"

"We met in Prag. I went to live with my brother and sister-in-law. I wanted to be a dressmaker." Katrenka examined her swollen fingers and lamented that she couldn't very easily pass a needle through a piece of cloth now.

"We—my brother Kornel and his wife Silvie ..." Katrenka saw Silvie in a group of women nearby and nodded to her. "We were living down the street from Johann and his mother—and their bookshop on Benátská Street in Nové Mešto."

She absently pulled on threads of her blouse. "I often stopped and looked at the window displays of books on my way home from work and saw him in the back sorting and stacking books."

She brushed the top of her skirt, smoothing out folds with trembling fingers.

"I really couldn't afford to buy anything, so when I went into the shop, I just browsed. If I found a book I liked, I stood in front of the shelves and read a few pages at a time. I always kept a lookout for Johann. And not only because he was so handsome." She laughed. "I was afraid he didn't want me to read a book without intending to buy it. But he started coming over to me, to look at the book I was holding and tell me about the author or ask me how I liked it."

She placed her fingertips on her forehead and massaged the area just above her eyes and her temples.

"Then he showed me other books I might like, or he set them aside and said I could 'borrow' them, as long as I would go out with him for coffee and tell him what I thought."

Katrenka swayed and leaned on her right side, easing pressure on her left hip, then ran her hand along the edge of her leg, back and forth, down the thigh.

"We went to the coffeehouse down the street." Katrenka smiled at the memory. "And he let me do most of the talking." she took a breath. "He knew so much about history and politics and music, but he listened to what I had to say first, and then patiently answered my questions.

And I had so many questions."

She put a hand to her back and pushed on her spine to stretch. "One time when I was 'shopping' in the bookstore, Johann put a record on the phonograph. It was a symphony by Beethoven. The Third Symphony. It was wonderful. I heard horses galloping, cannons exploding. I collapsed on one of the chairs and didn't move a muscle until it was over. When I realized he had been watching me, I got flustered and dropped my purse and the books I was holding. I bumped into a table and knocked over more books. I was so embarrassed, I just wanted to disappear."

Katrenka brushed her nose and face with her fingers and palm. "But he was so kind. He came over and helped me pick up the books. When I put the last one back on the table, he laid his hand on mine. 'You liked the music?' he asked. 'Oh yes,' I said, and I have to admit that I just gushed. 'It's like nothing I ever heard before,' I told him, then I went on and on about how thrilling it was, but mournful too, in parts. How exhilarating. How the music made me feel so ... so uplifted. He smiled and held my hand and said, 'Then we must go to a concert.' And we did—go to concerts and plays—or we just sat ... and talked ... before the Occupation."

A tightening of muscles, a contraction, a string of pain ran up her back. Katrenka winced. "A spasm," she explained in answer to Weber's worried look.

"It is kind of you to ... listen to all this ... while you have to watch over me." Before he could respond, she patted his hand. "I may not have heard exactly what the sergeant—Kleinschmidt is it?" Weber nodded. "What Sgt. Kleinschmidt said, but I could see that he wanted you to take me off his hands."

"It is no..."

"Let's go this way," Katrenka interrupted, leading him past the group of old women at the far end of the gymnasium who, in place of rosary beads, were counting on their fingers and murmuring *Zdrávas, Maria, milosti planá*, the Hail Mary.

"I have talked enough. Tell me something about you."

"My wife Sára is Czech, like you."

Katrenka smiled as she slipped her arm under his.

"Her, Sára's, family is from Unhošt."

GERMANIZATION

"Oh, right down the road from here."

Weber nodded. "We moved here last year."

"Where were you living ... before?"

"In Berlin."

"Why come down here?"

Weber fidgeted with the buckle of his belt. "For her ... for Sára. We—she and I—have been trying to start a family for years, but she has not been able to carry to term."

"I am so sorry." Katrenka squeezed his elbow.

"She had two miscarriages ... in three years. The doctor was so worried, he thought we shouldn't even try anymore. I ... we ... thought that if we moved to a smaller town ... to be close to her family... Her brother has a butcher shop—in Unhošt. I thought it would be better if we moved here, to Kladno, to a place where I could still be a policeman and a place that was not so ..." He searched for the word, "... so hectic." Weber did not want to use the words he had been thinking of—brutal, intolerant, sometimes rabid.

He remembered the unsettling changes he had seen in his own hometown, beginning nearly ten years ago, when Brownshirts, hundreds of them, marched down Unter den Linden, waving huge red, black and white Nazi flags and challenging the people lined up on the streets. Wise up, they told the townspeople. We have enemies—enemies within our own country, enemies who capitulated and ended the Great War and who are still sabotaging the Fatherland, rotting it from the inside out. "Come, follow us," the Brownshirts shouted, "to Germany's greater glory. Come follow us, and we will get rid of our enemies. We will get rid of the people who are polluting our race and making us weak."

After them came the Gestapo, who herded up the Jews from their homes, led them to trucks and drove them away, then ransacked their homes, throwing all the their belongings out into the courtyards of their buildings, grabbing what they wanted and burning the rest.

The Schupo he worked with in Berlin soon followed suit. In the early days of the Nazi regime, the men did small things, like knocking a shopping bag out of a Jewess' hand and kicking the groceries away from her, or sticking a foot out in front of a Jew so he would trip. Later on, they did far worse.

GERMANIZATION

Weber remembered a time when three of his fellow Schupo had surrounded an older Jewish man, then started pushing him back and forth between them, turning him round and round and spitting on him. They tore off his hat and coat and trampled them in the street. They pulled his arms behind him, shoved his head down, then grabbed his legs out from under him and laughed while they dragged him, letting his head crash onto the curb and then scrape along the cobblestones.

Weber could tell himself he took his wife away from Berlin for her health, but it was because of the disgust he could barely disguise from the other Schupo, the disgust he felt when he saw the reactions of ordinary Germans who witnessed the attacks on Jews in the streets. The shopkeepers in their tweed suits, the waiters in their white aprons, the clerks in their rolled-up sleeves stood by, nudging one another and nodding in agreement. "This is what is rotting the Fatherland," he heard some say. It was because of the feelings he had had when his younger brother appeared in the doorway of his home, proudly wearing his Wehrmacht uniform, and announcing that he was going off to fight for the purity of his race.

"Your sergeant," Silvie said as she approached, "needs you—over there." Weber saw Kleinschmidt leading the interviewers away from the tables toward the door and waving for the Schupo to follow.

"I will take care of her," Silvie said.

Feeling Katrenka flinch, Weber questioned her with his eyes.

"My sister-in-law," she said.

"Your sergeant said I could take over for you," Silvie said. "Don't worry," she said, taking Weber's place. "I will take good care of her."

CHAPTER NINETEEN

"It's happening, Sergeant!" Silvie waved to Sgt. Albert Kleinschmidt as he entered the gymnasium. She ran towards him from the back of the room, pointing behind her at Katrenka, who was covered with the remnants of her meager breakfast, crumbs on her chin, her shirtfront and her skirt, an arm suspended in mid-air, her fingers tensing, shaking, releasing slivers of bread. Warmth and wetness flowed between her legs, a stain blossoming on the front of her skirt. Katrenka put her weight on one arm and tried to push off the floor, but her arm collapsed, and she fell onto her elbow. She tried to gain enough traction to rise, but her legs slid away, her body rolled to the side and her head struck the floor.

Silvie grasped Kleinschmidt's arm. "We need to get her away from here—get her somewhere where she can have the baby."

"I can see that," he said shortly, unwrapping his arm from Silvie's hold.

Kleinschmidt called over two Schupo guards as he bent his head close to Katrenka's ear. "We will help you," he told her. The guards put their hands in Katrenka's armpits and tried to bring her to a standing position, but her legs could not hold her weight and her feet splayed out sideways. She lifted her head and looked at the Schupo, at Silvie, at Kleinschmidt. "No. I don't want you," she said, wrestling her arms away from the Schupo's grasp. "I don't want to go with you," she told Silvie. She felt a cramp in her side, a flutter in her chest, a rush of dizziness. She let her arms fall to her sides, her chin to her chest.

*

"Look at that. All that fussing over *her—again.*" Chessie turned to see what Jana was talking about. At first, she didn't understand—Kleinschmidt and Silvie, Schupo guards, the corporal named Weber, huddled at the end of the room. Then she realized: It must be Katrenka.

K. M. Sandrick

GERMANIZATION

Chessie stopped tearing chunks of bread into smaller portions and wiped her fingers on her shirt front. She turned to watch as Weber bent over, his cap in his hand, and lifted Katrenka's chin to speak to her. She saw Silvie smooth Katrenka's hair, the pair of Schupo take hold of her upper arms and back and Kleinschmidt direct everyone's movements. She watched the group around Katrenka as they led her across the floor of the gymnasium. Chessie noted, out of the corner of her eye, the reactions of the women in the room—Jana and Berta and Dorota and others—dropping their heads and turning away from Katrenka as she passed, hissing under their breath.

CHAPTER TWENTY

"We line up now," Kleinschmidt announced, "by color." The Schupo sergeant had returned to the gymnasium and was standing in the middle of the floor, tapping a manila file folder against his leg. "Color—of the badges," he added quickly when he saw the women's confused expressions.

"We start with the blue group—the children—only the children in the blue group." He opened the file and sifted through loose-leaf pages with lists of names arranged under colored headings: blue, black, red.

"The children will line up here," he said, gesturing to his right. "The ones with blue badges should come now, and line up there, in between those Schupo." He pointed to two pairs of guards. "Then we ...," Kleinschmidt stopped speaking when he saw women grab their toddlers' hands and pull the children behind their bodies. He watched as mothers folded their infants in their clothes, fashioning pieces of cloth over their faces. He frowned and squinted as mothers gathered older children together and held them, as single women, old and young, placed themselves in front of the mothers and their children and linked arms to form a protective barrier.

Kleinschmidt turned his attention to the gymnasium door as the Schupo guards shifted position, closing ranks, adjusting helmets, moving their rifles from their shoulders to the front of their bodies, bending at the knee and leaning forward.

"None of that," Kleinschmidt ordered, facing his men. "We don't need any of that." He turned back to the women and made a circular motion with his hand. "We will all cooperate, won't we?" He pushed the papers back into the file and closed it before walking slowly in front of the women. "We want to help the children, don't we?" He stared into Dorota Benda's eyes. "Don't we?" He raised his voice. Dorota dropped her gaze to the floor.

"Don't we want to get food for the children?" Kleinschmidt moved on to stare at Berta, then Irenka and Jana. "Ja? You want food for them?" He challenged them. "Well?" He smacked the file against his leg smartly.

GERMANIZATION

"You—" he stepped away from the women and spun his finger in the air, "You have all been complaining, 'We don't have enough food for the children,' " he said in a sing-song voice. " 'Where is the food for the children?' Isn't that right? You say you don't have enough food for the children." He waited for acknowledgment. "Right?"

Small, hesitant voices agreed.

"Right?" he called out. "Well?" He lifted and pumped his hands like a choir conductor urging more volume.

"Yes," scattered voices acknowledged.

Kleinschmidt extended his arms and lifted his shoulders. Shaking his head, he said, "You complain that there is no food. And now you resist, now, when we are getting ready to take the children to get food."

Women began to squirm; they loosened their hold on their children and their bonds with other women, but they did not break them entirely. They moved from one foot to another, brushing hips and shoulders with one another, looking questioningly at their neighbors and worriedly at their children.

"But why," Václava called out, "Why did you say only the children? Why can't we go with our children?"

Voices gained strength:

"Yes. Why only the children?"

"Why can't we go with them?"

Resolve strengthened: Women renewed their grip on their children and linked their arms again with the women next to them.

Kleinschmidt paced along the front row of women, stopping every few meters and turning toward them. He evaluated the ragged clothing, the bent heads; he assessed reactions, registering each flinch, each wince, each blanch, marveling that the women maintained their solidarity. Women who were not strong enough to shield the children were themselves being protected: Marketa was held up by Milan on one side and Paní Vasko on the other; Paní Mares and Paní Benda were sandwiched in between Klaudie and Václava Janda. Kleinschmidt was surprised by the intensity of their defiance. "No lousy Kraut is going to tell me what to do," he overhead Paní Tichy mutter as he passed in front of her.

The Schupo sergeant finished his march along the cordon and

GERMANIZATION

stood still, his eyes running from woman to woman, his index finger tapping lightly on the file folder. He sighed.

"All right." He strode smartly to the center of the room. "If this is what you want. You can stay here—all of you—just stay here. Let your children starve for all I care."

He turned his back on the women and walked toward the entrance to the gymnasium. He stopped suddenly and turned back. "You know," he said, "we are trying to help you. To help your children." He held out the file folder like a pointer. "Look at them—listen to them. Listen," he commanded. "Now," he insisted. "Hear them? That little one," he said, pointing to Elina, who was sniffling. "And that one." He pointed to Lizbeth. "We can get them food. We can take them now and get food." He paused. "We can take ALL the children—now—and we can— Get. Them. Food." He paused again. "But," he shrugged, turned around and started walking back toward the gymnasium entrance.

"But there's no reason why we can't go with our children," Václava objected.

Kleinschmidt continued walking toward the door.

"Why can't we go with our children?" she pressed.

Kleinschmidt extended a hand to push on the door. "Enough with you," he called back over his shoulder, as he laid his hand flat against the wood.

"Stop!" he heard isolated voices call out.

He smiled, listening to sudden snatches of conversation:

"Shut up, Václava."

"Václava, you bitch."

He pushed the door open a crack.

"No!" He heard the women's voices echoing each other:

"No—don't go."

"They need food."

"Don't leave."

"Please."

"Our children..."

Kleinschmidt let his hand relax and stood still, facing the door.

"No, you can't let them take the children," Václava implored the women.

"Václava, for god's sake," Klaudie retorted. "Look at them. The children are..."

"Well, what do you want?" Kleinschmidt put his hand back on the door.

"No, no, don't listen to her."

"She's just causing trouble."

"What?" Kleinschmidt tilted his head to one side and cupped a hand around his ear. "What?"

"Help us."

"Don't leave."

"Take the children."

*

Klaudie folded her children in her arms and rested her cheek on her son Tomás' head. "We will have to say goodbye now." She forced the trepidation from her voice. "But it will be only for a little while."

She crouched down so she could look in their faces. So beautiful, she thought, as she gazed at her daughter Adéle. Only 13, and already she was stunning. Her pale blond, shoulder-length hair and creamy complexion were highlighted by her soft brown eyes and thick dark lashes. Her body had not fully adjusted to her recent growth spurt, so she was not yet proportional. Her legs were a bit too long and thin and her shoulders were a bit too broad. But her bosom was developing, and her waist was compact. She would have the kind of hourglass figure many women yearned for. "Stop that," she told her daughter, who was twirling strands of hair under her nostrils, sniffing them, then licking the ends. "You know I hate it when you do that." Adéle grudgingly dropped the strand and sulked.

Klaudie turned to her son Tomás. So smart. Even in this dismal place, she had seen him practicing his mathematics, his eyes alert behind his glasses, his brow furrowed in concentration, his legs crossed in front of him, quietly determined to find the answers to his own questions.

GERMANIZATION

"You know your father." She stroked her children's arms. "He is working to get us all back together again. He knows people here in Kladno and in the factories. Once you go ... with the ...," She paused and looked for Kleinschmidt, eventually finding him to the side of the open, arched double doors. "Once you go and get your food, you will be coming home to us. I will have the house all cleaned up and ready for you. I will have your books on your desk. I know how you like them—in order," she said to Tomás, laughing at his fastidiousness. "And I will make sure your dress is finished for the party on Saturday," she said to her daughter.

She gave each one a hug and kissed their cheeks.

*

Chessie bent down to face her son. She fussed with the buttons of his shirt, straightened his shirt collar and tucked his shirt into his pants. She licked her fingers and pulled some unruly strands of his hair through them, trying to tamp down his stubborn cowlick, but Ondrej was restless, stepping away from her.

She reached out to stroke his cheek, but he was already turning his head toward Kleinschmidt, watching the Schupo guards and sidling away. She grasped his shoulders, pressed his body to her chest and held him as tightly as she could, trying to meld his essence with hers, their spirits and souls with each another.

She tried to kiss the top of his head, but he pulled away from her. "I have to hurry, Mama. I don't want to miss my group. I am one of the special ones."

"But I don't know where you are going, when I will see you."

"Mama, please. I have to hurry." He wiggled out of her grasp, pushed against her body and freed himself, leaving her with her arms open, but empty.

She watched each of his movements as he strode toward a Schupo who was standing guard next to a growing line of children—the slight skip of excitement in his step, the nervous snapping of his thumb against his index finger, the quick turn of his head, appraising the children in line next to him—Ivona, Radek, Klaudie's daughter Adéle.

*

"Now we line up the women with the blue badges."

"How about that, Václava?" Jana jibed. "Make you feel better?"

"No, all of us should go together, no matter what badges. We should go with our children. Our families should stay together."

"Oh, shut up," Jana replied.

"Marik, Stanek, Kohout," Kleinschmidt called out. "Come now," he said. "You come," he looked up and down the rows of women, "Kohout, Marik, Stanek, you come—stand here—behind the children."

"Last," Kleinschmidt said, "are the babies."

Zuzana Sykora tugged a corner of the shawl she had wrapped around her infant Petr and adjusted the baby's blue badge. She stepped in line after Irenka Kohout.

Klara Hruska rocked her fretting infant Filip in her arms as she took the next place in line, and Lucie Kriz and her baby Bara followed.

Kleinschmidt approached the three women. "Your surnames?"

"I am Kriz," said Lucie.

"Hruska."

"Sykora."

Kleinschmidt scrolled down the list of names. "No," he told the three women. "You are not on the blue list." He pulled their clothing aside. "See?" He pointed to their badges: two red, one black. "You are in other groups."

"But, I have to go with Petr," Zuzana said. "I am still nursing."

"No, no, we will get a wet nurse," Kleinschmidt said, pulling baby Petr away from his mother.

"No," Zuzana wailed, as she reached out for her infant. "No, you can't take him," she said grabbing onto the sergeant's arm.

Kleinschmidt shrugged away her grasp and handed the baby to Dorota. "You," he said to her, "you come and take this baby."

"No, no, that's not right," Dorota said.

"You do it," Kleinschmidt thrust the infant into her arms.

GERMANIZATION

"And you," he said to Zuzana. "Wait over there until we line up the black group."

"No, I won't," Zuzana said, rushing toward Dorota to recapture her baby.

"Take her," Kleinschmidt said to a Schupo. The guard stepped between Zuzana and Dorota, pushing his rifle into Zuzana's face and body. He pressed the butt of the gun against her mouth and forehead, moving his heavy body against her, propelling her backward.

"And you," Kleinschmidt said to Magda. "Come and take one of these babies." He pointed to the other two infants.

Magda hesitated. "Here, Magda," said Klara. "Please take my baby. I can see they are going to take her away, away from me, no matter what I want or what I do. I don't want one of them," she indicated the Schupo and Kleinschmidt, "to ... you know ... have her." She placed one hand under the baby's head and the other under her knees and extended her arms. She raised the baby slightly as she looked from Kleinschmidt to Magda. "Please, Magda. I know you will take care of her." She placed the baby in Magda's arms and stroked her infant's head before she turned away from the blue line.

Irenka took a few steps forward and approached Lucie, who had her face buried in her baby's clothing. Irenka put her arm across Lucie's shoulder and rested her head next to Lucie's. The two women stood together until Lucie turned her face away and let Irenka take her baby from her.

*

Kleinschmidt admired the children and the women in the blue group. Excellent selections, he told himself. Excellent.

"We leave now." He directed Schupo to lead the group out of the gymnasium.

"Hold hands," Magda called out to the children. "Hold hands so you can stay together—the way you do in school. Go ahead," she urged.

Ondrej and Ona began walking in ranks, swinging their arms back and forth.

GERMANIZATION

Ivona stepped up next to Elina, who was standing frozen in place, rolling the end of a shirttail between her fingers, waiting for her mother to come to her. "Go on," her mother called out, motioning Elina ahead. "Yes," Ivona said to Elina. "Come along with me, like your mother said. Come. I will be right here beside you."

Jarmil extended a hand to Radek, who brushed it aside and laughed when Jarmil stumbled.

The women sent their children off with gestures of encouragement. Some smiled weakly and nodded, mouthing, "It's all right." Some fluttered their fingers in a wave. Some pressed their fingers to their lips and blew kisses.

Chessie waited, her hands at her lips, ready to wave goodbye or blow a kiss, but Ondrej didn't look back at her. He gazed at the Schupo standing at attention instead, and mimicking the guard's stance, pulled down his shoulders and straightened his back. Holding hands with the neighbor boy Ona, he high-stepped like a Nazi soldier, marching out of the half-open double doors into the harsh morning light.

CHAPTER TWENTY-ONE

Chessie absently fingered the red badge on her shoulder as she kept pace with those in front of her, stepping over the threshold of the gymnasium and then down three steps to the passageway in front of the building. As she walked, she noticed that the pale-yellow stucco high school was U-shaped. A four-story central section housed classrooms with desks in orderly rows as well as offices with file cabinets lining the walls and tables piled with papers. To one side was a five-story dormitory, its rooms vacant—bare mattresses on wooden frames, empty chiffoniers waiting for students to return after summer holiday. To the other side was a five-story church with a pair of green, copper-tipped spires and a Baroque bell tower.

She was struck by the contrast: Wherever she looked there were signs of ordinary life, life as it was before the war. Through the tree branches that hid the school from the street, she could see automobiles in start-and-stop city traffic, shoppers in a hurry to fill their baskets and bags. Ahead of her, the women were moving quietly, in single file, as if they were taking a stroll on a fine summer day.

But she couldn't escape the evidence of the Occupation: heavily armed men on either side of her making sure the parade of women was orderly and quick and efficient; military vehicles idling in the parking area behind the school. In addition to the canvas-covered transport to which she was being led, there were large gray-green vans commonly used to carry furniture. A pair of Gestapo limousines was departing, the drivers honking their car horns to move an incoming ambulance out of the way.

Although Ondrej and the other children had left the gymnasium only moments before, there was no sign of them in the parking lot or the grassy area next to it. In between the parked vehicles, Chessie could see a pair of figures: Silvie was tugging on Katrenka's arm, leading her toward the ambulance; Katrenka was hunched over, waddling, holding her side.

"We'll be home soon." Klaudie nudged Chessie and pointed to the truck parked a few meters in front of them.

"Without our children? That's not the way I want to go home."

"They'll come later."

Chessie was silent.

"Doesn't it make sense that the children go for food while we go back to Lidice?" Klaudie persisted. "You saw what the town looked like. We need to get home and clean everything up. We need to get our own food for them. Then the children will come back."

"Doesn't make any sense to me."

"But Sgt. Kleinschmidt told me he was going to talk to Ctibor. As soon as he did, I bet everything was straightened out."

"Stop it with all this Ctibor nonsense," Jana said. "Kleinschmidt didn't talk to anybody. He's not *going* to talk to anybody, especially not that blowhard husband of yours."

"You just shut up. What do you know about Ctibor? The kind of influence he has? What do you know about anything?"

"No talking," a Schupo shouted.

Klaudie took her place on one side of the truck bed so she could see out over the tailgate once the vehicle started moving. She watched the last woman in the group—Václava—as she stepped up into the truck, folded her skirt around her and eased herself down onto the floorboards. Hearing the shot of the tailgate bolt, the firing of the engine, the whine of the wheels, she turned and watched the route the vehicle was taking. She first saw a street sign for Masáryk Road, the golden crown above the door of an apothecary and a spouting fountain in the center of the town square. As the truck drove out of the city, Klaudie saw a squat, dirty gray concrete-block railway depot, a blue wooden bench in front with a young woman leaning forward and looking down the track leading to Krupá. From the suburbs of Kladno and its small, square, single-family homes, the truck moved into the industrial section. The Poldi steelworks were in full operation, streams of smoke billowing from the

GERMANIZATION

red-and-white-striped tips of its yellow-gold chimneys.

The truck slowed as it passed over a rutted wooden bridge and a bubbling stream. At the intersection to the main road, the truck stopped. Klaudie rose on her knees, grabbed the top of the tailgate and stuck her head out of the back of the truck, anxious to confirm her expectation that the truck would turn left—south —toward Lidice. She caught her breath, sat back and shut her eyes when it turned right—north —toward Germany,

*

"You," Kleinschmidt announced gruffly as he surveyed the line of women and children with black badges in the gymnasium, reaching past a Schupo guard and pulling on Milan's sleeve. "You don't belong here." Milan stood next to his mother, his head down, his eyes staring at the floor. His arms collapsed into his body trying to make himself too small for the sergeant to see him.

Kleinschmidt clutched the back of Milan's collar and yanked on the fabric. He stepped forward, pushing his face next to Milan's and hissed in the boy's ear, "You are not one of these." Milan squeezed his eyes shut and tightened his stance. "You should be with the others in the red group." Kleinschmidt raised his voice.

"But they are already gone," a Schupo informed Kleinschmidt. "The truck left..."

"Ach," Kleinschmidt complained, pulling on a fold of material at the front of Milan's shirt. "You come with me. We have to figure out what to do with you."

Milan turned his head away from Kleinschmidt and hunched his shoulders. He moved closer to his mother's side, wrapping her arm under his, placing his head against hers, resisting the force of Kleinschmidt's movements.

Kleinschmidt dropped the manila file folder he was holding on the floor and tugged on Milan's upper arm. Milan wrenched away, elbowed Kleinschmidt in the chest and locked onto his mother's arm. Kleinschmidt stepped forward, caught hold of Milan's shoulder and pulled the boy's upper body toward him. He hooked an arm around

Milan's neck, jerking his head to the side and then hit the back of the boy's head with the heel of his hand.

Milan stumbled under the force of the blow. Losing his balance, he fell into Marketa's side, his elbow thrusting into her ribs.

Marketa teetered, her knees buckling. Without Milan holding on to her, she slipped down to her knees and then slumped to one side. Her hip, then her arm and head struck the floor.

"Mama, no!" Milan cried out in anguish. Trying to free himself, he thrust his body against Kleinschmidt's. He raised a foot and stomped down hard on Kleinschmidt's boot. As Kleinschmidt's grip eased, Milan pulled himself forward. He reached across and slapped a hand on top of Kleinschmidt's. He wormed his fingers in between Kleinschmidt's until he was able to isolate one of his fingers. He twisted the finger back, raised it to his mouth, and bit into the knuckle. Kleinschmidt grimaced as Milan's teeth clamped down and sliced into the flesh of his finger. He kneed Milan in the abdomen and moved his other hand so he could grab Milan's ear. He pinched the top of his ear, then grabbed hold of the lobe and pulled down. Bringing his forearm and hand to Milan's face, Kleinschmidt pushed his palm into Milan's nose, his fingers into Milan's eye sockets. He looked over his shoulder as Schupo guards shouldered their rifles and moved toward the boy. "Here," Kleinschmidt told a Schupo, grunting through gritted teeth. "Take him—here." A Schupo stepped around Marketa and grabbed a handful of Milan's hair, placed a hand on his throat and pressed a thumb into the space under Milan's chin until the muscles around Milan's mouth slackened, and Kleinschmidt could pull his finger away.

Guards stepped in front of Kleinschmidt, balled their fists and punched the boy: a blow to the side of his head, another to the stomach; a volley to the ribs and chest. A jab to the face, another to the nose. The crunching sound of shattering cartilage. The explosion of blood from torn capillaries.

Milan coughed as blood cascaded from his broken nose into his mouth. Gasping as one of the Schupo increased pressure on his larynx, Milan slapped at the Schupo's arm and hand.

The Schupo released his grip on Milan's throat to grab his hand. He pulled the boy's arm up behind his back. He bent Milan's body at the waist and kicked the back of his knees, then shoved his head and chin into his chest and grabbed Milan's other hand, twisting it behind his

GERMANIZATION

back and bringing his wrists together. He raised a boot and pressed his foot into Milan's lower back, forcing the boy's body down while pulling back on his arms. The Schupo pushed Milan's head toward the floor, then released his hands and let the boy's head smack onto the floor of the gymnasium. He smiled and stepped back as other guards continued to rain blows on the bloody stump of Milan's nose, on his forehead, his legs and shoulders and back until his torso curled and his breath slowed.

*

"We're ready. With the vans," a Schupo shouted from the doorway.

"All right." Kleinschmidt wrapped his finger in a handkerchief, picked up the file folder and restored its scattered pages. "Get them moving." He motioned toward the remaining women and children.

Kleinschmidt moved to Marketa's side. He crouched down next to her and placed a hand on her back. He saw that her eyes were open but uncomprehending. "Do you hear me?" he asked.

Marketa gave no response.

Kleinschmidt asked again: "Do you hear?"

But Marketa was silent and unmoving.

Kleinschmidt stood and looked around the gymnasium. He spotted a pair of guards and indicated they should come to him. "Take her," he told them, extending his bandaged finger toward Marketa.

"What do you want to do about him?" one of the Schupo asked.

Kleinschmidt looked past his bloodied finger at Milan and shrugged. "You take care of this," he shouted to Gruber as he strode to the door.

"But the trucks were full. They're gone," Gruber complained.

"Then figure out something else." The door slammed.

"I can't just drag this kid out and shoot him in the middle of the city of Kladno," Gruber shouted to the empty space Kleinschmidt had left behind.

"There're no more transports," he muttered. "No way to get this body out of here." He hurried over to the boy. "So what the hell am I going to do with you?"

Gruber paced back and forth, nudged Milan's ribs with the barrel of his rifle, then kicked his shins and shouldered his weapon. "I'm not going to waste any more time here. I'm just going to leave you here—as an example. This is what we do to anyone who dares to defy us. You can tell people all about it—when you can open your mouth again."

*

"...Kid?"

Milan's eyelids twitched.

"Hey, kid."

His eyes blinked open.

"Kid? You all right?"

Milan turned toward the sound of a woman's voice. He groaned as his body woke to the effects of the beating by the Schupo. He peered up through swollen eyelids at the woman who was leaning over the handle of a push broom, a babushka holding back her gray curls, a flowered housedress hanging from her thin shoulders.

Milan focused his gaze along the floor, past the woman's scuffed and torn boots, toward the walls where Schupo had stood guard, the doorway where they had led the children, the place where Sgt. Kleinschmidt had stood pointing his bandaged finger at him, the spot where his mother...

"Where?" Milan croaked to the woman.

"My mother." He strained to form the words through chipped and broken teeth and split and bloodied lips. "Where is she?"

BETRAYAL

Chapter Twenty-Two

"What are you going to do about this?" Paní Čurda slapped the back of her son Karel's head with the notice she had pulled off the fencepost on the outskirts of the fishing village of Nová Hlína in the chain of lakes region of southern Bohemia.

"You see this?" She waved the rolled-up poster in front of his face, then flattened out the creases and spread it flat on the kitchen table in front of the cup of coffee he was cradling. "Names ...," she tapped a finger on a list in heavy black type, "of mothers, fathers, children, grandparents—entire families. Names of people who were executed by the Nazis because they knew one of the assassins or harbored them or gave false information."

She pulled a chair roughly away from the table. "You are going to get us all killed. Your otec, your bratr, your teta, even your prarodiče."

Paní Čurda sat and rested her arms on the table. "I told you not to do this. I told you not to run off. But you had to be a hero. You had to get involved with the Czechoslovak Army Abroad and learn what? How to smuggle in radios to guide the British bombers? Make bombs to blow up the Škoda armament factory in Plzén? How well did you do with that? The Gestapo found all your radios in a matter of days, and you never got even close to Plzén, did you?"

Paní Čurda intertwined her fingers and pounded her hands up and down. "And now he's dead. Heydrich is dead. The most important Nazi in the Protektorate is dead. And your Czech Army buddies are the ones who did it. How long do you think it will take for the Gestapo to find you—to find us?"

"How will they find out about me? Kubiš and Gabčík were the ones who did it," he said. "I didn't have anything to do with the assassination. I wasn't even in their group. They were in the Anthropoid Operation. I was in the Out Distance op. We didn't even fly back into the country at the same time. Or land in the same place."

"Oh. So you think that makes a difference? You're still one of them.

BETRAYAL

One of the paratroopers who has been working with the Czech Home Resistance."

Čurda had followed the same path to Britain as the assassins Kubiš and Gabčík. Soon after the Nazi Occupation in 1939, he left his post as supervisor of a Czech Army unit that operated out of Olomouc joined the French Foreign Legion's 1st Infantry Battalion of the Czechoslovak Armed Forces in southern France. After Paris fell to the Wehrmacht, Čurda, Kubiš and Gabčík sailed with Czech military units to Liverpool and then bivouacked with more than 3,000 Czech foot soldiers, machine gunners, engineers, telegraphers and artillery officers on the grounds around Cholmondeley castle, near Chester.

By 1941, Čurda had become weary of the seemingly pointless exercises, the soccer games—the Czechoslovaks taking on the Norwegians or the Belgians in the Allied Army League—and the propaganda. Posters lauded the Czechoslovak Army and Air Force in Great Britain, proclaiming that the British Commonwealth and its Allies would destroy Nazi tyranny, but the major battles were being fought in North Africa and the Mediterranean. A massive Allied invasion on the European Continent or an operation in Czechoslovakia was highly unlikely, at least in the near future.

So Čurda had jumped at the chance to become a member of Special Group D. SGD was establishing training schools in remote areas of England and Scotland to prepare small groups of Czechs for clandestine operations behind the Wehrmacht lines and in Occupied territories. Like Kubiš and Gabčík, he became skilled in sharp-shooting, man-to-man combat, intelligence-gathering, telegraph and radio operations and bomb making. It still took another year before he parachuted into his homeland, and then the Czech covert activities went to hell.

"They weren't supposed to do it—the assassination," Čurda said, raising the cup to his lips and taking a sip, then wrinkling his nose at the faint odor of fish that emanated from the cup and its contents. He looked at his mother. "The Leadership of the Home Resistance—the ÚVOD—was going crazy. At least twice, ÚVOD tried to get Beneš to call it off."

Čurda remembered the panicked communications he and the other members of the Out Distance Operation had received from the transmitters at their parachute drop point near Ořechov. SGD leader Alfréd Bartoš had warned the head of the Czech government in exile, Edvard Beneš, that the assassination would threaten the lives of hostages and political prisoners, lead to unheard-of reprisals and destroy whatever remained of the Resistance in Czechoslovakia.

"But Beneš, the naïve fool," Čurda explained, "thought the Germans were pushing their armies too hard, would soon fail on the frontlines and sue for peace. Beneš wanted to prove to the Allies that there was a strong Resistance movement in the country—and show that *he* was in charge of it. He said that the sacrifices after the assassination would be worth it." He rose from the table and took his cup to the washstand.

"What does that matter—what your group leader did or said, what you said or did—*then?*" Paní Čurda studied him. "What matters is what you are going to do *now*. How are you going to keep us all from getting killed?"

"I said it before." Čurda turned away from a pot next to the washstand filled with live carp and faced his mother. "The Nazis are looking for the assassins—Gabčík and Kubiš. They're not looking for me. How could they find out about me?"

"How do you think they find out anything? There are plenty of people who would be only too happy to turn you in. Paní Fucha, for one. You think she doesn't know you left the country to join the Czech Government in exile? You think she doesn't know you're back here now ... after the ReichsProtektor was assassinated? You think she wouldn't just happen to give your name to the Nazis—in return for a million Reichsmarks?" Paní Čurda shook her head. "And what about your paratrooping friends? Do you know where they are?"

"Not exactly, but I have a pretty good idea." Čurda knew where the Resistance safe houses were in Plzén, Pardubice and Prag, like the Novák apartment on Stránského Street and the Moravec flat on Biskupcova Street in the capital city's Zižkov District.

"And they know where *you* are? Wouldn't they just happen to mention they know a paratrooper who came from Nová Hlína?"

"I never told them where I was from when we were in training

BETRAYAL

together, and then we went to different special services units," Čurda said. "Our operations weren't even close in time or location. They air-dropped in December, near Prag. Our operation didn't start till March, and we were hundreds of kilometers away. Besides," he added, "they have poison pills. They won't say anything if they're captured."

"You know this. For sure."

"Of course."

"Well, I am not so confident," she said. "So I am telling you. You have to *do* something."

Čurda didn't tell his mother that he had already done something. He had sent a letter to Gestapo Headquarters explaining that he could give them the names of the assassins as well as the families who were most likely hiding them. No reason for his mother to know that in a few days he would be leaving this stinking little town and her stinking little house. No reason for her know that he would do to his compatriots the very thing she worried they would do to him—turn them in to the authorities and claim a million Reichsmarks.

CHAPTER TWENTY-THREE

Karel Čurda, so confident when he sent his letter to the police post in the Central Bohemian town of Benešov, now stood before Heinz Pannwitz, leader of the committee charged with finding Heydrich's assassins, in Pannwitz' office in Petschek Palace—and stuttered. While others on the investigation committee were ready to dismiss Čurda as a crackpot or an opportunist, Pannwitz was desperate for leads, so he decided to test the man.

Pannwitz led Čurda to an interrogation room that displayed 20 similar suitcases on a tabletop and asked him to pick out the one that belonged to one of the assassins. Čurda immediately identified a worn leather case, lifting a small tear in its side as the telltale sign.

"This is the one ... the one I saw in Svatos' apartment, the one that had a British submachine gun in it."

"Whose was it?"

"Gabčík's. Josef. He went by the name of Zdenek."

"Did he have a partner?"

Čurda nodded. "Kubiš. Jan. Known as Ota Navratil."

Pannwitz could barely disguise his excitement. For the first time, he had names, identities, something solid to go on.

"Where are they?"

"I don't know for sure ..."

Pannwitz grabbed Čurda by the collar. "Don't fuck with me ..."

"But ... but ..." Čurda twisted his head away. "There are these safe houses ... in the Žižkov area of the city. A family there ...," He tried to ease Pannwitz' grip. "... called Moravec. On Biskupcova Street. They would know ... something."

*

The Pear Tree

BETRAYAL

Two battalions under the command of SS Brigadefuhrer Karl von Treuenfeld were in place on the streets that ran alongside and in front of the Church of St. Charles Borromeo in Prag. Seven hundred Waffen SS troops maintained a double cordon around the area, and Gestapo guarded every sewage outlet and manhole as well as the rooftops of all the neighboring buildings. Troops had already closed the inner and outer perimeters, a gunner had mounted a 7.92 mm MG 34 light machine gun on a roof across the street from the church, and the Prag fire brigade had readied hoses to drive water into the crypts below. The men of the battalions, von Treuenfeld and Heinz Pannwitz now waited for the order from Karl Hermann Frank.

A million Reichsmarks? To him? Frank looked sidelong at Karel Čurda, the traitor to the Czechoslovak Resistance. That slimy little turd, Frank thought. No respect. No loyalty. No allegiance to his own country.

Frank had to acknowledge that if it hadn't been for Čurda's leads to the Moravecs and other families who had been harboring Heydrich's assassins, Pannwitz and von Treuenfeld's men wouldn't be positioned for an assault on the church where not only both assassins—Kubíš and Gabčík—but five other Resistance fighters were holed up. If it weren't for Čurda, Frank would still be making excuses to Hitler, hoping the Führer wouldn't end up sending him to oversee the death squads in Poland. He nevertheless loathed having to deal with Čurda. He couldn't wait for the assault on St. Charles Borromeo to be over so he could hand the money to the turncoat and wash off the taint of it.

Frank climbed the stairs to the rooftop next to the church on Resslova Street. "The battalions?" he asked.

"They have surrounded the church and the area," von Treuenfeld affirmed.

"The machine gun ..." he started to ask, but then noted that the gunner was sighting his weapon. Frank checked his wristwatch: 4:14 a.m.

At Frank's signal, a squad of Gestapo, led by Pannwitz, climbed the front steps of the church and rang the bell. Pushing aside the janitor who unlocked the heavy wooden door, the squad rushed into the sanctuary and found the altars empty. With only the vacant eyes of saints within their picture frames bearing witness, they turned to the metal grille that closed off the stairway to the choir. Just as they were forcing it open, a grenade rolled down from the top of the stairs. Landing on the bottom step, the bomb exploded, tearing the metal latticework away from its hinges, hollowing out sections of the stone walls and floor and setting fire to the wall hangings on either side of the entry.

The explosion prompted the machine gunner and the SS riflemen on the nearby rooftops to open fire. Steady bursts from their weapons rained down shards of leaded-glass windows and ricocheted bullets on Pannwitz and his men, but they did not reach the Czech Resistance fighters, who were hiding in the niches between the supporting columns of the church roof.

A hastily called ceasefire: "For Christ sake, you're hitting *us*," Pannwitz radioed to the shooters surrounding the building.

A regrouped SS squad: "Remember," Pannwitz cautioned his men. "We want to take them alive."

An assault on the narrow stairs leading to the choir: Grenades tossed halfway up; fusillades from automatic weapons aimed at the ceiling; a two-hour unremitting attack, then a slow, careful ascent to the top of the stairs where Heydrich assassin Jan Kubiš was bleeding to death, his suit shredded by grenade fragments and pieces of the wall that had imploded behind him. Just beyond, Resistance fighter Adolf Opálka lay dead from a gunshot wound to the left temple, blood pooling behind his nubby gray V-necked sweater, his right arm at an odd angle, a bone protruding from the sleeve. Next to him was Josef Bublík, froth at the edges of his mouth—the residue from a cyanide capsule.

"That can't be all of them," Pannwitz told Pastor Vladimir Petrek. "And none of these men fits the description of the other assassin. So where are they? Where else are they hiding?" Pannwitz released his pistol from its holster and hefted it in his palm. "You don't want to sacrifice your life for these ... these killers?" Pannwitz placed his index finger on the trigger and cocked the weapon. "Do you?"

The pastor fingered the crucifix on the rosary he had withdrawn from the pocket of his cassock. He brought the cross to his lips as he tapped his foot on the stone floor. "The catacombs."

BETRAYAL

"How many?"

He bowed his head and crossed himself.

"Four."

"Why aren't you storming the cellars?" Frank demanded, a walkie-talkie to the side of his head.

"We can't risk it," Pannwitz answered. "We could kill all the rest. You know Himmler wants them alive."

"So how do you plan to get them out of there?"

Pastor Petrek leaned into the loudspeaker that had been placed on the outside of a grille at the entrance to an air shaft at the back wall of the church: "It is hopeless, my boys," the pastor said. "Save yourselves. Come out."

Muffled shouting:

"We're Czechs, fighting for our country!"

"You'll be treated as prisoners of war. The SS have assured me. All you have to do is surrender. There's no need for more bloodshed. Surrender ..."

"Fuck you, father."

"We'll never give up!"

Karel Čurda, handcuffed with young Ata Moravec to the Gestapo, tried next. "Surrender, boys. I tell you," he said. "It will be all right."

Catcalls. Whistles.

"Who the fuck are you?"

"I am one of you—Operation Out Distance."

"You're not one of us if you're with them."

"Listen to me. They promise..."

"They promise. They promise. Here's to their promises."

Ripples of gunfire from underground.

"Enough of this." Pannwitz summoned the chief of the Prag fire brigade. "Get going with your hoses. Flood them out."

*

Prag fireman Juri Fischer folded a small-bladed knife and slipped it into the pocket of his trousers before unrolling the heavy tubing connected to a water-pumping unit. He and a pair of other firemen thrust the hose into the vent leading to the church catacombs and opened the water main.

A geyser of high-pressure water burst from the side of the hose.

"It's leaking," a fireman yelled to his commander.

"For Christ sake," the commander shouted. "Get this thing out of here. Fischer," he called out. "Get another hose."

The torn section of tubing removed, the firemen reconnected the hose and began pumping 600 gallons of water a minute into the crypts.

Within moments, the end of the hose was flapping erratically, its sides severed and the tatters pushed out on to the street from below. Bottles with flaming pieces of cloth sparking from their mouths sailed into the air, crashed and rolled over the cobblestones. The Resistance fighters had placed a ladder under the nozzle of the hose, slashed and thrust the tubing out of the airshaft, then lofted a volley of Molotov cocktails.

Fischer and the other members of his fire crew hurriedly backed away from the building while Soldats flattened their bodies against the side of the building, then released pins from tear gas canisters and tossed the grenades down the air shaft.

"Push the end of that hose back down there," Pannwitz shouted to Fischer and his men, pointing to the remnants of tubing that snaked wildly over the street.

"The water must be escaping through some kind of drainage canal or underground passageway," von Treuenfeld told Frank, after torrents of water had been released and there was still no sign the Resistance fighters were weakening. "They could follow the water and find a way out. We should storm the crypt—before they get away from us."

"We could have stormed the crypt six hours ago if all we wanted to do was kill the bastards. We need to take them alive," Pannwitz argued.

"I've had enough. We look like fools," Frank said, assessing the number of troops and fire brigades and lorries and the heads of witnesses peeking from windows and around street corners. "All this, and we can't ferret out a handful of Czech Resistance fighters? Let's get this done."

On his order, SS combat troops ordered Pastor Petrek to lead them to the entrance of the crypt, concealed under a stone slab on the west side of the nave. After blasting away the flagstone, Soldats descended a steep set of stairs, dropped into waist-deep water and moved toward the Resistance fighters, gas masks protecting their eyes and noses. At the same time, more Soldats blew open a bricked-up entrance to the crypt near the altar and began their own descent.

Four pistol shots from below, then silence.

"*Fertig,*" a Soldat called out ten minutes later. "All dead."

Josef Gabčík, the man who had faced Reinhard Heydrich at the turn of Rude Armady on V Holešovičkách Street, the sight of his automatic weapon trained on Heydrich's forehead, was propped against an exterior wall, his short-sleeved shirt drenched in blood, dead from a shot to the head with his Colt automatic. Three other Czechs were nearby: Jaroslav Švarc, Jan Hrubý and Josef Valčík.

*

Karl Hermann Frank bent over the body of one of the Czech Resistance fighters lined up in the alleyway next to the Church of St. Charles Borromeo. He tugged at the man's collar and pulled his head off the ground. "This one?" he asked Čurda, who stood to his right, his hands shoved in the jacket pockets of his tweed suit.

"Bublík," Čurda said.

"One of the assassins?"

"No," Čurda said. "He was with me … in Operation Out Distance."

"So where …?"

"Here," Čurda pointed to Jan Kubíš, whose body lay next to

Bublík's, the jacket of his dark pinstriped suit unbuttoned.

"And the other?"

"There," Čurda said, indicating the body of Josef Gabčík, his shirt still buttoned but now torn and stained with blood.

"And they are from?"

"He," Čurda kicked Kubíš' oxford shoe, "is from somewhere near Poland, in Moravia. The other one is a Slovak."

"Anyone one named Horák here?"

"No."

"You know anyone named Horák?"

"No, never heard the name."

"Or Říha or Maruščáková?"

Čurda shook his head.

"So, no one from Lidice?"

"Lidice?" Čurda laughed. "That little town? I doubt anyone in that town even heard of the Resistance."

*

Juri Fischer passed behind Frank and Čurda, his fire helmet held to his chest, his eyes downcast but flashing as he surreptitiously acknowledged the dead bodies of his compatriots. He stooped to pick up the ends of the fire hoses, stopping to palm and hide in the depths of his pockets a pair of tear gas grenades lying on the ground.

LIDICE

Chapter Twenty-Four

Karl Hermann Frank resisted the temptation to interrupt Kommandant of the Reichsarbeitsdienst Alexander Commichau who sat in front of his desk at Czechoslovak Protektorate headquarters in Prag. Commichau was ticking off items on the first sheet of the checklists he had compiled to track the progress of the demolition in Lidice. One hundred men from the Reich Work Forces were working every day to eliminate all traces of the town. Already, 83 buildings had been destroyed and 140 family gravesites, 60 tombs and 200 individual graves had been plundered—the tombstones salvaged so the stones could be used for the foundation of the new Reichsarbeitsdienst barracks in Prag-Veleslavín.

Work crews still had huge tasks ahead of them: plant the explosives that would divert the course of Lidice creek; dam what remained of the creek during dredging and hollow out new channels; uproot and carry off trees, bushes and farmsteads; move and level 84,000 square meters of soil; bury all signs of Czech presence—blood and bones—with German ploughs; prepare topsoil for sowing grain and grazing sheep; haul in German soil to replace Czech dirt.

Frank's eyelids fluttered as he listened to Commichau drone on. A tiresome man, Frank decided. Also, full of himself. Frank recalled the letter Commichau had recently sent to his superiors. "The young men of the Reich workforce see that the German sword descends heavily, and without remnants it will destroy the sources of unrest, not only at the front but also in the rear areas, and especially wherever the secret front forms, and dark forces are at work," the man had written. Commichau would know about the rear. He never got near any fighting at the front lines. Sanctimonious prick.

Frank had heard enough. "Just leave the lists," he told Commichau.

"But what about these?" Commichau pulled photos from his briefcase. The Reichsarbeitsdienst, or RAD, was using the destruction of Lidice as a training exercise. It filmed or photographed every aspect of the operation for the young engineers and laborers who made up the workforce: the initial razing of the buildings; the shootings of the men;

the sorting and removal of huge piles of debris; the construction of a narrow-gauge railway to cart away the bricks and stones.

"Leave them, too."

Alone is his office, Frank prepared his own report on Lidice:

173 men shot to death and buried in a mass grave

200 women sent to Ravensbrück forced labor camp

4 pregnant women, two dead in childbirth

104 children taken: 82 exterminated at Chelmno, 6 suitable for Germanization and sent to the Lebensborn project, 16 in forced labor

7 Czech Resistance paratroopers killed at the church of St. Cyril and Methodius, including the two Heydrich assassins—Gabčík and Kubiš

254 relatives of the paratroopers killed at Mauthausen

Frank thumbed through the photographs of RAD's work: mounds of dirt next to the bridge across Lidice creek; cemetery slabs scattered along the road; young RAD workers spooning lunch from their tins.

He glanced at a picture of the Terezín Jews digging the mass grave for the men of the town. Something to the side of the burial plot, he noticed. He raised the photo up and squinted. Picking up a magnifying glass, he examined it more carefully. Next to a small tree, its branches broken, leaves curled and shriveled, were a pair of boards that appeared to be fashioned as a grave marker, next to a small mound of newly turned earth. Another grave? Why a separate one? And a Soldat standing next to it. Rostock? He would have to ask him about that.

*

Paní Sophie Vavra hovered over Milan's torn lips and cracked teeth. "Tsk, tsk," she commented as she observed the extent of the damaged tissue. Paní Vavra had sneaked Milan into the root cellar of her house after the Schupo left him on the floor of the Kladno gymnasium. She was nursing him but being careful to hide him from inquisitive eyes, including her husband's. Lukas Vavra was frightened of the Nazis, she told Milan, and she didn't dare tell him she was caring for a boy who had been singled out for a beating by the Schupo.

"Stop your fidgeting. This is good for you," she admonished as Milan shrank away from the swabs of mercurochrome on his broken skin. He sucked in his breath in reaction to the pressure she applied. "Shush," Paní Vavra said. "Now don't you think for a minute that I believe your people had anything to do with that assassination business. But even if the people in your town did kill Heydrich, I don't care. He was," she paused to make the sign of the cross. "A son-of-a-bitch. If you ask me, it's good he's dead. Lukas, he is afraid of everything. Not a brave bone in that old Czech body of his." She smiled and winked at Milan. "If he knew I brought home one of the 'Lidice assassins'....Tsk." She crossed herself again.

*

Paní Vavra folded bread and fruit in a kerchief and tied it to the walking stick. "I'd like you to stay longer, boy."

He had been hiding out at the Vavra's for days, gradually recuperating. He had not yet fully recovered, but he was getting around better every day, and he was anxious to get home, especially after he heard Pan Vavra tell his wife that truckers in the Kladno tavern had seen a lot of traffic and smoke coming in and out of the area near Lidice.

"And what if it is true, what Lukas said? What if your town has been blown up?"

Unable to speak because of his cracked and bandaged jaw, he sat mute. His stiff body gave the only clue that he would not listen to such speculation.

Paní Vavra adjusted the edges of his head and chest bandages. "You know how to get there from here? It is many kilometers, maybe 20."

He shook his head.

Paní Vavra traced a route in the dust. "You see this?" she asked. "It is the route to Lidice along the main road. You will probably have to go through the forest to be sure the Nazis don't see you, but the trees are pretty dense along there. You should be able to keep out of sight and still follow along next to the road."

She waited a few minutes, then asked: "You are getting a picture in your mind? Of the way to go?"

Milan studied the lines of the roadmap drawn on the ground. He nodded.

"The Lidice Valley Hill you should see from the road. Your town will be on the other side." She watched his face to be sure he understood.

"You be careful, boy," she said as she scraped away the markings with her boot.

*

Walking was slow and laborious. Paní Vavra had tightly wound strips of sheets around his fractured ribs to help the bones fuse together, lessen the pain and allow his lungs to expand. But stabs of agony still shot across his torso, convulsing his airway whenever he made sudden movements. She had also placed cloth around his head to hold the tips of his cracked jawbones in place and cover his shattered nose and swollen eye socket. But the wrappings made it difficult for him to see anything that interfered with his path. The heavy, T-shaped walking stick Paní Vavra had fashioned to ease the pressure on his wrenched knee and ankle was cumbersome and became easily caught in the underbrush.

His route was meandering and confused. He had been walking for days, camouflaging himself in the forest as he traced a path back to Lidice along the road from Kladno, past the suburbs of Prag, wary of the increasing numbers of Wehrmacht transports carrying men and tanks and armaments from Germany to the Eastern Front. Now about ten kilometers, he guessed, on the other side of Prag, he longed for some recognizable landmarks to confirm that he was even in the right area. He was close enough, he thought, to be able to see the bell tower of St. Martin's Church, to detect the honey and lemony scents of the lindens and the grassy, piney larches mingled with sweet-smelling stacks of hay. But there was nothing familiar here. Did that mean Pan Vavra was right? About what he said? What he said about Lidice?

A quartet of trucks rumbled down the road to his left. Young men in dirty khaki uniforms were crowded on the truck beds, jostling one another and singing.

Milan slipped out of sight into the trees. He stumbled over the tangles of weeds that covered the ground and cursed his injuries. He waited until sundown when he was sure the blacked-out road would be quiet. As the sun's rays turned orange, he scrambled up Lidice Valley hill, using his fingers to find spaces among the loose stones and uneven flagstones and pull himself forward. He lifted his head over the top of the hill and strained to see through the sunlight in his eyes. It must be the glare that makes it so hard to see, he thought. But shouldn't he be able to make out the pastures with grazing milk cows and horses? The homesteads with rows of vegetables and farms with fields of grain? The houses and streets and barns and silos? Why couldn't he find the village square, the town council, the schoolhouse?

He pulled himself over the crest of the hill and lay down in the tall fields of wildflowers. He was so tired, and it was getting dark. It will be better in the morning. He would be able to figure out where he was—in the morning.

*

Milan woke with a start, shaking off the vestiges of a dream. He looked past the purplish clumps of bromegrass and the broad, brown paper-like clover that had served as his bed the night before. He tried to make sense of what he was seeing—a vast area of yellow grass—and what he was not: the church, the granary, the butcher shop next to the bridge over the creek; the library and the school on the other side of the stream; Paní Marushak's dry-goods store and the Three Crows tavern, all close together on Armády Street.

He scanned the countryside for distant signs of Lidice, and thought he must not have walked far enough. Milan sat up and extended his legs out in front of him. He leaned back and let his rump slide down the hill. Near the foot of the hill he used the walking stick to pull himself upright, then stood in the field trying to decide which way to go. He got his bearings from the position of the sun to his left and began to walk south.

A few meters ahead, he noticed the thin trickle of a stream. He knelt down and cupped his hand into the water for a drink. After a second

LIDICE

drink, he took off his shoes and cooled his feet on the rocks. Picking up his shoes and socks, he walked barefoot across the creek and into the center of the valley, careful to step over snaking vines and tendrils. His foot kicked into something. Stones, it felt like, a small pile of stones. Milan bent forward and moved the weeds away. It was a pile of stones, nine of them, the largest supporting four layers of smaller ones: two in one row, then a larger one by itself, three in the next row and two on top. The marker. At the site where he had buried the torn body of his pet bunny. He remembered digging the hole with his fingers, searching Lidice creek for just the right stones, polishing them on the sleeves of his shirt, and positioning them, one by one, on the grave. Milan eased down to the ground, grabbing hold of the top of a small pear tree, gnarled and browned by flame damage, with only a smattering of leaves on a half-dozen stunted branches. His town. This is—was—Lidice.

In a pile of rubble, Milan found a pair of weathered boards broken in half, in the form of a cross, sticking haphazardly out of the ground. He tugged on the boards until they were free, then carried them to the animal's gravesite. He took the boards apart, peeled away the jagged portions and brushed the remaining fragments smooth. He unwound bits of fabric from his cheeks and nose and twisted them around the intersection of the boards. Then he tapped the new, sturdier smaller marker into the ground with his walking stick. With his palms on the arms of the cross, he said a soft goodbye to his pet, to his friend Ceslav, to his brother, to his town. With the branch of a small pear tree as support, he stood and scanned the countryside, wondering where he should go and how he could find his mother.

RAVENSBRÜCK

Chapter Twenty-Five

It was nearly the end of the workday. Chessie could sense it, with the cramps in her fingers, the widening separation between her skin and her cuticles, the accumulation of dust choking her nostrils and throat. She knew she didn't have much time. She had to find at least a dozen more strands of straw, strip them clean and weave them smoothly into one of the stylish handbags and other straw articles the Nazis were selling on the black market in Berlin. There were quotas for everyone and if she didn't meet hers, the entire crew would be punished. The shop boss, Gustav Binder, slapped women throughout the shift if they weren't on target. He forced the women in the straw-weaving shop to stand at attention for hours after evening roll call if the goods made by any one of them didn't pass muster. She didn't want that to happen tonight. Not on letter-writing night.

Chessie spit on her fingers and slicked back the wisps of hair escaping her gray-and-white-striped kerchief. Her hair was growing back—darker and thicker than before the camp overseers had shaved her head when she came to the Ravensbrück forced labor camp. It felt good to have a bit of hair to run her fingers through. It felt good to be free of the shame of baldness.

The end-of-shift siren bleated long and low.

Chessie and the other women at the worktable folded their hands in their laps as Binder examined their products. He ticked off the number of handbags and pairs of sandals each woman was expected to weave, picked up a representative sample from each woman's pile and uttered an occasional "adequate" as comment on the quality of the merchandise. Satisfied, Binder dismissed the women, then went to his office to enter the results of his inspection in the daily log.

Chessie carefully removed the cloth slippers the inmates were required to wear in the straw-weaving workshop and stepped out into the evening. It was gloomy, with hovering storm clouds heavy with humidity. Her bare feet sank into the mud and made sucking sounds with each step she took along the path from the weaving plant to the

K. M. Sandrick

RAVENSBRÜCK

Appellplatz.

She nearly fell as she slipped rounding the corner of the building and entered the passageway that led from the 4 meter-high, brick-exterior perimeter wall and along a 3-meter-high concrete partition to Lagerstrasse, the main road within the camp. The railroad tracks that ran parallel to and on the other side of the perimeter wall were silent. They rattled with cargo only twice a day: in the early morning hours when trains carried in new inmates, supplies and SS guards to the camp; and late in the evening when they transported the dead or nearly dead away from it. The space next to the partition erupted with end-of-shift activity as inmates, civilian workers and SS left the Waffen workshops and storage facilities, the armaments factory, the potato cellars and the political department building where prisoners' records were kept, on their way to roll call.

At the entrance to the living quarters for SS guards and their families, which branched off Lagerstrasse about a quarter of the way to the camp center, Chessie could see a group of five new three-story homes, each with a set of three dormers jutting out from their slanted roofs and an open-air porch on each of two lower levels. Building-crew inmates filled wheelbarrows with the earth they had dug to make room for more of the same structures, then pushed them toward the kennels and gardens at the far edges of the camp. Others placed the picks and shovels they would use the next day against a concrete foundation that had been partially poured. Further on, in front of the SS canteen, infirmary and laundry was the Appellplatz roll-call area, bounded by the Kommandant's headquarters, the camp kitchens and the inmates' barracks.

As she made her way toward roll call, Chessie stole glances at the city of Fürstenberg through the bulrushes along the edges of Schwedt Lake, which formed much of the southwestern boundary of Ravensbrück. The city was commonplace, with its white-faced homes, the imposing spire of the parish church, the city smokestack. The people must be able to see the camp across the lake. What did they think was happening here?

Chessie entered the roll-call grounds in front of the squat, dark-brown, single-story camp kitchen buildings, their oblong chimneys puffing smoke and unappetizing smells from the ovens. Electric currents crackled as bulbs in the tall light poles on either side of the kitchens came to life. She found a place in the line of workers from the camp sewing rooms, pulled her kerchief forward to protect her face from the sudden heavy rain, and waited for the overseers and barracks-block seniors to begin their head counts.

*

Klaudie spun the typewriter roller until the last page of the report she had been typing was free. She tugged the edge of the paper away from the carbon papers underneath, careful not to stain her fingertips and smudge the copies. She collated the original typed sheets and clipped them together, then did the same with the carbon copies. After stacking the reports in the outbox at the edge of her workspace in Ravensbrück's political office, she turned to the sack of mail that rested against her chair.

Klaudie pulled out bundles of letters and parcels that she would soon deliver to inmates in their barracks. Sorting the letters first, she grouped the correspondence so she could make quick work of the mail drop. The Poles received the most mail, so she ferreted out those letters and made several small piles in front of her typewriter. Next to them, she placed letters for the French and German prisoners. Last were the handfuls of letters for the Slavs. Some of the envelopes were thick with multiple sheets, but she knew from experience that most would not be legible through the heavy crayon marks or big black "X's" made by the camp censors. Some of the envelopes were lumpy— most likely filled with pages that had been sliced to pieces and stuffed back into their thin enclosure. A few were totally empty.

Next, she pulled out the packages. All had been ripped open, their contents thoroughly searched. Sausages, pastries and loaves of bread had been cut open or pulled apart to be sure nothing was hidden inside. Forbidden items—cigarettes, coffee and alcohol—as well as the finer items—caps, gloves and scarves in winter, stockings and shoes in summer, books—had already been confiscated by the SS. Klaudie tried to protect whatever was left for the inmates, but she couldn't keep track of all the packages and often noticed coworkers leaving the administrative office on mail day, their pockets bulging.

With the mail organized to her liking, Klaudie repacked the mailbag, finishing just as the roll- call horn sounded. With the other office inmates, Klaudie made her way to the Appellplatz, all the while avoiding eye contact with the women she knew from Lidice.

Soon after arriving in Ravensbrück, Klaudie had pestered the camp officials, offering herself to SS officer Konrad Dreschler and the overseer Hannah Hoyt, until they agreed to transfer her from the straw-weaving plant to administrative duty in the office next to the Kommandant's headquarters, and to move her from the squalid Barracks Block X to one of the so-called elite barracks, where she had a bunk to herself with a pillow and blanket, a bank of showers to use every day and three small but fairly hearty hot meals a day. She saw her former friends and neighbors at daily roll calls and knew they watched her closely, comparing their tattered and unwashed uniforms with her regularly laundered skirt and blouse, their muddy bare feet with her scuffed shoes and stockings, their bloody and infected fingernails with her smooth, clean hands.

She didn't begrudge them their feelings. Every month on mail-delivery day she saw their deteriorating living conditions: More than 250 women crammed together, two or sometimes three to each bare mattress, all sharing a single washroom with only 15 to 20 sinks and an open latrine. She heard the consumptive coughs, smelled the sweat and dirt, felt the itch of lice clinging to their hair.

She did wish they could understand a little about her situation— what she had to do for Dreschler and Hoyt to get her job and keep it, how many hours she had to work, what she learned about the operation of the camp, the overseers, the Kommandant. But then she realized they would not want to know the things she was finding out.

*

Roll call went smoothly for once, so in little more than three hours Chessie was able to grab her bowl and spoon, elbow a place for herself at the common table, and wait for the bucket of soup to arrive at barracks Block X.

"So what do you think we will be served for dinner tonight?" a French woman asked. "I hope it's not chateaubriand. I get so tired of it. Or wiener schnitzel. How terribly pedestrian." She raised a pinkie in the air.

"I don't suppose it will be fish and chips or bangers and mash.

The Pear Tree

RAVENSBRÜCK

Such barbarian food," Chessie laughed.

"No, it's none of that," Jana noted after glancing into the soup pot and finding the same fare as lunch—cabbage broth with maybe a few potatoes hidden below the surface. "It's one of our true delicacies—holubki."

"As long as they didn't make it the way you do," Chessie teased Jana. "I mean, adding tomatoes to cabbage rolls and sauerkraut? You can't possibly be one of us. You must be Hungarian."

The women lingered over their bowls of soup, trying to make the nourishment last as long as they could, then peeled off one by one to wash their utensils, use the latrine and get ready for letter-writing.

Chessie was already at the table, alternately scratching the point of the pencil and biting off slivers of graphite as she marked out the lines she would write on the tabletop before putting them on paper. She was allowed only 30 lines and wanted to get the most out of them—when Klaudie entered the barracks, dragging the heavy mail bag behind her.

*

Klaudie focused her attention on the bowed heads of the women seated at the common table in the middle of Barracks Block X, the women who carefully selected the words they wrote so they would not exceed the total permitted line count and could avoid the censor's heavy black marks. A group of Poles was comparing lists of the items they would request from their relatives. An "old political," imprisoned before the war had even started, was jotting down notes about the birds she saw outside the barracks window so she could describe them to her husband, also imprisoned, in Dachau.

Not a single woman from Lidice—except for Chessie—was writing, opting instead to hum folk songs or pray or work on small handicrafts. One by one, the women from Lidice had given up writing letters. Why should they? No mail ever came for them, and most camp overseers could not be induced to smuggle outgoing letters. The overseers accepted as truth the rumors they had heard: the town had been destroyed, the men shot dead, the children gassed to death. "Why take chances smuggling out letters," the overseers said, "when there are no addresses in that town anymore?" Klaudie worried that Chessie's persistence would attract attention and raise questions. She didn't want the SS guards or overseers to do anything more than they were already doing to safeguard records about inmates, or suddenly decide to restrict access to records to someone like her—an inmate from Lidice—and make it even harder for her to get the information she was looking for.

Klaudie followed the routine she had established months ago in the barracks. Before opening the sack and passing out the mail, she asked if any of the inmates needed help writing their letters. Three of the Poles raised their hands and asked Klaudie to translate words or phrases into German to meet the requirements of the SS censors. Two others asked her how to fill out forms they had been urged by the SS to complete, asking for divorces so that their men could marry and impregnate more suitable women. She passed Chessie on her way to the women seated at the back of the common table, but Chessie did not look up.

*

"Dear Ondrej," Chessie wrote. "It is hot here today. We had a big storm. I thought of the time when <u>someone</u>," she underlined the word, "(I won't say who), left the window open and soaked his Sunday shirt so he didn't have to wear that starchy collar."

She rubbed her chest with her knuckles to calm her rising feeling of desolation. She worried about what might have happened to her son. She was afraid for him; he was so young and naïve, so easily influenced. She remembered how quickly he had picked up the mannerisms of the Nazis. After the Gestapo had come to Lidice and taken Ana Maruščáková and farmer Horák away, Ondrej had talked constantly about the SS officer and his sleek, black uniform and peaked cap. practicing the straight-arm salutes and goosesteps in the front hall mirror. But she had worried that underneath it all, he was still afraid. After all, he had woken up in the middle of the night and bundled and shoved his urine-soaked nightclothes and sheets under the bed.

Where was he? She scanned the rows of three-tiered bunks covered with filthy straw mattresses, the women doing their best to keep themselves clean: checking one another for fleas or lice; picking mud out from under their toenails; stripping off their striped tunics and wiping the sweat from their underarms. Only a few of the women and children taken to the Kladno gymnasium had received the blue badges.

The Pear Tree

RAVENSBRÜCK

They—and her son—must be on a farm or in a school or some other special place—not in a place like this. No one could convince her otherwise. No one had actually seen what happened to the children. Had they? Who could say that the children *weren't* in a special place? Who could say she wasn't right?

"Don't forget to eat your ...," Chessie returned to her letter, applying only minimal pressure from the pencil on the thin sheet. But the paper slipped away from her, pulled by Jana, the thief of the labor camp, whose fingers were quick to claim anything that lay unattended, even momentarily, and squirrel it away under her mattress or in the lining of her uniform jacket.

Chessie lunged for the paper, trying to trap it on the table with the pencil, but Jana had already brought the sheet close to her eyes, squinting to make out the words.

"She throws your letters away, you know," Jana said, handing the letter back and gesturing toward Klaudie. "She throws them in the garbage. Your precious letters. To your precious son."

"What?"

"Go ask her, if you don't believe me," Jana said, smirking.

"You do this? What Jana said? Throw away my letters?" Chessie asked Klaudie.

Klaudie turned her head to the side to avoid Chessie's angry eyes while filling the mailbag with the letters written by Block X inmates.

"Tell me," Chessie insisted, grabbing Klaudie's arm.

Klaudie stood motionless, her shoulders slumped, her head down.

"*Tell* me." Chessie tightened her grip.

Klaudie nodded slowly.

"But my *letters*?" Chessie said, waving the paper in Klaudie's face. "To *throw away* my letters?" Chessie stared down at the letter, slowly crumpling it. "I knew you weren't important enough—in that office of yours—to be able to find out where the children were sent ... what was happening to children like your Adéle and my Ondrej, the ones who are different. But I thought you were giving the letters to the SS or the

overseers or whoever *did* know. And all this time you were just *throwing
... them ... away?*"

Chessie slapped Klaudie's face. "How could you?" She held on to
Klaudie's arms and shook her. *"How?"* A sob rose from the depths of her
soul as she stared into Klaudie's eyes and saw shadows of grief circling
her irises. Chessie released her grip and turned away. She raised her
shoulders, tucked in her chin and held her head in her palms to soften
the throbbing spreading from her temples to her neck.

"When did you start ... ripping up my letters and throwing them in
the trash? Last week? Last month?"

Klaudie rested her hand on the back of Chessie's head, but Chessie
twisted away from the touch.

"When?" Chessie faced her. "Not from the first day. Tell me that's
not when it started."

Klaudie remained silent, her head down, her eyes focused on the
floor.

"On the *first* day? The first letter-writing day? You decided to make
it easier for yourself? You didn't want to bother with any extra work. Or
was it just because you know better. That must be it. You always know
better, don't you? Always smarter than everyone else. Your husband's
smarter. You're kids are smarter. Always Klaudie, the smart one."

Chessie placed her fingertips on top of the table and looked at the
letter she had been writing. "All this time," she moaned. "Ondrej," she
said, her voice low, husky. "He never got a single letter telling him that
I was thinking about him—all this time—not a single letter telling him
that I was loving him..."

Klaudie gently squeezed Chessie's elbow and moved to take the
letter away.

"No." Chessie grabbed and crushed the paper in her palms. "If
anyone is going to throw away this letter ..." She raised her head and
wiped her nose on the sleeve of her uniform. "It is going to be me."

Chessie stood in front of one of the holes in the latrine's concrete
slab. Her hand shook as she extended the letter over the mounds of filth.
Lifting her eyes to the lines on the sheet, the curls of the "s's," the slants
of the "l's," the points of the "i's," she turned the paper to make the letters

dance. She pulled the paper to her chest and folded both hands over it, then slowly backed away.

She sat back down on the stool next to the common table, picked up her letter, flattened out the wrinkled spots and found the place where she had left off: "Don't forget to eat your—," she paused, then wrote, "kohlrabi" and laughed. Ondrej would like the joke. He always hated kohlrabi.

She held the paper out so she could proofread it. She, crossed out an extra "e," added a missing comma and at the bottom of the page wrote, "Love, Mama."

Chessie ran her finger along the edge of the paper, caressing it. Making a small tear in the top right-hand corner of the page, she tugged until the paper split in half, then folded and repeated the exercise until only thin strips remained. She put the strips in her mouth, one by one, gagging on the dryness. The scraps of paper deep in her mouth, she gnawed at them and then forced them down her throat, swallowing the letters, the words, the punctuation marks, the lines on the page—the only connections she had with her son.

Chapter Twenty-Six

"Look." Chessie barely heard the whisper above the drumming of the rain on the muddy ground during morning roll call.

"Look ... over there ... at the end of the line—on the right." Jana spoke out of the side of her mouth, her words muffled.

Chessie scanned the groups of women who had just entered the camp and were in the beginning stages of intake. They stood naked in the downpour, their belongings in sodden heaps in front of them. She remembered the degradation when she first came to the camp: forced to parade naked in front of the SS guards; then to wait for hours for doctors to arrive for a medical examination; then waiting again for a uniform, a colored badge and a number. They had remained quarantined for weeks in a "tent," with nothing but cement blocks to sit or lie upon.

Then she saw the woman Jana was talking about. Chessie didn't recognize her at first. The long, bushy, waist-length dark-brown hair was gone, revealing the curve of Silvie's crooked spine and misaligned hips. But the defiance was still there. Silvie did not cover her breasts like the other women. She stood with her hands on her hips, her chest thrust forward, legs apart—almost daring the SS to watch her, to want her, to penetrate her.

"Jesus," Jana exclaimed. "The scars ..." She hung her head as an overseer approached. "Something you want to say here?"

"No, Mistress."

The overseer eyed Jana and the other inmates. "What? I can't hear you."

"Nothing, Mistress." The entire line of women called out.

"Good. That's what I want to hear—silence."

Cautiously, Chessie focused her eyes on Silvie. She dropped her gaze to Silvie's legs. Although she had seen these kinds of scars before, she still had to stifle a gasp. There was a nine-inch scar on the outside of Silvie's thigh and another five-inch scar on the calf. Both were red, thick and raised with puncture wounds where stitches had held the skin together.

A "rabbit," Chessie thought, placing Silvie in the category of other women at Ravensbrück who were given that nickname because of the way they hobbled. Most of the "rabbits" were Poles, who were quartered in their own barracks and did only light work, like knitting socks or mufflers for the Wehrmacht soldiers on the Eastern Front, so Chessie had no first-hand knowledge of what had happened to them. But she heard that they had been taken to the infirmary soon after arriving in the camp and had operations performed on their legs. One of the Poles told Jana that she had woken up once days after her surgery. A doctor probing a wound so deep she could see bone. She had watched as his fat fingers pulled out pieces of metal seat-cushion springs, wood splinters, strands of horsehair and pieces of glass before he wrapped her leg in plaster.

Silvie must have had an operation like that. Chessie watched her grimace with each step she took toward the quarantine tent.

*

Unlike the other arrivals, Silvie had no sense of modesty. There was no need to cover her pubis, the rough razor cuts and scrapes still visible beneath the tufts of hair that were beginning to reappear. No need to worry that she would be subjected to a vaginal examination to search for hidden valuables. Before the surgery that scarred her leg and left her lame, her vagina had been fully probed, her mouth and ears thoroughly examined, her breasts palpated, her legs carefully groomed and smoothly shaved—not like her pubis—her knees tested, her calves squeezed, the tendons and muscles along her shins stroked. No, she had been through physical scrutiny as bad or worse than the intake procedures these new Ravensbrück inmates faced. She stood in front of the quarantine tent, her clothing kicked to the side. Her head up, her eyes fierce, she dared the overseers and SS guards to take a step closer, to aim a flashlight toward her eyes and ears, or point a speculum in her direction. She would have none of it. Her body was proof enough that she had passed inspection.

K. M. Sandrick

RAVENSBRÜCK

She laid back and enjoyed the warm, soapy water that rose up to her chin. A bath. An actual bath. After weeks of punishing 11-hour days in the sewing rooms of the Sachsenhausen forced labor camp, cold group showers, delousings and disinfections, she marveled at her fortune—one of six inmates who had been singled out for duty with the camp doctors. Finally, Silvie thought, her abilities were being recognized. She had proved to Kleinschmidt and the rest of the SS staff at the Kladno infirmary that she was a capable midwife during Katrenka's delivery. It was about time they took advantage of her clinical skills.

Admiring her clean toenails, she slipped her feet into a pair of terrycloth slippers. Her skin still wrinkled from her soak, she unfolded a blue-and-white striped hospital gown, letting her fingers linger over the neatly ironed edges of the pleats. She fell into line as the overseers led the group to a hospital ward with six beds in two rows opposite one another, each covered with crisp white sheets. While the other inmates in the group whispered worriedly about their fate, Silvie stoked embers of anger. She wasn't going to become a camp midwife—she was a patient!

She studied the ward: The beds were positioned close together with only enough room for a single person to maneuver in between them. The walls had been freshly whitewashed, the light- gray linoleum floor shiny clean. There were no windows. The door leading from the bathing area was open; the other on the opposite wall was closed. The heavy wood desk that occupied one corner of the room was uncluttered;, three precisely aligned stacks of spiral notebooks the only evidence it was ever used. A small metal table at the end of the rows of hospital beds was covered with a short white cloth.

She barked a laugh. This is what it had come to—her cunning, the steps she had taken to capitalize on Kleinschmidt's interest in Katrenka, the belief that she could use that interest to prove her worth and improve her lot with the SS and the Schupo.

A nurse swabbed her forearm with alcohol, tapped the barrel of a syringe and pushed the tip of the needle into a vein. Silvie felt the infusion enter her bloodstream, leaving her arm limp as it coursed up the blood vessel. Her eyelids became heavy, her head swam, her last thought before unconsciousness: What a joke!

*

The Pear Tree

RAVENSBRÜCK

Klaudie finished typing the last order for punishment that had been sent by the overseers and approved by the Kommandant's office. The list would be read aloud in the Proclamation of Punishments at morning roll call. The overseer of Block V was being especially harsh. She had ordered canings for three of her wards for stealing handfuls of potatoes and turnips. Her entire block would stand from 4:00 a.m. until the noon lunch break for breaking the code of silence during roll call. The overseer also refused to allow letters to be delivered to Block V for a month, confiscated all packages and assigned one woman to the Punishment Block for talking back.

Relieved that the punishment list was complete, Klaudie turned to the requisitions for work details outside of the camp walls. Only a few today: Two of the farms on the outskirts of Fürstenburg requested ten inmates to work in the fields for the next three days, and the railroad line renewed its request for a construction crew of 40 inmates to repair the banks along the tracks.

Next on her work list were the inmates' applications for brothel duty in the whorehouses at the nearby men's work camps and in the bordellos frequented by the SS officers. The number of applications was increasing as conditions in Ravensbrück worsened, and inmates learned about the advantages of becoming a prostitute. In the men's work camps, brothels were set up in nicely furnished barracks. The prostitutes were expected to work two hours a night and take care of eight men in that timeframe. In return, they could keep one of the two Reichsmarks they were paid. The bordellos for the SS officers, or so-called Lebensborn facilities, were most commonly located in homes that had been confiscated from Jewish families. High-quality food and drink were plentiful. The women were dressed in silks and lace, and they had their choice of fine lingerie and cosmetics. But only certain types of women were sent to the SS bordellos, and it was Klaudie's job to screen applications to identify the ones who might qualify.

Among the applications on her desk, Klaudie selected the ones from women who most likely had the appropriate heritage, such as Germans who had been imprisoned for criminal acts but who still might be patriotic to the Third Reich. For applications in later stages of review, she checked to be sure other necessary documents were included: a full family history; a medical examination certificate; a personal history questionnaire; recent photographs. She gathered the applications together, the fully completed ones on top, and carried them over to the line of filing cabinets that separated the camp's administrative work areas from the SS offices.

She pulled open the J-L file cabinet drawer and flipped through the folders until she found the one labeled Lebensborn. Klaudie lifted the folder out of the drawer and scanned the pages inside.

"Klaudie, Klaudie, Klaudie." Dreschler thrust his pelvis against her. He took the file and the papers out of her hand. "Don't want to be a hooker ... in one of these places, do you?" He put the folder and the applications on top of the filing cabinet. "Then what would *I* do?"

Dreschler turned Klaudie's body toward him, held her arms out to the side, and pushed her into the cabinet. He lowered his head and ran his lips and tongue along the side of her face and neck. He tightened his hold. "You are curious, my Liebchen?" He bit her earlobe, then whispered, "Don't be."

*

"Don't think I don't know you steal from me," Silvie snarled, extending her good leg out in front of Jana as she passed the low-level bunk Silvie had commandeered from a young Gypsy girl. She grabbed Jana's wrist and twisted her arm behind her, then reached into her tunic pockets and retrieved a pair of short, knitted socks.

"The others may put up with it, but I won't." Silvie pushed Jana into the common table. "These are mine. I make these things all day long. I deserve my own pair." Silvie shook out the socks and pulled them on, folding the extra fabric down on her ankles. She sat back, stretching out her damaged leg on the mattress and enjoying the attention she was attracting.

The door to the barracks was kicked open. The kitchen workers carried in the dinner kettles.

The Pear Tree

RAVENSBRÜCK

"She was your friend, wasn't she?" Silvie asked Chessie as she eased herself down onto a stool and rested her bowl and spoon on the table.

"Who are you talking about?" Chessie asked.

"Who am I talking about?" Silvie looked past Chessie's head toward the other Lidice women who were sitting nearby. "Who do you think? That Kraut cunt. My sainted sister-in-law. Weren't you a friend of hers?"

"You mean Katrenka?"

"Do I mean Katrenka? Of course, I mean Katrenka." Chessie remained quiet, dipping a crust of bread into the broth that had been ladled into her bowl.

"Well—don't you want to know what happened to her?" Silvie persisted.

Chessie wiped the bread along the inside of the bowl, unsure whether she wanted to hear what Silvie had to say.

"She's dead." Silvie kept her head down, swirling her spoon in circles in the thin liquid. Slowly lifting the spoon to her mouth, she whispered, "and so is her baby."

Chessie dropped her spoon and took hold of the table edge.

"There was so much blood," Silvie began. "Torrents of it, spilling out of her onto the birthing table and the sheets, onto the floor." She took a sip of broth. "And she had a lot of difficulty breathing. I could hear bubbling in every breath. Even when she did speak, she wasn't making any sense. I kept telling her to push and showed her how to breathe between contractions, but she wasn't helping me at all, just mooning about her Johann and talking crazy—about that bird of hers. It was so bad—the blood, I mean." Silvie waited as women in the barracks leaned forward to hear her story. "It was gushing out of the birth canal. I could see blood in her eyes and nose, even leaking out of a cut on her arm. It was coming so fast I couldn't tell if the baby was crowning. I couldn't see past it." Silvie paused, taking a sip of broth.

"She was twisting around so much I had to get a Schupo to hold her down when the baby started to come. I had such a hard time grabbing hold of the baby. It was so slippery and Katrenka was bucking so much she nearly fell off the table. But then all of a sudden, she stopped moving. Her eyes rolled back. Her arms and legs dropped onto the table. And then the baby came."

Silvie looked up at the faces of the women. "It was a girl." She looked back down at her dinner. "She was dead, of course. The baby. The baby never uttered a sound." The women who had gathered caught their breath, then hung their heads.

"They didn't need me after that ... the Nazis." Silvie complained. "No, they didn't want to have anything to do with me ..." She picked at the edge of a fingernail. "So they sent me to Sachsenhausen. Where I got ...," she pointed to her leg, "... these. These—" She traced the rows of stitches, "are what I got for trying to help her, to help Katrenka."

"That'll be the day that you help anyone, Silvie. You were just in it to save yourself," Jana said.

"And now I'm with you all." Silvie ignored the comment. Raising her spoon in acknowledgment, she smiled coldly. "With all my lady friends from Lidice."

Chapter Twenty-Seven

"Isn't she stupid?" Jana grabbed Chessie's letter out of her hand and held it toward Silvie, who had just finished washing her bowl and spoon after dinner and was slowly making her way down the passage between the bunks and the common table. "She," Jana nodded her head toward Chessie. "Keeps writing to him." Jana pointed to Ondrej's name in the salutation. "But he's dead, isn't he? They're all dead, aren't they?"

Silvie glanced at the words on the page Jana was holding in front of her and nodded, flinching as Chessie reached out to retrieve the letter.

"Why don't you tell her, then?" Jana urged. "Why don't you tell her what you told me?"

Silvie glanced sidelong at Jana, stroking the edges of her mouth with a thumb and forefinger. She squeezed her nostrils, then turned her head away and stepped toward the bunk directly behind Chessie. She held on to the wooden frame and eased herself down onto the mattress. "We were waiting for the ambulance to take us to the infirmary, Katrenka and I."

Chessie continued writing as if Silvie weren't speaking.

"We were standing outside the gymnasium in Kladno, with Kleinschmidt and the Schupo." Silvie smoothed the cloth of her tunic skirt. "When the children came out. We saw them line up and get into these big, green vans, the kind you carry furniture in. You know the ones I mean?"

"Oh, yeah, they're—" Jana began, then stopped as Silvie grabbed her wrist and pressed it tightly against her thigh.

"I told you before. Don't you dare steal from me." Silvie removed a mass of wadded-up wool from Jana's hand and increased the pressure on her wrist even after Jana whimpered.

"The vans," Chessie prompted, her head down, her fingers squeezing the pencil. "What about the vans?"

Silvie unrolled the wool and shook it out. "The other one." She held out her hand to Jana, palm upward, and wriggled her fingers until Jana dropped another bunch of wool into it. Silvie smoothed out the crumpled wad and searched for the opening at one end. She pushed her hand inside and extended her fingers as far as they could go. She rested her hand on her thigh and stroked the mitten that covered it.

"I didn't think anything about those vans," Silvie continued, absently tugging on the other mitten. "But then we passed one of them on the road." Silvie admired the way the mitten covered her fingers. "It was parked in the grass by the side of the road. The Schupo were standing in between the trees, watching a group of Jews digging in the woods." Silvie paused. "I thought it was strange." She rubbed her hand over her mouth. "The engine was still running but there was no exhaust coming out of the tailpipe. You know how those old vans are. How they belch out all that smoke. But not this one. And there were sounds coming from inside the van, like pounding against the metal."

"They didn't *all* get in the same vans, did they?" Chessie interrupted, her voice cracking, her chest constricting. "The children with the blue badges as well as the ones with the black badges? They went to different places, didn't they? There must have been different vans."

Silvie scowled and bit on a fingernail. Shifting uncomfortably on the bunk, she removed the mitten, folded one hand over the other and rubbed her thumb over her knuckles in tight circles. "What do you mean?" she asked.

"Well, they went to all the trouble of separating us—the Nazis did. There was the blue group and the black one and us." Chessie pointed around the barracks. "The ones in the red group. All of *us*—" she indicated the other women in the barracks, "are in the red group. No one from any of the other groups is here. So the others, the ones in the other groups, must have gone to different places, too."

Silvie leaned forward and picked non-existent nits off her skirt, enjoying the worry in Chessie's words.

"Certainly not all of the children were put in those vans, the ones you're talking about," Chessie continued. "The ones you're talking about had the black badges. The children with the blue badges were different. They wouldn't have—"

"*All* the children got into those vans," Sylvie insisted.

"Why did they give them different color badges if they were going to treat them all the same?"

RAVENSBRÜCK

"Why do the Nazis do anything?"

"I don't believe you." Chessie's voice rose. "The children with the blue badges were ... are different."

"Well, I don't know what you're going on about. *I* was there," Silvie insisted. "I *saw* it. I *heard* it. I heard *them*, pounding on the walls of the van. They were screaming and crying and choking. They were praying the Zdrávas Maria, calling out for the Son of God, the Holy Ghost, the Mother of God."

Silvie shoved her face close to Chessie's. "*All* of them were in the van. *All* the children. Your Ondrej, his friends. *All* of them. I saw it happen."

"It can't be true." Chessie picked up the letter she had been writing and pressed it to her heart. "You're wrong. It makes no sense." She turned away from Silvie, returned the pencil to the paper and started outlining letters and forming words on the page. She rocked forward and back. "It's not true. Not true. Not true." She began to wail. "Not true. Not true. Not true."

Klaudie dropped the packages she had started to deliver, stepped in between the two women, pushed Silvie aside, and wrapped her arms around Chessie's shoulders, holding on even after Chessie's panic roared into flame and burned into her own skin.

She sat quietly on a stool next to Chessie, bearing witness to the clash of emotions as her friend slowly came to acknowledge the apparent validity of the suppositions surrounding her. The assassination of one of the most important leaders of the Third Reich had been linked by camp guards, overseers, fellow inmates and the leaders of the Nazi Party to Lidice. Chessie had begun to realize the dark conclusions: Her town had been destroyed; the children of the town, her son, had been killed.

"You believe this? What she...?" Chessie asked Klaudie, watching as Silvie lifted her damaged leg onto the mattress. "That's why you were throwing my letters away? You knew this?" Chessie grimaced.

Klaudie shook her head. "Let me tell you something." She reached for Chessie's hand. "There's something ..."

"Not now." Chessie rejected Klaudie's outstretched arm.

Chessie sat staring at the letter on the table long after the lights

K. M. Sandrick

RAVENSBRÜCK

had been extinguished. The only illumination came from intermittent shafts of light as the guards in the watchtower rotated their beacon. As the barracks windows revealed increasing signs of daybreak, she picked up a corner of the paper so she could feel its texture and the imprint of the pencil markings. As she had done for weeks, she folded the bottom of the page so the edge rested directly under Ondrej's name, then creased the fold with her thumbnails and folded again and again, until the letter was only an inch long. She tugged on the edge of the paper, listening to every rasp and feeling every small change in texture as the fibers separated. She struggled to breathe as she placed the strips in her mouth and gulped. This time, unable to keep the paper strips down, she doubled over, her hands around her stomach, ran to the latrine and retched.

RESISTANCE

CHAPTER TWENTY-EIGHT

Milan jerked in his sleep. His foot kicked out, dislodging a patch of mold and soot from the cellar wall. His nostrils twitching, throat tightening, he woke from his dream. Snorting and coughing, he cleared his air passages, then rubbed his fingers over his face, now free of bandages and only slightly darkened and swollen.

He crawled across the musty floor to the corner of the cellar. He rose on an elbow and put his eye to the open space in the mortar he had scraped away from the edges of a pair of bricks and peered into Trojická Street in Prag, now dim in the waning twilight. He cautiously loosened one of the bricks so he could get a better look at the bakery just to the left in his line of sight. He was waiting for signs that the baker and his wife had closed up shop so he could rummage through the leavings at the back of the bakery. He had to time his foraging carefully—he wasn't the only one looking for scraps.

Keeping to the shadows, he crept along the building walls until he was directly across from the doorway near the alley that ran behind the bakery. He half-hopped over the cobblestones, slightly dragging a pigeon-toed foot and knee, the remnants of his beating by Kleinschmidt, and flattened himself within the doorframe.

A rush of movement caught his eye. Hurried steps drew close. He sucked in his breath to shrink back as far as he could from sight.

Three young men, kerchiefs around their noses and mouths, guns held close to their sides, jogged past.

Milan waited, not moving a muscle, until the footfalls faded into silence. He leaned his head and shoulders forward and peeked up and down the street. No sounds, except the rustlings of rats beginning their own forays in the gutters. No sights, except the shadings of sunlight winking off blacked-out windows.

He slipped into the alley, found the metal trashcan and eased off the lid, placing it carefully on the ground. Reaching into the trash, he separated paper from items of food. He grabbed a few pieces of hardened bread and pastries—rozkys, apricot it looked like, with specks of blue and white mold.

Gunshots, close by, shocked him. He dropped the food and stood still, waiting. Hearing nothing more, he reached back into the trash, pulling out bits and pieces and shoving them into his pockets. He raised the lid to replace it but dropped it when noises came from the street.

The same three men were running, blood on their clothes, bulges in their pockets, heads turning to watch behind them. At the sound of the metal lid hitting the ground, one of the men stopped and hissed to the others, "Someone's there."

The man crept to the alley entryway, pinched his nostrils through his red-and-white checked kerchief, and flattened his cheek and curly dark-blond head against the corner of the building. His green eyes squinting, he peered into the dimly lit space and spying Milan, brought his pistol to eye level.

"Wait." One of the other men, taller, huskier, darker, put his hand on the barrel and lowered the weapon. The man tugged on his black-and-blue patterned kerchief until it loosened enough to reveal the bulge of cartilage over the tip of his nose. He approached Milan, his arm extended in a calming gesture, his eyes giving Milan the once-over, noting the boy's torn trousers gathered at the waist and held up by a rope belt, his grime-encrusted shirt sleeves, his high cheekbones, his thin and now-crooked nose.

"I have black horses," he said to Milan in Czech. He stepped closer. "You understand?" he asked gently. Czech fireman Juri Fischer then removed his kerchief so Milan could see the moustache that curled over his upper lip but did not hide a pair of slightly bucked front teeth, the scarring that covered his left cheek, the shriveled and distorted ear lobe that appeared in between tufts of straight dark hair. "I have black horses," he repeated.

Milan stood silent, his fingers clutching his pant legs.

"C'mon, Juri." The man standing at the entry to the alleyway raised his pistol, worriedly jerking his head back and forth between the alley and the street behind him. "We can't..."

"Just wait, Saimon," Juri told him, nodding his head in encouragement to Milan.

"I have black horses," Juri said to Milan.

"The black horses are mine," Milan whispered.

"I thought so," Juri said, smiling and backing away from Milan and gathering the other men beside him.

"But..."

"Don't worry, Saimon." Juri wrapped an arm around his friend's shoulder. "The kid's all right. He knows that old Czech nursery rhyme, the one about the horses."

"I don't know, Juri." Saimon looked suspiciously at Milan.

"C'mon," Juri urged, leading his men away. "Let's get out of here."

"It's OK, kid." He turned back and winked at Milan.

Milan hobbled to the alleyway entry in time to see the tail of Juri's shirt disappear around the corner to the right on Podskalská Street. He returned to the trashcan, pulled out the food he had found, then carefully replaced the lid.

He stood again at the alley entrance. Preoccupied with checking for signs of Juri and his men, he forgot to keep close to the building and out of sight. Too late to take cover, he froze as heavy boots approached and a man shouted in German: "You there."

Milan stood still, afraid to turn and face the men.

"Hands up," a nervous voice called.

Milan lowered his head, closed his eyes and complied with the command.

"He's not one of them," a Schupo told the others. "Just look at him." The Schupo nudged Milan's clothing with the barrel of his pistol. "See that?" The policeman used the tip of the pistol to point at Milan's leg. "He's a cripple. There weren't any cripples back there, were there?"

The Schupo placed the barrel of the pistol under Milan's chin and raised his head. "What did you see, boy?" he asked. "Anyone running past you? In the last few minutes? Down the street here?"

Milan opened his eyes and looked at the Schupo's face. Dead eyes, he thought. Eyes like Kleinschmidt's. He blinked quickly to disguise his hatred.

"They went there," he murmured, indicating Pod Slovany Street. "To the left. They went that way."

*

Milan made his way down Trojická Street toward the bakery. He had not been on the street for more than a week, aware that Schupo had been policing the area, perhaps on the lookout for the crippled boy who led them on a goose chase. He glanced down Podskalská Street, wondering where Juri and the other men had gone, whether they had been able to elude the Schupo, whether he would ever see them again.

He slid along the sides of the brick buildings, trying to melt into them, then quickly rounded the corner into the alley, fairly confident he would have the pickings to himself. One thing about Schupo patrols, they kept a regular timetable. Find out how they synchronized their watches and you could get in and out without them knowing you were there.

He hurried toward the trashcan but found that the lid was off.

"Looking for these?"

Milan turned toward the sound of the voice and saw Juri as he stepped away from the back door of the bakery, chunks of stale bread and dried-out pastries in his hand.

"I thought you'd turn up here once you figured out the Schupo schedule." Juri tossed the food to Milan.

Milan backed away, letting the food fall to the ground.

"No, wait." Juri came over to Milan and placed a hand on his arm.

Milan jerked away, holding on to his arm as if Juri had set fire to it.

"Sorry, kid," Juri said, holding his palms up and away from Milan.

Juri stepped back and adjusted the patent-leather helmet that hung by its chinstrap over his arm. "Go ahead and take it." He indicated the bits of food. "Looks like you could use it."

Milan brought the food closer with his foot, but still did not bend to pick it up.

Juri took a few more steps away from Milan. He lifted the helmet and with his head down, concentrated on the brass badge just above the bill: a fire ax and a pair of ladders formed the background behind the Czech lion crest.

Milan inched his hands down his thighs. His eyes still watching Juri, he reached out quickly, grabbed and stuffed the food in his mouth, and took a step back.

"We could use you, you know," Juri told Milan. "Our group." He spoke without raising his head.

"We could use someone who looks harmless, someone the Nazis would ignore, someone too crippled for them to worry about." He noticed Milan wince in reaction to his last words.

"But you're a fireman, aren't you?" Milan gestured toward the helmet. "I can't ..."

Juri slipped the helmet under his arm. "Many of us—the volunteer firemen—are in the Resistance—the Home Resistance, the ÚVOD, not the Communists who are working with the Soviets. We are working with Beneš and the Czechoslovak Government in Exile in Britain. Well, we're working with them as much as we can. It's gotten harder to get information from Beneš or even to keep in touch with our members—since the assassination, that is."

"So what do you do?"

"We disrupt," Juri said, smiling. "Whatever we can—the Nazi troop trains, the munitions factories. We steal whatever we can—mainly weapons. We spy whenever we can—on the SS, the Schupo, the Germans who have taken our jobs. We have kerosene, we have trucks, we have manpower that can stand with our liberators when it is time to take our country back."

"What would I be doing?"

"You could help us a lot by acting as a lookout. Maybe doing a little eavesdropping or scouting around and following Nazis, finding out where they live, what's in their garbage." Juri paused. "You're good at picking through garbage, aren't you?"

"Would I have a gun?"

Juri laughed. "Maybe ... someday."

"Would I be able to find other people? Other people like me?"

"What do you mean, 'like me?'"

"From Lidice."

Juri peered at Milan and stroked his chin. "Is that ... your town?"

RESISTANCE

Milan nodded.

"What do you know? About Lidice—what happened?"

"It's gone. I saw it."

"Were you there … when the Nazis …?"

Milan shook his head. "They took me and my mother and the other women and children to Kladno before they … " He paused. "They held us there for a couple of days. Then they sent them all away and left me … "

"Why did they leave you?"

"I nearly bit off a Nazi pig's finger."

"I'm surprised he didn't shoot you on the spot."

Milan shrugged.

"He'll be sorry he didn't, eh?"

A smile tugged at the corners of Milan's mouth.

Juri laughed. "I knew it. I knew we could use you. You would do well for us."

"What will you do for me?" Milan asked. "Can you help me find the others? The ones they took from my town?" He rubbed a hand in front of his mouth, muffling his words so Juri wouldn't hear the longing in his voice when he said, "Help me find my mother."

Juri reached out to squeeze Milan's shoulder, then thought better of it. "We'll see what we can do. In the meantime, we need to get you cleaned up. Come to the old Jewish cemetery tomorrow night—midnight. If I am not there, come the next night."

"Where … in the … "

"I will find you.

CHAPTER TWENTY-NINE

"Kleinschmidt's the one we should be going after." Milan was standing in front of the kitchen window in the safe house near Slaný. At the table, Juri was sipping the top layer of foam from the beer in his mug. Saimon was circling his mug with the tips of his fingers. "He's the one who was in charge—in Kladno."

Juri took a drink, then held the mug in front of his face.

"He's the one who took the women away... and the children. And he's just out there—walking around like nothing happened."

Juri tilted the mug and watched the light from the ceiling bulb play off the contrast between white foam and gold ale. "He's a high-ranking Schupo in Kladno. What do you expect us to do?" He looked up at Milan. "Storm into police headquarters and demand answers? Trail him home and interrogate him in his living room? Just how do you think we can accomplish that?"

"But he did this." Milan extended his twisted leg and pointed to his crooked nose.

Juri put the mug back on the table.

"How about the one called Weber?" Milan flashed his eyes at Saimon, seeking support. "He's not around anymore, or we haven't been able to spot him. Maybe he defected. He didn't seem like a Nazi. He helped that pregnant lady, the one who was married to the German. He might tell us where they took her ... and my mother. Or Gruber. He's still on duty—in Kladno."

"For god's sake, Juri." Saimon Dolak stopped Juri from lifting the mug. "Are you listening to him? We can find out what happened to the people in Lidice. Milan knows this Weber was involved. If you don't want to go after Kleinschmidt—too big a fish for us? We can try to find Weber. We can use the network to find him."

Juri sat back in his chair and wiped his mouth with the edge of a kitchen towel. He looked from Milan to Saimon. To Milan, he said, "I know how much this means to you." He rose from the table, stood at

Milan's side and touched his shoulder. "But the situation with the network is precarious. Spies have infiltrated some of our cells. Aside from the fact that I don't know who we can trust anymore, we can't afford to go out and start asking questions and raise suspicions. It's just too risky. We don't want to overplay our hand, not now, now that the Allies are on the move."

"Overplay our hand? We're not even in the game!" Saimon shoved the mug of beer across the table. "What are we waiting for? You think we're going to get help from the Allies? Why now? They haven't done all that much for us. Oh, yeah, we got a few transmitters—only to hear Beneš making speeches. It's all well and good for him and his cronies in exile to hate everything German, to talk about what we're going to do to the Germans *after* the war. He's more interested in making sure he's *in charge* after the war. But he doesn't know what's going on here and now. Allies—Beneš—be damned. "

"Saimon," Juri said as he pulled his hair over his scarred ear and cheek and let his fingers trace the raised red blotches on his skin. "You know about all the arrests. The Gestapo got five of Sigma's people over the last three weeks, and just yesterday it was their second in command. They're getting very close to us. We have to be careful. We can't afford any kind of activity that shines a light on us."

CHAPTER THIRTY

Milan had waited long enough. Since he had come to Prag and joined Juri Fischer and his group of Resistance fighters in the summer, he had been nursing his wounds. Now, with the first dusting of snow on the ground, he felt strong enough to be on his way. The bruising and swelling around his broken nose had disappeared. His cracked ribs had mended, at least partially. The injuries around his right knee had left him lame—his lower leg and foot turned inward—but he could walk, and he had steadily improved his gait and stamina by serving as courier, carrying memorized messages back and forth from Juri's network to the Sigma Group, whose headquarters were sometimes as far as 15 kilometers away.

He was anxious to find his mother. He needed to learn what had happened after he had been beaten and left unconscious, where the Schupo had taken the women and children, how he could begin his search. He had to go to Kladno and find answers.

"Ridiculous," Saimon Dolak insisted, watching Milan wrap cloth around his fingers to protect them from the cold. "You're going to Kladno, and get the Schupo to tell you their dirty little secrets? Get them to sit down and have a glass of beer with you and a chat? I'll bet you don't even know where to find any of them. Well—do you?"

Milan flexed his toes inside his high-top leather boots. Enough room to move even with the extra pair of socks. He shook out his overcoat, then pulled a knitted cap and scarf from one of its pockets. He draped the coat over his shoulders, slipped his arms inside the sleeves and picked up the heavy tree branch he used as a cane.

"It's suicide," Saimon spoke from the doorway. "You don't know how to get around. How to find out things. Who will lead you in the right direction? You'll start asking, and the Schupo will have you arrested before you finish the question."

No response.

"You'll be shot."

The Pear Tree

RESISTANCE

No response.

"Who will I get to carry Juri's messages to Sigma?" Saimon laughed.

No response.

Saimon blocked Milan's passage through the door. "This is not just about you," he said. "If something happens to the Schupo in Kladno, the Gestapo most likely will suspect the Resistance. Our network will be targeted, our men singled out and killed, our work..."

"If something happens, I will turn myself in. It will be on me, not you or the network or the Resistance."

"Juri won't let you jeopardize our operations."

Milan stood firm, his eyes challenging Saimon's. "Juri doesn't have to know that I'm going. Does he?"

Saimon nodded and sighed, grabbing his coat from the rack on the wall. "No, he doesn't." He shrugged on the jacket and opened the door. "We'll make sure, won't we?"

*

Anton Gruber waved a backhanded farewell to his Schupo colleagues who still had full glasses of beer sitting on the bar on front of them. He stumbled slightly as he pulled open the door of the Kneipe and stepped out into the snow. Leaning against the doorjamb, he fumbled in his pockets for his gloves, then cursed as they fell to the ground. He bent forward, his cap sliding onto the bridge of his nose, his coat flapping out behind him, and reached for the fingers of leather curling up toward him. Waving an arm to keep his balance, he snatched up the gloves, returned the cap to the top of his head and wrapped the coat around him. He held a hand in front of his eyes and thrust it into a glove, but the fingers didn't fit. He examined his half-gloved hand, turning it front to back. Then, frustrated with the entire exercise, he pulled the glove off, paired it with its partner, and shoved the bundle into a pocket.

He swayed as he moved down Polská Street, taking several steps to the side for every step forward. To mark his way home, he peered at address plates on the single family homes that housed the Schupo while they were on duty in Kladno. Most of the men, including himself, did not invite their wives and children to live in this god-forsaken town. Better that families stayed home in Sudetenland. Better for the men anyway, he chuckled.

Number 14, the last house on the block, was separated from the others by a garden—he loved to tend his roses—there was a garage for his automobile and a shed for his tools. He turned the knob, pushed open the door and slid over the threshold. Bumping the door closed with his ass, he spun himself around as he struggled to unbutton his coat. He muttered, "Thank you," when he felt someone steady his movements, slip the coat off his shoulders and sit him down on a kitchen chair.

"Who?" he asked, focusing his eyes in the gloom on the teenage boy who was sitting across from him.

"What?" he mumbled as thick strips of cloth were wrapped around his upper body and secured behind him, the same process repeated with his hands and feet.

"Look at me," Milan ordered Gruber.

Gruber squinted. "Am I supposed to know you?"

"The gymnasium in Kladno."

Gruber shrugged.

"After Lidice."

Gruber stared at Milan but said nothing.

"You have no regrets, no remorse for what happened?"

"Don't be silly. We took all the Aryans. Sent them where they belong—to Germans who can't have children of their own or who need women to bear children for the New Reich."

"The others?"

"What about them? What do you do with vermin? Kill them, ja?"

"You didn't kill me."

"I don't know who you are."

"I was there—in the gymnasium—with my mother. Marketa Tichy. She was pregnant."

"Was she that beautiful one? The one with the German husband who died on the Eastern Front?" Gruber closed his eyes and licked his lips.

Milan shook his head.

RESISTANCE

"Ah, too bad. She was exquisite. No, we sent her to the infirmary to have her baby. Oh, yes, we wanted that baby."

"What infirmary?"

"The one in the center of town near the hospital. But it isn't there now. Not enough Aryans around here anymore to keep it open." Gruber laughed.

"What happened to the other women, the pregnant women?"

"There weren't any other pregnant women."

"Yes! There were!" Milan came over to the other side of the table and grabbed Gruber's collar. "My mother was pregnant."

Gruber closed one eye and analyzed Milan with the other. "We wouldn't have wanted another child like you."

"What happened?" Milan slapped Gruber's face. "What happened to the women?"

"What I said before." Gruber smirked. "We killed them." He dared Milan with his eyes. "I was the one who drove them—in a gas van. We stopped next to an empty field and let the motor run. Know what happens in a gas van? The people inside feel the van stop. They think they're going to get out, to move and breathe fresh air. But then the gas pours in. And they start to scream and stamp and pound on the walls ..."

Milan covered his ears.

"And their heads pound. And their eyes bulge. And they puke their guts out. And the clouds of gas keep coming. And they cry and kick and ..."

"No. No. No! It did not happen. I don't believe you. You're lying!"

"Oh, poor, poor boy. Lost his mommy."

Saimon stepped up and elbowed Gruber's cheek, then swung his forearm across Gruber's nose.

Milan stood still, his head down, his fingers pressed to his ears, his shoulders shaking. Then he raised his head and stared in Gruber's face. "I see it," he said, smiling. "What you are doing. You sick bastard. Making all this stuff up, because you don't know what happened. You low-level asshole. You just want to make me scream and cry for my 'poor mommy.' Well, it's not going to happen."

He turned to face Saimon and smiling slightly said, "Go ahead."

RESISTANCE

Saimon stepped behind Gruber and tipped his chair backward until it crashed onto the floor. Taking a pillow from the bed, he covered Gruber's face, pressed down and held it in place until the man stopped struggling. He removed the cloth bindings and tossed them in the potbelly stove, then raised the chair and pushed it under the kitchen table. Saimon positioned Gruber's head on its side next to a bottle of schnapps and an ashtray. He lit a cigarette and left it on the edge of the ashtray, the burning tip next to a splash of liquor. He straightened up the rooms, replacing the pillow on the bed, hanging up Gruber's coat and hat, laying his gloves neatly on the bureau.

Saimon peeked out the front window to be sure no one was nearby, then opened the door and led Milan outside. "Behind the house," he directed him. He watched Milan round the corner of the house and move toward the back, then shut and locked the door from the inside. He waited until the cigarette ignited the liquor before he opened a back window, climbed outside and joined Milan.

"He lied," Milan said. "You saw that, didn't you?"

1945

REVERSAL

CHAPTER THIRTY-ONE

Saimon Dolak was camped at the edge of a clearing. It was almost the end of the third day of his watch. Each morning he had made his way to and from the safe house near Litoměřice, riding his bicycle as far as he could toward the second of the three paratroop drop areas he had scouted out in the woodlands in the midst of the rolling hills of northern Bohemia. Then he took off cross-country, wheeling the cycle between the trees until the going got too rough, then finally settling himself until nightfall.

At the landing site, he tied and untied the sacks he had brought with him, time after time checking the supplies: bandage rolls in case one of the paratroopers sustained injuries while landing; a couple of bottles of beer; a half-dozen wrapped sandwiches; his pistol. When he got hungry, he unwrapped the waxed paper around a sandwich and lifted up the edge of the bread. Usually finding only a few slices of cheese and cucumbers, or butter and jam, he refolded the paper and stuffed the sandwich back in the bag. Not that he could be choosy, but this was not to his taste. He would wait.

Saimon was both the most logical person for this assignment and the least suited for it. He was the best choice because he was a forest worker. He was familiar with the surroundings, and therefore could find drop zones that were well hidden and yet accessible. His forest-worker identity papers permitted him to come and go pretty much as he liked. He was, in fact, known by the local Gestapo, who waved or nodded as he rode his bicycle along the highway or over rough-cut paths, his tools clanking against the front wheel from inside a canvas tool bag.

But he was the worst choice because he was restless. He rushed headlong from one task to the next, took over projects when others weren't working fast enough, paced and interrupted when others took too long to get to the point. Waiting alone in the woods, unsure when the plane would be circling or where it would release its cargo, was torture.

The sky was bright with only a smattering of clouds. "Now would be a good time, wouldn't it?" he asked the squirrel eyeing him from a low-hanging branch.

Saimon was thankful that flights behind enemy lines had finally resumed. The Czech Government in Exile had stopped sending teams of paratroopers after Heydrich's assassination and the ferocity of the reprisals. In addition to the massacre at Lidice, the Gestapo had destroyed the village of Ležáky when agents found that its residents had hidden a radio transmitter. Gestapo had roamed from village to village, searching every house for contraband, weapons, incriminating documents. Its special Nachrichten Referate section accelerated its recruitment of informers and armed its own spies to infiltrate underground organizations. The result: more than 3,000 Czech citizens arrested; nearly 1,500 of them executed; and 4,000 of their relatives rounded up and deported to forced-labor camps. The effect on the rank-and-file Czech Resistance: hundreds of "V fighters" imprisoned and killed; and the rest in hiding, able to communicate only fitfully using dead boxes, such as an upside-down prayer book in the last pew of a church, or through designated couriers.

Quick and effective communication was now more important than ever. New Resistance fighter networks were popping up across the Occupied territory, eager to pave the way for the British and American forces advancing through France and the Soviets who were attacking German divisions in Belorussia. Saimon hoped the radio operators and transmitters that were on their way to his landing site would give Juri the kind of information he needed to get his Resistance unit on the move, the kind of information that would help the kid Milan find a way to get to Kleinschmidt, or even to find that missing Schupo, Weber.

Saimon tilted his head to the side, willing the plane to appear, while he chopped thick branches into kindling with his hatchet. He didn't know how much longer Milan would put up with his new assignment. The kid had already waited a long time.

*

According to leader of the Czech Resistance unit in Prag Juri Fischer, Milan was ideal as a street operative in the guise of a street sweeper. The uniform—a dark woolen jacket buttoned to the neck, baggy gray work trousers, polished shoes, a dark fisherman's cap—and the straw broom at his shoulder gave him the freedom to move around the city, track the movements of Protektorate officials, and examine their garbage with few people taking notice. The current target was a banker and his family.

A banker? Milan had scoffed when he first heard who he would be tailing. Why bother? Weren't there better things for the network to do, or better targets, like the SS, or officials at the Protektorate's headquarters on Hradćany Castle hill?

But, as Juri explained, the Nazis had been funneling Czech gold into their own coffers to pay for the war effort ever since the Munich Agreement allowed Germany to annex the Sudetenland. Fourteen tons of gold were sent to the Third Reich in 1938 to fund currency in the Sudetenland. The following year, a special commissioner for the Reichsbank forced the directors of the Czech central bank at gunpoint to sign letters transferring another 23 tons of gold to Germany. The Resistance suspected that bankers who had been relocated to the Czechoslovak Protektorate from the Sudetenland were continuing to loot. So, by eavesdropping on conversations among bank guards, Juri had told Milan, he might learn about the comings and goings of armored vehicles slated to carry away more Czech gold. By tailing a banker, he would have a finger on the pulse of standard banking operations. Any unusual activity could be an early warning sign that the Protektorate officials were planning to raid the bank and make a run for it. At least that's what Juri said.

Milan was still not convinced his surveillance was critical, but it had its advantages. Foremost among them, he was developing detective skills. From conversations with janitors at Česká Národní Banka, he learned that the new commissioner at the national bank, Otto Wolffe, had come to Prag at the end of 1942 with his mother and 11-year-old son. Before arriving in Czechoslovakia, Wolffe had managed the central bank in Aussig in the Sudetenland. He was 42 years old and had been married for many years, but his wife died soon after he relocated to Prag. Her body had been cremated and the urn with her ashes placed in a niche in the Columbarium at the eastern end of Vinohrady Cemetery. Wolffe and his family occupied a first-floor apartment on Slavík Street near Riegráče Park in Vinohrady, not far from the cemetery.

By shadowing the banker and his family, Milan had developed a sense of their personalities. Otto Wolffe was orderly and predictable. Most days the banker could be seen at the window of his first-floor apartment at 7 a.m., coffee cup in hand, looking down Chopinova Street toward the city center. Between 7:20 and 7:30 he left the building, walked to the tram stop at Kubánské Námesti and rode the trolley to the Námeští

Republiky. By 8 a.m. he was entering the bank building on Na Přikopě.

The banker was proper and formal, courtly even. He bowed his head slightly whenever he encountered one of the bank secretaries, came around to the front of his desk to adjust customers' chairs as they seated themselves, sat with his back straight and his chin tucked, his vest and suit coat buttoned as employees explained ledger entries.

He did not socialize much with his fellow bankers. While a small group of bank officials enjoyed long lunches of sausage and sauerkraut at Kolkovna Savrin, Wolffe typically dined alone, often at his desk. On the rare occasion when he did join his colleagues, he returned to the bank immediately after the restaurant bill had been paid. He left work in the late afternoon or early evening, declining to join coworkers for drinks at Marie Teresie except for special celebrations—birthdays, promotions, holiday parties. Wolffe most often rode the tram back to the stop at Kubáneské and was next to his apartment window with a thin aperitif glass on the table beside him, reading spectacles on the tip of his nose, the afternoon newspaper spread out before him 90 minutes later.

One peculiarity Milan had noticed: Wolffe appeared to be uncomfortable with Nazi formalities. On the rare occasions when he traveled by limousine, he did not display the swastika flag or offer the Heil Hitler salute. He seemed almost embarrassed by Nazi etiquette. He often waited in the doorway of his apartment building, watching for passers-by. When no one else was on the street, he walked quickly to the car, hunching his shoulders, and ducking and turning his head to the side, as if the Hitler salute from his driver was an assault.

Frau Wolffe, the man's mother, also eschewed special treatment. Although her son had access to full housekeeping services, the old woman took care of many of the household duties herself, especially the cooking and shopping. Milan could see her moving back and forth in front of the kitchen window at the back of the apartment, draining water from cooking pots, steam swirling and fogging up her glasses and moistening hair tendrils at her temples. He had followed her a few times on shopping trips in the neighborhood, noting how she made careful use of her ration cards. She was not content to grab just any item offered in the bushel baskets and wooden pushcarts. She took the time to test the ripeness of the fruits and vegetables, appraising the color of the strawberries, hefting and squeezing a peach, sniffing the center of a tomato. The woman was attentive to shopkeepers and neighbors, calling each by name and exchanging pleasantries, wishing them a "Guten Dag."

Wolffe's son Oskar was a puzzlement. He was respectful and cour-
teous, at least to his family. He made sure a wreath of fresh flowers was
placed on the marble marker in front of the niche that held his mother's
ashes every week. He was attentive to his grandmother, taking her elbow
as she stepped down from the curb and in awe of his father. He hurried to
keep up with him, trotting along next to him, talking rapidly, grabbing his
father's arm to emphasize the points he was making and literally melting
into his father's side when the man pulled him close in an embrace. He
yearned for his father's approval and deflated into himself whenever his
father reprimanded or lectured him.

But he was also aggressive and cold to strangers, and unlike his
father, he embraced Nazi ceremony. Although there were no formal
Hitler Youth groups or activities in the area, it was not unusual for him
to wear the uniform as he strode down Chopinova Street to the shopping
district. He walked closely behind young boys or girls, intruding into
their conversations, or stepping on their heels to attract their attention.
He spoke loudly and harshly as he twirled the edges of his neck scarf and
fingered the buttons on his shirt to show off the characteristic Youth
Corps emblems. When he spoke, he pushed his body forward until he
hovered over the heads of the smaller children, or stood only inches away
from the older children, punctuating his remarks by wagging a finger or
grabbing and twisting a boy's collar or a girl's curls.

On more than one occasion, Milan had seen outright cruelty. One
time, Oskar was sitting at a table in the outdoor eating area of Riegráče
Park, listening to a group of boys seated across the aisle. When one of the
boys' friends approached, balancing a tray of food in his hands, Oskar
turned his head away while simultaneously extending a foot in front of
the boy. Ducking his head to smother his smile, he feigned surprise when
the boy tripped and fell to the ground.

Milan wondered at his own reaction to the boy. Rather than
dismissing him as just another young Nazi thug, Milan felt sorry for
Oskar. The boy seemed so conflicted, so unsure of himself, so familiar.
He thought he might know the boy, might have seen him somewhere
before, or perhaps saw something of himself in Oskar. He wondered if
Oskar was just yearning for acceptance, or if the boy was compensating
for something, pretending to be someone he wasn't.

Chapter Thirty-Two

Pop. Pop. Gunfire. Near the drop zone.

Saimon stopped wheeling his bicycle between the trees and stood still, orienting himself to the sounds and the direction they had come from. He could hear gruff, low-register German consonants, but he could not make out the words. A word of two of Czech, in pained, pleading tones.

He took a few more steps into the forest. Clear Czech shouts: "No." "Stop." The click of a cigarette lighter. The scent of lighter fluid. The fusty smell of soiled, heavy clothing slowly catching fire.

Now, not fully intelligible screams. The smoky scent of cooking meat.

Saimon slipped behind a stand of linden trees, eased his pistol out of his belt and peeked around the flaking bark of one of the trees.

Two Gestapo were sharing a cigarette while a Czech partisan's body, his paratrooper gear still on his back, hung from a branch by a rope wound around his chest. His hands were bound behind his back; his legs were engulfed in flames, kicking wildly.

Saimon rested his pistol hand against the side of the tree and trained his eye on the Germans, who were sitting on the ground, their rifles beside them, helmets pushed back on their necks. As one raised his head to look at the sky, letting the cigarette smoke curl out of his mouth, Saimon fired, hitting the man in the throat. As the other reached for his weapon, Saimon fired a second, then a third shot into the man's upper back.

Approaching carefully, his pistol held in both hands in front of his eyes, Saimon looked for signs of life. The first Gestapo lay bleeding heavily and gurgling from the wound in his neck. His eyelids fluttered, his breath choked, his body stilled. The second Gestapo quivered, his fingers crawling along the dirt toward his weapon. Saimon placed the pistol at the back of the man's head and squeezed the trigger.

He pulled the uniforms off the Gestapo and wrapped them around

REVERSAL

his hands and arms. He grasped the Czech paratrooper's legs and lower body and smothered the flames. He rolled the bodies of the Gestapo near the tree and piled one atop the other, then climbed on them so he could reach the rope that suspended the paratrooper, then cut the rope and tumbled to the ground, the paratrooper in his arms.

Saimon lay the man on his back, untied the ropes, and checked for a pulse at the side of his neck. He could feel the man's heart fluttering, hesitating but still beating. He unfolded the clothing from the man's lower body. Skin had been charred away. Muscle, tendon and fat had melted into one another. Bone was visible.

Saimon placed his fingers on his lips and then on the man's forehead. He rose quietly, pulled his weapon from his belt and shot the man in the temple.

*

Milan turned the corner on to Poříčí Street and dropped his broom to the ground, brushing dust and dirt from the base of the buildings across the cobblestones and off the curb.

Despite the crowds of commuters and shoppers, the only person to notice him on this section of Poříčí Street was the doorman at the entrance to the Imperial Hotel and Café. From his post just inside the polished, wood-framed glass double-doors, he shooed Milan away. "Off with you," the doorman said imperiously, appropriately enough. "We have our own people for this," including himself apparently, as he unfurled a handkerchief and rubbed the edge of the tall metal planter next to the door until it sparkled.

Milan kept his distance while he swept his way past the doorway and down the block until he could take a position next to the full-length windows fronting the café. He paused to tug on the back of his jacket and, partially hidden by the half-open, sheer curtains, scanned the interior of the room to locate the Wolffes. The family was sitting at a table in front of a carved wooden column. Their dinner plates were being cleared and dessert menus were propped in their hands. Milan busied himself making small, determined strokes with his broom, until he found a safe spot from which to observe.

The family's visit to the Imperial Café had become routine. Every Saturday afternoon, Wolffe walked from the Česká Národní Banka past

Powder Tower, the remnant of Prag's medieval history, to the restaurant near Zlatnicka Street. His mother and son Oskar took the tram from home to the shopping area near Náměští Republiky and, parcels in hand, met him for an early dinner.

To counteract the monotony of surveillance, Milan relied on the exercises he had invented to focus his mind on the details he was observing. Glancing up from his broom, he noted the line of office workers waiting for the tram in the street outside the cafe. A short man in a drab suit, broken threads from the cuffs testifying to its age, tucked a copy of *Der neue Tag*, the official newspaper of the Protektorate, under his arm. The woman next to him wore a dark green striped dress, black thick-heeled shoes and hose, the seams running up the backs of her legs slightly askew. An old woman hunched her shoulders and cradled her pocketbook in both arms as if in fear of thieves.

A crash of crockery and shouts from inside the café drew Milan's attention. Oskar Wolffe stood at the table, his chair knocked back on the floor behind him, his hand grasping the waiter's arm and pointing to an overturned plate of pudding, streaks of tapioca spilling down the side of the starched white tablecloth. Shouting, his face red, Oskar pulled on the waiter's arm and held it over the table. He picked up the cup of hot coffee that had been freshly poured for his grandmother and dumped it on the man's hand, refusing to release his grip until his father pulled him away.

While Wolffe escorted the waiter to the back of the restaurant, the boy dabbed at blobs of yellow pudding on the front of his trousers. Milan looked from the boy's hands to his head and shoulders, noting his thick blond hair and square jaw, and then the yellow stain, and he remembered: Piss Pants.

Chapter Thirty-Three

Administrative head of the Czechoslovak Protektorate, Karl Hermann Frank, rested on the wrought-iron bench at the edge of the garden behind Černiský Palác and let the late April sun warm him. He faced the southern portion of the building, his back to the shallow pool and Kaňka Pavilion, which formed the western edge of Hradčany, the hilltop castle district overlooking Prag from the north and west sides of the Vltava River. He let his eyes trace the façade of the massive structure—150 meters across—and marveled.

Denigrated as nothing more than a barn without a barn door by Emperor Leopold I in the late 1600s, the palace had an unimpressive early history: It once housed a military hospital and apothecary; then an art museum and gallery; and at one time a silk factory. But it had been impressively rehabilitated, in Frank's opinion, as the Czech government's Ministry of Foreign Affairs in the 1920s. To his mind, the blemishes of wartime that were added after the building became the headquarters for the Nazi Occupation in 1938—the bomb shelters, the concrete frames along the roof, the reinforced barriers around the ground floor—did not diminish its dominance and power.

Frank picked up the dispatches he had received over the last few days. The first informed him that Soviet forces were encircling Berlin, but Wehrmacht Field Marshall Felix Steiner was unable to mount a defense, because he had no divisions or combat weapons. The next reported that Nürnburg, the seat of Nazi pomp and circumstance, had fallen to the U.S. Army after a five-day siege. The war on both fronts was going to hell.

Frank left his seat and entered the main archway leading to the palace courtyard. He followed the cobblestone pathway around the central grassy area bordered by eight newly flowering trees and entered Staircase Hall. Turning to his left, he ascended the first flight of gray marble stairs, his hand tracing the creamy gold-marble handrail. At the bottom of the central staircase leading to the offices and living quarters on the next level, he looked up at the ceiling. Sunlight from the eight recessed windows at the top of the octagonal space winked off the dramatic Clash of the Titans fresco depicting the victory of the Olympian rulers over the Giants. Gods versus Goliaths. Select Brethren versus Subhumans. Purity versus Degeneration. Myths. Fantasies. Fairy Tales. A pretty picture, but the opposite of what was happening here—now —in this place.

He checked his wristwatch. The delegation he had assembled would be arriving soon. Could this group of Czechs and Germans—a pair of industrialists, a politician, a retired general, a law professor and himself—negotiate with the Allies for a separate peace to guarantee the safe passage of Germans out of Prag, and to slow the Soviet advance? The ReichsKommisar of Holland was planning to negotiate a cease-fire with the Americans in exchange for the importation of coal and food for Dutch civilians. Could he do something similar—for himself and the German citizens of Prag? Could he negotiate a separate peace and deal with the forces of chaos, the mongrels who had found a way to topple the gods?

*

Klaudie slipped the Book of Births off its perch atop a filing cabinet in the Ravensbrück camp's central office and flipped through the pages until she found the most recent entry. As she had done during other quiet times, when the SS guards and overseers left the inmate office workers to their bookkeeping while they occupied themselves with cards or drinking games, Klaudie pored over the details in the registry that listed the name of each infant born in the camp and the date and time of its birth, as well as the mother's name, her camp ID number and classification. She couldn't help herself—the entries, the numbers, just didn't make sense.

According to the Book of Births, 150 infants had been born in the last two and a half months. But according to her own loose tally, Klaudie believed there were many more births, births to anti-Nazi politicals or asocials, that weren't recorded. Like Eduard, the boy who had been born just yesterday to Jarmila. Neither his name nor his mother's was in the book. On occasion, she had found that some babies were mistakenly listed as "stillborn." Helena, for example, was reported as dead, even though the prison midwife had told Klaudie how beautiful and healthy the infant was when she was born a week ago. Also suspicious were the slips of paper Klaudie had found crumpled and discarded in the office trashcan, with the same scribbled notation next to an infant's name—"Lebensborn"—the place where SS prostitutes were sent. A note this morning juxtaposed "Lebensborn" and two infants' names, but no details about either birth had been entered on the most recent page of the Book of Births.

After replacing the book, Klaudie opened the file cabinet and looked again for the Lebensborn file. She slipped her fingers in between the sheets and spread them apart, moving quickly past papers she had seen before—the completed, date-stamped and "approved" forms for prostitutes who had been transferred from Ravensbrück to one of the Lebensborn facilities early in their pregnancies. She paused when she found another birth-book registry with columns listing the date and time of an infant's birth, the name of the infant and its mother, a physical description of the mother and her baby, the nationalities of both parents, the place of birth and the place to which the child was taken: a "Lebensborn home."

A waft of warm breath, tainted by liquor, touched the side of her face. A hand stroked her breast.

"So, Klaudie," Konrad Dreschler said, turning his face away from her as he lifted a bottle of schnapps to his lips. "Will you come with me? When I go to the West? When I go to the Americans?"

Klaudie pulled her fingers from the papers and nudged the file drawer closed with her hip.

"You know that it's all over, don't you?" Dreschler stood unsteadily next to the file cabinet. "The Soviets are in full control along the Oder River, the Wehrmacht demolished. And the Americans are near Magdeburg—only 180 kilometers from here. It won't be long before the Allies are on our doorstep." He wiped his mouth with a knuckle.

"Better for us," he said, tapping the SS emblem on his collar with the top of the bottle, "to get as far as we can from the Soviets." He extended the bottle toward Klaudie and raised his eyebrows, inviting her to take a drink. He shrugged when she shook her head and returned the lip of the bottle to his mouth. "Better to go to the Americans."

He turned his attention toward her: "Better for you, too." He brushed his lips against her hair. "The Soviets are madmen, raping young women and old ones, children, pregnant women. They don't care who they rape or how often. Women are only cunts to them."

He pushed the bottle against Klaudie's chest. "So it would be good for you to come with me to the Americans. The Americans won't rape you. At least I don't think they would. And maybe they would let me live—the Americans—if they saw that I was with you, that I took care of you. Maybe I could be your husband, eh?"

"Dreschler," Ravensbrück Kommandant Fritz Suhren called out from the doorway. "Get yourself together." Suhren walked quickly to Dreschler, pulled the liquor bottle out of his hand and slapped him across the face.

"The buses are coming," Suhren told him. "The Red Cross. We need to at least look like we're in control here."

Suhren glanced quickly around the office and motioned to one of the female overseers. "Get him some coffee," he said, pushing Dreschler toward her, ordering her. "Then go start finding the women, the Danes and the Norwegians. We promised those pompous asses from Sweden and the International Red Cross he could take the Scandinavians. And we don't have much time. They will be here early in the morning."

"Dreschler," Suhren called out to the SS officer's departing back. "Once you can see straight again, get to work on these files." Suhren slapped the file cabinet. "Get rid of them in the crematorium." He watched Dreschler lurch toward the back of the office area. "Dreschler?"

Dreschler nodded his response.

*

The plane that would carry Frank's delegation to the American lines revved its propellers, forcing Richard Bienert, leader of the Occupied Czechoslovak Government and his Minister of Agriculture, Adolf Hrubý, to hastily grab hold of their hats as they approached the aircraft. The last to board, Bienert and Hrubý squeezed past retired General Vladimír Klecanda, the former Czech military attaché in Switzerland, Austrian law Professor Hermann Raschhofer and the businessmen. The hatch secured, the plane rolled down the runway.

*

Dreschler saw Klaudie watching him pull handfuls of files out of the cabinet drawer and, without opening them, toss them in the trash-can. "You are interested in these, ja?" He raised a pair of files thick with sheets of different colored paper, then dropped them with a crash. "I see you looking in here." He flicked his fingers over the file-folder tabs. "This one?" he extended the Lebensborn file toward her, then pulled it back quickly. He opened the folder and licked his index finger as he turned page after page. "This one." He lifted a page in the air. "Ja, you would like to know about this one." He put it back in the folder. "This one, too." He placed his finger on top of the page.

He closed the file. "See what I am doing here?" Dreschler slipped the file into a worn leather briefcase resting against his calf. "I am going to take this with me ... when I go on the Red Cross buses." He leaned back in his chair. "This and ..." He tilted the briefcase toward her, revealing jumbles of gold—earrings, necklaces and wristwatches.

"Yes, I am going with the Scandinavians." He tipped the bill of his cap up on his forehead. "The deal, the one Himmler made with the Red Cross, the one that is getting the women out of here, requires SS to be on every rescue bus. So when the buses leave tomorrow morning, I am going with them."

Dreschler turned back to the task of gathering up camp records and dumping them in the trashcan. Without looking directly at Klaudie, he asked: "You want to come, too?"

Chapter Thirty-Four

At 1:30 a.m., a freshly painted white bus with large red crosses painted on its top and sides, drove slowly onto the grounds of the Ravensbrück work camp. *"Achtung! Achtung!"* came Kommandant Suhren's voice over the loudspeaker. *"Alle skandinavische Fangen vortreten."*

Danish and Norwegian women hurried to their barracks and picked up their few remaining belongings, as well as the civilian clothes that had been doled out from the camp's clothing department. The women assembled in the bathhouse, washed and dressed, then lined up as their names were called and crossed off a master passenger list by one of the overseers.

*

Klaudie pulled the edges of a scarf down over her forehead and cheeks and tightened the knot under her chin. She stood behind a pair of Danish women, keeping herself hidden from the overseer she had worked alongside in the camp office for the last three years and waited to hear the name Dreschler said he would add to the list.

"Hagen." Klaudie held back in case there actually was a woman named Hagen in camp.

"Hagen?" the overseer repeated, ready to place an "X" next to the entry.

Klaudie stepped into line and held her breath, afraid the overseer would recognize her. But the overseer was focused on the next name on the list: "Hansen."

Klaudie accepted the hand of a Swede clad in a gray Red Cross uniform, noticing a kindness she had not felt in many years, then climbed into the white bus and took a seat at the back as Dreschler had advised. She watched the bus fill with women, wary that at any time the bill of an SS cap would appear at the entry, a pair of eyes would search the passengers' faces and land on her, and a clipped voice would order her to disembark.

But the bus filled without incident, a motorcycle dispatch driver approached and spoke with the driver, the motor rumbled and the bus trembled.

The rear door squeaked open and Dreschler boarded. Slamming the door shut, he shouted, "Ready," to the driver and took a seat across the aisle from Klaudie, placing the briefcase on his lap.

He took hold of Klaudie's arm and squeezed it before waving a salute out the window.

The bus rumbled along on roads rutted from the passage of lorries to and from the Eastern Front, new roads that had been hastily built alongside those that had been torn apart by bombs dropped from Soviet planes. It passed narrow trails recently pounded into the earth by the footfalls of refugees and Wehrmacht soldiers escaping to the West, rolling hills gouged by firebombs, trees scarred by strafing.

The bus pulled over to the side of the road and shuddered to a stop next to an open field where the passengers could relieve themselves.

The women relished the smells as well as the tastes of the sprouting herbs, picking and digging up plants, savoring the sweetness of dandelion leaves and the texture of wild root vegetables. They enjoyed lying flat or rolling on the ground, gazing at the sky, thin with clouds, reluctant to return to the stale confines of the bus.

Klaudie strolled through the underbrush, kicking at the tangles. Her foot butted against something hard—a rock with a rough, serrated edge on one side. She pushed the rock deep into her pocket underneath handfuls of dandelions she had just picked.

*

The members of Frank's delegation huddled outside the headquarters of Field Marshall Albert Kesselring in Neubiberg, Bavaria.

"I say we just go back to Prag," Bienert said. "If Kesselring isn't sure where the front line is, how can we even begin to find the Americans?"

"We can't go back with nothing. Why don't we go to the SS headquarters in Bad Tölz and try to negotiate an exchange of prisoners?" Hrubý suggested.

"I could try to get in touch with the archbishop of Milan and petition for a papal intercession to cross over to Switzerland," General Klecanda offered.

Bienert rubbed his chin, frowning. "All right. We will split up and see what else we may do."

*

Still drowsy, Klaudie opened her eyes and glanced out of the bus window. More than 24 hours after leaving Ravensbrück, the bus was nearing the border of Denmark, a neutral country untouched by the war.

She rubbed the sleep from her eyes with the heels of her hands, then looked up and down the rows of seats. Women were waking, stretching cramped muscles, smoothing wrinkles from their blouses and skirts. Across the aisle, Dreschler, now clad in a faded blue work shirt and brown pants, was sitting sideways with his back toward her. Wearing scuffed, unlaced brown shoes, he shoved his jackboots under the seat in front of him. On top of the boots, he placed the neatly folded trousers and jacket of his SS uniform. The billed cap sat on top of the pile.

Dreschler sat back and watched carefully as the bus passed a sign indicating that Flensburg was a few kilometers away. Peering down the center aisle of the bus, he assessed the road ahead. He was looking for signs of Glücksburg Castle, the Renaissance fortress on Flensburg Fjord, a landmark near the dividing line between Germany's Schleswig-Holstein area and Denmark's Syddanmark region.

He turned toward Klaudie, surprised she had been watching him. "Liebchen? You are awake. Good." He pulled her close. "We will leave soon. Once we pass that—," he indicated the black-tiled peaks on the castle's four towers, "—and the bus slows down, we will jump out of the back." He loosened the latch on the back door, checked the buckles on the front of the briefcase to be sure they were fastened and monitored the vehicle's progress.

*

"So the mission was a total failure," Frank queried General Klecanda, who sat on the maroon-and-cream patterned settee in the Czernin Palace's living quarters, massaging his stocking feet. He had walked and hitchhiked back to Prag from northern Italy.

"You and Raschhofer couldn't even get closer to the archbishop?" Frank asked. Klecanda shook his head, then added with disgust in his voice, "And then Raschhofer ran off to hide with his parents in Salzburg." Frank paused.

"Bienert came back to Prag the day after you and Raschhofer left for Italy. Hrubý went into hiding himself in Bohemia a day later, once he learned there weren't any prisoners to exchange for at Bad Tölz."

"What are you going to do?" Klecanda asked. "I heard that the Soviets are in full assault on the Berlin Reichstag. Their rocket launchers have all but demolished the railroad station in Potsdam. In a matter of days, Italy will most likely surrender."

Frank turned his back on Klecanda, pulled back the navy-blue textured drape and stared out the window, crushing the heavy fabric in his fist.

"What of Hitler?" Klecanda asked when Frank did not respond.

Frank scoffed. "He's accused Göring of high treason for taking over leadership of the war effort, even though he's hunkered down in his bunker below the Reich's Chancellery. He's arrested Himmler for trying to surrender to Eisenhower. He barks out orders for non-existent armies to come to his aid." He paused and thought: What of him?

*

Klaudie cringed. Dreschler was pounding into her, his head raised, his chin back, his hips thrusting—hard. She closed her eyes and waited for his collapse.

At last, he pulled out of her and rolled away. He lay back on the straw and sighed.

Klaudie rolled on her side and waited until she could hear his slow, deep breathing and was sure he was asleep. Then she rose, reached into her pocket and pulled out the stone she had saved for just such a moment. She walked to the other side of the mattress, raised the stone in her hand and brought it down on his nose and his eyes and his mouth and his forehead. Again. Again. Again. Again.

She dropped the stone on the bed, found his discarded shirt on the floor and wiped the blood from her hands, her face and her body. She pulled on her clothing, sat on the edge of the bed and hung her head. She rose and took a step toward the door, cursing as she stumbled over the bedding. Pulling it away, she saw something lying under the bed. There on the floor, with only a corner showing—the briefcase.

CHAPTER THIRTY-FIVE

Silvie lay curled on the mattress, her forehead beaded in sweat, her body shaking with chills. Although her breathing came in fits and starts, she was afraid to try to fill her lungs with air. She kept her breath shallow to avoid the coughing that caused such sharp pain in the right side of her chest. She shuddered, unable to stop a cough from rising up her air passages and covered her mouth with her hand. She pressed down hard on her mouth but could not keep the bloody mucus from escaping, dripping past her fingers onto her tunic, the ticking and the patches of straw that protruded from tears in the mattress.

A camp overseer nudged her foot. "You. Come with me," she said. "The Kommandant wants to see you—you and all the other 'rabbits.'"

The overseer took a step back and put her arms behind her back. "Now," she insisted, raising her voice.

Silvie drew her knees up to the deep hollow of her abdomen, then pressed her upper body onto her legs. Using her bloody hand as leverage, she pushed herself up on a hip, inched her legs to the edge and over the side of the bunk and placed her feet on the floor. She held on to the wooden frame as another cough erupted.

Unwilling to wait any longer, the overseer took hold of Silvie's arm and pulled her upright. Silvie staggered, her hand covering the hard, painful spot in her chest.

*

"Here's the last one," the overseer told Kommandant Suhren, who was seated behind a trestle table in one of the camp headquarters' common rooms. Next to him was a bloated, ruddy-faced man wearing a green leather jacket. A peasant's hat rested on the table in front of him.

The overseer pushed Silvie's shoulder until she was standing next to a pair of Polish women who also bore scars on their legs: Jadwiga had long, wide, darkened areas on her outer calf forming two uneven horizontal streaks that followed the lines of the muscles, as well as a vertical triangle across the front of her ankle; Zofia had an indentation on the side of her leg that began just under the knee and ran parallel to the bone.

"These," Suhren told the man, pointing to the women's legs, "aren't so bad. Others are in far worse shape."

The other man remained silent, his penetrating eyes focused solely on the deformities, while Suhren nodded a dismissal to the overseer.

As she exited the room, Silvie heard the man warn Suhren: "You must not do anything to these women until you get a decision from the high command. Others who have already been released, have provided evidence of these experiments. The war is nearly over. If something happens to these women now...."

*

"They wouldn't dare kill us," Jadwiga insisted to Zofia and Silvie as they walked from the Kommandant's headquarters down Lagerstrasse toward their barracks. "That man, the one with Suhren. You heard him. He knows that if they shoot us now, they will be admitting to the Allies that they were doing experiments and are trying to cover them up. We don't have to worry about anything."

"What does it matter?" Silvie asked. "We'll probably be dead from the TB or the typhoid before the Allies get here anyway. Maybe it would be better to be shot today ... to get it over with." Silvie bent over, her body shaking with convulsive coughs.

"But the buses," Zofia offered, her voice hopeful. "You heard the Red Cross buses are coming."

"Who knows if those are really Red Cross? Who knows where those buses are going? They could end up in some field where they will shoot us and dump us in a hole or leave us on the road waiting for a gas van," Silvie responded.

"Did you hear?" a woman called out excitedly as she ran past the three "rabbits" toward the camp's front gates. "Ambulances ... " the woman pointed. "Red Cross ambulances..." she paused, "at the gates. More than ten of them!"

REVERSAL

Silvie didn't even turn her head to see what the woman was pointing at. She kept on her way, her head down, her arms holding on to her ribs, separating herself from Jadwiga and Zofia.

"Aren't you going?" Jadwiga called after her. "To line up for the ambulances? You're so sick, I'm sure they will take the sick first."

Ignoring Jadwiga, Silvie kept walking to her barracks, away from the inmates rushing toward the front gates and crowding next to the brick walls of the guard station.

*

She entered the barracks and tried to sidestep the furniture, but bumped into the corner of the common table and tripped over the leg of a stool. She reached out but found nothing to break her fall. Her shoulder butted into the frame of one of the bunks, her legs gave way and she landed on her knees. Heaving with deep but unsatisfying breaths, she collapsed onto her hip and sat, her hand pressing down with every rise of her chest.

"Here, let me help you." Silvie shrugged off the hand on her arm and shook her head.

"Come on, Silvie," Chessie said, finding Silvie's armpits and pulling her up. "Don't be such a pain in the ass."

"A pain in the ass?" Silvie smiled between hurried breaths. "So I am a pain ...?"

"You bet," Chessie confirmed. "Now come on." She led Silvie to her bunk and eased her down on the mattress, then pulled out a stool and sat down next to her.

"There are ambulances here, you know," she told Silvie. "Our overseer was just here, looking for the sick. She said the ambulances were going to take more than 100 women to Denmark and Sweden. You should get yourself together and go over to the offices where they are lining up."

Silvie shook her head. "You remember the last time they said they were going to take the sick? They let those women stand in the rain all night and then just led them back to the barracks the next day. And those were the Europeans. What do you think they're going to do for us? The

Slavs? And worse yet, the women of Lidice?"

"These are Red Cross ambulances, with Swedes driving them."

"So?"

"At least it's a chance—a chance to get out of here—a chance to get some medicine."

"It's too late."

"No, it's not. As long as you're still breathing."

Silvie coughed out a harsh laugh. "You call this ... "

"OK, you're really sick, but maybe they can do something for you."

"You don't even believe it. I can hear it in your voice."

"You can't give up, Silvie. You can't let them win ... those bastards. Come," Chessie said, reaching out a hand. "I will help you. You ... and me ... we'll show those sons of bitches."

Silvie stretched out on top of the mattress. "No," she said, folding her arms over her chest. "No, I am too weak." She closed her eyes. "Too tired."

She felt Chessie's hand on top of hers. She looked from Chessie's ripped and scarred fingernails to her eyes. "Why are you doing this? Why are you ... with me ... when I have ... Why are you trying to help me?

"I didn't help others ... when they needed it," Chessie said. She thought of Katrenka and her own son in the Kladno gymnasium. "I'm not going to let that happen again."

"I can barely breathe." Silvie's chest heaved with the exertion. "Leave me. Let me die ... "

"No," Chessie replied softly. "Too many people have died ... with no one to attend to their passing. If I can't help you live, I will be here while you die."

Silvie turned on her side, holding Chessie's hand in between hers.

"Not so many people have died as you think," Silvie said to herself, wheezing between the words.

*

REVERSAL

No discipline, Ravensbrück Kommandant Fritz Suhren lamented as he surveyed the work camp. Homes once lively with SS officers' wives and children were melancholy shells, occupied by men who spent their time taking idle potshots at the rats scurrying along the foundations of the buildings. Storage facilities were barren, raided by men who wrestled with one another over the smallest valuables or the civilian clothes that would help them establish new identities after the war. The camp's grounds were littered with debris, men too listless, morose, or drunk to perform standard maintenance, too weary to maintain even a semblance of order. This was not the SS way.

Suhren kicked up curls of dirt as he rounded the officers' canteen on the way to his headquarters, intensifying the force of each step as he pondered his dilemma. Instructions from the Führer made it clear that, at all costs, Suhren had to prevent the prisoners from falling into enemy hands. But he had no specific orders about mass evacuations or executions and no way of getting orders, since radio links to his superiors and the high command had broken down. So it was up to him: Should he evacuate all the inmates who were able to walk? If so, when? Should he kill the sick and the lame? If so, how could he get rid of the physical evidence when the crematorium was belching out flames continuously and still had cartons of documents to torch?

A decision had to be made soon, before the Soviets overran the camp. The Red Army front lines were only about 50 kilometers away, as evidenced by the bursts of artillery fire and rising clouds of smoke in and around the city of Prenzlau, and the relentless lines of refugees who were lugging sacks of belongings on their backs, dragging carts that sandwiched the elderly and frail in between pieces of furniture, tugging on the leads of scrawny pigs and cows.

Suhren entered the Appellplatz, sidestepping piles of vomit left by inmates who had broken into the kitchens and stuffed themselves with food their shrunken stomachs could not process—milk, cheese, sausages. He grabbed a shovel that had been abandoned by a work crew, tossed it to an overseer and pointed at the mess.

Inside camp headquarters, he stood in front of his desk, its drawers pulled out and emptied, only a smattering of papers on top. There would be no more Swedish White Buses or Red Cross ambulances, he realized. They had come and gone, removing most of the European women. It was time to take care of the rest.

*

Chessie eased Silvie's head to the side and wiped the sweat from her forehead. Her eye sockets were darkened and hollowed, her cheeks red, her eyes glistening with fever. Her body shuddered with each breath. She mumbled. Chessie leaned closer.

"What I said before ..." Silvie sputtered through bubbles of blood and mucous. "What I said about Katrenka's baby ... She ..." Silvie sighed. "The baby ... she ... didn't ..." Silvie wet her lips. "The baby ... didn't ... die."

"I have it!" Silvie exclaimed to the matron who headed the birthing ward in the Kladno infirmary. Silvie eased the baby's head and shoulders out of the birth canal, cradling them in her palms. Once the legs were free, Silvie pinched off the placenta, then held the baby upside down and slapped her back. The newborn responded loudly—her mouth wide, her eyes shut, her face red.

Chessie tightened her grip on Silvie's arm.

"The Schupo," Silvie continued. "They took her ... the baby ... away from me."

Silvie wiped the baby's face and body with the corner of a towel, then wrapped the towel around her. Refusing to hand the baby over to the matron, Silvie carried the bundle into the hallway outside the ward. The matron followed, reaching for the infant.

"No." Silvie held on to the girl. "No, you can't take her."

"Sergeant," the matron shouted. "Come. Hurry. The baby. It is here."

Schupo Sergeant Albert Kleinschmidt stepped into the hallway. "The Lidice baby?"

The matron dipped her head.

As he approached Silvie, he opened his arms to accept the infant, but Silvie held the baby closer.

"Weber," Kleinschmidt called out.

Motioning for Weber to stand next to her, Kleinschmidt moved directly behind Silvie. He placed his hands on her shoulders and pushed down until she loosened her grip enough for Weber to take the newborn and hand her to the matron.

Silvie watched Weber and the matron depart with Katrenka's baby, noticing for the first time that a pair of SS guards was coming toward her. She turned toward Kleinschmidt. "But I thought—if I helped her—if I helped you with her—if I took care of the birth for you ..."

"What happened to the baby? Where is she? Where did they take her?"

"I don't know. They ... the SS ... took me ... to Sachsenhausen ... right away."

Chessie covered her face and rubbed her eyes. "How could you lie to me about this?" Tears welled in her eyes, spilled down her cheeks and fell in streaks down the front of her uniform. She released her grip and let her hands fall into her lap. She pulled the kerchief roughly from her head, grasped it tightly between her fingers and began twisting it, the tendons in her hands and arms bulging. Her head down, her body shaking, her breaths short and rapid—for the first time since she had been taken from Lidice, Chessie wept.

*

"Get moving," the barracks overseer shouted from the doorway. "We're leaving. Right now." The overseer walked briskly past the common table, kicking the outstretched legs of women in their bunks. At the edge of Silvie's bunk, she paused, leaned over and peered into Silvie's face.

"This one's dead," she shouted to her fellow overseer. "One less to worry about."

CHAPTER THIRTY-SIX

Juri Fischer stood against the wall of the abandoned brick factory that the Czech partisans had been using as a base since their hideout on the outskirts of Prag had been discovered and their mole in the Protektorate police had been arrested. Juri and his group had been relocating their radio transmitter every two days as the SS intensified purges of the police, firemen, railway and munitions workers sympathetic to the exiled Czech government in Britain and the Allies. The end of the war was near, the partisans were sure of it.

Juri folded his arms across his chest, trying to keep calm as he watched his radioman Valentin brush a strand of hair from his eyes, lick the tip of a pencil and scan the jumble of letters and symbols in the latest message from Czech underground headquarters.

"What's this?" Saimon Dolak hovered over Valentin's shoulder and tapped his finger on the hurriedly scrawled markings. "That means Hitler, doesn't it?"

"The codes change all the time," Valentin said, sighing in exasperation.

"Stop making Valentin so nervous," Juri said, gently drawing Saimon aside.

"But it's so close." Saimon rapped his knuckles on the wall. "Can't you feel it?" He turned to Juri. "Hear it? The bombing? The Allies are close."

"Yes," Juri agreed.

"But who? Is it the Americans? The Soviets? And where are they? How much longer do we have to wait?" Saimon returned to the table where Valentin was working. "Why do you take so long? Can't you do it any faster?" he demanded.

Valentin pushed his chair back from the table. "You're so smart? You tell me." He held the paper out to Saimon. "Tell me what you think it says."

"Just do it," Juri admonished Valentin, pulling Saimon away. His arm around Saimon's shoulders, he asked: "Are you ready? Are your people ready to get the weapons out of their dug-outs? Do they know where they are supposed to go? What they are supposed to target?"

"Yes, yes, yes. Of course." Saimon turned his back on Juri.

Juri called out to Milan: "What about you?"

"Ready," Milan replied, searching his pockets for the scraps of paper with his notes about the movements of his German banker

"What's the situation with your family?" Juri asked.

"There has been a lot of activity—at the house," Milan said, unfolding the paper scraps. They—the old woman and the boy—are doing their own cleaning. I can see them through the windows, cleaning out cabinets, wrapping things up in newspapers. They are bringing in boxes and travel cases. Five of them," he said, referring to his notes, "in the last three days. And a steamer trunk. I saw the man haul a trunk from the car just yesterday."

"As I thought," Juri said. "They're getting ready to make a break for it." He rubbed the edge of the scar on his cheek. "What about the bank? What's happening there?"

"He leaves for the bank every day at the same time, 7:30 in the morning, but instead of coming home at the end of the day like he used to do, he goes back to the house two or three times a day, usually once in the morning and again in the middle of the afternoon before he comes home for the night. And he carries in these big briefcases. They're the same ones he takes to the bank in the morning, but in the morning, they seem to be empty, they are so thin. At night, he tries to hide them under his jacket, but they're sometimes too heavy for him to carry with one hand."

"Good work," Juri said, walking over to Milan and ruffling his hair. "Keep it up. We need to know where he is and what he does so he doesn't get away from us—and take our money with him."

"It's the Soviets," Valentin said, sitting back in his chair. "Patton is in Bohemia, but the Soviets will get here first. They're close to Olomouc."

"So they will be here in a few days. Today is the 4th; they should be here by the 9th of May, or maybe the 10th," Saimon interrupted, ticking off the days on his fingers, then rubbing his palms together.

Valentin glanced at Saimon, then turned to Juri. "And another thing," he said. "The Allies can't confirm them, but there are reports out of Hamburg Radio." He paused and grinned, exposing the gap between his teeth. "Hitler is dead."

REVERSAL

*

Karl Hermann Frank stood watching the bonfire until the documents of the Czechoslovak ReichsProtektorate were little more than ashes, a few blackened wisps spiraling in the breeze. Radio broadcasts still echoed in his mind—the Soviet Hammer and Sickle was flying over the Berlin Reichstag, and Hitler's successor, Admiral Karl Doenitz, was discussing surrender with British Field Marshall Bernard Montgomery.

He strode through Czernin Palace, passing the massive sandstone sculpture of Hercules battling the Hydra in the vaulted Entrance Hall before stepping out to the parking area in front of the building and the Loreta church beyond, the 27-bell carillon in its Baroque tower chiming the hour. At the side of the first of four limousines that would transport him and his family to the only suburb of the city still controlled by Wehrmacht troops, he took one last panoramic look at the building, down the line of 30 Palladian half-pillars and the diamond-pointed rustication below them. With a wry smile and a tip of his cap, he eased himself into the automobile.

*

"Here. Here. Here!" a pair of overseers shouted, marking where women should form lines outside the gates of the Ravensbrück forced-labor camp. The overseers assembled groups of inmates in the Appellplatz, crowding the women together and leading them in orderly columns of five abreast to the camp entrance. On either side of the main gate, guards filled small wagons with the remnants of camp life left behind in the homes of SS families as well as their own personal belongings and attached them to the backs of bicycles. Two of the guards stepped forward to lead the women past the Kommandant's Headquarters building, through the iron gates and along the edges of Schwedt Lake, moving south of the city of Fürstenburg.

Chessie struggled to keep pace with the others in her column. She clutched the Red Cross package she had been given on the way out of Ravensbrück, thankful she had received food but aware, from the broken seal and collapsed cardboard, that there wasn't much of it.

She marched, head down, eyes on the ground, afraid of being singled out by the guards. Step after step, she dispelled all thoughts from her

REVERSAL

mind. One foot down, then the other, into the countryside, west of the finger lakes and estuaries of Schwedt Lake.

Rain made pock-pocking sounds on her kerchief, accentuating the rhythm of her steps: Pock-pock-pock-pock: One foot down, then the other. Pock-pock-pock: One foot down, then the other.

Reverberations from bombs and artillery fire and rumblings from overhead aircraft made background music in between each step. A burst artillery shell followed by four steps. A distant drone followed by 12 steps. An overhead engine followed by 20 steps. A whistle, then a boom.

She side-stepped women who had fallen or were too weak to continue. She climbed over fallen tree branches and through small pools of water. She scraped her arms on sharp edges of bark, twigs and branches. She slapped at swarms of insects whose nests were disturbed by the procession.

Day into evening into night, one foot down, then the next.

*

The guards leading the procession of women from Ravensbrück slowed down, parked their bicycles and wagons on the roadside, and directed the women to a field where thousands of inmates from forced labor camps in northern Germany were sprawled on the ground, chewing leaves and grass, digging holes in the earth hoping to find ground water.

Chessie collapsed on the dirt, positioned her back at the base of a tree, stretched her legs out in front of her, pulled the kerchief over her face and shivered.

K. M. Sandrick

REVERSAL

Chapter Thirty-Seven

From his position on the hill at the upper end of Riegráče Park in the Vinohrady section of Prag, Milan could see the bedlam in New Town and the city center. Could this be the start of the Liberation? Men dressed in the suits and ties they wore to work every day ran from doorway to doorway, flattening themselves in the entryways, checking side streets to see if the coast was clear, shouting, gesturing to compatriots. Men in dungarees and work shirts scrambled over rooftops. Hunched and wary, they stopped at intervals, fell on their knees, unshouldered rifles and dropped into sniper positions, balancing the weapons on parapet walls.

He thought by now there would be columns of Soviet tanks and trucks rumbling over the cobblestones, troops pounding the pavement, aircraft buzzing Hradčany Castle. But as he scanned the city, Milan could see no massive movement of "liberating" men and materials across the Vltava River north of Josefov, none to the south of Nové Město or east of Vinohrady. The skirmishes in the city were small, sporadic. They must not be part of the Liberation, at least not yet. Saimon believed the Soviets wouldn't get to Prag till the 9th or 10th. It was only the 5th of May, so the partisans and the people of Prag must be doing all this on their own.

Milan had first become aware of the seeds of uprising when he heard shouts and cheers spilling out of the windows on Vinohradská Street as he made his way from the train station toward Riegráče Park in the early morning hours. "Did you hear that?" a woman called out to him, throwing up the sash. "The man on the radio said, 'It is just six o'clock,'" she gulped excitedly. Noting Milan's confusion, she explained: "He said it in Czech. Not German. Listen—Czech folk songs." She stepped to the side of the window so Milan could hear. "Songs that were forbidden by Nazi censors," she said, swaying slightly. "At last ... our words, our music."

"Rise up!" The radio announcer exhorted. "Come, help us every-one. We are fighting the Germans."

Milan had to jump out of the way as women, children and men rushed out of doorways and down the narrow streets toward the Legerova

220

intersection, steps away from the radio station. He watched dust and dirt fly off rifle barrels and handguns that had been hidden under floorboards as women tossed them out of their windows to the outstretched hands of their husbands and sons, neighbors and friends. He heard the clatter of boots on clay tiles as partisans shouted to people on the streets from the rooftops: "Barricades. We need barricades to stop the SS, the Nazi tanks from coming." Women dragged trash barrels to the middle of the streets, children added chunks of cobblestone and wood panels, men followed with sandbags and mattresses. Czech citizens destroyed evidence of the Occupation on nearby Bélehradská Street—traffic signs in German, store windows with photos of the Führer, banners bearing Nazi insignias. Partisan mobs attacked individual German Soldats, seizing their weapons. Partisans angled a truck across Vinohradská Street. Nearly a dozen assembled in front of J. Kameníček's shop, their hats pushed back on their heads, jackets loose, weapons loaded, ready to defend the radio station against the SS.

Milan turned his attention to the apartment building on Slavik Street across from Riegráče Park. He stretched out as much as he could in the cramped space behind a hedgerow. He twisted a prickly branch until it snapped so he could extend his crippled leg out on the ground and rub the muscles and tendons to get the circulation moving. He slipped his leg into a hollow he had made over the last few days, ever since his quarry had stopped his morning and evening commutes. He waited now for the banker to appear at the window of his first-floor apartment, or call for his limousine from the front stoop, or walk with his mother and son along Chopinova Street. The banker's movements were no longer routine, which complicated Milan's surveillance.

Ever since he had first begun to observe the banker from the bushes in the park, he had admired the brick-red stucco façade of the seven-story apartment building that housed many of the Germans who had taken over the country's businesses and industries from the Czechs. Cream-colored ornamentation formed peaks above the windows on the lower floors, outlined the balconies on upper ones and created a line of scallops just under the roof. It reminded him of his mother's birthday cakes with their raspberry-tinted icing and white sugar curlicues squeezed from a frosting bag.

The music blaring from open windows—now the waltz tempo of the sousedská—made him think of his mother holding a kerchief as she swirled on the dance floor at his cousin's wedding, his father and grandmother scowling in disapproval, turning their backs on her as she passed by. She had jerked her head in their direction, raised her eyebrows, rolled her eyes and winked at him. He wished now that he had jumped up and joined her on the dance floor, defying his father's and grandmother's censure.

Popping noises suddenly sounded as small weapons fired. Rifle ricochets shattered the air. Milan flinched. Thundering undertones of heavy vehicles. Deafening bursts from low-flying aircraft. Radio static screeches. Tense words from Czech radio broadcasters. "Czech people are being murdered at the radio station," they announced. "Everyone," they implored. "Come here immediately. Come help us."

Milan saw a movement in the window of the first floor apartment—the banker shielded his eyes from the noon sun as he looked down Chopinova Street toward the streets at the bottom of the hill where Czech men in the city center were reloading and firing at the SS tanks crashing through the barricades, where women were throwing kettles of boiling water out of their windows on German Soldats, where children were aiming stones at the windshields of the Nazi troop carriers. Just below the banker's windows the men, women and children of Vinohrady were gathering whatever weapons they could find and running toward the fight.

Milan looked back and forth at the apartment building, the banker standing in the window, the city center and the partisans taking up arms against the Nazis. Should he join them or stay at his post?

Hands on his shoulders pulled him out of the bushes. A heavy-booted foot on his chest, a pistol aimed at his face. "Why are you hiding in there?" a gruff voice demanded. "Can't you see what's happening?" He pointed the barrel of the pistol toward the city center. "What are you? A coward? Hiding in there, afraid to help your country? Or are you one of them?"

A man in a lightweight gray wool suit reached down with one hand and grabbed the collar of Milan's shirt. He jerked Milan upright, then grabbed his shoulders as Milan's twisted foot gave way under his weight. "Oh, I didn't see," the man said. "You're a cripple."

A second man in a navy-blue jacket, a loosened blue tie under his collar, held onto Milan as the boy steadied himself. "Don't feel sorry for me." Milan pushed the man away and brushed the front of his shirt.

REVERSAL

The men backed away.

"Hey," Milan said, reaching out his palms. "Hey, I can still shoot a gun."

"I don't know..."

"Oh, let him have a gun," a compatriot said. "We need all the manpower we can get."

One of the men pulled a pistol from the back of his waistband and turned the grip toward Milan. "I'm not sure about this, but ...," he said. "Now let's get going," he said to his compatriot.

Milan glanced at the banker's window but saw nothing except sunlight glinting off the glass. He stared at the empty window, hefted the pistol in his hand, then turned toward the city and followed the partisans down the street.

*

Chessie's heart leapt in her throat. Trucks. She could hear the sounds of the engines, the brakes, the doors opening, the snatches of conversation. She could distinguish between the SS guards—native guttural German—and the truck drivers' lilting accents. "There in the field," she heard. "You have 20 minutes."

She soon saw men in Red Cross uniforms enter the area, spread out among the crowds and hand out parcels of food.

"Where are we?" Chessie asked the man who handed her a package.

"In the Belöw woods near Wittstock," he answered, then asked how she was. "We will be coming back to evacuate the sick to Grabow. Do you need assistance?"

She shook her head. "I am not as bad as others."

"The Americans," the man whispered, "are not so far away—in Lübz—about a day's walk northwest through Freyenstein and Negenburg." The man moved to the next inmate as a guard took a step closer.

Chessie opened the Red Cross package, took out a biscuit, dipped it in a tin of jam and took a few tiny bites. She rested her head against the tree as waves of nausea rose. She waited until they passed, then looked up at the tops of the trees, the clearing sky, the clouds breaking up.

*

Milan sat behind a postal box, leaning his head out so he could look down Vinohradská Street without being too obvious about his position. Across the intersection, a crowd of men pointed toward the windows of the radio station where shots were being fired. In front of them were five bodies: two women lay face down, one in the gutter, her hands on either side of her face as if she was cradling her head while napping; the other with a hand on her nose and forehead, blood streaming from her head onto the cobblestones. Three men lay nearby, their hats still on their heads, their legs frozen in time, immobilized just as they were taking a step.

Rifle fire from the nearby Old Town Square was constant, explosions intermittent as tank mortars were loaded and then released. Heavy boots, German epithets, pistol shots in the radio station building tracked the progress of the SS. Frantic announcements confirmed that the Soldats were near the broadcast booth. The last words from the broadcasters begged for help from Allied aircraft.

*

Chessie heard rustling in the trees. Guards were changing clothes, stuffing their pockets with valuables from their wagons and walking away with their bicycles.

She watched areas of darkness move as inmates crawled toward the wagons, searched for usable clothing or other items and left the forest, walking in the opposite direction.

Chessie closed her eyes and debated whether she should just succumb to the void and let her spirit leave her body, let her mind know peace. She thought about her husband, that dear man whose understanding and kindness had made her feel whole; her father, whose pride in her and love had assuaged her insecurities. She thought about her son, whose life had not even started before it was cruelly cut short; her friend Katrenka, who didn't even see her baby's face before she died; and Katrenka's baby—alive but who knows where.

She hunched over and tried to ignore the pain. The soles of her feet were raw, the skin worn down to the muscles and tendons; her toenails

REVERSAL

were torn, her toes blackened; the flesh on her arms and legs was shredded so thin in places it barely covered bone. Her head was pounding, her heart beat rapidly, her lungs constricted.

Is that it ... life? One long journey of misery?

She pulled her legs underneath her, then pushed herself up from the ground. She brushed off her uniform, straightened her kerchief, tucked the Red Cross package under her arm and moved further into the forest.

Chapter Thirty-Eight

News that the Third Reich had capitulated, that the Wehrmacht had unconditionally surrendered and would cease all hostilities at midnight on May 8ᵗʰ, rippled through Prag. But the Soviets had not yet liberated the city, and the people were restive. Some in the Czech capital benignly accepted weapons from surrendering Nazi Soldats, slapping them on the back and letting them go on their way. But others hunted Third Reich citizens as well as Soldats. Ignoring white flags and arms raised in the air, Czechs dragged Germans from their barracks and homes, beat them with fists and clubs and painted Swastikas on the backs of their shirts.

The arrival of the Soviet Army on May 9ᵗʰ intensified the fury. Saimon watched as Soviet soldiers sprayed gasoline on Soldats hanging from trees and set them on fire. Like a handful of other Czechs, Saimon used the sparking flames to light his cigarette.

"What the hell do you think you're doing?" Juri asked, dragging Saimon away from the conflagration.

Saimon took a deep drag off the cigarette, relishing the flow of smoke down into his lungs and up into his nostrils. "Why are you surprised?" He leaned against a light pole, flicking ashes at the burning bodies. "I'm only doing what Beneš told us to do. Don't you remember the radio broadcast from Britain when he said that retribution will most certainly come and it will be horrible, that every act of violence against the Czechs will be revenged a thousand times over? I am just following the orders of the exiled leader of my country."

"But this." Juri covered his nose and pinched the nostrils. "This is barbarity." He took Saimon's arm and tried to draw him away from the scene.

Saimon wrenched away from his grasp and narrowed his eyes. "Leave me alone," he said. "Let me enjoy this."

"Saimon," Juri implored. "You have no idea who these men were, what they even did."

REVERSAL

"They're wearing Nazi uniforms, aren't they?"

"Did you see them—before the flames? They were barely more than boys."

"Don't give me any lectures. A Nazi is a Nazi."

"But that's the kind of thing the Nazis said about the Jews, isn't it?"

"Don't get all sanctimonious with me. You're just as happy to get rid of these people as I am. To get them out of our country."

"Not this way."

"They stole from us. Made us lick their boots. They *killed* us. Have you forgotten Lidice? Milan's hometown?"

"Of course not."

"It's no different than what they did to our people, the paratrooper—in the forest—near Litoměřice."

Saimon took a final drag from his cigarette and flicked the butt into the flames. "Hey, Tonda," he called out to a partisan in a pack of men running down the street. "Where are you going?"

"To the hospital," Tonda said. "We're going to get rid of all those Germans taking up the beds that should belong to us."

Saimon withdrew the pistol from his waistband and checked the ammunition. "Wait for me," he said.

*

The line of unmarked black automobiles crossed the Berounka River in the hilly wooded area near Western Bohemia's beer and iron-works center, Plzén. As it approached the city of Rokycany, the convoy was halted at an Allied checkpoint. Rifles drawn, GIs stepped down from the Jeeps that blocked the intersection, split into two lines and walked cautiously down each side of the roadway. Karl Hermann Frank, in the backseat of the last automobile, was ordered to surrender. His hands raised, he stepped out of the vehicle and was placed in custody.

*

Rows of German men, women and children crowded the streets

leading to Prag's Old Town Square. They sat solemnly, perched on leather suitcases, small parcels of their belongings in front of them, layers of clothing on their backs. They were silent, afraid to question where they might be going: Would they be selected for safe passage out of the city, or dumped into makeshift camps and jails until they could be put on trial for espionage or collaboration or wartime profiteering?

"Which one?" Saimon nudged Milan. "Which is the banker? Is he here?"

Milan looked carefully at each of the men. Not that one, the man with the receding hairline facing away from him, nor that one, wearing large, round, dark-rimmed eyeglasses, a fedora angled on the side of his head. That one? Or that one? No, no.

There. In the middle of a group of women. The boy. The boy was next to his grandmother, his head up, eyes bright, defiant. The banker stood a few meters away.

Milan raised his arm. "That one," he told Saimon. "The one in the gray coat."

"You!" Saimon shouted to the man. "You!" he repeated when the banker did not respond.

Saimon kicked his knees into the backs of the women sitting directly in front of him, forcing a small path through the group. As he reached for the banker, the boy knocked his hand away.

"Oskar, don't," the banker said.

Saimon grabbed the boy's wrist and twisted it back.

"Leave him alone," the banker shouted at Saimon. "Leave him alone, and I will come with you."

"No, Papa! Don't let them take you."

The banker rose and touched his son's cheek lightly. "It is all right, Oskar."

"Mama," the banker turned to his mother. "Watch out for him," he said, nodding towards his son. The old woman kissed his palm and his knuckles.

"C'mon, c'mon. Let's get going." Saimon yanked on the banker's jacket and pulled him away from the crowd and into the street. He

REVERSAL

twisted the man's arms behind him and tied his wrists, then went through his pockets. "Where is all the money you stole from us?"

Saimon pulled the man's pockets inside out, removing pieces of paper, glancing at the writing on them, then crumpling them and tossing them on the ground. He tugged the man's pocket watch loose and smashed the face with the butt of his pistol. He shoved the man forward until he stumbled and fell onto the cobblestones.

"You stop that," the boy screamed, lunging toward Saimon. He ran headfirst into Saimon's chest, knocking him off balance and kicked his shins with his heavy boots.

Saimon pistol-whipped the boy's face, then shoved the heel of his hand against his chin. Reaching around the boy's body, Saimon raised his wrist and arm and at the same time kicked the back of his knees until he fell forward.

"Stop, stop, stop," the old woman cried, trying to pull Saimon off the boy as the teenager shrieked.

"He's not German," she told Saimon.

"Shut up, old woman," the boy snarled at his grandmother. Turning to Saimon, he said, "Don't listen to her. She doesn't know what she's talking about."

"You listen to me," the woman implored Saimon. "He isn't one of us, like my son and me. Germans, citizens of the Third Reich. He's one of yours." She tried to loosen Saimon's grasp.

"No, grandmother. No. I am German. Like you. Like my father."

"He is Czech."

"Stop it, grandmother. I warn you."

"He is Czech," she continued, ignoring the boy. "He's from that town, the one that doesn't exist anymore. You know the one." She struggled to find the name. "Lidice. He's from Lidice."

Saimon turned toward Milan. "Do you know him?"

Milan stepped up next to the boy and took a good look at his face. Milan's eyes flashed in recognition and malice. Remembering the incident in the Imperial Cafe, the bubbling black coffee and blistering skin, he said, "No."

*

Red-tinged piss swirled around the toilet bowl in Cell #108 of Pankrác Prison, Prag. The cell was crowded; ten men were crammed into a space meant for one, or at most two. Five sat along the far wall under the barred window, the cell's sole dingy, stained mattress cushioning their backs. Three sat across from them, next to the metal grating and the solid iron door. One stood at the sink, cupping water to drink from his palm. The other, German banker Wolffe, was at the toilet, shaking the last drops of piss from his penis.

Wolffe buttoned his fly and rubbed the right side of his back with his knuckles. He worried that the pain and the bloody piss meant his kidneys had been bruised when he was taken into custody.

The bolt of the iron door shot open. An eye appeared at the peephole. "You," a gruff voice called out. "Drinking at the sink. Your turn for court."

Like the other men in the cell, Wolffe had been formally placed under arrest by police who had suddenly changed allegiance from Germany to Czechoslovakia. He had been led through the streets to the prison and exposed to beatings from the townspeople from metal pipes, bricks, wooden boards. He was not badly injured, he thought. Although he had sustained plenty of blows his body, his head and face had been spared. That was not the case for his son Oskar.

The boy was propped up against the concrete wall, legs splayed out on the floor, jacket torn at the shoulder, trouser pocket ripped. His lips were swollen and bloody. Two teeth were chipped and loose. One of his eyes was blackened; the bruising spread up to the hairline and down into the hollow of his cheek.

Wolffe had initially worried that the boy's orbital and cheekbones had been fractured, but gentle probing with his fingers had reassured him. If there had been bone fragments, Wolffe was sure he would have detected them.

Wolffe was touched by Oskar's devotion: The boy was willing to risk his own well-being to stand at his father's side. He and his mother had tried to protect Oskar from the Czech ruffians, but the vigilantes wouldn't listen. Oskar hadn't helped, insisting all the while that he was a faithful Nazi.

REVERSAL

The banker now watched his son, noting his youth—he was barely 14 years old. He didn't belong here. He was not a criminal. He wasn't even German. Wolffe remembered when he and his wife first saw Oskar; he was called Ondrej then. A bright, feisty boy, rushing down the hill in front of the Lebensborn home in Bavaria pursuing the boy who had just tagged him.

Wolffe stepped over the legs of the men in the cell and approached his son. "Oskar, please listen to me." He winced as he eased himself down to the floor. "When it is our turn to go to the court, please accept it when I plead for you, when I beg them to let you go. Please."

The boy leaned into his father's shoulder and sobbed.

*

The German banker Otto Wolffe and his son emerged from the underground passageway that ran between Pankrác Prison and Pankrác Courthouse and entered the main courtroom. A panel of four judges sat in high-backed leather chairs behind the curved wooden judicial bench in the center of the far wall. Above the judges hung the national emblem of Czechoslovakia—a two-tailed lion facing to the right, its tongue extended, claws bared. The judges' bench branched into two wings: at the right were the prosecutors' tables where six men in dark suits passed papers to one another; at the left were the defense tables where three men conferred, their heads close together, papers in hand. In front of them: a long, low wooden bench was occupied by ten bruised and bloodied men in shackles. A man stood in the semicircular wooden stand on a raised platform in front of the judges that served as the prisoners' dock. He received his sentence: 20 years imprisonment. The standing-room-only crowd of observers erupted in cheers, catcalls, whistles. As the line of prisoners was led out of the courtroom, the observers stomped their heavy boots, beat their chests with their fists and spit epithets: "Fuck you, Kraut." "And fuck your mother, too." "Don't forget your dog. Fuck him, too."

Wolffe and his son joined a line of eight men, the next group to be charged with crimes against the state. Defense attorneys hurriedly matched each man's name with a list of crimes, then explained the situation: More than 95 percent of defendants would be convicted, and 88 percent of them would spend 10 to 20 years in jail. As for the rest—the ones receiving death sentences—don't worry, the attorneys said, only those accused of crimes against persons, like murder or infliction of grievous bodily harm—would be sent to the hangman within two days. To the defendants' questions about calling witnesses or supplying any other proof that they had actually committed a crime, the attorneys shrugged. Oh, they added, there were no appeals.

*

"Wolffe," an attorney said. "I have something … somewhere." He lifted papers lying on the counter, patted his pockets, opened compartments in his briefcase. "The letter. I have it…" He spoke to Wolffe as he continued searching. "From a Frau Wolffe."

"My mother," Otto Wolffe said.

"About the boy." The attorney looked at Oskar. "He's not German, I understand."

"That's right. I … we … my wife when she was alive and I adopted him. He's Czech." Otto Wolffe raised his shackled hands and grasped his son's arm. "You remember what we talked about," he said to Oskar. "Do this … for me."

"He's pretty young. What? 13?"

"14."

"Ah, here it is." The attorney tapped the folded, hand-written page against his temple. "Wait, just a minute. I take it…." The attorney left the defense table and walked behind the judges' panel. He squatted down between two of the judges and began talking to them. He pointed to the letter, then to Oskar, then listened and nodded and scratched his chin. He stood and scanned the courtroom gallery. Spotting Frau Wolffe, he encouraged her to rise and then directed the judges' attention to her. He stepped back and waited while the judges conferred, filled out and signed a document and affixed the court seal.

*

"You can go," the attorney told Oskar. "That way—with him—the deputy of the court."

"Papa, I don't want to leave you." Oskar reached for his father.

REVERSAL

"Go, please, Oskar. Please," his father said.

"But what is going to happen to him—to my father?" he asked the attorney.

"I will do what I can do." The attorney turned to face Otto Wolffe and began to speak rapidly.

A court deputy took Oskar by the shoulder and guided him past the first row of men, women and even some small children who were watching the proceedings gleefully, their faces red and glistening, their mouths open, lips pulled back in wide grins, eyes dancing. How wrong his father was. "I am not one of these people," he muttered. "I belong with him." Looking back over his shoulder, he watched another court deputy direct Otto Wolffe to the dock.

*

"Here," the court deputy told Oskar. "Wait here." The deputy removed the boy's shackles and pressed him down onto a bench in the vestibule next to the courtroom.

"Oskar. Oskar." Raising his head, he saw his grandmother waving at him. She turned her attention to the deputy, handing him a manila envelope. The deputy opened the flap and pulled out its contents, shaking the envelope to be sure he hadn't missed anything. He read the first page, then the second, glancing from one to the other and turned the pages over.

"Him?" he asked Frau Wolffe, indicating Oskar.

She nodded and began speaking rapidly, but so softly Oskar could not understand her words.

The deputy thrust the papers back at Frau Wolffe and stepped aside.

Frau Wolffe trapped the papers next to her chest with her pocketbook. Hurrying toward Oskar, she eyed his injuries. "You are safe now, my boy." She gingerly touched his face. "You don't have to fear." Extending the papers toward him, she explained, "Your Czech citizenship has been reinstated. I told them in the Ministry of the Interior—the dolts. Do you know it's filled with Communists? They're taking over the government. Oh, never mind that. I gave them your real name."

"My name is Oskar Wolffe."

"No, no, before you came to us."

"My name is Oskar Wolffe." He sat back against the wall, his arms folded.

"Please Osk...Ondrej. You must accept this citizenship."

He grabbed the papers and spit on them. "That is what I think of 'citizenship.'"

Frau Wolffe smiled and nodded at the deputy, mouthing, "It is all right," when he made a move toward her and Oskar.

"You don't know what is happening," she whispered to her grandson. "They are expelling all the Germans, seizing all our—the—property, forcing Germans into camps or marching them to the Austrian border. Whether or not they were Nazis. This way," she pointed to the documents, "we can stay ... here in Prag. We can keep our apartment. This is the best way ... for you ... for me."

"And my father? What about him?"

"He is going to prison. Nothing we can do about that. For 20 years, probably."

"For what?"

"Oskar, they said he stole millions from the central bank and sent the money to the Reich to pay for the war. They claim he is an embezzler."

"He was doing a job. He was a banker."

"Please, Oskar." The old woman, wary of the deputy, urged the boy to rise. "Come." She smiled at the deputy, tugging on the boy's sleeve. "We are going," she said to the man. To Oskar, she said, "Home."

AFTERMATH

CHAPTER THIRTY-NINE

Since the Swedish Red Cross had brought her to the American frontlines outside of Lübz, Chessie had been shuttled from one refugee assembly center to another, gradually moving from northern to southern Germany. In the first collection center for refugees, her fingers had been cleaned and scraped, swabbed with antibiotic ointment and covered in gauze. Her hair had been washed and trimmed, her clothes and body dusted for lice. The reddish-brown swelling and blisters on her feet had been debrided, and the doctors were confident that the gangrenous sites would heal without the need to apply maggots to eat away the dead tissue.

With new leather shoes and thick cotton socks, she could walk without disturbing her bandages and aggravating old wounds. She was beginning to eat more, adding bread, vegetables and small amounts of meat to her soup bowl, and to savor again the taste of strong coffee, ignoring the grounds that accumulated at the bottom of her tin cup. She was regaining her strength and health—physically.

After handoffs between American soldiers, local townspeople and Red Cross volunteers, Chessie had been sent with other refugees from Eastern Europe to the displaced-persons camp in Deggendorf, south and east of Nürnburg. She was thankful for lodging in a structure that had been built as a hospital and army barracks in the late 1800s, for food that was hearty if monotonous, for clothes that were clean if mismatched and for medicine. She especially appreciated the little things: her own private space behind a plywood partition, a pillow, a feather-filled comforter, a selection of battered and dog-eared library books.

But Deggendorf was still a camp. She and the other "DPs" were confined to the buildings and grounds—they had no homes, apartments or gardens of their own—and regimented into routines for mealtimes, mail call and clinic visits. Their lives were under the control of others—kitchen workers, doctors and nurses, screeners who determined which of them would be allowed to remain in the camp and who would be released to make room for those in greater need.

AFTERMATH

Despite the similarities to her previous camp life, the adjustment was difficult. At least in Ravensbrück, Chessie had a job in a workshop where she spent most of the day weaving straw into handbags she had come to take pride in creating and an exhaustion at the end of the work day that was so profound it blocked many of her thoughts and feelings.

Here, she had time on her hands. She busied herself in the dressmaking shop shortening the legs of donated trousers to fit children's small limbs, repairing rips and tears in the new shipments of blouses, shirts and bloomers, and often tended the rows of vegetables in the camp garden. But she worked only a few hours a day so the other women in Deggendorf would also have things to do. In her many hours of off-time, she bit off the threads that held together the seams of her skirt and the pockets of her jacket, saving the strings so she could resew the hems. She attached buttons, pulled them off and reattached them. She knotted strands of thread together in a pattern, mimicking the crochet stitches she had learned from her grandmother.

In Ravensbrück, she had her friends from Lidice weaving straw next to her at the worktable. They all ate and slept together in the barracks, groomed one another on their mattresses, stood together in the wet and cold and heat and sweat of roll call.

Here, she was alone. Deggendorf was filled with refugees from the Jewish concentration camps in the Baltics and Russia, women and men who spoke languages she did not understand, who had religious services and customs foreign to her, isolating her not only in time and place but in human interaction. She watched the men learn to lay bricks as they built new structures to accommodate the hundreds of DPs entering the camp. She stood in the doorways of classrooms where children read and wrote on blackboards. She saw groups of men, women and children talking animatedly as they sat around tables, passing plates of matzo, their faces illuminated by the candles in a menorah. Although these activities happened a few meters away from her, they were unreal, unfamiliar and distant, alienating her by reminding her that many of the refugees were connected by faith, culture and friendship, while she was alone.

She was suffocating, berating and punishing herself for her mistake. Now that she realized what life was going to be like without her son, her friends, her home, her town, she wished she had been more careful in the forest at Wittstock. She had found a place she thought was well-hidden—in a furrow behind a felled linden, the tree's gray-brown bark nearly matching her dingy uniform. If only she had taken more care to cover herself, she now regretted, then the Swede would not have found her. If only she had taken a few more minutes to hide the ends of her kerchief completely. That had been such a good chance for her—the first time there was no shop steward to hover over her work, no guards to monitor her every step to and from the workshop, no overseers to watch her eat and sleep and shit. It had been the chance she had thought about ever since she learned of Ondrej's death—the chance to let herself die.

*

"Tichy. The first name is Marketa. She was last seen in Kladno," Milan told the woman who represented the United Nations Relief and Rehabilitation Agency in the Deggendorf displaced- persons camp.

Friends in the Czech underground had told Milan that UNRRA was an offshoot of the international refugee and relief organizations started in the 1930s after World War I. Since 1943, the organization had been handling the flood of refugees fleeing their towns and homes and the concentration camps in the wake of the Allied advance. By the end of 1944, UNRRA had 200 13-member teams that helped the Allied military operate refugee assembly and transit centers and camps. With the end of hostilities in Europe, UNRRA was now setting up a Central Tracing Bureau to collect information that might be used to find and connect refugees with missing loved ones. The Central Tracing Bureau in Deggendorf was the closest to Prag.

"In Kladno." The UNRRA volunteer jotted down the name.

"Where?" she asked.

"In a gymnasium—in a school."

"She was a schoolteacher?"

"No. She ... we were all taken there."

"Who?"

"Me, my grandmother, the people in the town."

"The people in the town?"

"Yes."

AFTERMATH

"All of them?"

"No, just the women and the children."

"The women and children of the town were taken to a schoolhouse gymnasium?"

"Yes."

"Where did they come from?"

"Lidice."

The woman studied Milan's eyes. "Lidice? But ..."

"Here, let me handle this," a supervisor told the volunteer. "This way."

She directed Milan to follow her past a partition of hanging drapes toward one of many wood-framed cubicles set in six long rows that extended to the back of the room. The supervisor's cubicle contained a table, pair of chairs and a glass-fronted cupboard that rested on two two-drawer filing cabinets. The supervisor twisted the bare light bulb hanging from an overhead line that carried electricity throughout the work area.

"We have a little information about survivors from Lidice." The woman motioned for Milan to take a seat at the table while she pulled out a two-page form from the top filing drawer and a stapled packet of papers from the bottom one. "We know the women and children were taken to Kladno, separated into groups and then sent to various locations. We have found some of them, but it has been difficult to ..." She paused as she felt Milan tense up.

"Well," she continued, licking her thumb and separating the sheets of paper. "You are looking for ..."

"My mother."

"Her name?"

"Tichy. Marketa."

The supervisor folded the papers back and scanned a list of names. "Not here," she said finally. "She's not on the list of women we so far know went to Ravensbrück." She consulted another list. "Or here. The ones who were sent to Sachsenhausen."

"She was pregnant."

K. M. Sandrick

AFTERMATH

"Ah," the supervisor said. "She may have gone to one of the Lebensborn homes." The woman closed the drawer. "You'll need to fill out one of these." She handed Milan two carbon-copied pages with wide blank spaces following a series of typewritten questions.

"Can you find her? My mother?"

"We will see what we can do, son."

*

"Milan?" He heard a soft voice calling his name. "I saw you come to the Tracing Bureau. I was waiting for you to come out." He squinted at the dark figure standing in front of him. The glare of the sun backlit a woman with short hair, a long neck, a baggy skirt falling to her knees. He shaded, then quickly dropped his eyes when he realized the woman was Chessie Sabel, Piss Pants' mother.

"I had to do that," Chessie told him. "Fill out the form, I mean. The Tracing Bureau made me do it, even though I don't have any relatives ... anymore ... from Lidice ..." She paused, rubbing her hip with the heel of her hand. "I don't know if you remember me or my son? Ondrej? You were in school with him. Of course, you're a few years older than he was, and I know how older boys are, not wanting to be associated with the little kids or pay much attention to them."

Milan remembered: Piss Pants ... pouring hot coffee on a waiter's hand in the Imperiale Café, denying he was Czech and protecting his German "father" from Saimon Dolak and the Czech police.

He flinched when Chessie sat down next to him and brushed his thigh. He turned his head away as she scanned the line of his crooked nose and the scars around his eyes and chin. "The last I saw you ..." she began.

"I have to find my mother," Milan interrupted, hunching over the form from the Central Tracing Bureau. "I have to finish this."

"Of course. I was just so happy to see you, to see someone from our town. There is no one here ..." She sighed. "Well, you don't want to ..." She rose and started to turn away. "Will you look for me?" She turned to face him. "When you come back?"

"Come back?"

AFTERMATH

"They can lose things here. They don't mean to, but ... It is a good idea to come back every few days to make sure they are working on this."

*

"Milan. Hello." Chessie joined the boy as he walked away from a desk at the Central Tracing Bureau. "How is it going?"

"They say they are not able to find records." He slapped a set of typewritten pages against his leg. "She was not in Ravensbrück. She was not in Sachsenhausen. She was not in Lebensborn. So where was she? Where *is* she?" He crumpled the pages in his fist.

"Here," Chessie said, drawing him close to her. "Come with me." She led him by the hand past the mess tent, past small groups of men seated in front of their refugee barracks, past women shaking out wet clothes and pinning them to clotheslines strung from poles next to the camp laundry, children racing in between.

The two entered a two-story brick barracks and rose the dark stone stairs, their shoes scuffing into the indentations in the middle of the steps.

"My place," she said as she entered a small wooden cubicle. She pointed to a chair next to a small set of shelves where she kept her soup bowl, cup and sewing, then sat down on the bedding folded at the end of her mattress.

"Let me see this." She took the papers from him, pulled out a small table that hid under the set of shelves and smoothed the wrinkles from the pages. She flipped quickly through the information about Ravensbrück. "I was there," she told Milan. "She was not. I am sure about that." She then reviewed the information about Sachsenhausen. "I know someone who was at that place. She never said anything about your mother and I think she would have ... if Marketa had been there."

Chessie spread out the Lebensborn report pages. She found the names of the Lidice schoolteacher, Magda Marik, and the little girl, Ivona Mares.

"What is this thing? This Lebensborn?" Milan asked.

"I don't know for sure, but they told me at the Tracing Bureau that some of the women from our town—the pregnant ones—went to one these Lebensborn places—I wonder if they had infirmaries ..."

Milan jumped. "What about infirmaries?"

"Well," Chessie said, scanning the lists of Lebensborn facilities in Bavaria and Germany. "My friend," she turned to Milan. "Maybe you remember her? Katrenka Becke? She was pregnant with her... "

Milan nodded. "Yes, yes. She was in Kladno. Kleinschmidt and that one Schupo and Paní Tůma took her away when ..."

"There's supposed to be an infirmary near Kladno. Silvie—Paní Tůma—told me they took her, Katrenka, to an infirmary where she ... had her baby."

"My mother was pregnant, too. I think she went to that infirmary, but no one can tell me what happened to the people who went there."

"There must be some way, Milan, to find out."

"But that's what I thought I could find out here." He took the papers from Chessie, folded them lengthwise and slipped them into a back pocket of his trousers.

"I'm so sorry." Chessie reached for him, but he pulled back.

"What will you do?" she asked.

He sat quietly, his eyes focused on the floor.

She stood and carefully approached him. She laid one hand on his head and the other on his shoulder. He turned his face to the side as she drew him to her. She pulled his arms around her legs, gently brushed his hair with her fingers and embraced him as he began to weep.

"You knew my mother?" Milan asked, as he wiped his nose with his shirttail and sat back in Chessie's chair.

"A bit, yes. We were not close friends, but I lived a few streets over from her house when we were growing up, and I knew her from the Daughters of Mary group at St. Martin's Church. Your mother used to bring these wonderful apricot tarts to our meetings around Christmas time."

"Could you talk about her? Anything you may remember?"

"Of course."

*

Milan climbed the barracks stairs and walked into Chessie's living space. He coughed and announced himself. "Hello? Are you there? Paní Sabel?"

"Yes," she said, smiling at the sight of him. "Come in. Come in and see what foolish things I do." She showed him the thread she was winding around her knuckles. "How I wish I had a crochet hook. I could...," she pointed to the thread. "... make something of this." She eased the thread off her hand and placed the circle of fibers on the table.

"Sit, sit," she told him, patting the seat of the chair.

He placed a small parcel on the table, its wax-paper wrapping unfolded to reveal a doughnut dusted lightly with sugar.

"Oh, my dear boy. How wonderful." She swiped a finger along the side of the doughnut and sucked on the sugar granules. "Wherever ...?"

"The black market."

"The black market." She scrutinized him. "You are indeed a man of the world, aren't you?" She laughed. "Well, you must have some of your ... some of the spoils of your adventures." She flattened out the wax paper and invited Milan to pull off a piece of the pastry.

He shook his head. "You, you go ahead."

Chessie placed a bite of the doughnut in her mouth and closed her eyes. "Wonderful." She sat back and smiled.

*

"Your mother loved St. Nicholas Day." Chessie stood with Milan in the doorway of the Deggendorf camp's new sketch class. Four men dressed in solid or pin-striped suits with easels propped on their laps were roughing out pencil drawings of a model seated in front of them. An instructor moved from one to another, suggesting changes in the way they outlined the woman's profile and the drape of her suit. Chessie enjoyed watching the drawings take shape and marveled at the beauty and detail of the black-and-white sketches pinned to the back wall.

Walking away from the classroom, Chessie hooked her arm through Milan's. "She hid in the bushes and waited for the procession. You know, with St. Nicholas in his beard and long red robe and bishop's staff, and the Devil with his tail and horns and chains, and the Angel in her white dress and big wings." Milan nodded. "Well, she waited until St. Nicholas doled out candy and nuts to the good children and lectured the bad ones who weren't eating their vegetables, or cleaning their rooms, or who were doing awful things. Then, when he wasn't paying attention, she pulled a hood over her head, ran out and tried to grab his bag. Or, when the Devil was last in line, she followed him, marching the same way he did to make fun of him, or pulling on his tail or his chains before she ran away. St. Nicholas and the Devil always claimed they didn't know who that hooligan was, but they did. They enjoyed the fun, too."

As they approached Chessie's barracks, Milan reached into his back pocket. "I have something for you." In his palm: a small crochet hook.

Chessie folded her hands over her heart, then raised them to Milan's cheeks, her eyes brimming. She brought his head close to her face and kissed his cheeks.

*

"Before your mother's wedding ..." Chessie held out a small crocheted circle so Milan could see it. "for the wedding invitation cookies ..." She paused, seeing Milan shift in his chair, rubbing his fingers on his trousers. "What's wrong?"

Milan hunched forward. "Paní Sabel."

"Chessie. Please call me Chessie."

He nodded. "Chessie. I am leaving ... here."

"Leaving? But where? Where are you going?"

"Back to Prag. There is nothing for me here ... anymore ... and the trials ... of the Schupo ... of Kleinschmidt, the one who ..."

"Yes." She placed her hands over his. "I remember him."

"His trial will begin soon. I must be there ..."

"Of course."

Chessie pulled the crochet hook through a loop in the threads. "I will be going there myself soon. They—the officials here—need space for new refugees so they are sending us ...," she paused. "Old timers, I guess you could say, to the cities, where there is work we may do, apartments

AFTERMATH

where we can live in groups. I don't know about this. This plan. I don't know where I will be or how I will get along. A big city for a country girl like me. I just don't know." She shook her head, then sighed. "But you didn't come to talk about me." She looked at Milan. "Tell me about you. When? When will you leave?"

"In the morning."

"Oh, so soon." She wiped a fingertip along her eyelid. "Well, young Milan." She smoothed his hair with the backs of her fingertips and then held his face in her palms. "Dear boy." She tilted his head and brushed her lips against his forehead. "Do take care of yourself."

Milan took her hands in his and kissed each one. Reaching into his shirt pocket, he pulled out a small folded piece of paper and handed it to her. "This is where you can find me—when you come to the big city."

Chapter Forty

Klaudie Cizek fastened the cloth-covered buttons of her brown gabardine suit, tugged on the bottom of the fitted jacket and smoothed the collar of her thin pink blouse over the lapels. She stepped around the bedspread lying in a heap on the thick wool carpeting and over to an oval glass-topped table. She sat on the upholstered easy chair next to the table, pushed aside a basket of fruit and picked up the top sheet of a stack of papers.

From the records SS guard Konrad Dreschler had stuffed into his briefcase before leaving the Ravensbrück forced-labor camp, Klaudie had collected and organized small bits of information: birth dates of infants born to prostitutes in the camp's SS brothels; arrival dates of children born to German women who were considered enemies of the Third Reich; and the dates and shipment logistics between Ravensbrück and one of its satellite labor camps. The data fell into a consistent pattern: Within a day or two of a birth or the completion of a new child's medical examination at the camp, orders would be issued for an SS limousine to arrive at the infirmary door. A day later, a receipt would document that a shipment had been made to the Lebensborn facility in Ansbach, Germany. The information provided further proof of what she had suspected—that there was a link between Lebensborn and the departures of young women and children from the labor camp. And they weren't just any women and children. The women and children destined for Lebensborn had pedigrees—they met a particular set of physical and genealogical characteristics.

Dreschler himself had hinted at the fact. He had openly dismissed her questions about Lebensborn. "Nothing for you to be concerned about. It is only for certain ... types," he once told her. But when she asked why, Dreschler had smirked and said it was for planting the seeds of the New Germany. At the time, Klaudie thought he was parroting the usual Nazi propaganda about the Master Race, but now she wondered if he had meant what he said: Lebensborn was a place for Nazis to seed the next generation with children who had been bred by the SS, as well as "certain types" of children stolen from their families.

AFTERMATH

She remembered the gymnasium in Kladno when the SS inter-viewers had questioned mothers and children, examined their heritage, measured their physical characteristics and separated children into different groups. She thought of her children: her daughter Adéle, her light-blond hair gleaming in the light, her heart-shaped face and pink cheeks; her son Tomás, his eyes made large by his spectacles, his crooked smile and slightly bowed legs. And the last she saw of them: Adéle leading the other blond ones, Kleinschmidt clapping his hands in admiration as they passed; Tomás standing to the side with other groups of children, shyly biting his lip. Had her children been selected as seeds for the New German Generation? Had they been taken to a Lebensborn site? Tomás because he was studious and intelligent—a future scientist? Adéle be-cause she was so confident and elegant? Klaudie shuddered.

On one of the pages of stationery on the table, she wrote down two names, a pair of brief descriptions, a date and a location and placed the paper in the pocket of her skirt. She opened her handbag and thumbed through the money she had made from the sale of one of the gold pocket watches Dreschler had purloined from Ravensbrück. She inserted the bills into a wallet, then gathered the labor-camp records together and slipped them into Dreschler's briefcase.

Before leaving, she took a look around the room. Her eyes moved from the pair of framed watercolors on the wall above the double bed, down the cherrywood headboard to the crumpled starched sheets and the yellow-gold patterned bedspread, past the sheer curtains, dark-brown valence and draperies and the basket of fruit on the table. She was in the Grand Hotel of Nürnberg, one of only a handful of buildings that had not been bombed to ruin by the Allies. The night before, she had dined at one of the shiny wood tables in the hotel's Brasserie on cream of chicken soup, broiled filet mignon, buttered peas and apple pie with vanilla ice cream. After dinner, she had listened to the pianist in the lounge, sipped Bordeaux wine and later lingered in her marble-tiled bath. Didn't she tell Chessie and Katrenka when they were girls that one day she would stay in a fine hotel? "Well," she said, a twisted smile on her face, "I made it."

*

AFTERMATH

"It's right up there," the driver Klaudie had hired to take her from Nürnberg to Ansbach said as he turned down a hard-packed dirt road. "You can just see the top of the house there. See the mansard roof? That's it."

Klaudie followed the driver's line of sight and saw the side of a four-story building, its lower three floors painted white, the top floor a set of three dormers poking out of the red-tiled roof.

As they drew near, Klaudie could see an arbor in front of the structure, vines: grapes?—running up and over the trellises. Two low garages, filled with American military vehicles, flanked the building, and a 12-step stairway led down from the arbor to the edge of a valley of tall grass.

The driver parked on the side of the road. "Don't want to get too close—the Americans, you know. Don't want any fuss."

Klaudie walked the rest of the way to the veranda that ran across the front of the building. She looked inside as she passed the windows on the first floor and saw empty wicker prams and wooden cribs, diaper-changing tables, toys in heaps. A framed photograph on the wall showed seven women standing behind two rows of small boys, 8 to 10 years old, dressed in shorts and long-sleeved shirts—Hitler Youth uniforms. This looks more like an orphanage—for babies and young children, she thought. She tensed. What if older children like hers were sent to some other kind of facility? She shook the thought from her mind. This had to be the right place, the place to find the threads that would lead to her children.

Klaudie approached a man sitting behind a desk to the side of the Lebensborn building lobby. He was dressed in a khaki uniform, a thin tie knotted tightly under his shirt collar, a set of chevrons on both sleeves, a black arm band with white MP letters on one arm. He was reading *The Stars and Stripes*. July 1945 headline announced: "Churchill Resigns" and "Nuremburg War Crimes Trials Set for November."

"I'm looking for these names." She spoke hurriedly to the man, rushing her words together. "For two children—a young girl, well, she would be 16 now, and a boy, a year older. They may have come here in the summer, the summer of 1942." Klaudie pointed to the names scrawled on the hotel stationery.

The man raised his eyes over the top of the newspaper, then folded it and placed it on top of the desk. "Do you speak English?"

Klaudie shook her head uncomprehendingly.

The man nodded, then held up a finger. "Wait." He pointed to the floor. "Here." Adjusting the white shoulder harness for his sidearm, the man rose, placed a white helmet on his head and grabbed a pair of white gloves. Walking to the doorway behind him, he called out, "Joe. Hey, Joe. We need a translator here."

A few minutes later, he was joined in the doorway by a similarly dressed but shorter, stockier man, a thick, dark moustache hiding the set of his mouth. His head tilted toward the taller soldier as he spoke. The man glanced at Klaudie, then patted the soldier's arm.

"How can I help you?" the man asked Klaudie in German.

"I am looking for these children." She held out the leaf of stationery. "If they came here, it would have been in 1942." She pointed to the date she had listed next to the names.

The soldier read the paper, pressing the embossed hotel logo between his thumb and index finger.

"Well, I don't know about any of this." He spoke haltingly. "When we got here," he paused between his words to be sure he had chosen the right ones. "There was an old caretaker and a lot of children—more than 100 of them. The doctors or nurses—or whoever the people were who took care of the children—were gone. Left them ... the children. God knows how long the kids were here ... alone." The soldier shook his head. "We sent them ... the children ... to the Red Cross—in Nürnburg. I don't have any names of the children who were sent there. I'm sorry. But I can tell you where the Red Cross is."

Klaudie stared at the man, wondering what she should do—go to the Red Cross in Nürnberg? But if this place housed only infants and children....

"Were any teenagers here?"

"No, no," he said. "No one was older than about ten."

"Are there any records of what happened to the children who came here—years ago—in 1942?"

"There's a shit—excuse me." The soldier swallowed the word. "There are rooms full of records."

"I am looking for my daughter and my son. They were stolen from me ... in 1942."

"Oh, lady. Oh, geez. Here," he led her to an easy chair. "Let me get my commander."

*

The caretaker of the Lebensborn facility was waiting for Klaudie at the side of the building when she came out.

"Not much help, was he—that commander." The caretaker smiled at Klaudie, taking her elbow. "So much information, in columns and rows, and in German, and hand-scribbling and all that. He doesn't know what to do, does he?"

"And you do?"

The caretaker's smile broadened. "But...."

"Not for nothing, eh?" she said.

"You are a wise woman. Let's go over there to the bench in the trees and have a chat."

"These are Czech names. The children here ...," he waved a hand at the building behind them, "... were given German names, no matter where they came from. German names when they got here. German names when they were adopted out."

It was as she had feared. "Where did they go? The adopted ones? Do you know?"

The caretaker held out his fingers and stared at his nails.

"I understand how difficult this is." Klaudie opened her handbag, eased the wallet open and flipped the edges of the bills inside. "I would appreciate any help you can give me."

The man reached for the wallet, but Klaudie jerked the purse away. "A little something? Earnest money?" he asked. She withdrew five bills, folded them and handed them to him.

He wiggled his hand. "Paper? And pencil?" She tore off a corner of the stationery and held it out to him.

After scribbling his name, he said: "Come tomorrow. Here—late in the afternoon—after the Americans lock up and leave."

AFTERMATH

*

Klaudie sat on the stone floor in the basement of the Lebensborn home between stacks of metal shelving lined with cardboard file boxes. The boxes were set in orderly rows, organized by year. Boxes labeled "1942" lay open, their contents spread in front of her, the documents telling the story: Transports of children from cities in Germany, Austria, Belgium, France and Holland. Clipped to an entry form for each child were details about the child's physical description, medical examination results and psychological profile. Interview forms chronicled every visit with prospective adoptive parents—the child's deportment, comments made by the prospective parents and observations from the Lebensborn official who oversaw the interaction. Disposition forms reported further outcomes: the child's placement with a family, referrals for counseling to improve his or her manners, disciplinary action to correct unacceptable behavior.

Klaudie pulled a sheaf of papers into her lap, then rubbed her forehead. None of the children named in the 1942 records for Ansbach had been old enough; none were older than 12 when they arrived. None of the children had been sent from Lidice or Kladno. A few newborns had been sent from Ravensbrück. Klaudie remembered two births that had occurred only a few months after her arrival: twins were born to a German woman who had been sent to the labor camp following her arrest for agitating against the Nazis.

Klaudie reorganized the pages and returned them to the box. She replaced the cover, then lifted and shoved the carton back into place. She scanned other boxes—dozens from 1941 and 1943— only a few from 1944. With the war going badly, the Nazis must have had other things on their minds, she thought.

Moving to the next aisle, Klaudie found boxes with more general labels: Administration; Personnel; Supplies. She lifted the lid from one of the boxes and found the names of Lebensborn facilities: Steinhoering, established in 1936, and other more recently established ones; Heim Taunus; Ardennen; Freisland.

Keys rattled on the other side of the door. "Finish up," the care-taker called out. "The Americans will be coming soon." Klaudie folded the paper she had been holding and pushed it into her pocketbook. She restored the box to its place, brushed off her skirt and joined him outside the records room.

"Find what you wanted?" the caretaker asked as they walked.

She shook her head. "What about these places?" She fished out the paper and showed him the names of the Lebensborn facilities. "Would Czech children have been sent to one of these?"

He shrugged. "You ask what I cannot answer."

"This place," she indicated the building behind them, "had only small children. What about older boys and girls? Where would they have been sent?"

*

Klaudie waited in the vestibule of an Augsburg convent that had been accepting orphaned and abandoned refugee children since 1940. Not a Lebensborn facility, but a Catholic nunnery that had also served as a children's home during the war years.

From the small reception area where she stood, Klaudie could trace the path of three separate wings. The first led to a series of dormitory halls with rows of small, white-sheeted beds. The next had a common meeting room, a classroom and a dining hall with the kitchen, storage area and office cubicles forming a "U-shape" at the end of the hall. The last wing had a chapel on one side with living quarters for the nuns across from it.

The children's center was relatively quiet. Younger children were bent over small tables or sitting on the floor of the meeting room, drawing pictures on scraps of paper with stubs of crayons. In the classroom, older children were listening to a nun recite a history lesson, then repeating her words one by one to help memorize them. Pairs of boys on the side of the reception area sat at oilcloth-covered tables, moving crude chess pieces across roughly drawn chessboards, their legs in knee-high stockings, feet in buckle shoes, restless.

Klaudie turned toward a clicking sound: Wooden beads hanging from the belt of the mother superior's habit rattled as she approached.

"How may I help you?" The nun led Klaudie to a pair of worn upholstered chairs next to a small rectangular table.

The Pear Tree

AFTERMATH

"I am trying to find a girl and a boy who may have come here in 1942. They were 13 and 14 at the time. The girl was ...The mother superior rested her hand on Klaudie's arm. "Were they Jewish?"

"No, why do you ask?"

"We had about 150 children at that time. Many of them were Jewish. Their families were afraid for them, as you can well imagine, so they paid a fee for their room and board. We not only cared for the children, but kept track of them in our card files so their families would be able to find them at the end of the war. Sadly, most of those children are still here."

"No, the children are Czech, Catholic. A man—from Ansbach—suggested they may have been brought here."

"Why would he think that?"

"Because you—the convent—took teenage children, children who had been separated from their families ..."

"I don't understand why you would think that. We have ... had ... few Czech children."

Klaudie was afraid to tell the mother superior the real reason she had come. She worried the nun would not want to acknowledge that the convent had also accepted payment from the Nazis to house children who might be adopted by German families.

"Could you please check your card files? My children would not have had identity papers. The time ... when we were separated ... was traumatic and ... Please check ..."

"Of course, my dear."

The mother superior guided Klaudie to an office cubicle and opened a large card index. "Here." She withdrew all the cards filed between 1942 and 1943 and handed Klaudie half of them. "This will take time because we organized them by name. We will have to read each one to find any who might be the right age."

CHAPTER FORTY-ONE

The interrogators assembled in one of the small rooms on the third floor of the Twelfth U.S. Army Group Headquarters in Wiesbaden, Germany. The investigating officer, Col. Dr. Judge Advocate Bohuslav Ečer, was representing the Czech Republic in the United Nations War Crimes Commission. He was joined by fellow investigators First Lt. Norman Miles from the War Crimes Branch of the Twelfth U.S. Army Group and Dr. Ernest Hochwald, plus an interpreter and a stenographer.

Col. Ečer removed his officer's cap, turned it face-front, and absently fingered the braided cord that circled the seam between the woolen cloth and bill and the metal Czech national insignia fastened above it. Despite the severity of the surroundings and its gravity of purpose, Ečer appeared amiable; the wrinkles at the edges of his pale eyes and the naturally curving corners of his mouth created a false impression of affability. Turning to each of the men in the room, he inquired with a lift of his gray-blond eyebrows whether the interrogation should proceed. Assured that the team was prepared, he pressed the intercom button, signaling the MPs stationed in the corridor to bring in the prisoner.

Since he had surrendered to the Allies on May 9th, Karl Hermann Frank had been incarcerated in a cell in the prisoner's wing of a massive five-story stone building commandeered by the U.S. Army a month earlier. During the war, Wiesbaden had been a stronghold, the headquarters of the Third Reich's Wehrkreis XII, a military district that encompassed large areas of Germany as well as France and Luxembourg. The U.S. Army was now in control. From the building formerly occupied by Wehrkreis, the army was mobilizing soldiers, supplies and engineers to secure and rebuild the area, and its intelligence group, along with investigators from the Allied and the Occupied territories, was gathering evidence to be used in the first international prosecution for crimes perpetrated by individuals during a time of war, such as Karl Hermann Frank.

Frank enjoyed the cat-and-mouse interplay with the questioners. It was a welcome relief from the boredom. For the past few weeks, he had been confined to a 3-by-2-meter chamber equipped with an army cot, small table and straight-backed chair. Until the interrogations, he had only one amusement: He tracked the habits of the guards who patrolled the edge of the roof behind a low parapet from the narrow barred window of his cell. There was the chatty soldier who stopped regularly at the corner of the watchtower and chewed the fat with the machine gunner, and the nervous one who could not keep his fingers away from the sleeves of his uniform or the brim of his helmet.

Interrogation also took Frank's mind off the constant surveillance. A guard stood watch, observing his every move, throughout the day and even at night. The guard was quiet, speaking only when Frank failed to follow the rules: Hands, head, and feet had to be in full view at all times. He was reprimanded, therefore, if he covered his face or his arms with his blanket while he tried to sleep, or if his feet could not be seen when he used the toilet in the shallow alcove adjacent to the table and chair.

He didn't like to admit it, but the presence of the silent sentinel was intimidating. In recent days, he had begun to sit cross-legged on the cold stone floor, his naked back to the door, so the guard's gaze would not catch his attention. But even as he sat with his head turned away and eyes fixed on the blank, gray, pockmarked wall, he still felt a sting of censure.

From muffled conversations he had overhead while eating beans from a small skillet in the prison mess hall, Frank learned that the Allies would not summarily execute members of the Third Reich for war crimes; they would prosecute war criminals in courts of law. Allied military lawyers were currently interrogating prisoners to decide what charges to file and against whom.

Word was that high-ranking leaders of the Nazi regime would be tried in Nürnberg, beginning in November, and lower-ranking individuals would be sent to courts in other German cities. While military, business and financial officials of the Third Reich would be held personally liable for the actions they had taken during the war, each would have the opportunity to defend himself. Each could choose an attorney to cross-examine witnesses, challenge incriminating evidence and present exculpatory testimony.

To help his own case, Frank was planning how he would answer his interrogators as part of an overall defense strategy.

First, he would demonstrate that he was not a powerful member of the Third Reich: He didn't have ultimate responsibility, others did. Göring, for example, had been in charge of economic measures. Himmler had exclusive responsibility for police and punitive actions, deportations into the concentration camps and the camp conditions. Goebbels mobilized labor, and Hitler himself was supreme commander of the war. Frank planned to emphasize in his next interrogation that Hitler ruthlessly imposed his will, even on experienced professional soldiers.

Second, he would explain that he hadn't done anything illegal or contrary to international law. The things he did were normal wartime activities—he had adhered to the unwritten rules of war. The questioners were military men, after all. Wouldn't they understand what he had to do? Heydrich's assassins, for instance: Surely the interrogators would agree that he had to aggressively hunt down the paratroopers. His regime had been infiltrated by a foreign power and the men had murdered one of the regime's most powerful leaders—in broad daylight. He had no recourse but to pursue the assassins, drive the sniveling cowards into the basement of the church, and kill them. Would the Allies have done any differently? And that Lidice business. Didn't the Allies do the same thing—destroy an entire town? He could point to Dresden: four raids between February 13th and 15th; more than 700 British and American bombers; nearly 4,000 tons of explosives, destroying 1,600 acres of the city center and killing 22,000 to 25,000 people. Lidice was nothing by comparison.

Next, he would argue—no, suggest, he told himself—that the whole prosecution was a sham. Who were the Allies to decide or define what constituted "crimes against humanity"? The victors would always exact the punishments and frame the history, but asserting that he and others in the Third Reich were guilty of "crimes against humanity" was pure sanctimony. He had taken actions to control and discipline a population, to foster and promote a racial purity that was threatened by separate and inferior influences. He had acted to protect his country and its people from an assault on its very existence. His actions were legitimate, justified; they were not crimes.

If the Allies persisted in this mockery of a prosecution and insist that he *had* committed crimes against humanity, he would demonstrate that he had been given no choice. He had to follow orders from his superiors or he would have suffered "unpleasant consequences." There had always been the threat that insubordination would lead to deportation to a concentration camp; he would tell them.

AFTERMATH

Finally, he would demand that the prosecutors provide evidence of any wrongdoing, any support for the contention that he was responsible for any crimes. He was sure there was little or no direct evidence: He had burned it all in the courtyard of Hradčany Castle.

Frank entered the small interrogation room and walked to the high-backed wooden chair that faced the questioners' table. The questioning began as all the others had, with the interrogator reviewing a typewritten sheet that listed specific questions under a series of topic headings, the stenographer flipping pages until he found a blank one and two MPs assuming their positions on either side of the door. Each interrogation adhered to legal formalities. Frank was given a standard legal oath, swearing he would tell the truth and nothing but.

He cleared his throat and began to speak. "I make the following additions to my prior statements concerning the appointment of Heydrich to the position of Acting ReichsProtektor." He wanted to take the initiative, get his comments on the record and establish his defense. "It was Heydrich's mission to introduce a more rigorous government into the late Protektorate. He had a long conversation with Hitler, the contents of which are unknown to me—I infer that he received instructions to take harsh steps."

A good beginning, he thought, to his argument that he had had little power in Occupied Czechoslovakia. "Heydrich never asked me in advance or consulted me in respect to the several planned actions. Heydrich acted with complete independence, and he was not a man to whom I had access," he continued.

Now to correct misconceptions about his role in the Protektorate: "I should like to add that my office was a territorial office; hence it embodied in itself all departments of state, and the impression could arise that I was a powerful man in Bohemia and Moravia. But that was a mistaken impression. It was also caused by the fact that the London Radio stigmatized me as the symbol of the German oppression of the Czech people, and that it marked me as a bloody butcher, literally a bloodhound. The agitation of the London and Moscow radios had a great effect on the Czech nation. It was impossible to prevent the listening to the London and Moscow radios by way of police or technical measures. In some instances, their orders were spread and obeyed within a few minutes after they had been broadcast."

AFTERMATH

A final comment on responsibility: "The supreme responsibility was borne by Adolf Hitler, who directed all decisive problems of the administration, of the Reich, and of the occupied and annexed countries, as well as of the conduct of the war."

Karl Hermann Frank settled back in the chair and waited for Ečer to begin, satisfied he had laid the groundwork for a solid defense.

AFTERMATH

Chapter Forty-Two

Paní Dagmar Skala squirmed in her gingham blouse, pushing it back on her bowed shoulders as she considered the meager portions of meat lined up behind the glass in the refrigerated display case of the Unhošt butcher shop. "Still not very much, is there?" she said to the man who stood to the side of a swinging door, his head down, eyes focused on the latest edition of *Mlady Svet*.

"Anything else? In the back room?" she asked, tilting her head to scrutinize the unresponsive assistant. "Where is Patrik? I think I should talk to him."

Patrik Pesko pushed through the door, a tray laden with cartons of freshly ground lamb in his hands. "Paní Skala. How nice to see you." He nudged the magazine out of his assistant's hand. "Take these," Pesko told him. "Put them over there—next to the ground pork."

Pesko wiped his palms on the front of his apron. "What can I do for you, Paní Skala?"

The woman watched the butcher's assistant as he balanced the tray of meat on his hip, slid open the back of the display case and adjusted the ground-pork containers to make more room.

Pesko smiled broadly, masking his wariness. "How is that daughter of yours? Due any day now, isn't she? How would she like a couple of chops? Good for her and that growing grandbaby of yours, no?"

Paní Skala continued to watch the butcher's assistant, squinting and lifting her eyeglasses so she could get a better look.

"When you're done with that," Pesko told the assistant, "get going on the rest of the lamb." Pesko stepped in front of his helper as he turned toward the swinging door, blocking Paní Skala's line of sight.

"Awfully interested in that magazine, isn't he?" Paní Skala whispered. "Are you sure he's ... alright? Hasn't been here too long, if I remember correctly. Came in, what? '42?"

Pesko held up a pair of veined lamb chops from the display case and placed them on a sheet of butcher paper. He dipped his head toward them. "What about these?"

The woman turned her attention to the chops. "They look good, Patrik. And how about some of that ground pork and some of the lamb? Can you divide the portions in half? I don't have that many cards left." Pani Skala opened her pocketbook and searched for the ration book.

Pesko placed the meat on sheets of cut butcher paper, wrapped them individually and taped them shut. He waved them in his hand as he moved to the counter and the cash register. He rang up the sale and deposited the ration cards under the till.

"Yes, Wim and my sister came in '42, just after the baby was born," Pesko told Pani Skala as he placed the packages in her string bag. "He's pretty worthless, if you know what I mean, as a butcher," Pesko said behind his cupped hand. "Still has trouble telling a chop from a filet. But what can you do? Have to take in the in-laws, worthless or not."

"Wasn't he—your brother-in-law—a policeman or something? I seem to remember old Pani Bartos telling me that—that your sister married a policeman, and you know what the police were like under the Nazis. Or maybe he actually was German. A Sudeten. Or was he from Berlin?"

"No, no, no. He worked in the factories, like everyone else. To be honest with you, he was pretty lousy at that too—that assembly line work. They ended up making him a guard on the rail shipments. That's probably where Pani Bartos got the idea that he was a policeman. No, Wim's not smart enough to be a policeman. Only thing he's good at is standing around, watching things. Well, you can see that, can't you?"

Pesko changed the subject. "You see my sister, don't you? And her little girl? She's three now. Prettiest little thing—all blond and pink. Maybe you see her—or that husband of hers," he motioned toward the back of the shop, "in the town square?"

"Can't say as I do."

"Well, next time you go through the square, if you see my sister, be sure to say hello to her. She would be happy to talk with you and tell you all about Mama Pesko. Mama's still running the chicken farm on the outskirts of town, you know. Won't consider moving. I guess I understand it. She's been there ever since my papa took over the farm when I was six or seven. It would be nice for her to be closer to me and my sister. Closer to her young grand-daughter. You should see little Katra.

The Pear Tree

AFTERMATH

She's so beautiful—and rambunctious. Always asking questions: 'What is this, Uncle Patrik?' 'What about that?' And always, 'Why this?' 'Why that?' 'Why, Why, Why?' I tell you, she's going to be a smart one. You stop by and say hello to her ... and my sister. But be prepared, that little girl may ask you a million questions." Pesko laughed.

He closed the cash register drawer, stepped away from the counter and escorted Paní Skala to the door. "You have a good day now," he told her. "I'll set aside some nice kidneys for you—for next time."

"What are you doing? Purposefully trying to look suspicious?" Pesko asked Wolfgang Weber, who was seated on a stool next to the meat grinder in the back of the butcher shop.

"Look at this." Weber spread out an article on the front page of the magazine. "An explosion at a munitions dump near Ústí nad Labem, and people blamed the Germans. Crowds of them pulled Germans out of their houses and shops and hauled them on to the bridge over the Elbe. They threw them into the water, Patrik." Weber stared at his brother-in-law. "Then there were more attacks on Germans in the town. Two hundred Germans killed." He paused. "This on top of the forced marches of Germans out of Czechoslovakia and into Austria and vigilante attacks of solders as well as civilians. And it's not just the Germans." He bit his lower lip. "It's the ones who," his fingers formed quotation marks in the air, "fraternize with Germans, who are being singled out. I am afraid, Patrik, of what might happen to Sára and Katra if people in this town find out about me."

Pesko took the newspaper from Weber, folded it and laid it on the butcher block. He stood next to Weber, an arm around the man's shoulder.

"I think I should turn myself in," Weber said. "Go to the National Court in Prag and be tried for war crimes."

"You didn't commit war crimes, Wolfgang. You were a policeman who followed orders."

"The Great Decree from the Czech government—you remember what it said. Section 5 on crimes against persons, like human trafficking or kidnapping of children ..."

"You didn't do that, Wolfgang."

"... shall be sentenced to death."

"Did you memorize it all?"

"Under Section 2: Whoever unlawfully restricted the freedom of a person shall be sentenced to prison for 10 to 20 years. For what I did—as a Schupo—I could be killed or imprisoned. For what happened in the gymnasium in Kladno after Lidice, I could be ... "

"You left them—the Schupo, the Nazis, after Lidice. You saw them for what they were, and you left."

"Yeah, I'm a deserter, too. Some father for my little girl. Some husband. Some ..."

"You were trying to do the best for my sister. You took her away from Berlin when you saw what the Brownshirts were doing. You gave my sister what she most wanted in the world—a beautiful baby. You took her and the baby away from Kladno when you saw what the SS were doing to those poor people from Lidice."

"That's what I'm good for—running away—and now, now that things could be catching up with me..." He rose from the stool and faced his brother-in-law. "What if they find out about Katra, the truth about Katra?" He turned and walked toward the meat locker. "If the government finds me, if someone like Paní Skala turns me in to the government, what will happen to Sára? They could call her a collaborator. Even if they don't do that, they could take Katra away from her." He pounded a fist against the locker door. "I should go to Prag and turn myself in before...."

"You have a baby girl to take care of. A wife who needs you. Don't be crazy." Pesko approached Weber. "You are not like them. The Nazis. You are a good man. Not such a good butcher, even after all these years." Weber smiled at Patrik's familiar gibe. "Just do me one favor," Pesko continued. "Don't look back. Act like you belong here. Do things everyone else does. Be one of us. And, if you could do one other thing—for me—*act* like a good butcher."

*

"Patrik? Are you here?" Paní Skala called from the front of the butcher shop.

AFTERMATH

"No," Weber answered as he pushed through the swinging door. "But how can I help?"

"I wanted to talk to Patrik."

"He is away for the afternoon. His mother. He's at the farm."

"Nothing serious, I hope."

"No, she needed some muscle ... to chop wood for her."

"Well...," Paní Skala hesitated.

"What can I do for you?"

"I was going to ask his advice." She squinted at Weber, deciding whether she wanted his assistance.

"Tell me the problem. Maybe I can solve it for you." Weber came around to the front of the display case and stood next to Paní Skala.

"I want to make velkonočna hlavka—something special, you know, for my son-in-law's family when they come. But you don't have much veal."

"Oh, yes, the usual recipe calls for about three pounds of veal, doesn't it?"

Mrs. Skala nodded. "I don't have to make it ... I was just hoping ..."

"We don't have nearly enough veal," he said, eying the meat in the display case. "But I could mix in some pork and chicken and get it up to three pounds. A couple more dashes of cloves when you're ready to mix in the yeast and the eggs, what do you think? You know," he said, turning toward the telephone, "I'll call Patrik and ask him to bring eggs from his mother's. Nice fresh eggs will help you with the bread. When are you making the velkonočna hlavka?"

"The family is coming tomorrow. If I could, I would like to make it the day after."

"Patrik will be home tomorrow evening at the latest. Let me call him."

"So you know about velkonočna hlavka?"

"What's that you say?" he asked, lowering the receiver.

"Oh, I was a little sur... No, no, never mind."

Weber opened the shop door for Paní Skala. "You let me know how your recipe turns out."

"I will. Thank you so much." Shifting her string bag, she shook his hand. "Give your wife my best," she said.

"And the best to your family," he replied. At the shop window, he waved to the greengrocer sweeping the walkway in front of his stalls, then turned toward the back of the shop. He smiled as he felt the small object he always carried with him, the object he was protecting for his daughter. He was determined: He *would* fit in here and seem like he belonged. He owed it to his family.

CHAPTER FORTY-THREE

Klaudie raised the sheet of paper and read it again. Yes—she scanned the numbers on the building façade in front of her—this was the address the mother superior had given her.

In their review of the card index at the Augsburg convent children's center, neither she nor the mother superior could find any notations indicating that a boy older than age 11 had been admitted at any time in 1942. There was no description of a boy even remotely resembling Tomás. But Klaudie had found a note concerning a 13-year-old girl who had been adopted near the end of 1942, but little else. Descriptions of the girl were difficult to read: They were smudged or carelessly written. The circumstances of her arrival were missing. The date of her arrival was blurred. The only fact Klaudie had to go on: The girl had been released to a German family who lived on Hauptstrasse in the city of Ulm.

Klaudie ignored the padlock on the house door and rapped her knuckles on the frame, dismayed to hear the echoes within. She rapped again, then peered through a smudged, half-boarded-up window, but she could see nothing through the stains and grime.

"Nobody's there," said a woman emerging from the adjacent building. "Haven't been here for at least a year."

Another woman chimed in. "Were the 'New Germans.' The family was. They moved into the house after the Jews were arrested."

"Don't know which was worse, eh, Greta?" the first woman said. "The Jews who lived there before. Dirty people if you ask me. Looked dirty. Smelled dirty. Had dirty dealings in their business. Or that girl, the one they adopted."

Klaudie held her breath. "What about the girl?"

"What a piece of work, that one," the woman named Greta responded. "Conceited, full of herself, thought she was too good to get involved with us—or her new family, for that matter. Wouldn't do chores. Sassed back. Always playing with her hair."

"What did she look like?"

"Oh, she was pretty enough, with that hair—silky blond. She was about 13 years old, I'd say. Filling out, leggy and slim at the waist."

"I'm almost surprised they abandoned her. Herr Nazi had an eye for her, if you ask me."

"So what happened?" Klaudie asked.

"They just left her in the street ... when they moved out," Greta added.

"Herr Nazi finished loading the car. Frau Nazi locked up the house. And they took off. Not even a wave at the girl."

"Where do you think they went?" Klaudie asked.

"Wasn't he an SS or something? Probably ran off to Argentina," Greta suggested.

"Never saw him in a black shirt."

"Well, then, where do *you* think they went?" Klaudie said.

"They probably lit out for the Austrian border and are now proud Viennese." Both women laughed.

"What happened to the girl?" Klaudie asked again.

"They're off doing the Viennese waltz." Greta curtsied to the other women and raised her arms, inviting her to dance.

"The girl? What happened to her? Did you take her in?" Klaudie insisted.

"Me?" Greta said. "Wanted nothing to do with her."

"What about you?" Klaudie asked the other woman.

"I tell you what I did. I saw them drive away. I saw that girl in the street. From my windows. I bade them good riddance and pulled the shutters closed and locked the door."

"So you don't know where she went, which direction she took?"

"Now, why would I care?"

*

"I am sorry the information was not helpful," the mother superior said. "But it was a long shot at best."

AFTERMATH

Klaudie was once again sitting across from the mother superior at the Augsburg children's center. It was just after lunch, and the children were cleaning the dining room and washing the dishes.

"Where else can I go ... to try to find information about my children?"

"There are DP camps not too far away. Ludwigsburg near Stuttgart has one ... and Landsberg just south of Munich."

Klaudie had heard about the terrible conditions in some of the camps under Soviet control. Gangs of children roamed the camp-grounds, stealing, fighting other gangs, goose-stepping into the dining rooms, wrestling with one another over food. She hoped her children were not in one of those places.

"What about the special search team?" suggested a young nun as she passed by the two women.

"What is it?" mother superior asked.

"The Allies created this group of investigators to look for lost or kidnapped children. In just a few months, the investigators found 1,000 missing children. I heard that there are small groups of investigators in the DP camps, but the main one, called something like the International Tracing Bureau, or Service, or something like that—it's in Bad Arolsen."

"How far is that?" Klaudie asked the young nun.

"Nearly 300 kilometers," mother superior replied.

Klaudie sighed. She had already traveled 40 kilometers from Nürnberg to Ansbach, another 80 to Augsburg, and then on to Ulm and back. She still had plenty of money to hire a car and a driver. People in the war-torn cities and towns were so desperate, they would do almost anything for only a few coins to buy a pack of cigarettes. So money was not a problem. Neither was the rough going over bombed-out roads. The trip to Bad Arolsen, the mother superior showed her on a map, was entirely within the American occupation zone—far easier and safer than traveling through the Soviet zone.

The problem was gasoline. Supplies were limited and tightly controlled. Her drivers had gotten by haggling with black marketers or siphoning the gas tanks of abandoned vehicles. That had worked for the short trips. She worried that she might have to make at least part of the trip on a horse-drawn cart or wagon.

Chapter Forty-Four

Milan opened the latest issue of the *Svobodné Slovo* and spread the paper on top of the bar in the tavern at the end of Táborská Street, a half-block from the tenement where he lived with other former members of the Czech Resistance. He adjusted his stool and motioned for the bartender to freshen his beer.

He had been following the Nazi trials since the first prosecution early in September. Josef Pfitzner, a former professor at Prag's German university, had been tried and convicted of complicity in the execution of the man he replaced as mayor of Prag, as well as for his membership in the Nazi Party and his bastardized teaching of Czech history. That trial had met Milan's expectations. It had been quick: The proceedings took only two days. It had reached the right verdict: death by hanging. And punishment was prompt and public: Within hours of the sentencing, Pfitzner was on the gallows that had been erected in a public square, and nearly 30,000 people watched as he died, his body left hanging for more than an hour.

Milan had been dismayed, however, by the changes made by the government since then. Worried that the spectacle of public executions was too reminiscent of the extravagances of the French Revolution, the Czech government ordered workers to dismantle and destroy the gallows scaffolding, and it restricted access to all future executions. Only those with approved passes could observe executions, which were now behind the walls of Pankrác Prison. This made it extremely difficult for Milan to witness the trials and the executions himself. He had to rely on Juri.

*

Juri Fischer wormed his way into the packed courtroom, squeezing in between the rows of men leaning against the back wall, squeezing sideways and forward until he had a view of the men on trial: Seven Schupo were dressed in dull green uniforms and white gloves but were bareheaded, their caps next to them. In the middle of the group, a sergeant sat ramrod straight, chest puffed out, head erect, eyes blank, hair slicked back. From Milan's description, Juri knew that Schupo was Albert Kleinschmidt.

The clerk of the court read from statements made by interrogators and signed by prisoners. "Members of Battalion Number 89, beginning in 1940, were actively involved in resettling native populations. On the morning of each resettlement, the men received cards bearing the names and addresses of individuals who would be evacuated by the SS. Battalion members removed these individuals from their homes and assembled them at a collection point. They escorted the native populations, most of them Jews or Poles, through the center of their towns to undressing barracks where the deportees removed their clothes and were searched. The deportees were told to wrap their valuables up with their personal belongings.

"Deportees were loaded onto special trains that transported them to their designated resettlement areas. The trips took two to four days, depending on the destination. During this time, deportees were locked in cattle cars; they received no food or water."

Juri tried to imagine what it had been like on the trains: Ordinary people crammed into boxcars, unable to breathe, some covered in vomit, all surrounded by flies.

"At their destination," the clerk continued, "the deportees often would have to walk for kilometers after leaving the train station. Some old, sick and young deportees were not able to make the trip. These were rounded up and kept behind, then led to open spaces in the woods. Deportees were told to lie down on the ground, while members of the battalion stood over them. Battalion members aimed their rifles at the deportees' backs, at a point just above the shoulder blades and fired on the Battalion chief's orders. Shootings often continued throughout the day. On two occasions, Battalion members ordered some of the stronger deportees to dig mass graves, then beat them with clubs before shooting them. On other occasions, Battalion members shot deportees who could not keep up or fell while marching."

Juri squirmed in his chair. The clerk's droning recitation of the facts made the horrors he was listening to seem commonplace. A list of events, disembodied from the actual circumstances, masked the enormity of the crimes and made it hard to separate out or visualize any of them.

He turned back to the clerk of the court. "In the period of one month, Battalion members transported approximately 2,000 Jewish or Polish men, women and children. In a period of one month, they shot more than 3,000. Over a year, the Battalion transported 45,000 individuals and shot nearly 40,000."

Juri glanced at the other spectators, all crowded next to one another, some standing three deep along the wall at the back of the courtroom. Many had stopped paying attention; they were yawning, shrugging their shoulders. A pair of men near Juri muttered: "So what? They're just talking about Jews. Seems that they're trying to impress the outside world. This has nothing to do with us." Not even the total numbers of individuals rounded up, herded onto cattle cars, shot and killed seemed to impress his neighbors in the courtroom.

Juri watched the Schupo as the clerk finished: "Each of these men has admitted these crimes. Each stands for his sentence: death by hanging." None of the former Nazi policemen showed emotion. Did they truly feel nothing about what they had done? What about their punishment? Weren't they afraid of the gallows?

The sentence woke up the crowd—brief bursts of applause, cheers and rebukes rang out before the room was graveled into silence.

*

"What did they say about Lidice? What did Kleinschmidt say about it?" Milan demanded as soon as Juri entered the tenement apartment they shared with their fellow former Resistance fighters.

"Nothing. None of them spoke."

"The court didn't even bring it up? Didn't even ask them or ask him?"

Juri shook his head as he pulled out a chair and sat at the kitchen table.

"But they should tell us what they did there. He—Kleinschmidt—should tell what he did, where he took the women and the children. They should—he should—tell how he took us away in trucks, starved us, examined us and made us feel like biology specimens. He should admit to those crimes—sending women like Chessie—Paní Sabel—away to the camps and my mother—god knows where—beating me up and leaving me for dead, blowing up our town so there was nothing. NOTHING. He should be made to account for that. He should ... suffer."

Milan was pacing between the sideboard and the table, alternately

AFTERMATH

wringing his hands and rubbing them over the top of his head and face. Juri loosened his tie and unbuttoned his shirt.

"Did you yell out to him?" Milan stopped in front of Juri. "Did you? To Kleinschmidt? Did you talk to the prosecutors, tell them to ask him about Kladno? Did you do anything?"

"Milan, there was nothing to do. The court was in session. It all moves the way the judges want it to."

"I should have been there. *I* would have done something. *I* would have gotten to Kleinschmidt ..." Milan moved to the sideboard where cups and saucers had been stacked. "I would have ..." He snapped the handle off of one of the cups and stared at it.

"What happens how?" Milan asked softly.

"He dies—Kleinschmidt and the others die tomorrow."

Milan squeezed the broken piece of crockery. "Can I get to see him? In the prison? Before ..."

Juri shook his head. "It's not possible."

"I don't know why I trusted you with this," Milan spit out the words. "Like always. You just can't seem to get it done. Every time there's something important to do, you have to stop and think, give all the reasons why you have to be careful."

Milan leaned over the table and glared. "I should have gone to Saimon. He's moving up in the Communist Party, bragging about all the things he can do. *He* could have gotten me in there."

"Milan ..." Juri pleaded.

Milan threw cup handle at Juri, and the sharp edge cut his cheek.

Chapter Forty-Five

In Oskar Wolffe's opinion, his father had deteriorated markedly since he had been imprisoned in Pankrác Prison for the embezzlement of Czech funds for the Nazi regime. Otto Wolffe had always been careful about grooming: his hair closely cropped and neatly combed; his cheeks and chin cleanly shaven; his moustache trimmed razor-sharp. Sitting on a stool in a cage opposite Oskar in the prison visitor's room, Wolffe was now slovenly. His hair hung in greasy hanks on his forehead and over the tops of his ears. His moustache covered his lips and raggedly framed the corners of his mouth. Patches of whiskers darkened his cheekbones.

Despite the warm smile he gave his son, he appeared haggard and dispirited. His face was ashen, his eyes hooded and dull. His dirty gray prison uniform drooped from his shoulders, covered his wrists and fingers and curled over the tops of his shoes. Oskar was not sure whether his father had lost weight or had been given prison garb that was several sizes too large.

Oskar fumed at the shame he saw in his father and other German inmates. He was disgusted that these men who had once commanded instant respect, who had been greeted with a smart salute, a tip of the hat, a bow of the head, were now so small, sinking into themselves as if they were little more than rag-picking rabble. He lamented that men who had been so confident in their step—head erect, back tall and straight, stride firm—were slumped figures who walked slowly, their heads bent, beaten men who waddled, hands behind their back.

He struggled to quiet an eruption of anger, fumbling in his shirt pocket for the pack of cigarettes he had brought so that his father could barter with other inmates or guards for better rations. He placed the cigarettes on top of a book that hid a few bills of money in the lining of the back cover. He passed along the cash so his father might one day bribe his way onto a work crew that would get him out beyond the prison walls.

Oskar examined the crudely white-washed walls, the rusty bars of the cage, the uneven floor tiles. His father should not be in this place, he grumbled to himself. Others who had committed crimes far worse than his father—Nazi officers, concentration-camp guards—had buried their uniforms, hidden their arms and forsaken their native tongue. Men who could easily be convicted of war crimes by the Allies in their holier-than-thou Nürnberg trials were peddling potatoes from pushcarts, laying bricks for foundations, cleaning out clogged drainpipes—hiding in plain sight!

Oskar pushed his fingers through the bars of the cage to touch his father when he heard the sharp bang on the metal door that signaled the end of visitation. He had to do something, he told himself, to get his father out of this place, if only for a few hours a day.

*

"Dolak. You son of a bitch. Get out here." Oskar heard the shouts as he neared the corner of the prison complex. A young man was teetering on the curb in front of him, raising a fistful of photographs in the air and hollering at one of the building windows.

"Dolak. I know you're in there." The man slipped off the curb and onto the pavement. "You get out here and tell me what this—" He shook the photographs, releasing two that fell to the ground. He stooped to pick them the pictures, swayed, then steadied himself. "You TELL me." The man organized the photos in a stack, then shook them at the building. "I'm not leaving until YOU TELL ME." He wiped a wrist across his mouth. "DOLAK!"

Oskar flattened himself against the side of the building and watched Saimon Dolak hurry toward the man in the street. What do you know, he remarked to himself—both of them—the ones who had fingered his father for the Czech police. There they were: the cripple—what was his name? When they were growing up in Lidice? And the arsonist—the man who burned Germans to death in the street after the Liberation. Oskar took note of Saimon's uniform—he was now a ranking member of the Communist Party.

"Milan, for god's sake, shut the fuck up." Saimon took Milan's arm and pulled him down the street.

"What the hell are these things?" Milan thrust the pictures into Saimon's chest.

AFTERMATH

"Not here," Saimon said. "Over there." He led Milan toward a tavern whose doors had just opened. "What do you think you're doing? Coming here ..."

*

Oskar waited in the tavern doorway until he spotted Milan seated at a table near the end of the curved bar. He moved toward a stool at the far edge of the bar after Saimon took two cups from the bartender and carried the hot coffee to the table.

"Christ, Milan," Saimon said, tapping the face of his watch. "It's just after noon ... and you're already drunk? What the fuck is going on with you?"

Milan pushed the mug to the side. "These—these are what's going on with me." He tossed the photographs at Saimon.

"You're supposed to keep these things to yourself." Saimon collected the pictures and covered them with his fingers. He glanced around the room to see if anyone had noticed, his eyes for a moment falling on Oskar, who was moving his head from side to side as if stretching his neck.

"It took a lot for me to get these," Saimon complained.

"What good are they? Some dead guy on a slab in the morgue, stitches running down ..."

"Keep your voice down."

"Head twisted to the side ..."

"Milan," Saimon warned.

Milan sat back. "*You* tell *me*. About those things." He raised his chin toward the photos.

Saimon brought his chair close to Milan and spoke softly. "They show he's dead. Kleinschmidt. After the hanging. I thought you wanted that—to know he was dead—to see him dead."

"What I *wanted*—" Milan wiped his mouth with the cuff of his shirt. "What *I wanted* ... was to talk to him. Or you to talk to him—before they hanged him. I wanted you ... someone ... *anyone* ... to find out what he did to the women from my town. What he did to ... my mother." Milan grabbed Saimon's arm. "*Then*—after that—*that's* when I wanted to watch

AFTERMATH

Kleinschmidt die. I wanted to see every twitch and muscle spasm, every bit of drool dripping from his face, every turd falling from his ass." Milan shoved his chair back from the table. "But you couldn't do any of that, could you?" He tugged the emblem on the lapel of Saimon's uniform. "Such a big shot with the Commies. Big fucking shot."

CHAPTER FORTY-SIX

The little blond boy bounced against the back of the tram seat, tucked his hands in his armpits and focused straight ahead. He was angry his mother was paying no attention to his pleas. He didn't *want* to go see his otec. The old man was smelly. His fingers were always dirty, and his face was all sunken—a big fat nose over a collapsed mouth that didn't have any teeth in it. And he never stopped complaining about the war. The boy didn't understand why he had to go all the way across town, walk six blocks and climb five flights of stairs only to end up sitting on the floor—his grandfather had only two kitchen chairs—and watch cockroaches squirm under the floorboards. His mother never said anything about the roaches—and he knew she saw them, knew she also thought they were disgusting. But she just sat listening to the old man mumble about the Nazis and the Communists and his goddamn neighbors and the ungrateful daughter who made him live in that lousy tenement. The boy ignored his mother's entreaties— "He's your grand-father. You should respect him"—and let the screech of the tram drown out her voice.

The boy noticed the woman who was sitting behind his mother. She was watching him—a smile lifted her lips, but not her eyes. He turned to face her. "It's all right," the boy said. "Don't feel bad."

"You're so much like my son," Chessie said, reaching out to touch his hair. The boy's mother wrapped an arm around him and drew him close. "We're almost there," she said as she rose and led her son to another pair of seats at the front of the tram.

Chessie looked out of the tram window and stared at nothing.

She was now living in a rooming house with a dozen other women on the south side of Prag. She had not yet found a job, although she had an appointment with a shop steward the next day. She hoped she could start working on one of the sewing machines at the garment factory. It would mean long work days, but she would have wages to pay for her lodging, and it would fill in some of the empty hours, the hours she now spent wandering the streets or riding the tram to and from different neighborhoods.

In her travels, she looked for places she and her friends, Katrenka and Klaudie, had visited when they were teenagers: the main streets down which Katrenka had practically skipped as she window-shopped, and the café where she chattered about the finest details of the latest fashions; the beauty shop where Klaudie carefully unfolded the pictures of movie stars she had ripped out of magazines to show the hairdresser. "I want a bob, just like hers ... what do you think about this?" Klaudie had once shown her an old photo of the American actress, Carole Lombard, and fluffing her thick, reddish-brown curls, suggested getting all her hair scissored off and dyed gorgeously blond.

Chessie traveled to some of the places Katrenka had told her about when she had lived in the city with her husband and his family: the special spot in Letná Park under the poplar trees, where Katrenka and Johann had sometimes munched on hot trdelniks streaked with cinnamon and nuts; the apartment above the book shop on Benátská Street where the newlyweds had lived until Johann was sent to war.

As she moved from place to place, Chessie marveled at the condition of the city. The streets of Prag were nothing like the ones she had seen while being transported between DP camps. The German towns were little more than shells, cascading piles of rubble, punctuated by isolated segments of wall, or scarred and charred facades fronting emptiness. Prag had few remnants of the war. The most obvious were in Staré Město—the top of the Old Town Hall tower had been blown away, and the front of its astronomical clock appeared to have melted, stopping the path of the 12 apostles across time in its tracks. But the twin towers of the high gothic Týnskýy Chrám church on the other side of the square were untouched, making Chessie once again think of a fairy tale castle housing a sleeping beauty within. Even more surprising was Prag's most famous bridge. Unlike the bridges she had seen in Germany—spans from either river bank ending in space—the Karlův Most was intact, the statues of its 30 saints continuing to watch over the pedestrians who crossed over the Vltava River between the two bridge towers. Chessie couldn't help but wonder if the old wives' tale had something to do with it—perhaps the eggs mixed with the mortar when the bridge was built in the 14th century actually did strengthen the sandstone bonds.

Still, there were small, unmistakable reminders of six years of

Nazi oppression—the shops on Celetna Road near Náměstí Republiky had gouges in the masonry where German signs had been pulled down during the Prag Uprising. And it was clear that the path to recovery would be long and slow: Store windows were largely vacant, goods strategically placed toward the front of the display areas to disguise the continued scarcity of supplies.

But there was no mistaking the energy and optimism. Shops were open for business, and shopkeepers made themselves busy arranging and rearranging their limited wares, talking with prospective customers or neighbors, painting signs in Czech to replace the German ones that had been destroyed. Men were going to work, lunch pails in hand; women were folding, pressing, fluffing, examining and repairing clothes and housewares; children were out playing with sticks and balls.

Chessie stepped off the tram at Náměstí Republiky and began walking toward Obecní Dům, the massive Municipal House, on her way to church. She passed the Church of St. Jakob the Elder, which was far too flamboyant for her small-town sensibilities, and made her way across the square to Kostel Svateho Josefa. The yellow stucco Church of St. Joseph stood behind a five-foot-high gray wall and a small courtyard. It was Baroque, like the Church of St. Jakob, but much plainer. Pews were simple brushed wood. Walls above and next to the altars were painted white and remained unembellished. A dark wood crucifix was the only adornment, hanging in the curve of the dome above the main altar.

She entered the confessional at the back of the church, knelt and waited.

The thin wood partition rattled slightly as it slid back. Through the dim light, Chessie could not see the face of her confessor, just the outline of his sharply beaked nose and prominent chin.

"Bless me, Father, for I have sinned. It has been two days since my last confession."

"I am surprised that you are back so soon," the priest said. "I recognized your voice. Is it about your son?"

Chessie swallowed a lump in her throat and nodded, then whispered "Yes" when she realized he couldn't see her. "What can I do, Father? What can I do to make it up to him ... to make up for the fact that he's dead ... because of me?"

AFTERMATH

The priest sat next to Chessie on a bench in the church courtyard. "We talked about this before," he reminded her. "You did nothing wrong."

Chessie tore at a handkerchief in her lap. "I should have fought for him ... not let the guards take him away from me ... in Kladno."

"You were alone. You could not have stopped them."

"I didn't try."

"You would have been killed."

"Better if I had died defending my son."

"God has a plan for all of us."

"Damn your god if he allows a young boy to be murdered horribly ... and buried in a pit ... no one knows where." She sobbed. "In a pit I could never find ... a place I could never go to ... to say goodbye ... to tell my son that I'm sorry ..."

"Do you know about the memorial ... in Lidice?"

"I heard about it. There was a story in the newspaper."

"Have you thought about going there?"

"Why? My son is not there."

"His spirit is."

*

Chessie rapped on the door of the four-story tenement on Táborská Street in the Nusle area south of Prag Central.

"I am looking for Milan—Milan Tichy. He said he lived here." She showed the paper Milan had given her in Deggendorf.

"The tavern," the woman at the door said. "Down there ... at the end of the street."

"Milan?" Chessie gingerly touched his shoulder. "Could I talk to you? It's Chessie," she said as she sat down next to him. "Remember when you and I were in Deggendorf?"

He turned his head toward the sound of her voice and squinted his bloodshot eyes.

K. M. Sandrick

AFTERMATH

"I wanted to talk to you about this place ..." She pulled out a copy of the *Svobodné Slovo* and pointed to an article circled in pen. "It's a memorial site at Lidice. A priest told me about it. The story is about the ceremony that was held—it was in June."

Her fingers rested on a photograph that captured Czech President Edvard Beneš as he walked past a row of five flagpoles, their banners at half-staff. In front of him stood a tall metal cross, a ring of twisted metal binding the two bars together. The cross stood behind rows of evergreen trees, one for each man killed by the Nazis almost exactly three years ago to the day. A second photograph showed a crowd of thousands, along with hundreds of wreaths and other floral displays and an urn with a perpetual flame, its smoke wafting in the breeze. More than 100,000 Czech citizens had made the pilgrimage, walking or biking to the valley where the city once stood, the newspaper article reported. The people had watched a procession of Czech and Soviet soldiers, schoolchildren in regional folk costumes and dignitaries march across a raised earthen bridge over Lidice creek, then listened to a military band and finally stood in silence as the monument was dedicated.

"The priest told me that Beneš, the president, before he even went to the memorial site—he vowed that no one would forget what happened ... to our town. The ceremony and the cross and the trees," she stroked the photograph. "Are meant to create a sacred place ... to honor ..." She coughed as the emotion rose in her throat, paused and then lifted her head. "It's meant for us, Milan. It's a place for us to ..."

"To what?" Milan circled the rim of his mug with a finger. "Nothing is there, you know. I went—" he slapped the photographs. "After Kladno. I saw ..." He wrapped his fingers around the heavy glass. "Nothing ... is there."

"We could go there—say goodbye. I could say goodbye to my son. Even if he is not buried there. He lived there once. His memory is there. And ... you ... could ..."

"What do I care about that? That place—where the town was—is dead."

"I don't believe that, Milan. Yes, many have died, most in our town have died. But there is also life. Parts of our town are alive, there at the memorial site. Others from our town are alive—somewhere—they're just lost. They're living ... somewhere ... away from us ... loving us as we love them, even if we will never know where they are."

The Pear Tree

AFTERMATH

Milan opened his mouth, ready to tell Chessie that he knew her son was alive, that he had seen him on the streets of Prag, but then he closed it without uttering a word. He wanted her to need him as much as he needed her.

"We could find peace, Milan."

"Peace?" he said harshly. "And just how is that going to happen?" He stared at her. "My mother is gone. No one can tell me where she was taken, what happened to her. No silly memorial ...," he waved at the newspaper, "... is going to change that."

"But, Milan ..." Chessie said, lightly touching his arm.

He shrugged off her hand as he raised the mug to his lips.

"What's happened to you, Milan?" Chessie tried again to touch him, but he rose, stumbled against the table leg, walked to the bar and slid the mug toward the bartender. She watched him as she folded the newspaper and put it into her pocketbook. She started to follow him to the bar, but then thought better of it and left the tavern.

*

"So." An elbow nudged Milan's arm. "So ... you know that whore that gave birth to me." He turned to see Oskar standing with his back against the bar, one leg crossed over the other. "I saw you with her—over there—heard her mewling about her son ... the one who is dead ... whose memory is in Lidice." Oskar put his elbows on the edge of the bar and folded his hands across his belt.

"She hasn't changed much, has she?" He raised an arm, turned his wrist inward, flexed his fingers and stared at his cuticles. "So easy to impress with ceremonies and rhymes and folk stories, as if the Czechs had anything to celebrate." He turned toward Milan. "You know how stupid those Czech stories are, with make-believe kingdoms and castles and enchanted lands, princesses. But she was always yammering about them. My mother, my dear sweet darling mother."

"You don't deserve her."

"Oh, so you've taken a liking to her, have you?" Oskar turned his head so he could see Milan's eyes. "What's to like?" He faced the bar, grabbed the edge of the curved wood and pumped his arms as if doing push-ups. "That stringy hair, square jaw, thick nose, dark-brown eyes."

K. M. Sandrick

AFTERMATH

"She made you, didn't she?" Milan kept his head down, not wanting to look at Oskar's face. "You were good enough for the Nazis, for your new 'father'—Wolffe."

"Just goes to show you how broad-minded my people are."

"*Your* people?" Milan turned toward him and let his eyes along the boy's body.

"Yes, my stupid friend. Some of us have good genes." He smoothed back his hair and brushed the front of his shirt. "No thanks to my mother."

"But she's your mother. I'd give anything to have mine—with me—again."

"Yeah, it figures. You're just as weak as the others of your kind."

"*Our* kind? You're one of us."

"Oh no, my dear boy." Oskar moved in close to Milan, his head inches away from Milan's.

"I'm nothing like you or her ... my mother." He tugged on Milan's shirt collar, then let go in disgust, turning to wipe his fingers on a bar towel.

"She doesn't know, does she? That I'm still alive." Oskar smiled and turned toward Milan again. "She doesn't know what happened to her son or ...," Oskar took Milan's mug and sipped the foam, "... that you've known all along that I'm alive. Her one and only son—is alive. Now, wouldn't she like to know? What if I go and find her and say, 'Oh, mama. I've been so lost without you. I've been looking for you—in so many places.' Better yet," Oskar laughed. "What if I find out when she's going back to Lidice, to that memorial site? What if I get there first and pop out of the trees when she's falling all over herself in grief over her lost baby boy? What if I put my arms around her?" Oskar wrapped his arms around Milan's shoulders. "And ask her why she believed I was dead. 'Oh, that's so sad that you didn't know about me,' I'd tell her. But then I'd say there weren't very many people who knew I was still alive.' 'There's that one—in Prag—that one boy—the one from our town—Milan—Milan Tichy. You remember him? He's the only one from our town I saw in Prag.' How do you think she would feel about that? Oh, thrilled to find me again, of course, but wondering: 'Why did that boy, Milan—Milan Tichy? Why didn't he say anything, when he knew I thought my son was dead? Why did he let me believe that?'"

The Pear Tree

AFTERMATH

"What do you want?"

"Tell that Commie friend of yours, that bastard Dolak, to get my father out of prison."

"How?"

"He's the smart one. Let him figure it out." Oskar tipped Milan's mug so the beer spilled over the edge of the bar. "Just get it done soon. I won't wait—to see my mother—for long."

Chapter Forty-Seven

Juri pulled the fire department van off the dirt road and onto the grass, guiding the vehicle over a small hillock before parking and switching off the engine. He glanced at Milan, who sat in the backseat, his head turned toward the road, his eyes unfocused.

He tapped the steering wheel. "We're here," he said to Chessie who sat n the front seat beside him.

"I'll just wait ..." His voice betrayed his uncertainty. The journey from this point was one only Chessie and Milan could make. He realized that. Still...

Chessie stepped out of the van, opened the back door and waited for Milan, but he did not respond.

"Aren't you getting out? Going down the road to the memorial? I wish you would, Milan. I think it would help."

She worried about him. He had become so angry and disillusioned that he was folding in on himself, withdrawing into solitude and despair, refusing to accept condolence from her or his friends. She thought this trip would be an opening, an acknowledgement that his sorrow was shared by many in a grieving nation, but he had been prickly, quick to anger from the moment he got in the van. Now that they were at the memorial site, he was calm and quiet but distant, his face and body closed.

Chessie removed a cloth bag from the backseat, cast one last look at Milan and began walking across the softly rising meadow between spindly stalks that swayed with the breeze.

"Why did you even come?" Juri asked as soon as Chessie was out of earshot. "Well?"

Milan was silent.

"There's a formal memorial, a commemoration of your town and all that was there, all that you lost," Juri persisted.

"What's the point? It was a graveyard when I saw it three years ago; it's still a graveyard, with a cheap metal cross in the middle of a bunch of trees."

"But each of those trees is for one of the men who was killed here ..."

"And what about the women?" Milan interrupted. "The women they took and killed and buried ... wherever ..." Milan's voice caught in his throat. "There's nothing for me here. My mother isn't here."

"Your brother. Didn't you tell me he was shot and killed here?" Juri paused. "Your friend Ceslav?"

Milan squirmed.

"Well, maybe you don't want to go for yourself, but what about her?" Juri indicated Chessie, who was joining a line of people who had left the road and were making their way across the meadow, carrying bouquets of flowers and mementoes.

"You told me you didn't want her to come alone."

"I meant when we were on the street—in Prag—I worried who she might run into ... and I didn't want her to be by herself." He scratched the back of his neck.

"Who? What are you talking about?"

"Never mind." Milan squeezed his upper arms. "I was just worried about her."

"What about now? When she's going to see what you saw three years ago? How did you feel then? How do you think *she's* going to feel?"

Juri opened the door of the van, released the back door handle, and grabbed Milan's arm. "Go. She's your friend. She needs you."

Milan stepped out of the van and walked into the field of goldenrod and false sunflowers, hat pulled down over his ears, eyes on the ground.

*

Chessie opened the bag she had brought from Prag, removed a nosegay of flowers and placed it at the front edge of a raised platform that sat to the side of and across the road from the memorial. As she moved past the platform, the scent from hundreds of floral wreaths, potted plants and garlands of red and gold chrysanthemums became nearly overpowering. She suppressed the urge to sneeze away the pollen particles that tickled the hairs in her nose and the spasms that tightened her chest.

She approached the near side of the memorial and stood at the corner of a low concrete boundary. She touched the spines on a pine tree branch and wondered: Which man did this tree commemorate? Katrenka's brother Kornel? Farmer Horák? Milan's brother Ignace? His friend Ceslav? Her neighbor, Pan Adamcik?

Continuing along the concrete edging, around the periphery of the memorial, Chessie let her fingers feel the needles of each tree. Grief, then anger, swelled within her. She mourned the tragedy that all these men had been slaughtered, sacrificed—but she resented them, too. The men here had a resting place, rows of living testimonials to their lives, a formal site where loved ones could come to remember, link with their yesterdays and ease the pain of their todays. But she had none of that. Her son had been slaughtered, sacrificed—yet there was no resting place for him, nowhere for her to go to weep over his loss or to enjoy the memories of his life with her.

A sob rose from her soul. She staggered and nearly fell to the ground.

"Here, dear," an old woman touched Chessie's elbow and began to lead her away from the memorial.

"This is your first time—I can tell," the old woman said. "It is not easy ... being here. It is difficult even for me, and I have been coming here every now and again for weeks."

The woman linked her arm in Chessie's. "It's not that I am from this town—the town that used to be here." She felt Chessie tense.

"It's all right, dear." She patted Chessie's arm. "Call me Tetka. I live a few kilometers away with my son and his wife. And I remember Lidice, the men going to and from work, the women and girls traveling to the city, the farmers bringing their crops to market. When I heard what happened, I had to come ... to see ..."

The old woman directed Chessie toward a flat area of dark-green and purple groundcover. "I have been walking this place ...," she indicated the rolling grassland, "... many times. It was important for to me to figure out where things used to be. Can you understand that?"

Nodding, Chessie she introduced herself, patting herself on the chest.

AFTERMATH

The old woman gestured toward the formal memorial area. "The trees and the cross are wonderful tributes, but they are not the essence of the town, if you know what I mean."

"Yes, yes," Chessie said, wiping her nose and eyes with the edge of a kerchief.

"Would you like to walk with me—to learn what I have learned?"

Chessie slipped her arm out from the woman's grasp and wrapped it around her waist. "Show me, please."

She led Chessie to an uneven path that angled away from the memorial area and toward a bridge spanning a gurgling stream. "This is not, of course, where Lidice creek was," the old woman said. "And that makes all the difference, don't you agree? If you know where the creek was, you can put other things in place."

The old woman stepped off the path and moved into a line of bluemist shrub. "The creek, you see, ran along that line of young trees." She extended her hand. "Can you see it in your mind?"

"Yes."

"And the bridge was there, just past the lindens in the midst of the bromegrass." The old woman paused. "Let me rest just a little," she said, as she raised a handful of berries to her mouth. She then put her hand back on Chessie's arm and took a few steps.

"So from there—where the original creek and bridge were—you can figure out that the church was up in that rocky area. The grain store was to the right of the church, and the butcher shop was down around there." She tilted her head to the side.

"Now, here is what I want you to see."

The old woman entered a thicket, stumbling slightly over rust-colored Joe-Pye weed and pointed to a small crooked tree, its trunk bifurcated, a thick scarred knob on one side and three young branches sprouting from the other.

"A pear tree," she said, "the only thing from Lidice that still lives."

Her hand to her mouth, Chessie looked back and forth between the tree and the old woman.

"It was just a stalk ... when I last saw it." Chessie caressed Tetka's arm and shoulder. "I warned Ondrej ... my son ..." She turned to face the woman. "I didn't want him to damage it. He was running around, throwing stones, calling it a ..." She paused to catch her breath. "A stink tree. You know how pear trees are in the spring ... how awful they smell?" Her voice caught. "I was so worried ... about that little tree, but I didn't have to be, did I?" Sobs took her breath away.

She rubbed her palms on her thighs, at first absently, then quickly and more purposefully. She closed her eyes and took a breath, groped for Tetka's support and lowered herself to the ground. On her knees in front of the tree, she rested her forehead against the base of the blackened knot that marked where the top of the tree had cracked and fallen to the ground after Nazi bombings and fire. She stroked the bark and the tops of the plants that had sprouted between the roots—whorls of German garlic and thick black spleenwort.

"Chessie?" Tetka asked.

"I am alright. I just need time ..." The tree, she realized, would be her memorial for her son. She would come here, plant flowers at its base, drop bits of oplatky wafers on the ground at Christmas time and cirak at Easter, add woven straw figures or small crocheted bands to its lower leaves, sit with an open sack lunch in her lap and remind herself of her son and the time they had had together.

As Tetka stepped away, Chessie began to tug at the underbrush, then into the dirt. She slowly uprooted plants, working systematically until she created a small open area. Flattening the foliage on either side of the space, she rested her cheek on the ground, then pushed her fingers as far as she could into the soil. She stretched out her body and pressed it into the earth as hard as she could and breathed a soft goodbye to her son.

*

Chessie rose, brushed off her skirt and blouse, kissed the blades of the leaves that grew in reddish-orange clusters where she had lain and turned toward the road, the truck, Juri and Milan. She was surprised to see that Milan had come onto the memorial grounds and was standing next to the rows of evergreens above the mass grave that held the bodies of the men of Lidice. Moving next to him, she let her shoulder touch his.

"It's so hard," he said, without turning toward her. "The men, the boys, Ceslav are ..." He pointed down. He paused. "She's dead, isn't she?" He looked at Chessie.

AFTERMATH

"I believe so, Milan."

"She's dead. My mother ... and I'll never ..." He stopped, his words strangling his throat, burning his lungs as they gave testimony to the reality he had tried so hard to disprove. He raised his head, threw it back and opened his mouth. With all the force of his being, he howled. He converted all the pain of loss and guilt and failure into a sound, raw and feral, that gave voice to his thoughts and feelings when his mother had collapsed at the sight of his dead brother, when she folded into herself and couldn't respond to his touch, when he took her limp, insensate arm in his and fended off Kleinschmidt's blows, when he woke to find himself alone on the gymnasium floor and his mother gone. It captured his feelings when he returned to Lidice and stumbled on the grave of his pet—the only clear sign of the town where he and his mother and family had lived and loved. The sound reverberated throughout his body, making his chest heave, his arms twitch, his shoulders shudder.

At last he dropped his head to his chest and gave in to the sorrow as it rose from his core and culminated in rapid, convulsive breaths. "Help me," he whispered as Chessie wrapped her arms around him. He let her hold on to him until the shaking stopped.

K. M. Sandrick

AFTERMATH

Chapter Forty-Eight

Saimon Dolak sat in Milan's apartment on Táborská Street, eying the boy as he measured ground coffee and spooned it into the metal basket, inserted the basket into the coffee pot and placed the pot on top of the potbelly stove. The boy had changed significantly in the weeks since his return from the Lidice memorial site. His hair was washed and neatly combed, his nails were clean, his shirt was pressed and tucked into his trousers. Saimon didn't know if Milan had stopped drinking entirely, but at least he was not perpetually drunk, and the signs of alcoholism were dissipating: His eyes were no longer red-rimmed and rheumy; his breath and body no longer smelled stale; his skin was pale but no longer gray and streaked with broken blood vessels. Saimon knew Milan was preparing to apply for a job with the Prag security force—something Saimon had wanted for him ever since Liberation but had thought was out of the question once Milan turned to the bottle. If he was able to keep it up and stay dry, Saimon just might put in a word for him, not only with the police, but the Communist Party as well. The Party could use his talents and courage.

He turned his attention to the matter at hand. Milan had asked Saimon to request a transfer for Otto Wolffe, one of the German prisoners in Pankrác Prison. Wolffe was not doing well in confinement: he was weak, often ailing, and for the most part couldn't pull his weight on the work crew. He was not a war criminal—a Nazi party official, or Gestapo henchman or a Soldat—whose release would send tremors up the line in the Communist Party. Wolffe also might have useful information. The Third Reich had plundered anywhere from 34 to 94 tons of gold from Czechoslovakia and funneled bullion as well as stolen currency, shares of stock and securities into secret Swiss accounts that were being credited or transferred to other countries, most recently to Argentina. The Soviet Union thus far had not benefited from its war efforts. The Soviets had expected to be rewarded with gold reserves from the Baltic States after their 1938 invasion of Poland, but none of it had ever been transferred from the Allied banks that ended up holding the bullion. So while the Communist Party in Czechoslovakia was adamant about punishing

AFTERMATH

Czech collaborators as well as "Hitlerites," Saimon believed he could plead a strong case for moving Wolffe from the prison to an administrative office so the Party could learn how the banker had managed ledgers, money transfers, safe deposits and accounts, and in the process, learn about some of the ins and outs of Swiss money-laundering. He just wondered why Milan was so involved.

"Isn't this the man, the banker, you were tailing just before the war ended?" Saimon asked.

Milan nodded as he touched the side of the coffee pot to check on the progress of the boil.

"When did you start looking out for ex-Nazis?" Saimon persisted.

Milan grabbed a pot holder from a hook above the stove and pushed the pot off the heat. "Well, you were talking about the Nazi money the other day, and I remembered Wolffe."

"So you followed up? Found where he was sent? What he was doing in prison?"

Milan dropped his eyes. "It's not like I did a lot of work here. I just remembered the guy and thought I'd pass along the information to you. If you're not interested ..."

"No, no, no. Let me look into this."

*

Milan was relieved that Saimon wasn't asking too many questions. He didn't have answers—at least ones he wanted to share with him. He wasn't about to admit that Wolffe's son Oskar was not German, to acknowledge that the boy had been born and raised in his own home town, had gone to the same school, was his friend Chessie's flesh and blood. Or to tell Saimon that he wasn't interceding on behalf of the Wolffes—father or son—or even to keep Ondrej/Oskar from telling his mother that Milan had known he was alive all along. No, he was doing it for Chessie. It was better for her to believe her son had been killed by the Nazis than to find out he had turned into one.

*

Karl Hermann Frank waited while the MP who guarded him

handed his belongings over to the prison clerk through the office window next to the entryway, then walked to the cage that served as the holding pen. He squinted as his eyes adjusted to the gloom and surveyed his surroundings: the barred holding pen in which he sat; the long hallway ending with floor-to-ceiling bars; the black-and-white-checked linoleum floor; the dingy walls with their peeling paint; the rectangular opaque windows set high in the walls.

Frank was being admitted, nearly two months to the day after his last interrogation, to Pankrác Prison in Prag. Unlike other leaders of the Third Reich, he was not going to be tried in Nürnberg or in any of the other courts in Germany. He had been extradited by the Allies to the Czech government and would be tried by a Czech court of law.

His strategy had backfired. He had made too strong of an argument, been too convincing to the interrogators and proved to their satisfaction, apparently, that he *was* an underling, not a member of the Nazi high command. His carefully framed answers to interrogators' questions had been crafted to give him a chance at exoneration or dismissal of all charges before the international tribunal and a trial in Nürnberg before professional judges, prosecutors and defense attorneys, but it was all for naught. His extradition to Prag meant almost certain conviction.

It was a travesty. He would *not* have the right to counsel; he would *not* be presumed innocent; he would *not* be judged on proof beyond any reasonable doubt. No, he would have *none* of that. He would be judged by a Czech People's Court that had four lay "judges" in addition to a professional magistrate—four people who would be little more than rabble off the streets or flat-out enemies to officers in the Third Reich—former concentration-camp inmates and Resistance fighters. How could these "judges" possibly understand the law or the arguments he had so carefully embedded in his statements to interrogators? How could they view him fairly if they were swayed by their own perceived concentration-camp horror stories? How could they look beyond the Obergruppenführer title to see *him*—a military man who had only been doing his duty, a man who had *absolutely nothing to do with the camps, or the Jews, or the so-called crimes against humanity?* No, he would be at the mercy of the mongrels.

*

"We're almost there," said the hay wagon driver as he clicked his tongue and flicked the reins on the back of his horse.

Klaudie nodded, not taking her eyes from the roadway and the remnants of the Wehrmacht airfield alongside. Several Messerschmitts, torn and disabled, lay in a field of high grass, their cockpits charred and wrenched open, propeller blades broken, camouflage-painted fuselages flat on the ground—casualties of the Allied air raids that began in 1943 and intensified as the German army and air force were driven out of Bavaria.

She was apprehensive. She was following up on a lead she had found in the records at the International Tracing Service in Bad Arolsen: a description of a teenage girl who had been taken to a Lebensborn facility around the time of the Lidice massacre, along with the name and location of the German family who had adopted her. But she was running out of options. If she could not find Adéle here in Regensburg, she would have to journey far to the east, to Poland, where the trails of several Lidice children ended. The idea of traveling through Soviet-controlled territory was frightening. If she had to she would, of course, but not without an armed escort. She was sure she could find one, but it meant more time, more money, more red tape.

She shook those thoughts out of her mind and turned her attention to Regensburg. The wagon was entering the Old Town area of the medieval city. Along the winding cobblestone streets, she could see little damage. Allied bombs had targeted the airfield and munitions plant to the west but left most of the city intact, including the Gothic Regensburg Cathedral, the 14th-century Old Town Hall and the buildings around the Haidplat city square. Signs of the war were more obvious near the Danube. The loading dock for ships and storage sheds was bombed out, and the top level of the concrete bridge that had been built in Hitler's name in 1938 had slid off its foundation blocks, but that might have been the result of Wehrmacht bombings engineered to stall Allied advances, not Allied bombers themselves.

The driver directed the horse to the semicircular roadway in front of the cathedral and waited while Klaudie slid off the wagon to the ground. He dipped his head to acknowledge that he would lead the horse and cart out of the city and wait for her at the side of the road near the airfield.

Klaudie set off through a residential area of three-story buildings lined up flush with one another. She slowed as she neared the address scrawled on the wrinkled piece of paper in her pocket, noting an open window on the second story and an edge of billowing blue fabric. Taking a deep breath, she knocked.

*

The upholsterer burst out of his shop doorway, feathers swirling around his head and shoulders. Chessie smiled as she walked past the man on her way to Milan's apartment and remembered the early January day when Katrenka had returned to Lidice from Prag.

Chessie had ducked out of the way of an arching snowball lofted by Ondrej from the bushes next to the Lidice schoolhouse and run into the middle of the street, nearly colliding with Katrenka. Katrenka was bracing herself against the chill, alternating between holding the collar of her threadbare cloth coat closed and shaking the cold from her thinly gloved hands. She walked slowly, head down, kicking through the banked snow as she made her way to a shoveled path. She was pale and sluggish.

Few from Lidice greeted her that day. Most of the men glanced up only briefly from their chores, then returned to chopping wood, shoeing horses, rounding up feed for farm animals. The women remained behind closed cottage doors. The only evidence of their presence was the flutter of curtains falling back into place as Katrenka passed by.

"Goodness," Chessie had said to Katrenka. "You must be deathly cold. Come, let me warm you up." She clasped Katrenka's fingers and rubbed them with her own. "Come home with me for a cup of hot cider."

"Thank you so much," Katrenka said, "but I need to get home—to see my brother. It's been a long trip and I am so tired."

Two snowballs sailed over in rapid succession. One directly hit Chessie's back; the other just missed Katrenka's head. "*Ondrej!*" Chessie shouted as a third snowball smacked the ground in front of her. She turned to see her son mounding another handful of snow. "Ok, that's enough," she said, but not soon enough to prevent another volley.

"Looks like you have your hands full," Katrenka laughed. "And I'd better get out of the way." Another snowball flew through the air, then another rolled up to Katrenka's shoes. "All right. You're in for it now," Chessie called to Ondrej as she turned to run towards him.

AFTERMATH

She hadn't seen much of Katrenka in the months that followed. The bitter cold of that winter kept people indoors most of the time. As the weather improved in the spring, Katrenka was still reclusive. But Chessie made it a point to stop by when she could, to serve as a sounding board for Katrenka's questions about pregnancy: "I am so sick. Almost all of the time. Was it like that for you? It is so hard for me to breathe. Was it like that for you?"

Chessie brought advice about home remedies and shared her knowledge about the gender of Katrenka's baby. "Carrying the baby high means it's a girl," she told Katrenka. "A needle suspended over the belly will swing back and forth if it's not."

Now Chessie knew from what Silvie had told her just before she died in the Ravensbrück camp that she had been right: Katrenka had given birth to a baby girl.

*

Karl Hermann Frank unwrapped the wool blanket he had been given by the trustee of Pankrác Prison. In addition to the blanket and a single, rough-textured white sheet, he found a bar of soap, a roll of toilet paper, a toothbrush and a can of toothpaste, shaving paste and a brush, plus a single-blade razor, a plastic cup and a bent metal spoon. The clothing he would wear in place of his Obergruppenführer uniform included a prison jumpsuit, brown sandals, green socks, a pajama top and bottom and a pair of dirty gray boxer shorts.

Frank threw the blanket and the items it held on the cell floor and dropped down onto his mattress. He stared at the guard who jiggled the keys to his cell as the man turned the lock, critiquing his Slavic face: a disgusting overhanging brow—like a primate; a bulbous nose; a hang-dog expression.

As he turned away from the guard, Frank called out: "I should have killed more of you people when I had the chance."

*

Paní Dagmar Skala felt the whiff of a cool breeze as she rounded the path that curved alongside the tower and nave of St. Peter and Paul Church. She paused before crossing the street that led to the Unhošt' town square and the market area to fasten the top button of her cardigan. Autumn had been slow in coming: Until the last week, most days had been quite warm, despite the waning hours of daylight. She welcomed the cooling temperatures, even though she soon would notice the effects of the changing season in her arthritic joints.

Paní Skala merged her steps with those of other women on their way to the open-air farmers' market at the opposite end of the square. Only two trucks, as far as she could see, were parked in the street with their tailgates open, and small groups of women peered inside them. Certainly not as many farmers as there had been before the war—Paní Skala could remember farmers' markets that had as many as six trucks crowded on the narrow street. But that had been years ago, before local farmers lost their property to the New Germans and growers sent their produce elsewhere—to the Wehrmacht or to the Nazi Oberlandrats. Since the peace agreement at Potsdam, the Allied Control Council had begun planning the transfer of Sudeten Germans from the Occupied territories to Germany. But the Czech government wasn't waiting. The Czech Third Republic, formed in April, just as the war was ending, had started confiscating property that belonged to Nazis and Nazi collaborators and distributing it to local peasants. Already, a few farmers in Central Bohemia had repossessed some nearby farm buildings and fields, and they were now bringing their harvests to Unhošť and other towns every few weeks.

Forced by the bowing of her upper spine, Paní Skala continually looked at her feet: black leather oxfords, seams split, laces shortened and frayed at the ends, moving across the patterned stone tiles, from light-gray to dark-gray squares. After traveling about 15 meters, she spied what she was looking for—the raised edge of stone that bordered the ground where one of the town square's six trees had been planted and the bench that rested next to it.

She was not in a hurry. From her experience over the last few weeks, she knew by this time of day, the produce in the farmers' trucks would be brown at the tips, wilted and musty. If she had been shopping for her daughter and new grandbaby, she would have been waiting for the trucks at dawn. But today, the trip was only for herself, more of an excuse, to her way of thinking, to sit in the square and watch the townspeople.

Paní Skala inclined her head so she could look at the trees and their colors. At the far end of the square was her favorite—a bushy pear tree that was always stunning in its transition from summer to autumn. It did not disappoint: The lower branches were still green, but the middle ones had bursts of fuchsia and the top was the color of a mandarin orange. She marveled at the tree's transformation. It was such a nuisance in the spring when it smelled like rotting fish, but then it became a flowering beauty, with clusters of white, five-petal blossoms. And in autumn—breathtaking.

As she turned to rise, Paní Skala noticed the butcher's brother-in-law and his young daughter.

*

Chessie was growing steadily stronger. She was able to walk across town and make her way from greengrocer to butcher shop to bakery and get supplies for herself and the other refugee women in the rooming house, then prepare innovative meals despite limited food options. She had put herself in charge of cleaning the apartment and was handling laundry and sewing, in addition to her work at the clothing factory.

The feelings of desolation were subsiding. She shook off remembrances of Ravensbrück, the forced march through the north German woods and the refugee camps when they bubbled up and threatened to plunge her into despair. She replaced the horror of evacuation from Lidice with memories of life as it once had been: tugs-of-war with Klaudie over whose doll was whose; tests on botanical names posed by her father during walks in the forest; long, slow love-making with her husband. The hole in her heart from the loss of her son could not be filled. She knew that. But her heart was opening up again—for Milan.

She lamented the changes in the boy that had been spurred by his drive to find his mother. The qualities she had seen when she first encountered him in Deggendorf—his self-reliance, determination and kindness—had steadily eroded as he came to recognize the futility of the search for his mother and to realize that she most likely would never be found, that her fate would forever remain unknown.

Since their trip to the memorial site at Lidice, she noted signs that Milan was finally healing. His generosity and sensitivity were re-emerging. Chessie believed he was growing into the kind of man she had hoped her son would become—strong and steadfast, but kind and compassionate. A few days ago, she had seen him separate two boys who had been wrestling in the street in front of his tenement. As he moved between them, he did not lecture or harangue the older, bigger boy who had bested the younger one. He complimented the boy on his skills but then suggested that he share his knowledge, instead of using it on those who were less experienced. Then Milan brought the other boy in close to him so the youngster could hide his tears in Milan's trousers. She was so proud of him.

*

Footsteps, children's voices, the click of a lock releasing. "Yes?" a young woman stood in the doorway, her body blocking the rush of three toddlers toward Klaudie.

"I am looking for Bauer." Klaudie gave the name of what she hoped was Adéle's adoptive family.

"No, no one here by that name." The young woman turned toward the interior of the home, calling, "Mama, can you come and take them?"

"Did a family with this name live here, maybe in 1942?"

Facing Klaudie, the young woman shrugged. "The people who lived here ... before us—a woman and a couple of children—left months ago. There are stories that she was afraid for herself and her girls ... because of the Soviet POWs. They had been released and were heading here. Women and girls living alone, they were most afraid ... afraid of the rapes."

"They said she drowned her daughters," said an old woman, standing behind the children. "The woman who lived here, that is. Drowned the girls and then herself—tied stones to their necks and pushed them in the Danube—so they wouldn't have to submit."

"Mama, you don't know that."

"Well, they did find some bodies ... downstream."

"Hush, Mama." To Klaudie, she said, "Don't listen to her. There were never any bodies downstream. Just some people telling scary stories."

"Do you know where I can find people who knew the Bauer family? Anyone who could give me information about them?"

AFTERMATH

"No, I'm sorry."

"There's a DP camp," the old woman called out. "Not far away from here."

"I'm sorry," the young woman repeated, slowly closing the door.

*

Chessie could not get Katrenka out of her mind since she and Milan had returned from the Lidice memorial site. In her mind's eye, Chessie saw Katrenka in the rocking chair in the garden of her mother's home, at the kitchen table sketching copies of the garments shown in the newspaper advertisements, dressed in traditional Czech folk costume at her wedding. Then her memory flashed to Katrenka crying out for her carved bird in the Lidice schoolhouse, holding Ondrej's hand behind the Schupo truck, sitting alone in the corner of the Kladno school gymnasium. She remembered Katrenka's eyes seeking and finding hers, the beginning of her smile, then the realization that even Chessie was abandoning her, her eyes then clouding and dropping to the floor. Chessie thought of Kleinschmidt bending over, speaking close to Katrenka's ear, the Schupo guards picking her up, Silvie and Weber following Katrenka across the floor of the Kladno gymnasium.

Words as well as images haunted Chessie.

"What I said before ...," Silvie had said, "... about Katrenka's baby. She, the baby, didn't die."

"The Schupo took her, the baby, away from me."

"The Lidice baby."

"The Schupo took her."

"The baby."

"The Schupo."

Weber.

*

Klaudie walked slowly back toward Regensburg Cathedral. Ahead of her, she could see the top of the Golden Tower, marking the entry into the city from the old stone bridge. Near the church was the

Adler-Apotheke, historic pharmaceutical bottles and formulating vessels in its front window. She kicked at small piles of debris at the edge of the pavement and watched as they swirled in front of her. Was she foolish—going off on her own to try to find her daughter, following up on the lead to the Bauer family that she knew was a long shot? The people at the International Tracing Service had been kind but blunt. Few of the Lidice children had lived, the woman at the Tracing Service said. The woman had tried to soften the story, but in the end she admitted that all indications had led investigators to believe the children had been gassed to death. "There were the gas vans. Green vans that were usually used for carrying furniture," the woman had said. Klaudie's mind flashed back to the parking area behind the gymnasium in Kladno. "They were rigged to send gas from the exhaust pipe into the cargo area of the van."

Some of the children from Lidice had ended up in Chelmno—the death camp in Poland where thousands of inmates had been gassed to death, their bodies burned in the crematoria. "It's possible one of your children—your daughter—could have been sent to the Lebensborn facility in Pushkau, near Poznan in Poland." Klaudie remembered the look on the woman's face, the tone of her voice, telling more than her words.

Was she chasing phantoms? Like Chessie? Like Chessie had been in Ravensbrück, when she insisted on writing letters to a boy everyone had told her was dead? Was she stubborn and foolish to believe that the situation was different for her? That her children were alive when Chessie's boy wasn't?

*

Paní Skala shook her head at the thought of how suspicious she had been of the butcher's assistant, Wim. How could she have thought he was hiding from something, that he was a Nazi sympathizer or even worse—a fighter on the German side in the war? She had come to like him. He was friendly and funny with customers in the butcher shop, and he had become more knowledgeable about cuts of meat and the ways to prepare them. Patrik must have given him a good talking-to, she laughed to herself. But most important to her changed opinion was the way he interacted with his daughter. Paní Skala had only a little experience with Nazi soldiers or officials, but from that, she had concluded that the men were distant, judgmental and demanding of youngsters. Wim was nothing like them. She had seen him walking hand in hand with his daughter, his ear cocked to her words, his eyes bright with excitement; or carrying her in the crook of his arm, a hand pressing her head to his shoulder; or sweeping the child up high in the air, then depositing her atop his shoulders.

In the butcher shop, on a small table he had set up next to the meat display case, he would crouch down to watch his child's crayon drawings take form, admiring the wide swaths of color she applied to sheets of butcher paper. "That's a nice little doggy," he once said while Pani Skala was waiting for Patrik to wrap her package.

"No, silly," his daughter reprimanded him. "It's a dragon. A big, old, nasty dragon."

"And when was the last time you saw a dragon?"

"You don't have to see one to know about them."

"How do you know they're mean?"

"They breathe fire," she said in a huff.

"Oh, of course."

Pani Skala couldn't help but notice the kindness in the man's manner, the patience in his tone when father and daughter were together as they were now, at a bench in the square. Wim was bent forward, his palms loosely on his daughter's waist as she stood in front of him. The little girl was talking animatedly, waving her hands and pointing to one of the pockets of his jacket. He shrugged when she grabbed the cloth, tugged the pocket open and pulled out a handkerchief and a pair of keys.

*

Reluctant to leave the city, Klaudie turned down a side street, the roof of the train station ahead. People hurried toward the tracks where lines of box cars stood open, much of their contents already strewn on the ground. She stopped and watched people dig through packages and cartons and papers: a dark-haired girl in braids; old men in tattered suits and uniforms; an old woman in a long dark coat.

A young woman stood with her back toward Klaudie, rubbing her lower back. As she bent to retrieve a parcel, Klaudie could see the outlines of her pregnancy. Dissatisfied with the contents of the parcel, the woman dropped them on the ground. Turning other packages over with her foot, she tugged strands of hair from behind her ear, ran them under her nose and then sucked on the ends.

Klaudie's breath caught in her throat. How many times had she told her daughter to stop doing that? She had not learned, had she?

"Adéle?" she called softly. "Adéle?" she said more loudly until the woman turned and she could open her arms to her daughter.

*

"Where to next?" Paní Skala could see Wim mouth the words to his daughter.

When the little girl pointed to a pants pocket, Wim rose up on his opposite hip and extended his leg so his daughter could reach inside. He laughed when she put her hands on her hips, unhappy that the pocket held only a ration book and a few coins.

Then she caught hold of his jacket lapel and pulled the fabric against the buttons. "Open it," she seemed to tell her father as he unfastened the front of the jacket. She pointed to the buttoned-down pocket on the right side of his shirt and bounced impatiently while he lifted the flap and invited her to explore. "There," she shrieked, squeezing the pocket and urging her father to remove the object within.

The little girl took the object from him and turned it over. It appeared to Paní Skala to be wood, carved into some form.

"Tell me, again, Papa," Paní Skala heard as she drew near enough to hear the conversation.

"This belonged to a woman who loved you very much." Weber adjusted his shirt pocket and refastened the front of his jacket, then lifted his daughter onto his thigh. "It was very precious to her and she wanted you to have it."

"Why?"

"Her husband carved it for her."

"Why?"

"Because he was going off to war and wanted her to have something special, something he had made himself."

"What happened to him?"

AFTERMATH

"He died in the war."

"Why?"

"He was in a battle and he was hurt."

"What happened to the lady?"

"She died, too."

"Why?"

"She was very sick,"

"Why?"

"She had some condition, I don't know what it was, darling, but she got very ill and she died."

"When?"

"She died right around the time you were born."

"Hello, Wim, Katra," Paní Skala said as she approached the pair.

"Hello, hello," Katra said, jumping down from her father's lap and hurrying over to the old woman. "Look at this." She opened her hand. "It's a bird."

Paní Skala extended a finger and felt the grooves along the top of the bird's head and its wings. "Yes, I see that. It's beautiful."

"It's for me. It's very special. Papa told me. He is saving it for me."

Weber rose from the bench, lifted his daughter up in his arms and gazed at the bird, remembering how he had found it.

The carved wooden bird lay on the floor of the infirmary, next to the birthing bed, and Katrenka's lifeless body. He picked up the bird, then bent to whisper: "Don't worry, Paní Becke. I am going to get your baby and carry her away from here. I am going to take care of her and protect her." He brushed strands of hair away from her forehead, closed her eyelids, then kissed each of her hands and folded them on her chest.

"I am leaving the police ... the Schupo, Paní Becke. I am going to stay with my brother-in-law, in Central Bohemia. We—my wife and I—are going to make a home for your baby ... a home you would be proud of. I ... and my wife ... will tell your daughter... Katra, we will name her... all about you." He pocketed the bird, tipped his helmet and bowed his head. "You will not be forgotten."

*

K. M. Sandrick

AFTERMATH

Chessie entered the tenement building on Táborská Street in the Nusle area of Prag, stepping to the side to make way for a Communist Party official exiting the building. She walked up the four flights of stairs and down the hall to apartment 4N, wishing the landlord or residents would brighten up the drab walls with fresh paint. She rubbed her palms on the front of her skirt and wrapped her fingers under the bottom hem of her jacket. She took a breath, raised her fist and rapped her knuckles on the dark-green, paint-flecked door.

The door opened, and Milan stood at the threshold, backed by the light from a single bare bulb hanging from a cord in the ceiling. She stepped into his open arms and brushed her lips against his cheek. Accepting a cup of freshly brewed coffee, she gazed at Milan while taking a sip. She marveled at him—all he had been through—his injuries and disability, the loss of his brother and mother and best friend, his work with the Resistance. All this, while so young and so alone.

She watched him now as he stacked the books and papers on security procedures he had been studying and placed them on one of the kitchen chairs to clean off the tabletop. She watched his hands carefully arrange the sheets in neat piles and his eyes: They were clear and focused; intent while he organized the paperwork; tender and shining when he looked at her. Chessie breathed deeply, stoking her resolve to broach an idea to him.

She had been fretting lately, restless about where she was and where she had been. She wondered why she had been able to circumvent the many threats to her life. She could have been singled out for death with the other women and children of Lidice. She could have died from typhus or tuberculosis in the Ravensbrück labor camp or left to starve in the forest at Wittstock. Yet she hadn't.

The same was true for Milan. He had not been herded up and executed with the men of Lidice; he had not died from his injuries or from starvation after Kladno; nor in Resistance fighting.

There had to be a reason they were still alive, and she thought she knew what it was.

"Help me, Milan," she said, reaching out to grasp his fingers, her eyes focused on his. "Help me find Katrenka's baby."

TITLES AND TERMS

Allied Control Council—joint body formed by the USSR, USA, Great Britain and France to oversee Germany after Nazi capitulation in 1945.

Appellplatz—open area in Ravensbrück and other forced labor camps where inmates gathered for roll call.

Aufkommando—construction detail that transformed the garrison city Terezín into a Jewish ghetto. The first details were made up of Jews.

Bratr—Czech word for brother.

Cirak—Easter cheese.

Gruppenführer—SS group leader, equivalent to US major general.

The Great Decree—law passed by the Czechoslovak Government on June 4, 1945 that defined punishment for Nazi war criminals as well as accomplices and traitors and established a system of 24 Extraordinary People's Courts that would include lay individuals as well as a professional chief justice and follow expedited procedures for prosecutions, convictions and sentencing.

Hitler Youth—education program for German boys and girls that began in 1936. Involvement was compulsory from age 10 through 18. Boys and girls were separated. Boys participated in military athletics; girls prepared for motherhood.

Hauptsturmführer—head SS storm leader, equivalent to US captain.

Hoelan Front—Sudeten German Home Front formed in 1933 to seek annexation of Czech Sudetenland by Nazi Germany.

Holubki—Slavic word for stuffed cabbage.

International Tracing Service—a center that gathers and preserves information about the Holocaust and individuals who were placed in forced labor camps during WW II.

Kneipe—German word for tavern.

Lebensborn—program set up by the SS Race and Settlement Office to increase the German birth rate. Meaning Fount of Life, Lebensborn created a network of maternity homes to "accommodate and look after racially and genetically valuable expectant mothers." The homes came to be seen as legalized brothels where SS men acted as "conception assistants" to unmarried and racially suitable women.

Lebesraum—"living space" that had to be expanded across political and geographic borders to restore Germany's national pride.

Lidice Memorial—a memorial created by the Soviets at the site of the original town. A service dedicated the site on June 10, 1945. Czechoslovak President Edvard Beneš spoke; women of the town who had been repatriated were honored guests.

National Court in Prague—created by the Czech government in 1945 to handle crimes committed during the Nazi Occupation.

Oberlandrat—local German administrative and police unit in Occupied Czechoslovakia.

Obersturmbannführer—senior storm command leader, equivalent to US lieutenant colonel.

Operation Anthropoid—plan by the Czech Government in Exile to assassinate Reinhard Heydrich.

Operation Outdistance—plan by the Czech Government in Exile to send men behind Occupied lines to aid the Czech Resistance.

Oplatky—Christmas wafers.

Ordungspolizei—Nazi police force.

Opa—German term for grandfather.
Otec—Czech term for grandfather.

Pan—Czech term for Mr.

Paní—Czech term for Mrs.

People's Courts—established by the Czech government under the Great Decree immediately after Liberation. The courts were placed in 24 locations across Czechoslovakia. They were authorized for one year and charged with adjudicating specific crimes associated with the Occupation. These courts included a professional chief justice as well as four members of the public who were appointed by the central government.

Prarodice—Czech term for grandparents.

Prague uprising—began in the early morning hours of May 5, 1945, when Czechs regained control over the Prague radio station. Fighting occurred throughout the city of Prague but was concentrated on streets near the radio station. Troops under the command of Soviet General Vlasov assisted Czech fighters beginning on May 6. The uprising ended on May 9 when a full contingent of Soviet troops entered the city and the Nazi government capitulated.

Rasse-un Siedlungshauptamt, RuSHA—SS Race and Settlement Office responsible for establishing and enforcing Nazi race laws.

Reichsarbeitsdienst—military work crew.

ReichsKommisar—leader of Occupied Holland.

ReichsProtektorate—term for Occupied Czechoslovakia.

ReichsProtektor—title for leader of Occupied Czechoslovakia.

Rožky—crescent roll pastry.

Schutzpolitzei, Schupo—name for German police.

Schutzstaffel—SS.

Sicherheitsdienst—Nazi security police unit.

Sléthnout se—Czech phrase meaning come together by flying.

Soldat—German term for soldier.

Sousedská—semi-slow, swaying Bohemian dance.

SS Reichsfurher—leader of the SS.

Stada baba—term for old woman.

Stardartenführer—SS standard leader, equivalent to US colonel.

Strýc—Czech word for uncle.

Sturmmann—SS storm man, equivalent to British lance corporal.

Teta—Czech term for aunt.

Trdelnik—rolled sweet pastry.

UNRRA—U.N. Relief and Rehabilitation Administration created in 1943 to repatriate and support WW II refugees who came under Allied control.

UVOD—Ustřední vedení odboje domácího, Central Leadership of the Czech Home Resistance.

Volk—German word used to mean "the people" as opposed to the state and ruling elites. The term was adopted by the right-wing in the 1930s to identify categories of people with varying worth. To be healthy, the German Volk had to be purged of asocials, homosexuals, Jews, and the mentally ill.

Wehrmacht—German armed forces.

White Buses—program led by the Swedish Red Cross and Danish government in the spring of 1945 that collected inmates from concentration camps and transported them to Sweden.

MAJOR CZECH AND GERMAN LOCATIONS

Ansbach—site of a Lebensborn orphanage in Germany.

Čzerniský palác—Czernin Palace, headquarters of the ReichsProtektorate at Hradčany Castle Hill, opposite St. Vitus Cathedral.

Deggendorf—site of a displaced persons camp in southwestern Germany.

Holešovice—near suburb of Prague where the leader of Occupied Czechoslovakia, Reinhard Heydrich, was severely wounded by a grenade thrown by a member of the Czech Army in Exile.

Hradčany—Prague Castle Hill area situated on a hilltop over the west side of the city. It includes the Castle District with Prague Castle, St. Vitus Cathedral, Old Roman Palace, Gardens, and the seat of the President of the Czech Republic.

Josefov—Jewish section of Prague.

Karlův most—Charles Bridge.

Kladno—site of Poldi Steelworks where some Lidice men worked during WW II and the city where Lidice women and children were taken after the town was attacked and destroyed by German police and SS.

Letná—public park on a plateau above Prague in the Holešovice area.

Lidice—18 kilometers northwest of Prague. Suspected of housing sympathizers or helpers of Heydrich's assassins, the town was destroyed in June 1942 by SS and German police. It was later rebuilt and includes a small museum just north of the original location of the village.

Malá Strana—Little Quarter of Prague near Hradčany.

Námestí Republiky—public square in Prague's Old Town.

Nehvizdy—landing site where Heydrich's assassins were airdropped.

New Reichs Chancillery—site of Heydrich's funeral in Berlin.

Nove Město—New Town and commercial district of Prague.

Nova Hlina—hometown of Karel Čurda, Czechoslovak Army in Exile member who betrayed fellow members of the paratroop squads.

Nürnberg—Nuremberg, Germany, where the first international criminal trials for war crimes were held following WW II.

Olomouc—city in Moravia with a large German population before WW II.

Ořechov—landing site where members of the Czech Army in Exile's Operation Outdistance were air-dropped in March 1942.

Paneský Brezany—chateau occupied by Reinhard Heydrich when he was head of Occupied Czechoslovakia.

Pankrác—courthouse and prison in Prague. Karl Hermann Frank was tried and executed by hanging at Pankrác in 1946.

Paderborn—site of a restored medieval castle were Heinrich Himmler installed a round table emulating King Arthur's court and held meetings of his self-described Teutonic Knights.

Petshův palác—Petshek Palace, headquarters of the Gestapo for the Czechoslovak Protektorate.

Plzeň—second largest city in Bohemia, site of the Skoda ironworks and armaments factory that was a target of the Czechoslovak Army in Exile.

Prag—German spelling of the city of Prague.

The Pear Tree

Major Czech and German Locations

Prinz-Albrect-Strasse—Berlin street where Gestapo Headquarters were located.

Reichstag—seat of German government in Berlin.

Rokycany—city near where Karl Hermann Frank was taken into custody by American Forces in 1945.

Slaný—location of the factory where Václav Řihá, author of the love letter that sent Gestapo to Lidice, worked.

Starě Mesto—Prague's Old Town.

Unhošt'—small town north of Prague.

Ústí nad Labem—site of retaliation by Czechs against German residents after a nearby munitions dump exploded on July 31, 1945. Crowds of Czechs attacked Germans and forced them into the river Elbe. At least 200 Germans died.

Václavské náměstí—Wenceslas Square in Prague.

Vinohradská Street—location of radio station where Prague Uprising began on May 5, 1945.

Vinohrady—near suburb of Prague.

Wannsee—suburb of Berlin where 15 key officials from ministeries of the Third Reich assembled to "implement the desired final solution of the Jewish Question." The Wannsee Conference was convened by Reinhard Heydrich and took place on January 20, 1945.

Wiesbaden—site of the interrogation of Karl Hermann Frank by U.S. Army and U.N. investigators charged with determining who would be tried for crimes committed during wartime at one of the international war crimes tribunals.

Zižkov—working class suburb of Prague that was a Communist stronghold even before WW II. It was the area where families hid Heydrich's assassins.

SOURCES OF INFORMATION

Assassination

94208718-Assassination-Operation-Anthropoid.pdf.

Himmler Eulogy: Wannsee House and the Holocaust, Ch. 6.

The History Place: Biography of Nazi Leaders: SS leader Reinhard Heydrich, 1997.

The History Place: The Triumph of History. The Gestapo Is Born. 2001.

The History Place. Biographies of Nazi Leaders. SS Leader Reinhard Heydrich, 1997.

Kostian F: Czech Press Agency: 70th anniversary of ReichsProtektor Heydrich's rule over Bohemia and Moravia.

MacDonald, C: The Killing of SS Obergruppenfuhrer Reinhard Heydrich. The Free Press, 1989.

Mastiny V: The Czechs under Nazi Rule. Columbia University Press, 1971.

Petschek Palace. Wikipedia; Falvey C: Petschek Palace Once the Headquarters of the Nazi Secret Police.

Reinhard Heydrich's funeral held in Berlin. News reports, 9 June 1942.

RuSHA Racial Criteria for SS and Germanization Candidates. Skadi Forum.

Silentstalker: Inconvenient Heroes. Part V by Vaclav Vlk, Sr., blog post, 22 July, 2014.

Wannsee House and the Holocaust, Ch. 6: Heydrich Grave, Himmler Eulogy.

Weiss S: Heydrich's Home, blog post, 20 May 2002.

Who's Who in Nazi Germany: Heinrich Himmler. 1997.

Reprisal

National Library of Australia: Sydney Morning Herald: Love Letter Led Gestapo to Massacre Lidice. 11 April 1947.

Germanization

Kidnapping of Eastern European Children by Nazi Germany. Wikipedia.

The Holocaust Revealed.org.

Malone A: Stolen by the Nazis: The Tragic Tale of 12,000 blue-eyes blond children taken by the SS to create an Aryan super-race. Daily Mail. 9 Jan 2009.

Betrayal

94208718-Assassination-Operation-Anthropoid.pdf.

Ravensbrück

General Ost—The Germanization of the East. Stormfront Forum.

Helms S: If This Is a Woman. Inside Ravensbruck, Little Brown, 2015.

Hitler's "Master Plan" Included Child Theft:

Lebensborn. WW II. Htt;"www.desertwar.net

The Lebensborn Program. Jewish Virtual Library. 2012 American-Israeli Cooperative Enterprise

The Nazi Party: The "Lebensborn" Program (1935-45). The Forgotten Camps. ABC News 20/20 Special Report, 27 April 2000.

Morrison J: Everyday Life in a Women's Concentration Camp 1939-1945, Markus Weiner Publishers, 2000.

Nina Osten's Escape from Ravensbruck. WW2 People's War. BBC.

Ravensbruck Concentration Camp. WW II Remembered. 2007-8.

Ravensbruck. A Teacher's Guide to the Holocaust. US Fla 2005.

Ravensbruck (Germany) Jewishgen.org/forgotten camps.

Resistance

Communal pear tree. A silent witness of Lidice's tragedy, www.lidice.cz/obec/historie/hruskaen.html.

Demetz P: Prague in Danger. Farrar, Straus and Giroux, 2008.

Luza R: The Hitler Kiss. A Memoir of the Czech Resistance, Louisiana

State University Press, 2002.

Novacek C: Border Crossing. Coming of Age in the Czech Resistance. Ten21Press, 2012.

Lidice

Fortinbras J: The Truth about Lidice. The War Illustrated. Vol. 10, No. 242, p. 355-6, Sep 27, 1946.

History Learning Site. World War Two. Lidice 1942. www.historylearningsite.co.uk/lidice_1942.htm.

Holocaust Education and Archive Research Team: The Massacre at Lidice, HolocaustResearchProject.org.

Illichmann CT: Lidice: Remembering the Women and Children. UW-I Journal of Undergraduate Research VIII, 2005.

Pamatnik Lidice: History of Lidice Village. www.lidice-memorial.cz/history_en.aspx.

Rapson J: Topographies of Suffering. Berghahn Books, 2015.

Reversal

Chen CP: Prague Strategic Offensive, World War II Database.

Clark RS: The Interrogation of Karl Hermann Frank and the Kristallnacht Documents. 3 Rutgers J of L and Relig Nuremberg 1.Prague uprising, Wikipedia.

White Buses, Wikipedia.

Aftermath

Blythe R: Dark Day, Da Capo Press, 2015.

Bolger N: The Convent Children. Book in progress.

Bower T: Blood Money, Macmillan, London, 1997.

Browning C: Ordinary Men, HarperCollins, 1992.

Bryant C: Prague in Black, Harvard University Press, 2007.

The Forgotten Camps: ABC News 20/20 Special Report. Hitler's Master Race Nazi Program Attempted to Create Racially Pure Children, 27 Apr, 2000.

Frommer B: National Cleansing. Cambridge University Press, 2005.

Gallagher RF: WW II Story. Ch. 22—Regensburg, Germany.

Hitler's Gold—Part 1. Robert Whiston's Seblog. Whiston.wordpress.com/2012/11/13.

Jewish Virtual Library: The Lebensborn Program. www.jewishvirtuallibrary.org/jsource/Holocaust/Lebensborn.html.

Overy R: Interrogations. The Nazi Elite in Allied Hands, 1945. Penguin Books, 2001

Regensburg. Wikipedia.

Wagner H: Prag 1945-1947. Documents on the Expulsion of Sudeten Germans, Report of September 27, 1950.

Wyman M: DPs: Europe's Displaced Persons, 1945-1951. Cornell University Press, 1989.

Zahra T: Lost Children: Displacement, Family, and Nation in Postwar Europe. J Mod History 81 (Mar 2009) 45-86.

ACKNOWLEDGEMENTS

I wish to thank Mariann Stephens, Kitty Malik and the late Karen Gardner for their patience as they read through my early attempts to write this story.

Special thanks to Bridget Boland and Jo Ellen Mistarz for reviewing the full manuscript and guiding me toward a better story, to the late Gretchen Edgren for her editorial review, and to Laurie Larson for editorial polishing.

Thanks to Northwestern University Professor Benjamin Frommer whose alumni course on "WWII—The Eastern Front" gave me the idea for this book, and all who supported me along the way, including but certainly not limited to: Ana Gil, Jim Aldworth, Mark Hagland, Carol Schultz and Helen Voris.

CPSIA information can be obtained
at www.ICGtesting.com
Printed in the USA
LVOW10s2340041217
558591LV00015BA/2191/P

9 781947 605015